PRAISE FOR *BLOOD'S PRIDE*

"Impressive . . . Pragmatic attitudes and goals mingle with the uncanny in a complex web of plots, as the perspectives shift between characters and cultures to gradually uncover a multitude of relationships, schemes, and secrets. . . . It's a remarkable feat for a newcomer and leaves me eager for the sequel, *Fortune's Blight.*"
—*Locus*

"Presents the tangled dynamics of two cultures at war with each other and within themselves . . . Plot twists, romantic entanglements, and political rivalries make for lots of melodrama."
—*Publishers Weekly*

"Manieri's debut novel combines epic fantasy and family melodrama to rousing effect, with emotionally complex characters on every side of every conflict."
—*Shelf Awareness*

"A cracking page-turner . . . *Blood's Pride* has everything: elegantly concise language, epic storytelling, cunning characters, a seductive desert setting, and stunning action sequences. The most impressive fantasy debut of 2012."
—*Rue Morgue*

"An intriguing tale of insurrection and divided loyalties."
—Col Buchanan,
author of *Stands a Shadow*

"Eve Manieri deftly portrays three clashing cultures about to be torn apart by violent rebellion. Against the background of war and revolution, three mismatched couples struggle to stay true to their families, themselves, and the ones they love. I found myself deeply engrossed in this fast-paced tale of honor and betrayal, hope and despair, secrets, revelations, and a whisper of divine magic."

—Sharon Shinn,
author of *The Shape of Desire*

"This clever take on epic fantasy, filled with unexpected twists and turns right to the end, will undoubtedly appeal to fans of Michelle West and Patricia Bray."

—Rachel Neumeier,
author of the Griffin Mage Trilogy

TOR BOOKS BY EVIE MANIERI

SHATTERED KINGDOMS

Blood's Pride

*Fortune's Blight**

Forthcoming*

BLOOD'S PRIDE

Shattered Kingdoms Book 1

Evie Manieri

A TOM DOHERTY ASSOCIATES BOOK
NEW YORK

This is a work of fiction. All of the characters, organizations, and events portrayed in this novel are either products of the author's imagination or are used fictitiously.

BLOOD'S PRIDE

Originally published in Great Britain in 2012 by Jo Fletcher Books

A Tor Book
Published by Tom Doherty Associates, LLC
175 Fifth Avenue
New York, NY 10010

www.tor-forge.com

Tor® is a registered trademark of Tom Doherty Associates, LLC.

ISBN 978-0-7653-6891-1

Tor books may be purchased for educational, business, or promotional use. For information on bulk purchases, please contact Macmillan Corporate and Premium Sales Department at 1-800-221-7945, extension 5442, or write specialmarkets@macmillan.com.

First U.S. Edition: February 2013
First Mass Market Edition: February 2014

Printed in the United States of America

0 9 8 7 6 5 4 3 2 1

To Mr. Robert Frick of Garrettford Elementary School, Drexel Hill, PA

Dramatis Personae

The Norlanders:

Arnaf — a soldier, Eonar's personal bodyguard
Beorun — a soldier
Daem — a soldier, Rho's friend
Eleana — Eonar's wife, mother of Eofar, Frea and Isa
Eofar — only son of Eonar, the governor
Eonar — the governor, father of Eofar, Frea and Isa
Falkar — a soldier, Frea's lieutenant
Finlas — a soldier
Frea — the governor's elder daughter
Ingeld — a soldier
Isa — the governor's youngest daughter
Jeder — a soldier
Kharl — a soldier
Ongen — a soldier
Rho — a soldier of noble birth
Varnat — a soldier

The Shadari:

Alkar — Shadari freedom fighter, loyal to Faroth
Beni — Dramash's friend
Binit — Shadari freedom fighter, loyal to Faroth
Cara — Dramash's friend
Daryan — the last daimon (king), Shairav's nephew
Dramash — son of Faroth and Saria, Harotha's nephew
Elthion — Shadari freedom fighter, loyal to Faroth

Faroth — twin to Harotha, Shadari freedom fighter
Hakim — a temple slave
Harotha — twin to Faroth, Shadari freedom fighter
Josah — a slave from the mines
Majid — Shairav's assistant
Meena — Daryan's aunt
Omir — a temple slave
Rahsa — a temple slave
Rasabal — a temple slave
Sami — Shadari freedom fighter, loyal to Faroth
Saria — Faroth's wife, Dramash's mother
Shairav — the last of the ashas, Daryan's uncle
Tal — a temple slave
Tebrin — a temple slave
Trini — Elthion's mother
Veshar — a temple slave

The Nomas:

Brigeth — a Nomas healer
Dannika (Danni) — second mate on the *Veruna*
Jachad Nisharan — the king, son of the sun god Shof
Mairi — a Nomas healer
Nisha — the queen, Jachad's mother
Raina — a Nomas healer

The Mongrel, also known as Meiran

BLOOD'S PRIDE

Prologue

Excerpt from the manuscript, *The History of the Shadar*, by Daryan (Daimon, ninth of that name)

You may believe this work you now hold in your hands to be an abomination. You may believe that in writing these words I have committed an unforgivable sin—but I will not waste ink and paper justifying my actions; I will say only that if I do sin against the gods, I pray that they will visit their wrath upon me alone. I pray they will spare their people more suffering, for they have already had too much heaped upon them.

This is my memory. When it happened I was a new baby, swaddled and hidden from the world, and though I did not then have the words to describe it, that does not stop me from remembering. I see it when I close my eyes, far away at first, then growing nearer and nearer, until I can smell the blood and the smoke and taste the salt spray on my lips.

The fishing boats came in on the dawn tide and the fishermen and their wives and children busied themselves unloading the evening's catch. It was a chill morning in the Shadar, the air still cold from the desert night as the sun came up over the sea and etched the peaks of the bordering mountains in gold. The ships were unloaded quickly and silently, everyone helping each other to pile the catch onto carts and haul it to the place where the women would clean and salt the fish while their fathers and husbands and brothers slept.

They glanced up from time to time at the temple, the red rock promontory towering over the northern end of the city. The ashas, the consecrated priests and priestesses of the Shadari, moved through the labyrinthine corridors hollowed out by ancient and mysterious hands, fulfilling their secret offices, gathering in the roofless chambers to inscribe prayers in the sand for the gods to look down upon. The gods winked back at them from the night sky and moved the sands in answer to their prayers, and so the ashas prayed confidently, content in the unfaltering routine of their work, content with the tithe baskets that overflowed with offerings. In a few months, the ashas would descend to the city by their hidden staircase to choose candidates for the initiation rites, to lie with their spouses and foster out their infants. The people on the beach felt secure knowing that their ashas had their gods' wishes firmly in hand.

The last nets were stowed and the Shadari started for their cozy homes. Soon the city would stir in earnest, with those who tended the vines and the groves and the animals rising and starting for the hills and the day's work.

One fisherman let his fellows walk ahead of him and lingered alone on the beach, gazing at the beauty of the sun on the sea until his eyes could no longer bear such brightness and he turned his back, feeling the warm rays caressing the dark curls on his head. He looked at the sleepy Shadar, with its crooked rows and circles of gold-tinged white houses, and marveled at how lucky they were that their gods had given them such a place to live. He looked up to the sky to give thanks to the gods before the sun chased them to their rest, and then he turned to look one last time at the endless stretch of the Sea of Misfortune.

And he saw that he was no longer alone.

A ship—no, three ships—were sailing for the Shadar.

The fisherman's sharp eyes picked out the three black spots, and realized these were much larger vessels than the simple fishing boats of the Shadari or the Nomas. As they steered into the harbor the fisherman could see that the great sails were in tatters and the ships were badly damaged. Odder still, he could see no one about, not in the rigging, nor on the decks: they were ghost ships. Yet they stayed in tight formation, one leading the way, the other two just behind.

A chill ran up the fisherman's spine and he shut his eyes tightly, hoping that when he opened them, the ships would be gone.

But they were not.

All that day the Shadari gathered on the beach, coming and going as their tasks permitted, gossiping, speculating, fearing, hoping. A thousand times someone volunteered to take a boat out to where the ships had anchored far off the shore in the deep water, to welcome the visitors to the Shadar. But each time the fears of their neighbors won out and they waited all together, doing nothing. They looked to the temple, wondering what the ashas thought of the new arrivals, hoping they would descend to the beach and give their people guidance, but they remained hidden.

The day passed slowly and as the sun began to slide behind the mountains, the fishermen prepared their boats for the night's catch. Phantom ships or not, there were fish to catch. As the gods began to show a faint presence in the sky, the drums called out the evening prayers. Life continued.

But the fisherman who had first seen the ships had not lost his uneasiness, and as he examined his nets, he kept looking out to the empty decks of the three ships. They looked as if they had come through storms and rough waters, as if they had been battered against rocks and tossed upon forbidding shores. Their crews must have seen the wide-open jaws of terrible beasts and smelled the seductive perfume of strange flowers. The Shadari did not cross the sea, and they did not cross the desert beyond the western mountains. The Shadar itself had always been enough for them. What calamity could have inspired a journey such as these ships had endured?

He waited for the stars to come out and watch over the Shadar; it would be all right then.

As the fisherman looked at the magenta sky, he saw a black splotch like a stain on the horizon, a shadow forming over the sea which spread and grew larger until he saw not shadows but black shapes: great flying creatures. The fisherman recognized them at once as dereshadi, the beasts that carry the souls of evildoers down into the depths of the earth after death. Phantoms swarmed from the bowels of the ships, crawling across the decks and into the landing boats and mounting the flying beasts.

The phantoms were giants to the Shadari. Their pale skin was the color of death, marred by oozing purple sores; grime matted their seafoam-white hair. They had the hollowed cheeks and gangly limbs of the starving, but they held aloft great, gleaming swords.

"Eshofa's children!" a woman screamed, naming the damned children of the goddess of traitors, and the city exploded into chaos.

These beings who appeared like walking dead, like living corpses, descended upon the Shadari like the wrath of hell, killing indiscriminately, splashing the town with red blood. They spoke not one word, made not one sound, as they moved in perfect tandem like a school of flesh-eating fish. Those Shadari who managed to inflict wounds saw their adversaries' blood flow the silver-blue of a shark's fin, but not for long, for the invaders thrust their swords into the fires and seared their wounds closed, and all the while they kept on fighting.

From the backs of their flying beasts, Eshofa's children, the Dead Ones, stole food and carried it back to their ships. The Shadari screamed out to the ashas, beat their drums and clawed at the forbidding sides of the plateau, pleading with those above, but the temple remained silent and dark.

When the sun rose again, the Shadari were free. The invaders had returned to their ships, leaving the burned buildings and the dead and dying as evidence of their coming.

The Shadari beat their drums and looked to the temple, but still no help came.

When the sun set the Dead Ones came again, this time fortified by their plundered booty, and the Shadari suffered as before, crying out to their ashas for help, defenseless without their protection, lost without their guidance. Silence was the only response.

On the third night, the invaders came again, but this time as the dereshadi spread out over the Shadar, the drums that the Shadari had been beating day and night finally received their answer. The Shadari came out of their hiding-places, rushing into the streets. Now, at last, the ashas would use their magic, calling up the desert sands to swallow their foes. The Shadari crowded out into the streets and onto the beaches, climbed to the roofs of their homes, looked hopefully up to the temple.

The fisherman stood on the beach, brandishing the spear that he had used countless times to pluck food from the waters; now it had tasted blood of a different kind. The fisherman gazed up at the temple, flushed with hope as he picked out the white-robed figures gathered on the roof, standing in a line along the edge high above the beach, lit by the moonlight for all to see. The bedraggled defenders raised a cheer, and fists were brandished in triumph.

When the first body plunged into the sea, sending up a column of white foam, the fisherman blinked. When the second body fell his eyes opened wide, and he stared in horror. The ashas—their protectors—were killing themselves.

* * *

We learned later that the ghostly invaders, the Dead Ones—Norlanders, they called themselves—watched with equal amazement as one by one the priests stood on the edge of the cliff and leaped into the sea. The long voyage from their frozen homeland had been fraught with dangers, but the pathetic, disorganized resistance of the Shadari had restored their confidence in this venture. Already they were picturing the mines they would dig to extract the black ore, that miraculous substance which had brought them to these unsuspecting shores. Already they could smell the sulfur from the smithies where they would smelt the ore into metal laced with their own pure blood. Already they could feel the great swords in their hands, swords that would obey their owners' thoughts as well as their hands: the secret property of the black ore only they had learned.

One by one, the drums ceased beating. The silence of the Dead Ones was complete.

Chapter One

"There he is," she told Jachad, in her ageless, sexless, expressionless voice.

Jachad stopped beside her and dropped his pack down onto the desert sand. He followed the gaze of her eye across the gray sweep of the dunes and isolated clusters of rocks and on up to the mountains in the east, where he saw a black shape winging its way toward them from the great square shape of the temple. Each majestic sweep of the creature's wings etched an arc against the silvery pre-dawn sky. Its long tail snaked out, piloting like a ship's rudder, while the needle-sharp claws on its hind feet raked the air. Mounted on its back on a broad leather saddle was a figure draped in a shimmering white cloak.

"Well, I certainly hope that's him," Jachad replied, "because if it's not, we're in real trouble." With a practiced flourish he unwound the gauzy scarf from around his head and ran a freckled hand through his shock of bright red hair. Then he turned to his companion, frowning. "You're sure you want to do it this way?"

In place of an answer, she reached into a hidden pouch inside her grimy multi-colored robe and brought out a small bundle swaddled in a scrap of red cloth.

He said, "You can't even be sure he remembers—"

She tossed the bundle to him.

"Careful!" he cried, snatching the object out of the air

and clutching it to his chest. He held it there for a moment, pressing it against his heart. Then he unwrapped the package with nervous fingers and held the contents up in front of his eyes. The cork of the little glass bottle was still sealed up tightly under a thick layer of wax, and the bottle was half-full of a syrupy dark-red liquid. Jachad sighed with relief.

"You could at least tell me if it works," he said, looking over at her. She wore her cowl low over her face, but he could see the faint glow of her silver-green eye. "If he's fool enough to try it himself, I'd feel better if I knew it wasn't going to poison him."

"You'll both have to take your chances." She turned away and left him behind without a backward look, resuming their eastward trek toward the Shadar alone.

"This won't take long. Don't get too far ahead," he called after her. But the stillness of the desert deadened his words and if she heard him, she made no sign.

Jachad called up an oily film on the palm of his right hand and flicked his fingers over it to spark up a little fireball, not much bigger than a marble. He worried it between his fingers. He knew it was in his own best interests to avoid a confrontation now, but he still felt a little cheated. It was sure to come sometime, and when it did, he wanted to be there.

Her long strides had already carried her some distance away by the time the beast dropped to a graceful landing among the rippling dunes and its rider extricated himself from the complicated harness. Jachad forced himself to turn his attention to his Norlander client. The tall man wore the cowl of his white cloak down around his neck and his gloves tucked into his sleeve; he wouldn't need them until the sun crested the horizon. True to form, his long white hair was pulled back and bound with a leather cord and the hilt of an enormous broadsword rose from behind his right shoulder. But Jachad also noticed that his pale skin lacked the slight iridescence—like a fish's scales—that his people, the Nomas, had always admired in the Norlanders, and that the flesh under his luminous silver-gray eyes sagged as if he'd been losing sleep.

"King Jachad?" rasped the Norlander.

"Lord Eofar," he answered, smiling. He opened his right hand and the little fireball snuffed itself out in a wisp of black smoke. "It's good to see you. You got my message, I see."

"I did. Thank you," said Eofar. His features remained so still, his face so rigid, that Jachad found it hard to believe his lips could move at all. The words he spoke fell to the sand like lead weights, devoid of any life or expression. It was no mystery why the Shadari still referred to them as "the Dead Ones" even after all these years. "I didn't expect you to come personally."

"Oh, but this is a very special commission. Plus, I had some other business out this way."

"Don't your people need you?"

Jachad laughed. "I would have thought you knew by now not to take my title too seriously. We Nomas need a king about as much as a snake needs a pair of boots."

The Norlander took a moment to unhook a waterskin from his belt and take a long drink, then he put his hand to his throat and massaged it. "It's very dry out here."

Jachad knew what Eofar expected, but even though this transaction would earn more than his tribe had seen in the last half-year, he still hesitated. "We can speak Norlander, if you prefer," he forced himself to say.

<Ah, thank you,> Eofar answered at once, only this time his words made their way directly from his mind to Jachad's without any of the mechanics of sound. Jachad wouldn't have minded so much if that had been the extent of it, but everything Eofar felt came along with the words: an assaultive jumble of relief, anticipation, anxiety, excitement, fear, and a host of other emotions too subtle to name, all accompanied by swirling colors and strange images. For reasons no one really understood, some people—most notably, the Shadari—couldn't speak

Norlander at all: the words and emotions simply didn't register for them. In Jachad's opinion it was one of the few ways in which they were fortunate. He pressed his knuckles to his temples and tried to stay focused. Surely the Norlanders did not experience each other with such intensity; life would be unbearable.

<No thanks are necessary,> he said. <I'm sorry to drag you out here to the desert, but the garrison's supplies aren't due to be delivered for another few weeks, and your letter said it was urgent.>

<No, I'm glad you suggested this,> Eofar assured him. <With Frea running the garrison now, nothing happens up there without her knowing about it. And I don't want her to know about this.>

<Lady Frea is in charge of the garrison?> As a rule the Nomas kept themselves well informed, but somehow the caravans had missed this important bit of information. <Then, is your father—I hope the governor's health has not declined?> said Jachad, trying hard to project nothing but mild concern. The Norlanders apparently had no trouble lying to each other, but he could never be certain of carrying off even the most innocent of deceptions—and in this case, he had no wish to share his feelings about old Governor Eonar with his only son.

<My father's still alive,> replied Eofar, his distress coming across like a splash of muddy ochre. <Frea has been running the mines for a long time, really. The only difference now is that we don't have to pretend Father's still making the decisions. That and she gets to bully the slaves all she wants.>

<What about your other sister?>

<Isa?>

<Last time I was in the temple, she looked nearly of age. I would have thought your father would have sent her back to Norland to be married by now.> *The sooner the better*, Jachad thought to himself. At least, he hoped it was to himself.

<She's still here,> said Eofar, but his emotions were so

murky that Jachad felt this subject was even less to his liking than the last.

<Well, we didn't come here to gossip, did we?> Jachad asked briskly. With a suitably dramatic flourish, he produced the little bottle and held it up between his thumb and forefinger. <Shadari divining elixir, as requested. It was rare even before the invasion, forbidden to any but the Shadari ashas, who used it to see into the future. Many speculate that the ashas took it when your people invaded and the visions somehow drove them to their famous leap. I can't verify any of that, of course, but I will guarantee you that this is the absolute genuine article. As far as I know, it's the only bottle to be had anywhere in the world.>

Eofar's eyes shone more brightly as he examined the merchandise. <It's not even half-full,> he said, but his attempt to feign disappointment was laughable; his desire was reaching out like a pair of grasping hands. <You didn't say in your message how much you wanted for it.>

<I'm asking thirty-five.>

<Sudras?>

Jachad shook his head apologetically. <Eagles.> He felt Eofar's dismay and pressed his advantage. <If we could negotiate the price in imperial ore instead of currency—>

<That's impossible.> The words dropped like iron ingots, dark and hard. <Frea has every ounce accounted for. The mines haven't been producing well lately. The emperor's ship is due any day now and we've only eight swords out of twenty-five ready to send back to Norland.> He reached beneath his cloak and pulled out a fat little purse. <I have thirty-one. I can't get any more right now without asking my father or Frea. Maybe in a few months . . . > His words tailed off.

Jachad scratched his head and desperately tried to conceal the fact that he had been prepared to take twenty-five. Finally he said, <All right, thirty-one it is.

And one back to you for luck, so that's thirty. We've known each other a long time, after all.>

Eofar's surge of relief nearly knocked Jachad backward. He wrapped the little bottle back up in the scrap of cloth and held it out with a smile. Instinctively Eofar reached for it. His hand came close enough for Jachad to feel the chill radiating from his skin before they both remembered themselves and pulled back.

<Sorry,> said Jachad. <I forgot you weren't wearing your gloves.> He deposited the little package carefully in the sand between them. Eofar picked up the bottle and left the purse lying in the same spot for Jachad to retrieve.

<Thank you, King Jachad.>

<Oh, no need to be so formal. And thank you, for a good bargain.> He flipped opened the purse and tossed a coin to Eofar, who caught it neatly in his pale hand. <Frankly, I could use the cash. The gathering is coming up in a few days and I have my eye on a perky little second mate with a fondness for bracelets.>

<The gathering,> Eofar ruminated as he undid the clasps of his cloak and carefully tucked the bottle into the pocket of his shirt. <It only lasts a few weeks, and then you're apart again. The women go back to sea in their ships, you men go back to your caravans in the desert, and another half-year goes by before you see each other again. I can't understand why anyone would choose to live that way.>

<No, you'd rather be under each other's feet all the time, wouldn't you?> said Jachad. <Nomas men love the desert, and our women love the sea. That's the way it's always been. It's pointless to ask either one to change.>

<You could compromise: spend some time in the desert and some time at sea—and all of it together.>

<Oh, that would make for a happy family, wouldn't it? Taking turns being miserable.>

<I still think there must be some of your men who would rather be with their wives than live in the desert,

and women who would rather be with their husbands than on a ship.>

<Some do, of course,> Jachad answered, trying to mask his impatience with extra good cheer. They'd had this conversation before, and his answer was always the same. The bargaining had gone as well as could be expected up to this point, and now he wanted Eofar to leave so he could catch up with his companion. He certainly did not want to waste his time defending his people's customs to a Norlander yet again. It was bad enough that once he reached the city he would have to contend with the open hostility of the Shadari, who even after twenty-odd years still blamed the Nomas for failing to come to their aid against the Norlanders.

He began walking casually toward Eofar's triffon, hoping Eofar would follow. <It does happen, once in a while—there's no law against it,> he continued. <Sometimes it works out; sometimes it doesn't. People should be able to do what they like with their own lives, don't you think?>

<I suppose so,> said Eofar, following Jachad to his mount. She lifted her massive head from between her front paws and sat up as they approached. Jachad patted her coarse fur, examining the small, round ears protruding from tufts of longer fur, the deep eye-ridges and long snout. With the ashas' secret passage in and out of the temple lost to history, the triffons were the only way to come and go, and Jachad was forced to ride on one of the creatures each time he came to negotiate with the governor for the garrison's supplies and sell trinkets to the soldiers. He had grown accustomed to it over the years; the last few times, he had even opened his eyes.

<Good girl, Aeda,> Eofar said as she bent her short legs slightly to make it easier for him to mount. He buckled himself into the harness and took up the reins, then stopped suddenly. <Who is that?>

Jachad turned and pretended to look where he was pointing. There was no sense in denying that they were together: Eofar's sharp Norlander eyes could easily spot her smeary footprints leading away, even in the tricky half-light. Jachad reminded himself that the best lie was simply an edited version of the truth. <Oh, she's just a business associate. I'm escorting her to the Shadar. She has some scars on her face, so I sent her on ahead. I know how you Norlanders feel about that sort of thing. I didn't want to upset you.>

<Should I ask what her business might be?>

<Only if you want to know,> said Jachad.

<No, I suppose not,> Eofar answered. <"Let all so afflicted . . ."> He trailed off.

<What's that?>

<What? Oh, nothing. It's from *The Book of the Hall*. Norlander scripture.> Eofar stared thoughtfully across the sands at the dwindling figure. <Did you know that in Norland they take deformed babies and injured soldiers and people like that out into the forest and leave them there to freeze to death? It's said that if Onfar—our god of life and death—decides that a person is worthy, he heals their affliction and sends them home again.>

<Yes, I had heard that,> Jachad said, clamping down on the anger this unexpected disclosure elicited. <And how many has he judged worthy so far?>

Eofar answered without looking away from Jachad's associate. <None.>

Jachad tapped his fingers together to disguise the little sparks sizzling between them and stepped back, out of the way of Aeda's enormous wings. <The sun's coming up. You'd better be getting back.>

Eofar whistled to his mount and she crouched low, then sprang into the air. A moment later the Norlander and the triffon were winging their way back to the temple. Jachad watched until their shadowy figures blended into the temple's stark façade.

Then he scooped up his pack and ran after his companion.

He tracked her easily, though her footprints had

shifted away from their original easterly direction. He began to see gaps here and there, as if she were stumbling, then the trail veered even further from due east and Jachad, looking round, saw the reason why. She was heading toward a low circle of sand-smoothed boulders a little to the north. He stopped and watched as she stumbled and fell to her knees a dozen paces from the stones. Reflexively he started toward her, but before he had gone very far she was on her feet again and a moment later, she had disappeared behind the rocks.

The dawn breeze whisked across the desert and rustled through Jachad's brilliant silk robes, offering him a greeting, a whispered welcome to the new day. The sand at his feet swirled and shifted, and the sun's first rays glowed behind the smudgy mountains. Jachad Nisharan, king of the Nomas, dropped his pack into the sand and knelt down to pray to his father, the sun god, Shof.

Absolute privacy, every day, at dawn and dusk, without fail: that was the condition she had imposed on him, the same condition she set for anyone who desired her services, and in the two weeks she and Jachad had been traveling together he had scrupulously honored his promise.

The wind began to gather strength, blowing westward from the sea.

He looked at the rocks and wet his lips. Dire warnings echoed in his mind. He had been putting off this moment, but they would reach the Shadar before sunset and he might never have another opportunity. He had to see for himself; if he let this chance slip by, he might as well have stayed with his tribe on the other side of the desert.

He stood up, and as he edged toward the rocks, the wind died down and the sand hissed back to the desert floor. Jachad dropped his pack and silently slid through a narrow space between two of the boulders.

He saw her immediately. She was laying face-up, her eyes closed, half-buried in the sand. The long fingers of her right hand were extended, scratching deep grooves into the dirt. He watched as a tremendous convulsion ripped through her and then left her lying flat on her back again, but now completely motionless. He dropped to his knees and crept forward.

Her soot-black hair, roughly tied back with a rag, spilled out from beneath her hood, contrasting ghoulishly with the gray glimmer of her skin. His eyes traced each scar on her face: the straight white seam on her broad forehead, the crescent-shaped mark on her hollow cheek, the jagged line that distorted the delicate shape of her thin, blue-tinged lips and pulled them up into a perpetual smirk. The cord of the eye-patch over her right eye split her features into separate sections, making her face look like something that had been broken, then clumsily repaired. But beneath the scars and the eye-patch, Jachad could still see the face of his former playfellow, the fourteen-year-old girl she had been nearly eight years ago.

"Meiran?" he whispered, reaching out his freckled hand to stroke the strands of black hair away from her damp forehead. He could feel a faint coolness rising up from her pearly gray skin. But the instant he touched her she bolted upright and her hand shot out and grabbed him by the throat.

"Who's there? Who are you!" she cried, one hand choking him while the other groped blindly at the air.

"It's me!" he gasped, trying to pull away from her, but her grip was too strong. Then he felt her fingers scrambling near his abdomen and suddenly she had his knife. Panicking, Jachad struck his hands together and orange flames licked over his palms. "Meiran," he shouted hoarsely, "it's me, Jachad!"

She released his neck but lunged at him, and her knee caught him squarely in the chest, knocking him flat. As the point of his own knife came screaming toward his face, he threw up his arms and a sheet of flame burst to life in front of him.

She recoiled from the crackling heat, falling backward between his scrabbling legs, and the knife went flying from her hand. It landed in the sand, out of reach.

"Meiran," he shouted again, crawling backward away from her, "Meiran, remember where we are—it's me—"

She drew back, panting heavily as she fell onto the sand, and Jachad, still reeling, watched as she drew in an unsteady breath, then snaked her finger beneath the black eye-patch and slid it over the silver-green left eye. It was the dark brown right eye, rounder and slightly larger than the one on the left, which focused on Jachad briefly before sliding away.

He exhaled in a long, relieved sigh and flopped down onto the sand in front of her. She sat across from him, staring at nothing, her scarred face expressionless. The desert silence pressed down on them.

"It's a lot worse than it used to be, isn't it?" he asked finally, but Meiran spoke at exactly the same moment, saying, "You broke your promise." And then: "That was a long time ago."

"I know," he admitted in response to both of her statements. She didn't look particularly angry; that was something. "*Seven years.* You can't blame me for wanting to know if you're all right. Seven years without a word—for the first three, we didn't even know if you were dead or alive. Then when word got around about this new mercenary . . ." He trailed off, watching her face. "More than once I thought about trying to find you."

He saw her lips part, but then they closed again, biting down on whatever she had been about to say. Jachad's skin prickled: he had come very close to getting her to say something she hadn't wanted to reveal.

"But I figured you knew how to find me if you wanted me," he continued, as if he hadn't noticed her reaction, "as evidenced by the fact that you're here. I'm only trying to understand you. You turn up at my caravan after all these years—just when the Shadari have put out the word they want to hire you, and with a bottle of elixir, just when that's needed—without any explanations." He got up and went to retrieve his knife, watching her from the corner of his eye as he slid it back into its sheath. Her breathing had slowed and her arms hung heavily at her sides; for the first time, she looked weary. But she was listening. He wandered back and sat down. "So, have you ever tried to find a cure?"

Her eye stayed fixed on the sand. "I have better things to do."

"What things? Things like going to the Shadar?" Jachad asked, allowing himself a hint of sarcasm.

"I'm being paid to go—and you're being paid to bring me, remember?"

He laughed. "You can't possibly need whatever money the Shadari slaves have managed to scrape together for their uprising—after all, you're supposed to be the greatest mercenary anyone's ever seen. In all of these years you've never lost a fight. You've done everything from commanding whole armies to besting champions in single combat. You took the tower at Treborn with a dozen men in a single day, after King Grayson had laid siege to it for almost a year. *To this day*, no one has figured out how you got the Chastian army out of the Kabor Pass." He smiled proudly. "Our Meiran."

She looked up at him. "That's not my name."

"Well, neither is 'the Mongrel,' and I'm certainly not going to call you that. Meiran is a good Nomas name—and you never minded it before." He ran a hand through his fiery hair.

She grunted noncommittally.

"Would you like to hear a funny story?" he asked, conscious of holding her attention at last. "It's about your pact with demons. They say that at dawn and dusk you sneak off and sacrifice a baby. You cut out its heart and eat it before the heart stops beating. Of course, babies aren't generally easy things to come by on a battlefield, but apparently"—he paused for effect—"you travel with your own supply." He grinned, and finally a dry, scratching sound that might have been a laugh escaped her. Jachad felt his freckled cheeks flush and he snapped up a few spits of flame and playfully flicked them at the ground.

Then Meiran stood up, brushed the sand from her robes, and replaced her cowl. She led the way out between the rocks and he recovered his pack and slung it over his shoulder. They struck out again for the mountains, Jachad trying to match his shorter strides to hers, until he stopped suddenly.

She walked on without him for a few paces, but then looked back.

Trying to ignore the cold knot in his stomach, he forced himself to voice the question he'd been too cowardly to ask before now. "Why go back, Meiran? Tell me, why now, after all this time?"

The sun was just beginning to crest the mountains, painting the tops of their low bluffs in molten shades of gold and copper. With her back to the sun, he could see nothing of her except her stark silhouette.

"There's a story I've been waiting a long time to hear," she said after a moment. "I want to hear it now."

He went to her as she turned back to the mountains. "And then what?" he asked, standing in front of her. Peering beneath her cowl, he saw her brown eye sweep over the landscape before her, taking in the low mountains that were hiding the little white houses of the city; the temple, carved by ancient hands or even more ancient magic out of a single mass of living rock; and beyond them all, the shining ribbon of the sea.

"I'm going to end it."

Chapter Two

Rho sat on the edge of his cot in the airless barracks room and watched with mild distaste as Daem took yet another candied fruit from the jar, peeled off the leaf, and popped it into his mouth. A drop of purple juice slid down the Eotan crest on his tabard and plopped onto the dusty stone floor.

<No need to stare. If you want one, just ask,> Daem quipped, stretching out on his rumpled bed.

<Thanks, I won't,> said Rho, pulling himself up from his own cot and ambling over to the room's one table, taking his boots with him. <I don't know how you can eat that sweet stuff so early in the evening; or at all, honestly.> He lowered himself into what he was convinced was the world's least comfortable chair, with the possible exception of the three others beside it, and poured himself a cup of wine.

<It's not early for me. That's the advantage of working day-patrols for so long; I'm back to living decent Norland hours. Don't pretend you're not jealous.> The syrupy scent of the fruit drifted across the square, low-ceilinged room as he chewed, mixing with the smells of lamp oil and rock dust and sweat. <You can't expect me to sleep on an empty stomach.>

From his cot in the far corner of the room, Ingeld called out, <*Nobody* can expect to sleep if you two triffons' asses don't *stop talking*.>

<Isn't that your last jar?> Rho asked Daem. <I thought you were saving them.>

Ingeld rolled over, favoring Rho with a view of his pale, slightly luminous backside. <You know, some of us have actual duties tonight,> he said.

<Yes, Ingeld, please do tell us again about all the things Lady Frea has ordered you to do for her,> mocked Daem. <We haven't heard nearly enough about it yet. Has she added polishing her boots to your list of empire-saving tasks?>

Rho leaned back in his chair and stretched out his long legs. He had never understood the weirdly fanatical loyalty that Frea inspired in the talentless idiots who made up a good portion of the Shadari garrison; after four years, he was nostalgic for the time when he'd still found it amusing. <Sorry we disturbed you, but we didn't think anything we were saying would make it past those magnificent waves of self-satisfaction you're displaying.>

<Come off it, Rho. I'm sick of your fine Arregador airs.> Ingeld's quick anger came at him like the swing of a hammer, but Rho had long ago ceased to take it seriously. <Who cares if you're from one of the twelve high clans? You're still stuck here like the rest of us.>

<Now, now, let's not bring clans into this,> said Daem.

<Says the Aelbar, of course,> Ingeld shot back. <You people from the high clans always stick together. Well, the way Lady Frea feels about *you*, Daem, good luck getting a transfer out—you'll probably be stuck here for the rest of your life.>

<Anyway,> said Daem, ignoring Ingeld as he unwrapped yet another sweet, <I don't need to save them now, because soon I'll be able to buy more. We'll be getting paid when the ship arrives from Norland, and that always brings the Nomas back—>

<—like flies to shit,> Ingeld finished for him.

<That's *enough!*> The last of Rho's roommates, Ongen, heaved himself up from his cot and swung his heavy

legs over the side. The strap had come loose from his hair while he slept and the tangled white strands clung to his thick neck. <Onfar's balls, didn't anyone ever teach you people how to keep your conversations to yourselves?>

Daem sat up and said, <In a room this small? Where do you think we are, the great hall in Ravindal? Speaking of which . . . >He trailed off as he fished under his tangled blanket. <I found *this* on the table when I came back from my patrol this afternoon.>

He flung the book across the room at Ongen, but the lack of effort he put into the throw sent it spinning toward the table instead. Rho snatched it out of the air, recognizing the plain leather cover; it was the only book Ongen owned, a poorly lettered copy of the battle poems from *The Book of the Hall.*

<Ongen, we're all happy you're learning to read,> he said, pleased to feel Daem's burst of malicious delight, <but you can't leave this lying around. You're lucky the slaves didn't destroy it.>

<Lucky?> Ongen snapped. <*They're* lucky, you mean.>

<Just lock it up in the strongbox next time, will you?> Rho bent down to pull on his boots.

<Why should I? Are we the masters here, or them? I don't give a damn about their religion.>

<Okay, forget it. If you want your book destroyed, go ahead and leave it out.>

<No, I'm sick of this,> said Ongen. <I shouldn't have to lock my things up because of *them*. If we made the punishment bad enough, they'd stop doing it.>

<No, they wouldn't. Governor Eonar has been here for more than twenty years, don't you think he tried that? It's their religion. It's important to them.>

<Their religion is stupid. They worship the stars, or the stars are gods, or something? What does that have to do with books? The problem is we're too easy on them. I'm telling you, if you cut—>

The curtain across the chamber's entrance moved aside and a barefoot slave in a shapeless, undyed robe and a brown headscarf slipped through carrying a basket of clean laundry.

<—cut off their hands or just went ahead and killed a few of them for it, they'd stop doing it.> Ongen watched the Shadari girl set the basket down against the wall and move noiselessly to retrieve one full of soiled laundry closer to his cot.

<Or you could make them learn to read and write,> Daem suggested. <That would really teach them a lesson.>

<Sometimes I think they only pretend not to understand us,> said Ongen. His silver eyes—too small for his heavy, square face—followed the slave toward the door. <That one there could be listening to us right now. I mean, how do we really know they can't? And why can't they? Other races can, lots of them.>

<Who knows?> said Ingeld. <Because they're from the desert, maybe. Who cares?>

<The Nomas are from the desert.>

<The Nomas get around,> Ingeld replied. <If you go back far enough, I'll bet there's even some Norlander in their bloodlines.>

<Do the Nomas even have bloodlines?> asked Daem. <I think it's really more of a puddle.>

Rho got up to retrieve his sword; the bickering was beginning to weary him, and it reminded him too much of his brothers.

<What are you doing up so early, anyway?> Daem asked him.

<I know where he's going,> sneered Ongen. <Lady Frea's passed him down to little Isa, just like a pair of old trousers.>

<*Lady* Isa's Naming Day is tomorrow, and I've been helping her prepare,> Rho replied, making sure that Ongen felt the full force of his displeasure.

<She's going to challenge Lady Frea after all?> asked Daem.

<Of course she is,> said Ingeld. <She's going to name her mother's sword, isn't she?>

Rho's own weapon felt heavier than usual as he lifted it up—it was a family sword, ancient and ungainly, with a huge uncut gem like a bird's egg set in the cross—and settled the scabbard over his shoulders. His four elder brothers had all passed it over in favor of new imperial blades, and he remembered the diligence with which he'd practiced wielding it for his own Naming Day. When the day came, his eldest brother Gavin had shown up so drunk he could barely stand, and the whole ceremony had turned into a joke. His brothers had been furious with him when they'd sobered up and found he'd named it Fortune's Blight.

<I wouldn't mind sparring with Lady Isa one of these days,> mused Daem. <Oh, relax, Rho. What do you expect? There are only two Norlander women in this entire colony, and the other one is Lady Frea. If you want me to think about someone else, get the emperor to start posting women here.>

<I don't understand why there aren't any,> said Ingeld. <There were plenty of women in the garrison at Thrakya.>

<That's the governor's doing, not the emperor's,> said Rho. <He stopped allowing any women posted here after his wife—>

He stopped short when he sensed Falkar coming down the hall with an urgency that was hard to ignore. The others felt it, too, turning toward the doorway just before the lieutenant—armed, and in full uniform—pushed the curtain aside.

<Get up and get dressed. Lady Frea wants everyone down at the mines. The triffons are already being saddled.>

<Everyone? Why, what's going on?> asked Ingeld,

bolting up and practically humming with eagerness. <Has something happened?>

<Ask Rho,> said Falkar, and left the way he'd come. The instant he was gone, all three of his roommates barraged Rho with questions.

<Calm down, will you? I overheard something last night at the mines. The slaves sounded like they were planning something—some kind of uprising—so I told Lady Frea about it. That's all.>

<Oh. I get it,> said Ongen, flopping back down onto his cot. The wooden legs of the simple frame creaked under his weight. <For once I thought we were going to get a real fight. You make me sick, Rho.>

<In that case, maybe you should change rooms. It's important not to neglect your health.>

As usual, Ongen didn't get the joke. <I can't believe the whole garrison is on alert, just because *you* want to worm your way back into Lady Frea's trousers.>

<He's got as much chance as an icicle in the desert,> said Ingeld, grabbing a pair of clean leggings out of the laundry basket.

Daem leaned back against the wall. <I hate to say it, Rho, but he's right about that.>

<If I don't go back to some place where there's real fighting soon, I'm going to go crazy,> Ingeld vowed as he strapped on his sword: a cheap, newish blade he'd somewhat hilariously named Valor's Glory. <What good is having an empire if all we ever do is stand around looking at slaves? How are we supposed to earn our place in Onfar's Hall?>

<I don't know—what does *The Book* give out as the fate for those who die of boredom?> Daem yanked his tabard off over his head even as the others were still dressing. <This place wouldn't be the empire's dumping ground if there was anyone here to fight. I think it's a good joke that we're here to make sure the imperial swords get made, but none of us are important enough

to own one. Onfar must have a sense of humor after all.>

<Why are you taking that off?> Rho asked him.

<*I* can't go. Lady Frea has me assigned to day-patrol,> Daem reminded him. <I'm not the kind of soldier who disobeys orders.>

<Yes, you are.>

<Not the orders I like.>

<Just get dressed.>

<This isn't about the imperial swords. I wouldn't name one if the emperor himself ordered me to,> Ingeld insisted. <Why do you think Lady Frea doesn't have one? A real Norlander doesn't defeat his enemies with tricks. The empire is *changing* us—being a Norlander doesn't mean what it used to mean. I was there at the taking of Thrakya when they brought in mercenary archers—*archers*! The bow is a coward's weapon. You'll see, when we go to Onfar to be judged, I bet he counts one kill with a steel blade like ours the same as ten with a black one.>

<Lord Eofar has an imperial sword. Are you saying that makes him a coward?> asked Daem.

<I didn't say that,> Ingeld replied hurriedly.

<Don't forget that Governor Eonar has one, too,> added Rho.

Ingeld, dressed now, had no answer for that; he and Ongen headed for the doorway, both of them grabbing their white sun-proof cloaks on the way out. Rho leaned against the wall and waited patiently for Daem to put his boots on. Then he noticed that once again Ongen had left his book lying on the table. He took the key from its hiding-place under the chair, unlocked the strongbox in the corner, and tossed the volume in with the rest of their books, papers, pens and ink. By that time, Daem was ready to go.

<I *did* hear them planning something,> he told his friend. He hated himself for letting Ongen worry him, but he couldn't help it.

<I believe you.>

<Frea's not going to be happy if I'm wrong.>

Daem's sympathy was reassuring. <Don't worry. I know just what you need.> He was still carrying the little jar of candied fruit; he took one out and pressed it into Rho's hand. <Here. *You* take the last one.>

Amused in spite of himself, Rho tucked the dubious gift into his pocket. <Thanks,> he said, <but I'll save it for later.>

Chapter Three

Eofar stood in the middle of his bedroom tipping the little bottle back and forth, watching the red liquid slide from one end to the other. He hadn't slept. In the darkness of his windowless room, he found it too easy to torment himself with the morbid fantasies he'd built up, layer by layer, over the last five months. Several hours before sunset he'd given up, dressed in the same limp shirt and trousers from the night before and sat back down to berate himself for the fact that after all the elixir had cost him, he lacked the courage to use it.

First he told himself that taking it would be foolhardy—he had no way of knowing what it would do to him. Even if it was harmless to the Shadari, no one could possibly know what effect it might have on a Norlander; it might even poison him. Then he had told himself that the elixir was too valuable to waste; they would need money to get far enough away to start a new life—the Antinean Islands, maybe, or Prol Irat—and he had spent everything he had acquiring it.

That had been hours ago, and the longer he hesitated, the less energy he had to deceive himself. He was afraid of the truth—that was the real reason. Everything else was just noise.

He tore the wax seal from the bottle and threw the pieces onto the stone floor. The cork felt warm to his fingers and the air trapped inside escaped with a faint pop as he pulled it out. A bitter aroma snaked from the bottle's mouth.

But at the sound of someone moving beyond the curtain out in the hall, he stuffed the cork back in and thrust the bottle into his pocket. He held his breath, listening: the footsteps were soft. A barefoot slave, perhaps—Daryan, with his clean linen and breakfast? But no, it was too early. Daryan would still be asleep in his little chamber down the hall.

His eyes strayed for a moment to his sword, Strife's Bane, hanging in its scabbard on the wall. He had the great honor of being the only other person in the Shadar besides his father to own a black-bladed imperial sword. It was a beautiful thing: twin triffons, worked in silver with shining gold claws and eyes, twined up the hilt and unfurled their wings to form the guard; a row of faceted red calipset stones marked out the crosspiece. His father had commissioned the hilt from Norland especially for him when he was still a boy. When he'd received it he'd thought he could never love anything as much as he loved that sword. His Naming Day had been the first really happy day of his life since his mother's death. Even Frea hadn't been able to spoil it for him; she had declared that a real swordsman didn't need to resort to cheap tricks to win a battle—but her bitter envy had only made him that much more proud.

Now the very sight of it sickened him.

Every time he looked at its shiny black blade he saw reflected the gaunt faces of the men who had slaved their lives away in the mines. He saw the hopeless faces of their families lining up for their daily bread, old men and women and children who would starve if their men tried to escape or died or became too sick to work. He thought of the young men and women snatched from the arms of their families and brought here, to the temple, to wait upon Eofar and his family and the garrison's soldiers, in darkness, for the rest of their lives.

The blade quivered in its scabbard, responding to his

attention, and the triffons' wings rattled softly against the stone wall. He decided to leave it where it was; he told himself that taking it down would make a noise, and if someone was spying on him, he wanted to surprise them.

He made his way past the low dais on which his bed was placed, and then past his few imported pieces of heavy Norland furniture—a carved chair, a small writing-desk, a trunk with a stout lock for his books and papers—until he was close enough to look out from behind the curtain. His chamber lay at the crossing of two passages, one running parallel to his room, north to south; the other beginning at his door and running westward about twenty paces before it intersected with another north-south passage running the length of the temple's western wall. That passage, like most of those along the outer walls, was pierced at intervals with small window openings, and from the door of his room Eofar could look straight down to one of these windows.

That's where he saw Isa. The shutter was still closed but the latch had been lifted, allowing a tantalizing sliver of light, glowing with the depth and color of a jewel, to creep through a tiny chink.

She had her hand in the light.

<Isa!> Eofar cried, springing forward. She snatched her hand away just as tiny tongues of blue flame rippled across her palm and she whirled toward Eofar, her long white hair fanning out around her shoulders. <Damn it, let me see your hand,> he demanded, grabbing her pale wrist and pulling her toward him as she attempted to conceal her hands beneath the wide sleeves of her gown. <Isa. Let me see it.>

<Let go of me,> she said, but he tightened his grip around her wrist and bent closer to examine the flesh. A few blue blotches marked her palm, but nothing worse. The veins underneath her semi-transparent skin shone with a healthy blue glow. There was no sign of the black

poison that resulted from a serious burn. <There—you see?> she told him. <It's fine. Nothing.>

<We talked about this,> he reminded her, but he relaxed his grip and she pulled her hand away. <You promised me. I told you I'd tell Father if I caught you again.>

<Oh, really? And how are you going to do that? Ask Frea to tell him for you?> she asked. She knew how badly it rankled that Father hadn't spoken to any of them except Frea in months.

<That robe might be a fine thing to sleep in, but do you really think you should be walking around like that? You're not a little girl any more,> he snapped back at her. She was cocooned in the folds of a shimmering gossamer gown, the kind worn in Norland over several layers of more concealing clothing.

<It's too hot for anything else,> she complained, but he saw her tug the collar a little closer around her throat.

<You'd be cooler if you braided your hair,> he said, simmering with impatience. <Or better yet, if you went back to bed until later. Which is what I'm going to do.> He turned and started back toward his room.

<Wait, Eofar. I need to talk to you. About Frea.> When he turned back around, her silver-gray eyes were sparkling in outrage. <She's still saying she won't fight me.>

<Well, I still agree with her,> he said, even though he knew this response was sure to prolong the conversation. <I've told you before, I think we should skip it. Just keep the sword, if you want it so badly. No one will know. And Frea doesn't care. It doesn't matter to her what you do.>

He'd known this moment had been coming, ever since Isa, ten years old at the time, had taken the opulently jeweled sword from their mother Eleana's tomb and stubbornly dragged it back to her room. As the eldest daughter, Frea had first claim to the sword, but she wanted nothing to do with it; for her own Naming Day she had commissioned Blood's Pride from the swordmakers at Ravinsur according to her own precise specifications. But there was still Norlander tradition: if Isa wanted to carry her mother's sword, she had to fight her older sister for the right to do so on her Naming Day. That was her seventeenth birthday. Tomorrow.

Isa's wordless fury struck him like a slap. <I don't understand you, Eofar. It's written in *The Book of the Hall*. How can you just ignore tradition—?>

<It's a pointless ritual, Isa,> he said, sick to death of the whole subject. <Two women bang their swords together a few times, the older one lets herself get pricked in the arm and then everyone goes off and gets drunk in the hall. It's just a chance to show off for the neighbors. We don't have any use for that kind of thing out here. We don't have anyone to impress.>

<That's not the reason you don't want me to fight. You think I can't win. Eofar, you don't know how good I am. Rho has been sparring with me, and he says he's never—>

<What I know is that Frea will hurt you—badly—if you're foolish enough to fight her.>

<What do you expect me to do when we get back to Norland, Eofar?> she pressed, flexing her long white fingers and then lacing them together. He could feel the undercurrent of her anxiety like a sinking in the pit of his stomach. <What do I tell people when they ask me about my Naming Day? That my family didn't think it mattered? Don't you care anything about our honor?>

Eofar shut his eyes. This wasn't a conversation he wanted to have with her, and he certainly didn't want to have it now. <Isa, it may be years before—>

<Frea says she's going to do whatever it takes to get us recalled before next winter.>

<It's not up to Frea. It's the emperor's decision.>

She looked away from him, toward the shuttered window, as if she could see through it all the way to the snow-covered mountains of Norland, far across the sea. <But we will go back some day. We have to. It's our home.>

<A home we've never seen,> he reminded her. <Maybe you wouldn't like living where it's always dark, high up on a frozen mountain. Maybe we've grown . . . different, out here on our own, in the desert.>

<That's ridiculous,> she said, but he could feel her shoving back some emotion she didn't want him to see. He had touched a nerve. <Of course we'll go back. There's nothing for us here.>

<There could be,> he told her. <Work. Friends—>

<Friends?> she asked incredulously. <Who? The soldiers? Or do you mean the slaves?>

<They're Shadari, Isa,> he reminded her, his blood warming. <They weren't always slaves, and one day they may not be again. And yes, why not?>

<Because I know what's proper and apparently you don't. Like that woman.> A blue flush tinted her pale cheeks. <It's not right for an unmarried man to have a female hand-servant. Father should never have allowed it.>

<Harotha is dead, Isa,> he said, imparting a note of warning. <She's been dead for five months. You know that.> He forced himself to stay calm. <Well, what about Daryan? He's my friend, and he was yours too, once—practically a brother. You've known him since you were five years old. For Onfar's sake, you used to chase each other up and down these hallways when you were little. Now you treat him like he's just another invisible servant.>

<So Daryan is your friend?>

<Yes.>

<And you trust him?>

<Yes, why not?>

<Why not?> Isa asked with bitter triumph. She beckoned him down the western hallway and around a sharp corner to the doorway of Daryan's room. Then she

thrust her white arm at the dark opening. <So where is he right now?>

Eofar stepped past her and glanced inside the little room. The straw pallet was disarranged and the bedclothes were half on the floor, as if Daryan had risen hastily. <I don't know, Isa,> he said, <maybe he's getting an early start on his duties. Maybe he went to the washroom. Maybe he's with a pretty girl. The more interesting question,> he said, stepping closer to his little sister, and looking into her eyes, <is how you knew he wasn't here—unless you had already been here looking for him?>

A complicated mix of consternation and pique sputtered out of her, but before she had time to respond she suddenly stumbled, as if she'd been pushed from behind. She lost her balance and fell down on one knee. Over her head, Eofar saw the person who had just come around the corner and crashed into her.

The female slave, struggling to keep hold of a gigantic bundle clasped in her thin arms, took a moment to realize who she'd knocked into and then let out a sharp cry that pierced Eofar's head like a dagger. "I'm sorry, my Lord! My Lady!" the slave whispered, frantically reverting to the low tones in which the slaves were taught to address their masters. Rahsa, that was her name. She was new to the temple, but he remembered the unusual reddish tint of the hair straggling out from beneath her scarf, and the odd air she had about her.

"They told me to open the shutters for the night and take these things up to the laundry. I didn't know— Let me—" And clearly without thinking, she shifted her bundle to one side and reached out for Isa's arm to help her up.

Isa cried out in pain as the Shadari's touch burned into her cold flesh—though of course Rahsa couldn't hear her—and wrenched her arm away violently, but not before the cold of Isa's skin bit into Rahsa's fingers. The slave choked back her own scream as the realization of her terrible mistake broke over her; she dropped her bundle and stared at Eofar and Isa, quaking, her big brown eyes stretched wide in terror.

"I'm s-sorry," she stammered.

"Go," Isa hissed at her menacingly in Shadari, and Rahsa turned and fled down the corridor, leaving her bundle behind on the floor. Eofar heard the sound of her bare feet slapping against the hard stone.

<Isa! Bloody Onfar, was that really necessary? I know it stings, but a little touch like that isn't going to kill you,> he fumed as Rahsa disappeared into the darkness. <You frightened that poor girl half to death. For all the complaining you do about Frea, you certainly do your best to act just like her sometimes.>

Isa stood up slowly. She compacted her emotions down into a dark brood and now she stood before him so still that she might have been a statue carved in ice. <I'll make Frea fight me,> she told him coolly, <without your help.> And she turned and left him alone in the hallway.

Her feelings were like blinding colors; a conversation with her always left him spent and disoriented. He wished she could have remained the little girl who had liked nothing better than to throw her skinny arms around his neck and rest her white head on his shoulder.

He tapped the hard lump of the little bottle in his shirt pocket, and started back for his room.

<Lord Eofar!>

Striding down the corridor in front of his room came two of the garrison's soldiers, dressed for duty in their embroidered tabards and white sun-proof cloaks, their broadswords sheathed across their backs.

<What is it, Rho?> he asked impatiently.

<Sorry, my Lord; I was just wondering if you'd seen Lady Isa. I went by her room but she wasn't there.>

<She was just here, but I don't know where she went,> Eofar told him. <Why?>

<I was supposed to spar with her tonight, but Lady

Frea wants everyone down at the mines. I just wanted to tell her.>

Eofar paused with his hand on the curtain to his room. <I wish you wouldn't encourage her, Rho,> he said. <I know this is a way for you to get back at Frea, but Isa could really get hurt.>

He felt Rho's anger, but the soldier was too well-bred to answer back to the governor's son. There had been a time when Eofar thought he and Rho might become friends—but then Frea had taken Rho under her wing and into her bed, and by the time she dropped him, it was too late.

<Come on, Daem.> Rho said to his companion, and Eofar watched them go, listening to the strike of their boots echoing down the featureless red rock hallways.

<Wait,> he called out after a moment and ran to catch them up. <Why does Frea want everyone at the mines?>

Rho's chill displeasure darkened to uneasiness. <There might be trouble tonight. I overheard some of the slaves talking. It sounded like they were planning something.>

<An uprising?>

<Sounded like it to me,> said Rho.

He would know, if anyone would, Eofar thought. With apparently minimal effort and even less intent, Rho had learned to speak Shadari more fluently than anyone else in the garrison, including Eofar, who had lived there his whole life. <Did they mention anyone by name?>

Rho betrayed a little flicker of suspicion. <No. Not that I heard.>

<All right.> Eofar looked at Rho and Daem in their immaculate uniforms and was suddenly painfully aware of his rumpled, damp shirt. He knew what the soldiers thought of him; the gossip that had circulated three months ago, after his father had given control of the garrison to Frea, even though he was the elder by nearly two years. He tried his best to ignore it; he had more

important things to worry about. <Well, good luck down there.>

He left Rho and Daem and returned to his room, ducking his head automatically under the lintel of the doorway never meant for someone of his stature, climbed up to the dais and sat down on the bed. He took the little bottle out of his pocket, tipped it one way, then the other.

He pulled out the cork, poured a few drops onto his tongue and swallowed them. And waited.

Chapter Four

Daryan's heart sank when he realized how late he was to arrive. He stopped in the doorway, guiltily glancing around at the other Shadari ringing the pyre, but every one of them had their watering eyes fixed resolutely on the flames. There were at least sixty people there, and probably more of the two hundred-odd slaves in the temple would have come if their duties had allowed it.

He moved in among the mourners as quietly as he could. The flames had already caught the hem of the dead girl's robe and before long were sweeping over her body and consuming the filmy veil covering her face. He watched the garments char away. The heavy, drowsy scent of the oils in which the garments had been soaked rolled through the room—it was oppressive, but at least it masked other less pleasant smells. Acrid smoke spiraled around the pyre and drifted into the room, but the draft pulled most of it up through the aperture in the ceiling and out to the stars. Suffocating heat pulled at his limbs, reminding him longingly of his bed, and he sighed heavily.

"I know. She was so young. And she'd only been here a few weeks," the young Shadari woman standing next to him commiserated in a tragic whisper. She had her hands pressed to her heart, but when she saw him looking at them she self-consciously curled them up under the sleeves of her robe; her knuckles were swollen and red with sores, most likely from scouring floors. "She would have been honored to have you here, Daimon."

A tall man on her other side, so tall that the top of the girl's head did not reach up to his shoulders, nudged her gently. "You're not supposed to call him that, Mariya," he reminded her in a low, deep voice.

The girl brought her swollen hand to her mouth. "I'm so sorry, Dai—" she began, and then stopped herself. "I mean, I'm so sorry, Daryan," she amended, emphasizing his name with a shy giggle.

"That's all right," he said, smiling back at her. He turned back to the fire.

On the far side of the pyre behind the leaping flames, he noticed his Uncle Shairav glaring at him from beneath his heavy black brows. Daryan dropped his smile.

The tall man—Omir, he remembered—looked up through the skylight. "Almost dark," he said to himself. Daryan looked upward as well, anxiously scanning the cobalt sky for any sign of the White Wolf's patrols. Anyone flying over the temple on a dereshadi might easily notice the smoke.

He looked round again at the ring of solemn faces. The Dead Ones had outlawed the burning of the dead as a waste of resources, just as they'd outlawed drums because of the noise, and a host of other Shadari rituals for offending their sensibilities in one way or another. The punishment for participating in this ritual—not to mention the related crimes of stealing oil and straw and exhuming the girl's body from the Dead Ones' tombs—would be unpleasant, to say the least. And yet here they all were, huddled in this unused room while someone kept watch out in the corridor, just to liberate the soul of a young woman most of them barely knew.

Shairav walked forward into the circle, taking a large jar of sand from one of the waiting Shadari. Daryan thought he looked ridiculous in his gaudy ceremonial robes with their silver and gold constellations crudely worked over a ground of flamboyant indigo, but his dark, deep-set eyes, straight shoulders and black hair shot through with silver were still impressive. Shairav poured the sand out onto the floor while the rest of the Shadari knelt down on the hard stone. Everyone—except for Daryan—assiduously averted their eyes while the old priest scratched the prayer into the sand; he was watching Shairav carefully, mouthing the words to himself as they emerged from beneath the asha's sharp fingers.

"You don't look away?" Mariya whispered to him with a thrill of fear in her voice.

"No—it's not a sin for me, because I'm the— you know," he whispered back. "Not many people know it, but it's one of the ancient privileges. All the daimons used to read and write. My uncle said my father and my grandfather never bothered with it, but I made him teach me anyway."

Mariya looked up at him, wide-eyed. "What for?"

He answered with a tiny shrug, but when she looked away again he allowed himself a secretive pat to his chest. Underneath his robe, he could feel the flat, square object hidden inside his pocket.

"We inscribe these prayers to the gods on behalf of their daughter Inada," Shairav was intoning solemnly, "that they may see her and take her spirit upward to join them in their eternal dance."

"The gods are merciful," murmured the assembly.

Shairav took the tattered hem of his robe in his hand and with a long, careful sweep of the fabric, smoothed away the sacred inscriptions so that none but the gods would ever look upon them. "Your daughter Inada's spirit has been freed from the flesh and returns to the winds and the sands. May the gods watch over us all this night, and all nights."

The ceremony was over. Obeying a gesture from Shairav, the rest of the Shadari scrambled to douse the fire with the mound of blankets they'd brought for the purpose. Daryan stepped back out of their way and collided gracelessly with someone behind him.

"I'm sorry," he murmured, but his apology was drowned out by a chorus of anxious protestations of concern on his behalf. "I'm fine, really," he started, but then he caught sight of an older man with a long nose and sharp, intelligent eyes. "Tal!" he called out, walking over and taking him swiftly by the arm. He pulled him back a little from the others. "Did you ask him? What did he say?"

Tal began to speak, but then the expression in his eyes suddenly changed. At the same moment Daryan's nose caught the stink of dereshadi.

"Ask me what?" His uncle stood behind him, already changed out of his asha finery and back into the brown breedmaster's robe in which he'd seen more than fifty of the stinking creatures into the world. His eyes were bloodshot from the smoke.

"We thought—" began Daryan, but Tal interrupted him.

"It was my idea, Shairav'Asha," Tal lied. "These ceremonies are so heartening for everyone; we thought that perhaps we could do something for Harotha—"

"Daryan and I have already discussed this," said Shairav, looking not at Tal but at Daryan. He finished tying his sash with an angry tug. "I cannot perform the funeral rites without a body. Have you found her body?"

Daryan's jaw tightened. "You know we haven't."

"Well then."

"But she has to be in one of the tombs. We just haven't found the right one yet. We're still looking—"

"You've been looking for five months." Shairav shook his head. "I'm sorry. There's nothing I can do."

Daryan, emboldened by the presence of Tal and the other Shadari surreptitiously watching and listening as they bustled around the room, pleaded, "You're our only asha—the last asha. Can't you just make something up? Make a new ritual? We're not asking you to use your powers. Just to say a few prayers for her. After everything she did for us—"

"Stirred up trouble, that's what she did," Shairav began, but Daryan was spared the rest of the lecture when the sound of footsteps echoed down the corridor toward them. The Shadari all turned toward the sound.

"They've found us!" someone cried out.

"The White Wolf!" gasped someone else, but Daryan recognized the rag-doll's tangle of reddish hair as a dark figure slipped through the door and hurtled toward them.

"Oh, Shairav'Asha, it's the governor's daughter, please, it's Lady Isa," Rahsa panted, throwing herself at the old man's feet.

"What's wrong?" Daryan asked.

Rahsa looked up at them, her eyes swimming in tears. "I was taking the laundry up, like they told me, and I—I didn't mean to—" She stopped to gulp down the sob rising in her throat. "I never expected anyone to be there so early. They were outside your room, Daimon—"

"Rahsa," Shairav interrupted, "you know you must never refer to Daryan as the daimon, even when only we Shadari are present."

Rahsa dropped her eyes. "Yes, Shairav'Asha, I'm sorry."

"My room?" Daryan asked, but she was already hurrying on.

"I couldn't see over the bundle I was carrying and I knocked into her, and then I tried to help her up, and I *touched her arm*—Please, I didn't mean to do it. Please hide me! I don't want to be—"

"Rahsa, calm down!" Daryan bent down and forced the hysterical girl to get to her feet, thinking how unfortunate she was to be pretty enough for temple service; the sensitive ones never fared well. "You couldn't have hurt her badly if you only touched her for a moment. It might have stung a little, but that's all. It was just a mistake. She's probably forgotten all about it by now."

Rahsa looked up at him with a reverential gleam in her eyes. "Do you really think so?" she asked.

"I'm going to take Lord Eofar his breakfast right

now—I'll talk to him about it. It will be all right, I promise you. Go on, now. You should be getting back."

Before he could say anything further another Shadari dressed in stableworkers' brown, Shairav's fawning new assistant, Majid, came through the door. "Shairav'Asha," he said in a low voice, "you're needed in the stables. The White Wolf is already awake and the whole garrison is preparing to ride out."

Most of the other Shadari, having quickly realized that Rahsa's dramatics did not concern them, had already left the funeral chamber to resume their duties. Just as Daryan turned to slip away with them, his uncle thwarted his escape, calling, "Walk with me."

"Of course, Uncle," he said, suppressing a sigh. He took his place at Shairav's side and they strode off toward the stables where his uncle's beloved dereshadi would be having their messy breakfast of rotting goat. The refectory where Eofar's breakfast was waiting to be fetched lay just beyond the stables. He could think of no good excuse for going a different way from Shairav but he knew what would happen the moment they were alone together.

Shairav did not disappoint. "I do not want to hear that woman's name mentioned, by you or anyone else, ever again," he said as soon as they were alone. The old man hated her, of course. Until Shairav had taken over as breedmaster, the dereshadi had been steadily dying out. Harotha had been the only one with the courage to point out that without enough dereshadi at their disposal, the Dead Ones might not have been able to maintain control of the colony.

Daryan found himself compulsively counting the empty brackets between the few torches the Dead Ones—who could see in almost total darkness—allowed the slaves to light. *Two, three, four, five . . .*

"Daryan. Did you hear what I said?"

"I'm not the only one who thinks she should be honored," he argued, carefully keeping his tone amiable.

"Her mother and father were both ashas. Her family has produced at least one asha in every generation as far back as anyone can remember—"

"And they died, along with the others. So her parents were ashas; she was not—the *presumption*, coming here and demanding to be shown the secret staircase, expecting me to ordain her—"

"So she could carry on if something happened to you," he put in. "Otherwise all the knowledge of the ashas will die with you."

"She wanted power for herself," said Shairav, "and she would have used it to destroy everything you and I have spent our lives preserving. Do you think it has been easy for me to keep my vow not to use my powers? And if I had broken my vow, do you think you and I would still be alive?"

"I know that," said Daryan, looking down at the stone floor. "If you hadn't brought me here I'd be choking on black dust in the mines or sweating blood in the smelting shacks, or laid out on a pyre, just like that girl." He had already forgotten her name. *Was it Inara?* "But what about the other things Harotha did? She and Faroth were organizing the resistance in the city, and she allowed herself to be brought to the temple of her own free will—"

"Which was foolish. And look where it got her."

"Dead," he murmured darkly, rubbing at his smoke-stung eyes. "Falling down the stairs." He shook his head with a grim laugh. "Someone like Harotha just hits her head and dies. It's not right."

"It was the will of the gods," Shairav intoned. "She was not your friend. She was using you."

"She wanted the daimon to be more than just a name," Daryan mumbled to himself. He could almost hear her, exhorting him to action in that firm but cajoling voice of hers. She had expected more from him; she had wanted him to expect more from himself. And here he was, months after her death, so useless that he couldn't even give her a proper funeral. "She wanted me to do something."

As they entered the stables the reek of spoiled meat assaulted Daryan's senses. The vast cavern, shaped like an inverted bowl with the bottom knocked out, was already abuzz with activity. Soldiers in white capes with great swords slung across their backs strode around waiting for their mounts to be saddled. The light was dim and the faint glow of the Dead Ones' skin stood out clearly. Dereshadi sleepily leaped or glided down to the straw-covered floor from dark berths chiseled high up into the cavern walls, and then lumbered about, rolling their massive heads, and endangering slaves and Dead Ones alike with lazy stretches of their fleshy wings. Slaves hustled about with complicated harnesses or lugged heavy saddles from the storerooms. Feet whispered among the straw, booted and sandalled and bare, and metal clanked and leather creaked, but no voices were raised except for the occasional sibilant whisper.

"You give our people hope," Shairav was saying, "the hope that the Shadari will survive this torment and will someday, with the gods' help, triumph. You are the preserver of our way of life—"

But Daryan was no longer listening to the lecture.

Isa was there.

Chapter Five

Isa whisked aside the red curtain hanging across the doorway to Frea's chambers.

<What do you want?> Frea asked without turning around. She was buckling her scabbard across her chest, and her long immaculately plaited braids swept across the unadorned hilt of Blood's Pride as she yanked the buckle tighter. <I don't have time for you now.>

Isa adjusted her white shirt where it had slipped off her shoulder. It was one of Eofar's cast-offs, and too big for her. The brown leggings were Eofar's as well. The black boots had been Frea's. Importing cloth and leather was expensive, and Isa, as the youngest, was expected to make do. Her father hated waste.

<Do you want to have the ceremony when you get back in the morning or wait until nightfall?> she asked boldly, stepping across the threshold and into the dark room. A single lamp burned on a tall iron stand in the corner. Around the walls hung her sister's collection of weapons, some from Norland, some from places Isa couldn't even name. Despite the desert climate, Frea had perversely covered her bed with thick animal pelts and her silver helmet with its figurehead of a snarling wolf gleamed atop the dark furs. The only other piece of furniture in the room was the carved wooden stand displaying her black-bladed imperial knife, given to her by their father on the day she had assumed responsibility

for the mines. It was nothing compared to Eofar's sword, of course, but he'd still needed special permission from the emperor to make it for her.

<I'm sick of you wasting my time with this,> Frea snapped as she grabbed the helmet from the bed and jammed it down over her head. <I've already given you the only answer you're going to get.> She extended her right hand and with a whir the imperial knife whisked itself into the air, flew across the room and slapped neatly into her waiting palm. She closed her fingers around the hilt with a squeeze of possessiveness and thrust it into the sheath strapped around her thigh. <Never. That's your answer.> She strode out of the room, walking past Isa without a single glance.

Isa hurried out into the hall after her sister. <You've always told us how important it is not to neglect the Norlander rituals,> she reminded Frea.

<What right do you have to name a sword you're never going to use?> Frea replied. Her words felt tightly wrapped, as if she had bound them in iron bands. She was walking so quickly that Isa had to practically run to keep up with her.

<What right do you have to dishonor our family by letting the sword go unnamed?> she countered as they turned another corner in the maze of passages and then pelted up a short, narrow staircase. Every corridor looked like every other corridor in the temple, and even Isa, who had lived here her entire life, still got turned around. When her father had first come to the Shadar as governor he had ordered markings placed on the walls, but the Shadari's abhorrence of writing of any kind was so deep that they'd scrubbed away the signs as fast as the Norlanders could put them up. <You could have claimed the sword for yourself and you didn't. That was your choice, not mine.>

<How was I supposed to know that you'd turn out to be such a coward?> Frea answered as they turned yet another corner.

<If I'm the coward,> she shot back, ignoring the familiar sting of her sister's contempt, <then why are you the one who's refusing to fight?>

They turned another corner and suddenly, right in front of them, was the archway leading into the stables. Through it Isa could see triffons lumbering across the floor, others lounging in their tomblike berths. The rustling of their wings sounded like a swarm of insects massing in the dark. Then the smell of damp hides, dirty straw and spoiled meat hit her. She drew back and reached her hand out to steady herself against the wall.

Frea turned to her, her silver-green eyes glittering in the darkness behind the visor. <I think you just answered your own question,> she said.

Isa snatched her hand away from the wall. She could do this—she *had* to do this.

<Don't make this about the triffons, Frea,> she called after her sister as she followed her inside. <You can't refuse to fight me because of that. I know. I asked Rho.>

<Rho?> Frea called back. <Really, Isa. Can't I throw anything away without you picking it back up?> She speeded up and vanished.

Isa stopped and looked around. She'd lost her. All around her were uniformed soldiers, meek slaves and triffons, but her sister had disappeared. Sweat crawled underneath her shirt. She could not see the way back to the archway they'd just come through. Worse, she couldn't see any of the other entrances either. And people were beginning to notice her. She could tell the Norlanders were gossiping about her precisely by what she couldn't hear them saying. And the Shadari: she could feel them staring at her, and whenever she looked they turned away with a particular expression on their changeable faces. The heat and the smell were stifling. It was getting harder to breathe . . . harder to think.

Then across the room she saw Daryan. He had been looking at her, she could tell, but when she looked toward him he turned away just like the others. She saw him touch another slave on the shoulder, perhaps asking him a question, but she knew by the way he clutched briefly at the curls straggling over the back of his neck that he was well aware of her gaze. A warm, unpleasant flush traveled down her arms and into her fingertips. Disgusted with herself, she turned sharply away.

And there was Frea again, standing beside her triffon, Trakkar, while the slaves finished buckling on his saddle. Her silver helmet turned slowly as she surveyed the preparations in the stables.

<I have an idea,> Frea suggested with a trill of cruel merriment. <We can have the ceremony down at the mines.> Even though the sun was already down, she had donned her white cape and now began pulling on her long riding gloves. Isa could feel her sister's enjoyment of the moment. She had made sure to speak so that the other Norlanders around her could understand every word. <All you have to do is come with us.>

This was usually the point where Eofar would step in and tell Frea to leave her alone, but Eofar wasn't there. <All right,> she tossed back with all the bravado she could muster. She tried to focus her eyes on Frea's helmet and not on Trakkar's bristly hide and fleshy, sweeping tail, or on the massive bulks of the other triffons shuffling all around her. How could anything so heavy and ungainly possibly fly? Even standing with both feet on the ground, she could feel the earth pulling at them, pulling at her, grabbing and pulling—

<Too bad Eofar isn't here,> Frea kept on. She had Isa exposed now, and her words dug like sharp fingers into the invisible wounds. Frea circled around Trakkar, eyeing the preparations of the slaves who were visibly trembling under her scrutiny. <It was fun watching him carry you back to your room that last time. You were in bed for two weeks after that, weren't you?>

Isa whirled around and addressed the first slave she saw. "Get my sword," she commanded. The words scratched and clawed at her throat and fell heavily onto the voiceless silence of the room. Then she picked another slave. “You. Saddle Aeda.”

Frea was right. What good would it do her to carry her mother’s sword if she couldn’t fly? She could do this. Eofar wasn’t here to stop her, and anyway, she wasn’t a little girl any more, relying on him for everything. No, this was possibly her last chance to prove that she was just as much a Norlander as anyone else here. Her mind was made up: this time would be different.

There was a subtle movement from the crowd around her and then Daryan was suddenly there, right in front of her. His eyes were wide, but his usually soft, mobile mouth was as hard as stone. “What do you think you’re doing?” he whispered to her. “You know you can’t—”

Frea clouted him from behind: a tremendous, sweeping blow with her forearm that snapped his head around with terrible force and dropped him to his knees on the hard stone floor. Then she thrust her stiff boot into his back, sending him sprawling onto his face in the dirty straw. The other Shadari gasped: a harsh, involuntary sound that rent the silence. <Eofar’s pet has forgotten his place,> Frea remarked. <I’ll speak to Father about it. A good lashing should solve the problem.>

The Shadari stared at Daryan, their tasks forgotten. Isa had the sense that they would have rushed to him if they hadn’t been too afraid of Frea. She saw him roll over on to his side, breathing hard. Blood—red Shadari blood—smeared the side of his mouth and his face was creased with pain. He kept his eyes fixed on the floor in front of him.

<Why wait for them to saddle Aeda?> Frea asked, walking back to her triffon and unhooking the reins from the pommel of her saddle. The silver helmet gave the illusion of casting its own light in the gloom. <I can ride with one of my men. You take Trakkar.>

Isa walked forward. Trakkar swung his big head around and she saw his slippery black eyes, like weedy, bottomless pools. <I left Mother's sword in my room,> she told Frea.

<One of my men will bring it to you,> Frea replied.

Isa hooked her left foot into the near stirrup, just over the point where the tough ridge of cartilage joined Trakkar's wing to his body, and then reached up and grabbed the pommel of the saddle. In one smooth motion, she lifted herself up and straddled her right leg over, then searched with her foot until she found the other stirrup. The floor of the stables looked much further away than it should have been. Frea's saddle felt hard and uncompromising, as if it knew she didn't belong there. In front of her was the harness, a complicated framework of tough leather straps and burnished brass buckles.

She saw that Daryan was sitting up now, wiping at the blood trickling from his mouth. He was not looking at her, but everyone else was. She could feel their eyes on her, Norlander and Shadari alike. She reached out for the harness, but when her fingers touched it, she felt nothing. Her hands had gone numb. She shook out her wrists and flexed her fingers but the tightness had started in her chest and the next breath she took lodged somewhere in her throat. She reached down and gripped the side of the saddle with both hands as her head began to swim. A drowsy blackness rolled through her and she felt herself listing. She was going to fall. Blindly she kicked her right foot out of the stirrup and brought her leg up over the saddle. She was trying to get down, but her left boot caught on the stirrup on the other side. She clung to the pommel, swinging crazily, until her foot finally came free and she crashed backward down on to the floor.

She didn't think about anything then. She just got up and ran away.

Chapter Six

Daryan raced past the refectory without stopping; his master's breakfast could wait, especially since he never ate it anyway. He dragged his fingers along the wall as he rushed through the corridors, a habit left over from childhood when the bad light and blank walls had made him dizzy; when he reached Eofar's room he found the curtain over the doorway still pulled shut. He halted before it, rolling his stiff jaw and calling softly, "Lord Eofar?" When no answer came he called again, a little louder; then, with a sour feeling in his stomach, he brushed past the curtain and into the room.

Sure enough there was his master, just as Daryan found him most evenings now: sprawled across his bed, half-dressed, sleeping off the wine he'd drunk the night before. It had been the same for three months now, ever since Governor Eonar had transferred command of the garrison to Frea instead of Eofar. The shift had begun even earlier than that, though. It had started a few weeks after Harotha's death, only Daryan had been too numbed by his own grief to notice or care that after twelve years of easy companionship, Eofar had suddenly shut him out completely. Now Daryan spent most of his time staring at the wall in the corridor outside while his master drank alone, envying even a servant's drudgery over the nights of mind-numbing boredom.

You're his slave—not his friend. He's lonely, that's all,

Harotha had told him when she'd first come to the temple, refusing to listen to his explanations about why Eofar wasn't like the other Dead Ones. It had taken three years to prove her right. He only wished he could hear her say she'd told him so.

He walked up to the dais, trying to think of some way to rouse Eofar out of this lethargy, for Isa's sake, but just as he was about to call his master's name more loudly, he noticed that there were no emptied jugs of wine or puddled dregs on the table, and that although his master appeared to be sleeping face-down on the bed, his hands were clutching the bedlinen so hard that Daryan could see the blue veins throbbing in his wrists.

"Lord Eofar!" he cried, leaping up to the dais. The Dead One's shoulders jerked at the sound of Daryan's voice and he twisted his neck around. His eyes were fixed and cloudy, as if he'd been blinded. "My gods, what's wrong?" Daryan gasped. "I'll get the physic—"

As he turned to jump down from the dais, Eofar reached out as if to grab his robe. "No!" he moaned, but his hand fell away and he pitched over onto his back, throwing an arm across his face as if the dim light hurt his eyes. Strands of his pale hair had come loose from the leather binding and stuck to his forehead. His skin was a sickly grayish color and his lips were no longer blue but nearly black.

"You're ill, my Lord. You need help," said Daryan, trying to remember to keep his voice low.

"No," Eofar said again, this time with a little more strength, "not ill—" His left hand scratched among the bedlinen as if he was looking for something. Suddenly, Daryan saw a small, shiny object roll off the bed. It landed on the stone dais with a musical ping and he scooped it up before it could roll down the steps. It was a tiny bottle, stopped with a cork, containing a few drops of some thick, dark liquid.

"What is this?" he asked, tipping the bottle from side to side, watching the syrupy stuff slide back and forth. He stared at Eofar with the bottle cradled loosely in his hand. "It looks like poison," he said thickly. "Is it poison?"

Eofar coughed and rolled onto his side away from him. "I don't know yet." He clawed his way to the edge of the bed, coughing hard enough to make him retch, though he did not. He tried to sit up, but instead slid off the bed and fell down on to the stone step, shutting his eyes and resting his forehead against the wooden bed-frame.

Daryan watched while his breathing gradually slowed, at a loss for any way to help him. Finally Eofar's silver-gray eyes slid open again. "Water, please," he requested thinly, followed by a long, relieved exhalation.

Daryan put the bottle back down on the bed, filled a cup from the cistern in the corner and set it down on the floor next to his master. Eofar's hand shook as he lifted the cup to his lips, but the water appeared to revive him. After a long moment, the Dead One picked up the bottle again. "You don't recognize it?"

"No, my Lord."

"This is made by your own people, to see the future."

Daryan stared at the little bottle in shock. "Divining elixir, my Lord?"

"You've heard of it?"

"Yes, but I didn't think there was any still around. I remember Har—" but he stopped himself there.

"Why did you think it was poison?" asked Eofar, slipping the bottle into his pocket.

Daryan swallowed. "I don't know, my Lord."

"I've had— There are things—" the Dead One started, but he couldn't seem to go any further. He looked past Daryan at the curtain still swinging gently in the doorway. "I'm surprised you think I'd do something like that."

"I don't think I would have," Daryan said carefully, "before."

"Before what?" Eofar asked in his expressionless voice.

"My lord, it's not for me to—"

"Speak."

"You've hardly left your room in months. You barely eat. You drink too much. You've stopped training. Why did you let your father give control of the mines to Lady Frea instead of you? And Lady Isa— I rushed here to tell you that she tried to fly out on Trakkar tonight, by herself." Eofar straightened up quickly. "Don't worry, my Lord," he reassured his master bitterly, "she didn't get off the ground—but you know her: she'll try again. I'm begging you, please do something before she gets hurt."

Eofar stared back at him, his face as smooth and immobile as a slab of marble. "You have more to say."

"No." He stared down at his sandals. "That's all, my Lord."

"Say it."

"I've already said more than I should have, my Lord."

"Daryan," Eofar said, even more quietly; he watched his own clasped fingers for a long moment, then slowly wet his lips and whispered, "why won't you say her name?"

For a moment, Daryan stood there, feeling the hurt pressing down on his chest. Then, speaking as quietly as his master, he said, "She's been dead for five months and you've never mentioned her—not once. We served you together for three years, and when she died, it was like you didn't even notice, like she was just another slave who didn't matter at all. She did matter. She was special." His throat felt swollen and his eyes stung. "I know people die, but nothing feels right without her. Nothing feels . . . finished."

He fixed his eyes on the ground, feeling his nerves singing.

"The elixir," said Eofar. "Do you want to know why I took it?"

Heart beating fast, he answered, "Yes, my Lord."

"I need to show you what I saw." Eofar stepped down from the dais and started toward his trunk, but his strength deserted him again and he sank down into the heavy wooden chair, shutting his eyes and holding on to the carved armrests.

"My Lord?"

Eofar fumbled under the table in front of him, produced the key to the trunk and laid it on the arm of the chair. "The writing instruments. Get them."

Daryan remained where he was, stock-still. "I can't," he said. "You know I'm not allowed to touch—"

"I know you've been stealing them," Eofar informed him and he flushed, but before he could protest or even apologize his master said, "Your rules, not ours. I would have given them to you if you had asked. Now get them."

Daryan went to the trunk, unlocked it and lifted up the lid. For a heady moment he breathed in the dry, musty smell of everything that made his life bearable: secrets and truth, dreams and action, *hope*. Inside the trunk were the flat squares of dried pulp—the Shadari had no word for them, but he had learned the Nomas word, "paper," along with "book," "ink" and "pen"—piled up among quills and little pots of dark, vinegary-smelling ink. On the other side of the trunk were leather and cloth-bound books imported from the Dead Ones' homeland. He reached for the writing implements, then stopped.

The large book with the tattered red cover on the top of the stack belonged to Isa. He had a vivid memory of her sitting with it in her lap, her white hair tumbling down her back, staring at it, while he'd jealously spied on her from behind a chair. With a thrill of trepidation he took a moment to lift up the book. It fell open near the middle. On the left-hand page swirled a Norland script so ornate that he couldn't tell where one word left off and another began, but on the right was a drawing alive with colors so bright they made his eyes ache. It showed a woman in a flowing cape of scarlet trimmed with gold, riding a dereshadi. Seated in front of her, wrapped up in her cape, was a little girl. In the distance a silver castle perched on a mountaintop like a wisp of cloud. The sky was dark, but bright yellow and azure flags fluttered from the castle's innumerable spires, and ornaments of a lustrous purple were shown in the lady's pale hair. The edges of the paper were smudged with dirt as if someone had turned to it many, many times.

"Daryan?" Eofar called out.

He flipped the book closed, scooped up the requested materials and returned to his master. Eofar led him to the desk, where he set everything down, but before the Dead One could begin to write, the clay lid of the inkpot began to rattle, and then the pot itself began to skid very slowly across the desk.

Daryan watched in confusion until he became conscious of a faint, deep grinding sound, coming from a long, long way down. "Earthquake," he announced in alarm, but almost immediately the sound died away and the inkpot trembled to a stop. "Just a tremor," he breathed with relief. "That's the second this month."

Eofar moved to pick up the pen, but instead, after a moment's hesitation he unbuckled the sheath of his dagger from around his leg and dropped it down onto the desk. "I want you to take this."

"My Lord, I can't!" Daryan glanced behind him toward the closed curtain. "You know what will happen to me if I'm caught with a knife—"

"Take it," his master insisted, pushing it closer to him. "I may have to go away tonight, and I might be gone some time, so keep it with you. Just in case."

"My Lord—did you see something about *me*?"

"I'm not sure. Maybe, but it was hard to tell," said Eofar. "Please take it."

The sheathed dagger lay on the desk in front of them; it wasn't going to go away on its own. "Are you ordering me, my Lord?" asked Daryan.

"Accept it as a gift—from a friend."

Finally he picked it up, and a little shiver of danger raced through him. It was too big to put in his pocket so he slid it underneath his robe and then tied his sash tighter to hold it in place. Satisfied, Eofar picked up the quill and dipped it in the ink.

Just as he touched the point to the paper he said, "I have been waiting for a message from someone." He spoke very slowly, as if finding the right words took some effort. "The message should have come a long time ago—I was worried that this person might be in danger, or—" He left the thought unfinished, but his meaning was plain enough. "The elixir was the only way to find out."

Daryan drew close enough to feel the Dead One's chill eddying around him. "What person, my Lord?"

Eofar's quill scratched across the paper. "I saw things—bad things—and a place I must find. This place."

Daryan watched the lines forming under his hand and felt an unexpected flush of panic. He looked again at the curtain. He really shouldn't be part of this.

"Do you know this sign?" Eofar asked, lifting his hand away.

"I don't know—I don't know what that is," he stammered, turning his head away from the paper, just as the Shadari at the funeral had turned away from the sand-written prayer. But despite himself he had already seen the character, a curving line with three small vertical lines beneath it: the Shadari character for "truth." A character that Eofar couldn't possibly know.

His hand ached with the desire to snatch up and rend that forbidden figure, to tear away the disaster that it surely boded. "Only the ashas were allowed to read and write. You know that. They're all dead." He laid his hand down over the paper, covering up the symbol, and looked at his master. "My Lord, who are you looking for? Who is in danger?"

Eofar clutched the quill even harder, and his eyes darted away. "I wanted to tell you—this secret, it was not my idea."

"Tell me what?" It was beginning to dawn on him that whatever Eofar had been hiding was far more serious than he had imagined. "My Lord, *who* is in danger?"

"My wife."

Daryan's face went slack with shock. "Your *what*?"

"We made plans to leave the Shadar. I helped her escape, so she could see her family again. She didn't tell me where they were; she said it wasn't fair to them. We had a signal for when she was ready to go. It should have been a few days, a week. I waited. I've been waiting for five months. I couldn't wait any more."

"Escape? But that would mean—"

"You have never seen a place with that?" In his impatience Eofar's voice had risen to a squeak like a rusty hinge. "A doorway, like this," he drew the shape in the air with his free hand, the other still holding the quill, "with this above it?"

Daryan shook his head. "No," he responded truthfully, still reeling, "I never have."

"Not in the Shadar? Before you came here?"

"I don't know what you saw, my Lord, but it could not have been in the Shadar," he said definitely. "No Shadari would ever make a mark like that—or allow one to be made."

"Harotha"—Eofar paused. His eyes blazed in the low light—"would she make a mark like that?"

"Harotha is dead." The words felt cold and hard leaving his mouth.

Eofar looked down at the desk. The lamplight tinged his white hair with amber.

"Harotha is dead," Daryan said again, blinking rapidly to ward off the sharp pain that had suddenly sprung up behind his eyes. Some unwelcome creature fluttered awake in his chest. "Lord Eofar, Harotha is *dead*."

Eofar set down the quill and looked into his eyes.

Daryan reached out and grasped the edge of the table. When he tried to speak again, the creature in his chest crawled up into his throat and choked him, so that he barely had breath enough to whisper, "*Isn't she?*"

Chapter Seven

"Move over, Dramash."

"You move over."

"No—you! My mother can see me from here!"

"No, she can't, Cara. The laundry's in the way."

"I didn't ask *you*, Beni."

"He's right, and she's inside, anyway," said Dramash. "Come on, let's go over there. We'll see better from there."

Harotha pulled her dark shawl closer around her face as the three children scuttled away from the side of the house. She heard their bare feet rustle through the dry weeds and caught a glimpse of their little figures as she shrank around toward the back. A moment later she heard their voices again, just a few feet away. She was trapped; if she moved too much further around the curved wall she'd be in view of the house opposite.

"I'm scared. I want to go home," said the little girl.

"There's nothing to be scared of," said Dramash. Harotha smiled at his gently patronizing tone; the girl was about a head taller than her little nephew. "Just wait. They'll fly right over us. You'll like it."

"You said if we stayed out until curfew we'd see something special. I've seen dereshadi before," said the other boy. He sounded older than Dramash and from his height she guessed he was eight or nine.

"Not like this," Dramash insisted, his enthusiasm undampened. "When they change shifts they fly in a big triangle. It *is* special. When I'm a soldier I'll have a dereshadi of my own. I'm going to teach it to do tricks."

"I don't think your mother will let you do that," said Cara. "She won't even let you go fishing on your cousin's boat."

"She's scared of everything," said Dramash, but even though he meant it as a complaint, Harotha could hear the sadness underneath. He was right, too; Saria *was* scared of everything. "It's okay—she doesn't know it yet, but I'm going to protect her."

"Protecting her is your father's job. Why doesn't *he* do it?" asked Beni. Harotha imagined a sneering, ugly face; she knew it was wrong to dislike a child, particularly one she had never even met, but she couldn't help it.

"He's busy," Dramash answered stolidly.

"How much longer do we have to wait?" Cara broke in, obviously anxious.

"Until it starts getting dark, dummy," said Beni. "Anyway, you *can't* be a soldier," he said to Dramash. "Only Dead Ones can be soldiers."

"I'm going to be one anyway."

"Then you'll be a traitor."

"No, I won't. I'll only do good things. I won't let anyone get hurt in the mines, I'll get more food for everyone, and I'll punish anyone who's bad."

"But you'd have to live in the temple with the Dead Ones," Cara pointed out in an awed voice. "Won't you be afraid?"

"I'm not afraid of the Dead Ones."

"You're not?" Cara asked, breathless. "How come?"

There was a slight pause before he said, "I can't tell you yet. It's a secret."

"You're just a big liar," said Beni. "You're never going to be a soldier. You're going to go into the mines or the temple, just like everyone else."

"I'm going to be a *good* soldier," Dramash persisted, "and my father's going to punish all of the bad ones."

"No, he won't. Your father's no good for anything. He's a cripple."

Harotha's jaw clenched and she felt that familiar sick cramp in the pit of her stomach. She had to remind herself that she was a grown woman, not a child; she was too old to knock Beni down in the dirt for saying nasty things about her brother.

"I'm going home," Cara announced. "I don't want to get in trouble. Okay, Dramash? What are you—? Ow! Something fell on me!"

The other boy made a similar noise and Harotha heard them both scrabbling in the dirt. "Look, those stones came from right up there. Stupid Mitharia should fix her wall. I'm bleeding! This is stupid. I'm going home."

"Me, too," Cara agreed hurriedly.

"Don't go," Dramash pleaded, "you don't have to be scared. It'll be fun—"

"*Cara!*" A shrill voice rang out from somewhere across the street and Harotha jumped. She didn't know the voice but she knew the tone right enough; every child who had ever stayed out too late or gone where they weren't supposed to go knew it well. She also knew that such a shout was likely to draw the head of every other mother within earshot out of the street's curtained doorways. No one could see her where she was standing but she drew her scarf closer anyway.

"*Coming!*" The girl bade her friends a hasty goodbye, then Harotha heard her running furiously across the street. Beni wasn't far behind, and to her relief, Dramash pushed through the drying laundry and circled around toward the front of the house.

Harotha sagged back against the wall. Nothing to do now but wait for Saria to come back out as she'd promised. The light was beginning to fade and the dry weeds pricked at her legs and made her swollen ankles itch. When she and Faroth had been children, this little scrap of land had been a tidy garden fussed over by their indifferent guardian, an unattractive, unmarried older cousin.

The cousin and the garden were long gone, but she still felt like she was trespassing just by standing there. From time to time she could hear the put-upon strains of Saria's voice through the whitewashed clay as she gave Dramash his supper.

She didn't know what to make of her nephew's bizarre ambitions. Saria loved to talk about her son when she came to bring Harotha food and water, but she had never so much as hinted at anything of this kind. That wasn't surprising, though; Saria was far too concerned with other people's opinions to ever say anything that might reflect badly on her family. Dramash couldn't be the only little boy to covet the dereshadi, but it troubled her that he aspired to be one of the soldiers who oppressed and brutalized his people. What had Faroth been telling the boy? Whatever it was, the message had become badly muddled.

"So you are still here," Saria whispered, rounding the wall of the house. "Anyone else would have had the sense to go back, but not you."

"What took you so long?"

"I told you, I have to have supper ready for Faroth when he gets home or he'll ask too many questions. But I don't know why you bothered waiting at all. You came all of this way for nothing—I'm not going to change my mind."

Harotha adjusted her shawl, took a deep breath and tried again. "Saria," she said, "I know you think something terrible will happen, but I have to talk to Faroth. Tonight. He's making a serious mistake."

"Absolutely not," said Saria.

"He's still my brother," Harotha reminded her.

"Yes, he is—and he thinks you're dead. He *mourned* you. I don't think you have any idea what losing you did to him. The gods help me, why do I have to explain this to you over and over again? Why did you come here when every time you asked me I told you to keep away?"

"I should have seen Faroth as soon as I came back. I

know you meant well, but hiding was a mistake. I've been doing nothing, sitting out there alone for the last five months, while this was happening." She grimaced. "This business with the Mongrel has got to be stopped."

"Listen to yourself!" Saria demanded, forgetting to keep her voice low until Harotha quickly shushed her. "You amaze me, you really do. You think you can just walk back in here and start telling everyone what to do again, don't you?"

"Of course not. That's not the point."

"No? I'm sorry I ever mentioned this Mongrel business to you. I think you're looking for an excuse to take over—ever since you realized you couldn't get that elixir. You just can't stand Faroth being in charge instead of you. You've always been like that."

Harotha adjusted her shawl again. Getting angry at her sister-in-law would accomplish nothing—and Saria had been extraordinarily good to her under the circumstances, in her own way. Saria was just an ordinary Shadari girl, a loyal wife and a doting mother. She'd never been interested in politics, though she'd pretended for Faroth's sake. "That's not why I wanted the elixir. I just need guidance. I need to know what the gods want me to do."

"A little late for that, isn't it?" Saria replied acidly.

Harotha laid her hands across her big belly and said, "That's not fair."

The light was beginning to fade but she could still see the anxiety tightening the corners of Saria's dark eyes. "Oh, so I'm not being fair? Is any of this fair to me? I've lied to my husband. I've taken food that might have gone to my son just to keep you and that baby alive. Well, I'm not going to let you throw your life away now: you're going back to that house, and you're going to stay there until—until you do whatever it is you're going to do."

"I can't do that, Saria. Things are different now. I have to—"

"Quiet!" her sister-in-law hissed, and pushed her

back against the hard clay wall, ignoring her stifled cry. "Dramash! What are you doing out here?" she called out loudly, stomping out from around the sideyard and into the street.

Harotha felt the baby wriggle inside her as she crept forward just far enough around the curving wall to spy through the gap before the first blanket hanging on the clothesline. She could see her nephew standing in the dusty track, his head thrown back and his mouth open as he stared up at the sky. Saria flicked the rag in her hand at the swathes of gold and crimson streaking the sky above Mount Asharamon and the smaller peaks on either side. "Can't you see how late it is? Get back inside!"

"I want to see the dereshadi," Dramash answered, gesturing vaguely with the scrap of bread in his hand. He tore off a bit of hard crust and munched it without lowering his eyes.

"Dramash, you'd better mind me," his mother warned him, seizing his arm. "They send people to the mines for being out after curfew. Do you want to go to the mines?" She gave the boy's arm a little shake.

"They won't catch me. I can just—"

"They can do whatever they like. They could send you to the temple—how would you like that? To have to work all night, and do whatever the Dead Ones tell you to do, and never see your cousins or your father and me ever again?"

"I could help take care of the dereshadi," Dramash suggested in a wheedling tone, as if he was asking to go play at a friend's house. "I could be breedmaster when old Shairav dies."

"Shairav?" his mother asked in surprise. "How did you hear about *him*?"

"From Papa. He said that Shairav must like it in the temple, because he would have come back by now if he didn't. How come he could come back from the temple if he wants to, but no one else can?"

"That's enough nonsense now," Saria said. She grabbed

him by the wrist and began pulling him back toward the house. "Get inside, and go to bed. If you're still up when your father gets back, he'll—"

Dramash stopped dead in his tracks and his other arm shot up in the air. "Look!" he shouted.

A triangular shape was drifting toward them. At first it looked like a single massive creature, but as it came closer, Harotha could pick out the six dereshadi flying in formation, one in front, two others wingtip-to-wingtip just behind and three more behind those. The day-patrols were returning to the temple. The six sets of wings beat together in unison, and the sun-proof capes of their riders rippled in the wind, reflecting the ruddy colors of the sunset.

Returning to the temple, where Eofar was waiting for her.

"Dramash!" whispered Saria, holding her boy tighter.

"Don't worry, Mama. I'll protect you."

Saria gave him another squeeze. "There, are you happy? Now get inside!" She swatted him on the bottom to start him off in the right direction. "And go straight to bed!"

As Dramash skipped into the house and disappeared behind the heavy curtain Harotha started to emerge from her hiding-place, but she froze when her sister-in-law said stiffly, "Stay right where you are. They're coming."

Harotha's heart pulsed in her chest and she crossed her arms over her belly and pressed closer to the wall. Saria remained standing where she was, looking down the street. Insects buzzed in the weeds and the houses cast long shadows into the street. Then Harotha too could hear the unmistakable sound of her twin brother's limping gait, and a moment later she saw Faroth stop in front of Saria. She had been seriously considering confronting her brother despite Saria's refusals, but she abandoned that plan when she saw that her brother was not alone.

"What's going on here, Saria? Did I see Dramash out here just now?"

"He only came outside for a moment—only a moment, Faroth," said Saria. "I made him go right back in."

"You have to keep him under control, Saria. You know the White Wolf is sending out more patrols these days. Why did you leave him alone? What are you doing out here?"

"Me? Oh, I was just down the street at Ahnisa's. Her daughter is sick. I told her I'd bring some fish broth over to her later." The ease with which Saria lied to her husband made Harotha think she'd had plenty of practice.

"You're too generous, Saria," said Faroth. "It's not like we have it to spare."

"Faroth, don't you think we should hurry?" asked one of the other men. "The sun's going down, and she'll be waiting in the tavern."

"Let her wait," Faroth answered back in that irritated way that meant he was anxious. He followed his wife into the house while the others waited outside.

Harotha studied the faces of the men; she'd known what to expect from Saria, but seeing them assembled here was still a blow. The most talented of their inner circle, her closest friends—Jai, Shovan, Elud, Thissela, and so many more—were all gone. Jai had been lost to the mines, Shovan to sickness. Elud had split after a bad quarrel with Faroth, taking many with him, only to be killed a few months later in a failed attempt to steal mining tools. Some of his followers had gone back to Faroth after that, but more than a few lost their taste for rebellion at their first sight of blood. Thissela had given up after the death of her only son in the temple; the others had similar stories. Three long years had taken a heavy toll.

She knew those who remained, too: worried Binit, somehow still stout and flabby despite that fact that no one in the Shadar ever had enough to eat; young Elthion, taller and thinner than when she'd last seen him, as if he'd been stretched, and still unable to keep his hands and feet quiet for a moment; broody Alkar, with his right hand missing all of the fingers except the thumb; and short Sami, eager to please, always exhorting the others to listen to Faroth.

She still didn't agree with Faroth's decision to hire the Mongrel, but she had more sympathy for him now. It was impossible to imagine these men overthrowing the Dead Ones without help—her brother could only do so much on his own.

He came back out of the house holding a bundle wrapped up in cloth, with what looked like a sword-hilt protruding from the top. The shape of the bundle was wrong for a straight sword, but she thought she could detect the outline of a wide, curved blade.

"They say she's killed hundreds of people," Saria was saying, clearly continuing an argument that had begun inside. "They say she worships demons, and she's got all sorts of unspeakable evil powers."

"Don't be childish," said Faroth, securing the semi-disguised weapon under his sash. "She's a mercenary. She gets paid to lead armies and to kill, and she's good at it."

"But I heard the ore is running out," Saria argued. "That's why the Dead Ones have doubled the shifts at the mines—they don't even have enough to finish the blades for this shipment, and the emperor's ship is due any day now."

"What of it?" Elthion asked. Harotha had known him since he was a troublesome, colicky baby, and he hadn't improved much over the years.

"I heard the Dead Ones melted down an imperial sword from some soldier who died and mixed in the blood of someone else, to see if they could re-use the ore," Alkar said.

"I heard that, too. It didn't work," Binit chortled. "The Dead One whose blood they used couldn't control the sword—he almost cut off his own arm!"

Faroth glared at Binit, who stopped talking and looked down at his feet.

"If the ore runs out, the Dead Ones will have no reason to stay here," Saria reminded them all. "They may just decide to go and leave us alone. If you get the Mongrel involved now, you'll be stirring up trouble for nothing."

"Where are you getting these ideas, Saria?" Faroth asked, his voice dripping contempt. "At the well? Gossiping with a bunch of brainless women?"

Harotha flushed with anger.

"What's going on?" called out an excited little voice, and Dramash stepped out in front of the curtain, rubbing at his eyes. His robe was askew and his belt untied. Then he caught sight of Faroth. "Papa!" he shouted, bounding toward him. "Where are you going with your sword? Are you going to kill bad people? Can I come?"

Faroth caught the boy by the shoulder. "How do you know what this is?" he asked.

"I . . . I saw you cleaning it last night."

"You were in bed."

"I woke up. You and Mama were talking too loud."

Saria stepped in front of Dramash and stood there with her hands on her hips. "You see?" she said bitterly. "You see what you've brought into our house? I want you to get rid of that thing. I won't let you keep it here any more."

Harotha could see Faroth's face clearly from where she stood. She'd seen that hard glint in his eyes once before: the night Harotha had told him that she was going to the temple to find Shairav, with his approval, or without it.

"Where are you going?" Dramash piped up again. "Can I come, too?"

Faroth looked from Dramash to Saria and back again. "Yes," Faroth said to the boy, "you can come. Tie your robe."

"Faroth, no!" Saria cried in horror, as Dramash let out

a wild whoop of joy. “The Mongrel? And the Dead Ones? He’s six years old! It’s after curfew, and the patrols— What are you thinking?”

“I’m thinking you coddle the boy. Maybe that’s what’s wrong with him. Come on, son.”

Dramash flew to his father’s side with a shriek of delight.

“Faroth, wait!” Saria cried out, rushing over to him. She seized his hand and drew him away from the others, close to the wall where Harotha was concealed as if she’d forgotten her sister-in-law was hiding there.

Harotha held her breath.

“Look into your heart, Faroth. Is this really what the gods want from you? Do you think this is why they spared you from the mines?”

He stared down at her. “*Spared* me?” he asked, with a nasty little laugh. “So that’s what you call being born with a crippled leg, is it? *Spared?* The gods don’t spare anyone, Saria. And neither will I.” He turned away and rejoined the others, and they hurried off down the street with Dramash gamboling like a puppy at his father’s side.

Harotha watched them until they disappeared from her line of sight and then remained with her eyes still focused on the same spot, staring at nothing. For months she had endured Saria’s harping on about her brother’s changed nature; she’d dismissed it all as dramatics. But now she had seen it for herself. She couldn’t believe he could be capable of such casual brutality.

“I hope you heard every word,” Saria said, pushing suddenly through the laundry and making Harotha jump.

’Yes,” she said after a moment, her hand still pressed to her heart. “I heard.”

“Well, now you see for yourself,” Saria fumed, twisting her face up in an effort not to cry. “He took my son away from me—my only child—just because I spoke against him in front of the others. That’s why he did it, you know: to punish me.”

Harotha wanted to deny it but she couldn't. Saria was right—she had been right all along. And now Harotha's situation, already complicated enough, looked far grimmer than it had at the evening's start.

Suddenly Saria reached out and touched her arm. "Do you hear that?"

"Hear what?" she asked, but in the next instant she heard it, too: a long, low rumbling, as if a heavily laden cart were rolling past them down the street. But the street was empty.

"Earthquake," Saria breathed.

"Just a tremor," Harotha reassured her. "Listen—it's already fading."

"It's the gods," said Saria. "They're angry at us. They've abandoned us." As Saria's anger faded, a faint look of hopelessness came into her eyes. Harotha's heart shrank. This was all her fault; she had put her sister-in-law in this position and it wasn't fair to her.

"You were right, Saria. I'm sorry," she said. "I'll go back."

Saria looked at her and the lost look disappeared as swiftly as it had appeared. "Good." She lifted the shawl from her shoulders and draped it over her head.

"What are you doing?" Harotha asked, surprised.

"I'm going with you to make sure you get back safely," Saria said.

"But the curfew, and the patrols—" she protested.

"Someone has to look after you—gods help me, Harotha, sometimes you act like I don't care about you at all!"

Chapter Eight

Jachad pushed aside the curtain of the tiny tavern, looked inside and muttered, "Thank Shof." There was Meiran, slouched on a stool in front of the stone bar with her cowl pulled close around her face despite the lingering late afternoon heat. He picked his way toward her around the battered furniture, glancing uncomfortably at the rounded ceiling arching just over his head.

"We're closed," the Shadari taverner called out with a sour glance at his Nomas garb.

"I'm meeting someone," Jachad informed him pleasantly, and then sniffed the air. "It stinks in here. What's in that lamp? Fish oil?" Then he noticed six or seven coins glinting on the bar and whistled softly: Norland imperial eagles. He squinted at Meiran. "Just how long have you been waiting here, anyway?"

A gulp. The clay cup smacked down.

"More," she rasped and tossed another coin on the bar. The taverner leaped forward to pour her another drink from the jug sweating in his hand.

"I've seen Faroth's men. He should be here soon. I tried to delay them, but they said everything's prepared for tonight." He leaned in closer. "The sun will be down soon," he told her quietly. "If you want to go, I'll wait here for Faroth."

Her only response was to produce a small silver

flask—one he had never seen before—and take a short, sharp pull.

"What is that you're taking?" he asked, eyeing the cup on the bar in confusion.

"Medicine," she said as she stowed the flask away again.

"You have *medicine*?" he asked. "Why haven't I seen you take it before? Why didn't you use it in the desert?"

"There's not much left. I've been saving it."

"Where did you get it?"

She didn't answer.

"Why don't you get out of here and leave her alone, sand-spitter?" the taverner interposed. "She's fine right where she is."

Jachad straightened up. "Now I know you can't be talking to me," he said smoothly, "because my name is Jachad. King Jachad Nisharan, of the Nomas." He tapped his fingers on the bar. "You understand?"

The taverner snapped the evil-smelling rag from his shoulder and began wiping up an invisible spill. "King of bastards," Jachad heard him grousing under his breath. "One of our girls gets in trouble, we don't call her brat the son of a god."

He struggled for self-control. "Insult me all you want, Shadari, but go carefully with my father, Shof. I won't stand for any blasphemy."

"Your father, the sun!" jeered the Shadari, thrusting his sharp-boned face across the bar. "I think you and those other swindlers have been living out in the sun too long. 'Shof' has baked your brains dry!"

Jachad rested his hands on the bar and looked across at the taverner. Wisps of smoke rose up from between his fingers and scorch marks etched black lines in the stone around his palms. "Careful, Shadari. If you want proof of who my father is, you'll get it."

"Tricks! Tricks and lies—that's all you people are good for!"

Suddenly the cups and jars on the shelf behind the bar began to rattle. The taverner stepped hastily aside just as a little jug on the far end shimmied its way off and crashed to the floor. Jachad felt the stone of the bar vibrating and snatched his hands back in alarm.

"Earthquake!" said Jachad and the taverner simultaneously. Jachad looked up at the ceiling, holding his breath, but as he listened, poised to bolt for the door, the faint rumbling subsided. He exhaled and wiped his damp forehead with his sleeve.

But the taverner was now staring at Meiran. He pointed at her with one crooked finger and asked, "Is she dead?"

Meiran was slumped over the bar, her arms outstretched amidst her overturned cup and puddles of wine. Jachad snatched up her flaccid wrist and tried to find the throb of her pulse: thready at first, then a weak but steady pressure against his fingertips.

She slowly removed her arm from his grasp and reached up under her hood. As she hooked a finger under the eye-patch and dragged it across to the other eye, the hood slipped down to her shoulders, leaving her face fully exposed. The taverner drew in a sharp breath and backed away, colliding with the shelves behind him and knocking some cups to the floor.

"They're here," Meiran said, as she leaned across the bar and liberated the wine jug dangling from the taverner's hand.

Four Shadari men and a little boy jostled their way into the tavern. The tallest man had a pronounced limp and he was red-faced, presumably from exertion. The other three were pale—presumably with fear. The leader nodded meaningfully at the taverner, who scooped up the coins from the bar and fled out into the darkening night.

Jachad came forward and smiled down at the boy, a wide-eyed little thing no more than six or seven years old, with long, curling black hair bouncing around his shoulders and over his eyes. "So, you must be Faroth," he said.

"I'm Dramash, son of Faroth, son of Ramesh'Asha, of the Shadari," the child corrected him, with all of the pride and solemnity due to such an impressive lineage. "This is—"

"I'm Faroth," said the man with the limp. He barely glanced at Jachad before turning his eyes past him toward the bar. "So that's her?"

"That's her."

"Good." Faroth reached beneath his robe and brought out a small purse, which he tossed at Jachad's feet. "You can go now."

"Faroth," called out one of the other Shadari—the youngest, scarcely more than a boy himself. He jabbed his finger toward the purse. "You're not going to pay this sand-spitter, are you? We don't even know if she's going to help us yet. You know what these Nomas are. Cheaters and liars, every one of them."

"You asked me to come here," Jachad commented mildly, "not the other way around."

"Oh, your sort will always turn up if there's a profit to be made. But where were you when we needed help? Where were you when the Dead Ones were butchering us?"

He sighed: this old song again—over something that happened long before this whelp was even born. "We're traders, not fighters."

"What about that fire trick you're so proud of?"

"Of all the ignorant—" he murmured to himself. "Only the kings of the Nomas have that power," he informed the man, "and only one is born in each generation. When the Norlanders attacked you, King Tobias was the only one of us not too old or too young to fight. Or would you expect one man to take on the whole Norland Empire?"

"I wouldn't expect anything from a Nomas coward."

"Enough, Elthion!" said Faroth. "The Nomas were

hired to find her and bring her here. She's here. So that's the end of it."

"You really should tie up your dog, Faroth," Jachad answered back, picking up the purse and weighing it doubtfully in his hand, "but there is some sense in his barking. You can't possibly have enough money to pay her to fight for you. So as a gesture of good will, I'll give my fee back to you, and she and I will leave. No one will ever know we were here. We'll forget this ever happened."

"You've been paid, Nomas," another of the Shadari said, stepping forward. All of the fingers but one on his right hand were missing, probably the result of a mining accident. "Get out."

"Oh, come now," pleaded Jachad, throwing out his hands. "*This* is your uprising? The four of you and one little boy?" The boy squeaked in outrage but Jachad had lost the desire to play. The more he looked into Faroth's hard, flat eyes, the more he regretted this bargain. He turned to Meiran. "Come on, let's get out of here. I told you from the beginning that this would be pointless."

"We don't want any more noise from you. We know what you do out in the desert, without any women," Elthion taunted. His hands were balled into fists and an angry vein stood out on his temple. "Go back where you came from, king of goats! Looking at you, I know why your women spend all their time at sea."

"You small-minded little—"

"It's not just us. There are dozens more of us outside right now," broke in the short Shadari hovering at Faroth's elbow. "And hundreds more at the mines and in the city, just waiting for Faroth's signal."

"Shut up, everyone," Faroth commanded in a quiet voice that chilled the room. He limped past Jachad and went over to the bar to stand next to Meiran. "We have money," he told her. "Maybe not as much as you usually get, but besides the currency we can give you—"

"I don't want your money," she said, cutting him off.

His eyes narrowed dangerously. "Come again?"

Meiran stood up. She unhooked the cloak from around her neck and let it slip to the floor, revealing her high Norlander boots, tight leggings and a sleeveless leather vest that creaked against the whipcord muscles of her shoulders. A striated pink and red mass of scar tissue crawled up her right arm from the wrist all the way up to the elbow. Dark blood slipped through the veins beneath her pale gray skin like eels in a stream. The Shadari could see what Jachad already knew: she carried no weapons of any kind, not even a knife.

"If you don't want our money, then why did you come?" Faroth demanded. Jachad saw him angrily fingering the handle of the sword stuck through his sash. It had only a rag for a scabbard. "We've risked our lives just to meet you here. This had better not be some Nomas swindle. Or a trap."

"I don't want your money," Meiran repeated, "but you do have something I want."

"What is that?" Faroth asked, voicing the question that had been plaguing Jachad for weeks.

"After the Dead Ones are gone," said Meiran, "I'll tell you then."

"You can't possibly expect me to agree to that. Tell me what you want, and if it's in our power to give it, it's yours."

Meiran hesitated. Here was the moment, the reason she had come back.

Warmth tickled in Jachad's palms and little flickers of nervous white and blue flame fizzed across his knuckles.

"Not now," Meiran said finally. "After."

"But that's ridiculous." Faroth's voice had risen; his composure was beginning to crack. "You could ask for *anything*—you could ask for the whole city, or for something we don't even have. What then? You'll come back with an army and kill us all?"

"If you want this enough you'll risk that possibility."

At that moment the curtain across the doorway flapped aside and a Shadari with a round, florid face hopped into the tavern. "Patrol," he panted as everyone's eyes swung in his direction.

As Elthion blew out the lamp—it was past curfew, and the tavern was supposed to be closed—they all heard the rhythmic crunch of booted feet on the road. Jachad held his breath. The footsteps approached. The moment lengthened. He waited for the sound of the footsteps to grow softer.

Instead, a surprised cry was followed by sandals slapping the ground, then more cries, more running, and the long scrape of swords being drawn.

"Damn!" swore Faroth, leaping toward the door. "I told them to stay hidden." He snatched up the child and swung him behind the bar. "Wait here, Dramash."

"Don't be afraid," Jachad whispered to the child, when he saw him peeking out from around the corner. When he turned back around he saw Meiran flicker past them all and dash out into the street like a shadow.

"She's not even armed!" Faroth exclaimed as all four Shadari men tried to get through the doorway at the same time to help their comrades.

"I don't think that matters," replied Jachad, grinning in spite of himself. He followed them out into the street.

And into chaos. Shadari were running everywhere, and a few were already dead, or dying on the ground. He noticed sadly that the majority of the rebels were very young, very old, too ugly to serve in the temple or had some kind of injury or deformity that had exempted them from service in the mines. Despite their numbers, they didn't look like they could take a bone away from a hungry dog, much less take their city back from the Norlanders. On the other hand, two Norlander soldiers had thrown down their capes and were lunging nervously at anyone who came within their reach. The Shadari could have overpowered them easily if they'd had the slightest notion of how to organize themselves.

Meiran wasted no time. She kicked the first guard

squarely in the chest with a sideways leap that knocked him down on his back and left him wheezing for breath.

When the second guard came running at her from across the street, she sidestepped him and tripped him as he ran by her. As he fell she grabbed his shoulders and brought her knee up hard against the side of his head, then snatched the sword from his loosened grip.

The first Norlander scrambled up again and rushed at Meiran with his sword aimed at her heart. She swept his thrust aside with a neat flick of her borrowed blade, then matched him blow for blow through a rapid exchange that left Jachad's ears ringing. His hands itched with warmth, but he didn't dare intervene. With a serpentine writhe she slid under the Norlander's shoulder and skipped out behind him. The soldier dropped his weapon and staggered back, blood spurting from his arm and pattering in silvery-blue droplets on the sand: she had drawn the edge of her blade across the back of his arm as she'd passed underneath it. The guard's feet became entangled in one of the cast-off capes and he crashed to the ground. Meiran wrapped her wiry arm around his throat and held on until his eyes rolled up into his head.

Meanwhile, Faroth had been trying to organize his followers: terse commands were given and men slipped away through the city streets; the wounded were helped up and whisked into the dark houses.

Jachad walked across the street to where Meiran stood looking down on the two unconscious Norlanders. He could see her chest rising and falling with the exertion of the fight. Just as he reached her she tossed the borrowed sword to the ground, brushed past Jachad and the Shadari converging on her and disappeared into the tavern. He followed her inside. By the time he had relit the lamp she was sitting at the bar once again, draining a jug of wine to the dregs.

A few moments later Faroth returned leading a small troop of shocked Shadari. They were dragging the two unconscious Norlanders along with them, carrying the guards' unsheathed broadswords carefully to keep the sharp edges from slicing their own flesh. The Shadari dumped the Norlanders on the floor.

Faroth checked on Dramash and then limped straight up to Meiran. "Are more of them coming?" he asked, brandishing his unstained sword.

"They didn't call out to anyone." She paused to take another drink. "Maybe no one was nearby. Maybe they wanted to kill me themselves. They wouldn't be the first to make that mistake."

Faroth glanced over at the unconscious guards. "But you didn't kill them. Why not?"

"Why should I?" She wiped a splash of wine from her mouth with the back of her disfigured forearm. "I don't work for you, remember? You didn't like my terms."

Jachad leaned back against the bar.

Faroth turned to the man beside him and exchanged his battered weapon for one of the captured broadswords. Then he hobbled over to the two Norlanders. Without pausing, he plunged the blade into the back of the first guard. Blue blood swelled around the wound. The body twitched for a moment and then lay still. Faroth awkwardly changed his grip on the sword and yanked it out of the dead man's body, then methodically repeated the procedure on the other man. He turned and handed the dripping sword to his follower, who dropped it as if it were red-hot.

Only then did Jachad notice the boy standing next to the bar, gazing at his father with the grave expression and the round, unblinking eyes of an owl. There was something truly terrible in that look. It had never occurred to Jachad that a child's innocence could be lost in a single moment, but if it were possible, surely he was seeing it now.

"You could never understand how much I want this," Faroth told Meiran.

Jachad saw her smiling back at Faroth. He shut his eyes.

"Then we have a deal?" asked Meiran.

"We have a deal," Faroth replied.

"Faroth, I think Dramash just ran outside," said Elthion, poking around noisily behind the bar.

"What? Why didn't you stop him?" Faroth's eyes flashed. "Sami, go and find him. He can't have gone far." To Meiran, he said, "The mines, then. Our people will be there, waiting for your signal. Before sunrise." He limped out of the tavern with his retinue, leaving Jachad and Meiran alone with the two corpses.

Jachad took a deep breath and gathered his thoughts. "Meiran, if you don't—"

He had intended to plead with her to call off this arrangement—or at least tell him what it was all about—but he never got the chance. Before he could get in another word, a dim rumbling shook the air and then built to a grinding roar. The lamp went out, drowning the tavern in darkness as the ground beneath him dipped. The shelves behind the bar crashed down, shattering winejars and mugs. He no longer knew where to find the door; all he could think of was the ceiling over his head, which he felt sure was about to crack and tumble down on them.

"Jachi!" he heard Meiran cry out, and a moment later he felt her hands on his arms, shoving him. The tepid glow of her skin made him remember himself. He rubbed his fingers together and a little point of flame danced above his hand. They had nearly reached the door when it all stopped.

Meiran let his arm go.

"Is it over?" he asked as a soft cloud of chalky dirt drifted down and settled on his hair and shoulders.

"I don't know." Her silver-green eye gleamed at him.

"Come on." His voice was unsteady. "Let's get out of here."

But she walked back toward the bar, found the lamp and the flints and lit the wick again. He checked the ceiling above him nervously, relieved to see that it looked solid enough, then crossed behind the bar and sifted through the wreckage until he found an unbroken jar of wine. He tore off the wax seal with his teeth and spat it into the dirt. "We have a deal," he repeated with a sigh. "Then I suppose I'm done here."

"Not yet. I need you to deliver a message."

"What message?"

"You need to go after Faroth. He's not going to be at the mines—he's going to get his long-lost sister back."

"Really?" asked Jachad. "That's nice for him. And what about you?"

She walked over to the dead Norlanders and picked up the bloody sword lying next to them, then aimed the point at the two corpses. "I need their heads."

Jachad took a long, deep drink, and said, "Of course you do."

Chapter Nine

Harotha shuddered, her spine tingling. Her back ached terribly after the long walk from Saria's house, and her ankles were so swollen that she could feel them throbbing. Waiting up ahead of them was a derelict building, mottled with dark patches where the whitewash had flaked away from the red clay bricks. The doorway was a black maw, stretching wide to swallow her up. This was the abandoned house where she had lived, alone except for Saria's infrequent visits, for the last five months: five months shut up in the dark, of no more use to anyone than if she really had been buried in the Dead Ones' tombs.

"I can't," she said faintly. "I'm not going back in there."

Saria stopped, too. "I'm sorry, but there's no other place for you to go." She looked away and with a soft, frustrated sigh she added, "You should have gone away with him, Harotha, like he wanted. You should never have come back here."

The two women were completely alone. The neighborhood around them had been abandoned long ago, the houses left to crumble where they stood. The Shadari population had been shrinking steadily since the coming of the Dead Ones, and the remaining families now huddled together in the center of the city, like a litter of abandoned pups. The Dead Ones didn't even bother patrolling here. The chalky-red face of Mount Asharamon, flanked on either side by the smaller peaks of Esramon and Sharamon, rose up in the near distance. Occasionally they could hear the tuneless tinkle of a goat-bell drifting down from the scrubby slopes of its low summit.

"I still don't understand how you could have let it happen, that's all," Saria grumbled.

Harotha looked into the dark doorway. "I didn't think it mattered what I did. I'd been *so sure* I could convince Shairav to use his magic, at least to open up the ashas' secret passage so we could coordinate a rebellion between the city and the temple, but nothing I said made any difference to him. Even getting Daryan on my side didn't help. After that, I didn't think I'd ever come back to the Shadar. There was no way to escape; I was trapped, just like everyone else."

"You didn't *want* to come back. You didn't want to tell Faroth he'd been right about Shairav'Asha."

"By then I had become Eofar's servant, so I could work on making Daryan into something like a real king without his uncle hanging over him. How could I have known then—? You don't understand, Saria. Eofar is different from the other Dead Ones. While I was up there in the temple—while we were together—everything was so simple. It all made sense."

"Because it was a secret," Saria said in her frank but not unkind way. "A secret in the dark. Shine a light on it and it doesn't look the same, does it?"

"No, it doesn't." She felt a hard lump in her throat and wished, not for the first time, that she had the easy gift of tears like other people. Harotha never cried; she couldn't even remember crying when she was a child.

"Do you think he's still waiting for you?"

"Yes." She rubbed her bottom lip with her thumb. "I think that's why he let the White Wolf take over the mines, to make it easier to run away with me."

"You know how I feel about what you did, and about

him," Saria said. She could never bring herself to mention Eofar by name. "And since only the gods know how these things are going to turn out I thought you should stay here until you were delivered. But now I think you should go—leave the Shadar, right now. Go and have your baby and forget this place ever existed. And let it forget you."

"I can't," she said.

"For the gods' sake, why not?"

She looked at her sister-in-law. "You remember earlier, you said you thought the gods had abandoned us? Well, they haven't."

Saria drew back suspiciously, and for a moment Harotha's courage failed her. But no: she needed Saria's help, and this was the only way.

"I want to show you something, but I need you to be brave."

"What is it?"

She knelt down, bending awkwardly to balance the baby's shifting weight. Then, unconsciously holding her breath, she began writing in the sand. Saria shrieked and backed away with her hands over her eyes.

"Stop, stop!" cried Saria. "How dare you! Oh gods, forgive her! Forgive me—"

"Don't be childish," Harotha snapped, not realizing until the words left her mouth that Faroth had said exactly the same thing to Saria just a short while ago. She was nervous, and that didn't make the situation any easier. She glanced up at the stars and saw them shining brightly now—maybe that would help. She chose the prayer that had worked for her more often than the others, though it still failed much more often than it succeeded.

"I convinced Daryan to teach me how to write," she explained to her sister-in-law as she carefully formed the letters. Saria was standing stock-still with her hands pressed firmly over her eyes, as if blinding herself would render her invisible to the offended gods.

"All right, Saria, look! Take your hands away." She struggled up off the ground and took hold of Saria's wrists, pulling her hands away from her face, but Saria just turned her head away.

Harotha looked over at the words she had written in the sand and waited. She bit her lower lip. "Please," she whispered.

Nothing happened.

Defeated both by her own failure and by Saria's all-too-predictable reaction, she walked back over to the letters and swept them away with her foot. "All right, it's gone. You can look now."

Saria slowly lowered her hands away from her face and looked suspiciously at the sand around her feet as if she suspected a trick. "What did you think you were doing?" she asked, quivering with outrage. "Who do you think you are?"

"I can do it—I have done it, many times. I just can't do it all of the time." She took a deep breath. "Daryan taught me how to read and write a few prayers when we were in the temple together. And I had all that time here, alone, so I began . . . I didn't want to tell you until—"

Saria stretched out a finger accusingly. "Only ordained ashas have the power. That's why you went to the temple in the first place. Shairav is the only one who can speak to the gods. Everyone knows that!"

"That's what we've been told, but it's not true," Harotha said. "Maybe it's because my mother and father were both ashas, or maybe something's changed. Who knows? Maybe it was never true in the first place." She took another deep breath, and moved closer to Saria. "So you see why I can't leave now? Why I have to tell Faroth about this before we end up at the mercy of the Mongrel?"

"Be quiet! Be quiet!" Saria shouted, clamping her hands over her ears. She walked to the doorway of the house and put a hand out to brace herself against the wall. "You and Faroth are so much alike it makes me want to spit. Even though the thought of what that baby represents makes me ill, I hoped that maybe if you became a mother, you'd have enough to worry about without trying to save . . ." Her words trailed off strangely and she looked up toward Mount Asharamon. Harotha saw an unfamiliar look of intense concentration cross her face.

"What—?"

"Quiet!" Saria interrupted in a tense whisper. Then she beckoned Harotha over. "Do you hear that?"

She stood by the wall next to her and listened. After a moment she heard the rumbling again, like a heavy stone rolling along, and felt a kind of buzzing under her feet. This time, instead of fading away, both began to swell in intensity; a shifting sound came from within the dark house and a wet crash broke the stillness, as if something heavy had fallen on the water cistern.

The women both jumped, and Harotha cried out, "Saria! Get away!" and pulled her sister-in-law away from the doorway. "It's the roof—it's coming down!"

Together they lurched over the sliding sands, making instinctively for the open space at the foot of the mountains. A house on their left collapsed in on itself with a terrifying roar just as they stumbled by, and Saria screamed. But in a few moments they were on open ground. They both dropped to their knees.

"Listen!" she shouted over the noise, squeezing Saria's arm tighter. Saria threw her other arm around her shoulders and pulled her close. "Listen! Do you hear that?"

"Like an egg, cracking," Saria cried in return. "What is it?"

She looked around for the source of the sound. The cracking sound grew louder, and then the rumbling grew louder as well, but this time the rumbling was coming not from underneath them but in front of them.

"Oh, no," she gasped, staring at Mount Asharamon. The moonlight was bright enough to show cracks zigzagging up the rocky face, more and more of them, even as she looked. "No, no—"

With a heavy thump the surface of the mountain face broke away and slid down in one long, majestic sweep.

"Run!" screamed Saria, pulling wildly at her arm. The view in front of them disappeared, choked with dust. Rocks and boulders bounced over the sand toward them.

"It's too late," she said and threw herself down in the sand. She grabbed Saria's legs and toppled her down onto the ground beside her. "Stay down," she commanded as she wrote another prayer into the dirt. "Cover your head!" She finished writing the prayer and then scrambled over next to Saria, tucking herself into a ball with her arms around her belly. Sand and dirt rained down on her and she shut her eyes and her mouth tight, listening to the concussive thud of rocks striking the ground all around them. Saria whimpered with fright.

And then it all stopped.

Harotha opened her eyes. A few small rocks skipped by but the ground was no longer rumbling. In fact, there was no sound at all. A heavy cloud of dust hung in the air, stinging her eyes until they watered. She wet her lips and stood up as quickly as her ungainly body would allow, arching her sore back and looking around thoughtfully.

Saria raised her head, eyes wide and glassy with fright. "We're still alive?"

"We appear to be," Harotha reassured her, and then added, trying to keep her voice calm, "Why don't you get up?"

Saria stood up, staring in disbelief at what Harotha was regarding with growing satisfaction. A dune had risen up from the sand in front of them, crested at the top like a wave that had frozen just as it reached its apex, at least twelve feet high and twice as long. On either side of the dune, rocks ranging in size from tiny pebbles to huge boulders lay strewn all about. Moonlight filtered through the dust. Behind them, the abandoned houses had been completely flattened.

Harotha began to laugh raggedly to herself. "I did it," she whispered hoarsely. "I really did it." She turned to Saria, triumph roaring in her heart. "I did it: I saved us!"

But Saria's face was dark with fear. "You did nothing," she said blankly. "It was the gods, not you." She backed away a step. "Not *you*."

Harotha walked around to the other side of the dune and looked up at the mountain. The landslide had left the mountain face even sheerer than before: almost completely flat, in fact, like a wall. *It was odd, an unnatural way for it to break,* she thought as she walked toward it. The dust was still settling, but the moon was bright, illuminating something on the side of the mountain that had not been there before; something had been unearthed from beneath all that red rock.

A shadow flicked over the ground, racing away over the rocks, then another one, right behind it.

"Dereshadi!" Saria cried out, and Harotha ran back to find her cowering under the swell of the dune as she looked fearfully up at the sky, where dereshadi were rising from every corner of the city. One skimmed by right over their heads, the moonlight shining through its wings to reveal a tracery of veins as delicate as a spider's web. They were all heading in the same direction.

"Trouble at the mines," said Harotha.

"I have to go," Saria said suddenly in a voice hushed with dread. "My son— I have to go. Dramash is out there."

"You can't go now. They'll see you," Harotha answered practically. "Listen, Faroth won't let anything happen to Dramash, you know that. Look, can you see that, over there?" She tugged Saria out from under the dune and pointed at the thing she'd seen: shadowy lines in the rock that moved against the natural grain of the stone, and below it, something black that might be a cave-mouth, though only a sliver was visible above the piles of fallen rocks. "There. Do you see where I mean? It's just above that—"

Saria slapped Harotha, hard, across the face.

For a moment everything turned red. Then Harotha slowly raised her hand to her burning cheek. Her mouth opened, but she was too stunned to say a word.

"You have no idea what's really important," Saria told her, regarding her with a cold kind of pity. "Maybe when you're a mother you'll understand." Then she turned away and fled in the direction of the mines.

Harotha watched her go, staring across the unfamiliar landscape of broken rocks, sand and fallen houses long after Saria was out of sight. The night air felt colder beneath the dune's shadow, and she shivered and wrapped her arms around her belly. She had never felt more alone.

Chapter Ten

Rho was watching Frea, who was watching one of the hands turn slowly in the air. Something in the way the small, delicate movements played in the dappled shadows of the torchlight had transfixed her. She was regarding the turning hand with such serenity that Rho could almost feel the soft, heavy silence of the snow-covered mountains of Norland—a place Frea had never even seen, except maybe in her dreams.

The moment didn't last long; even as she stood there watching, the hand wilted like a flower on a broken stem. The entombed slave to whom the hand had belonged had finally suffocated.

A formation of triffons thumped by overhead and Rho looked up from the collapsed entrance to the mine. The fly-over elicited a chorus of fresh screams from the hysterical slaves who were already flailing around Frea's normally well-ordered mining camp, beating their breasts or clawing uselessly at the stones, dirt and Shadari corpses blocking up the shaft. By his tally more than a hundred slaves had been trapped underground by the collapse.

<Kharl! Jeder! What are you playing at? Can't you see you're making them worse? Land those triffons and get down here. I want everyone clearing that shaft,> Frea called. Then she turned the eye-slits of her silver helmet on Rho. <And you,> she began, walking toward

him, <these slaves wouldn't revolt against the fleas on their backs. Where's this uprising you promised me?>

He looked around at the havoc playing out all over the camp. <That was before the earthquakes and this collapse. Frea, you can't possibly expect—>

Her warning clamped down like a suffocating hand over his mouth.

<Lady Frea,> he amended, stressing her title, feeling the acid burn in his stomach: yet another reminder that she'd nullified any claim he might have to familiarity. <I know what I heard. The slaves were definitely planning something for tonight.>

<Lady Frea.> Ongen rushed up with panic oozing around him like a stench.

<What is it?> she snapped.

<It's the blood jars, my Lady.>

Rho followed her gaze over to the southern end of the camp where the roofless smelting huts were huddled against the mountain-face. Frea wiped the sweat from the back of her neck. <What about them?>

<Some rocks must have fallen down from the slope—some of the jars are smashed. They're— they're empty.>

Frea gave no response beyond the sheer black wall of her mood, forcing Ongen to try again. <The blood from Norland—for the imprinting, my Lady.> His silver eyes twitched at their reflection in her helmet before he hastily refocused them elsewhere. <Half of it's gone.>

<Half?> Rho echoed in dismay. The continued wailing of the slaves behind him sounded like a chorus of shrieking gulls.

Frea sheathed Blood's Pride and charged off toward the huts, darting around a few hilt-less black sword-blades stuck in the sand to cool. She was swiftly followed by Rho and Ongen. Rho envied the guards who'd served in the early days of the colony, when all they had to do was mine the ore and ship it back to Norland. As soon as the empire began to expand, the raw value of the ore had made it irresistible to pirates, so they'd shifted to sending the blood for the imprinting to the Shadar and making the swords there. Imperial ships came twice a year now to drop off jars of blood for the new blades and to pick up the ones already made. Since the blades were only valuable to those whose blood had been used to imprint them, robbing the shipments now was hardly worth the risk.

She disappeared inside the hut while Rho stopped in the doorway. The place was in a shambles. Most of the furniture and equipment had been damaged, and large red rocks were lying among the wreckage. The crates were in the corner, smashed into splinters, and from between the broken boards the blood of Norland's finest warriors dripped to the ground like the silver-blue tracks of so many snails.

<You know what this means, don't you?> Ongen asked as they backed out into the cooler air. <We were already *way* behind—even without this collapse, who knows if we were going to find enough ore? Lady Frea's going to—>

Rho cut him off. <I know.>

<But the emperor's ship will be here any day now. Someone's going to have to—>

<Ongen, I know, all right?> he lashed out impatiently.

<You're a real little shit, Rho.> Ongen's anxiety shifted to resentment, pushing at him like a shove to the shoulder. <Why don't you make yourself useful instead of sniffing around Lady Frea's heels all the time, like some kind of mangy dog?>

<What's that supposed to mean?> he asked as Ongen drew his sword and lumbered off back toward the mine.

<You know what it means,> Ongen scoffed. <She's done with you. About time, too.>

As Rho started after him, Frea emerged from the hut and walked past him among the sword-blades. She looked up at the faint lights winking in the temple windows high above the city.

<Your father can write to the emperor and explain

what happened,> he said, careful to keep any trace of pity to himself. He wished that she would take her helmet off. Just looking at it made him feel claustrophobic. <It wasn't anyone's fault.>

<It's *always* somebody's fault,> she answered darkly. <You know what this place is. We're a joke.>

Rho had never cared about the garrison's reputation—his only goal had been to get as far away as possible from his family's infighting—but Frea had far grander aspirations, and her only chance of being recalled to Norland was to somehow impress the emperor with her management of the colony. Now it looked as though all of her efforts had gone up in smoke in a single night.

<Frea,> he said, moving closer to her, trying to reach the vulnerability that he knew was buried somewhere beneath the silver and leather, so much more alluring to him than the chiseled perfection of her face or the erotic promise of her flawless body.

<Shut up, Rho, and come with me,> she commanded, marching toward the center of the mining camp. His stomach muscles contracted. What had Ongen called him—a mangy dog? But he still followed.

The situation in the camp had not improved much. The slaves were frantically trying to dig out the shaft, but the more they dug, the more rocks and dirt—and dead—came pouring out. The ground in front of the shaft was already littered with crushed bodies, some unlucky enough to still be breathing. Those slaves who'd escaped the collapse were being rounded up, but many were just flopping around on the ground, howling and weeping.

<Lady Frea,> another soldier cried, rushing up to her, <I've just come from the temple. Your father wants to see you.>

<Now?> Frea asked, bristling.

But before the soldier could answer, a strange, taut silence swept through the compound, flattening the noise and confusion like a shockwave. The emotions of the Norlanders charged the air like an electrical storm; Rho felt his skin bristling with it. He turned and looked in the same direction as everyone else, over the entrance to the mines.

The Mongrel.

She was ethereal but unmistakable: the eye-patch like a hole on one side of her face, the tangle of black hair and the aura of invincibility pulsating through the air around her. She was bare-armed, and stood with both hands behind her back.

How the piss-poor Shadari had ever managed to hire the most notorious mercenary commander who had ever lived, he couldn't begin to imagine, but there she was, standing on a rocky outcrop over the entrance to the mines.

Just then a sibilant noise scratched at his ears: the Shadari were whispering. The Mongrel brought her hands out from behind her back to reveal a bundle hanging from each fist. The two round objects transcribed an arc against the moonlit sky and landed in front of Frea's boots with a thump. The metallic smell of fresh blood wafted up to him. With a twinge of satisfaction that shocked him, he recognized the one on the left as Beorun, her latest lover, his successor to her bed.

<Tell my father he'll have to wait,> Frea said. She slid Blood's Pride from its scabbard with a heady anticipation that flooded through Rho's senses like strong wine. He noticed her exaggerated gait as she stepped over the two disembodied heads, almost as if she could already feel the sway and roll of the ship that would carry her back to Norland in triumph. The mines, the colony, none of it would matter if she became the first—the only—warrior to bring down the Mongrel. Her name would be the toast of every hall; her chair would be pushed to the head of every table. To the rest of the Norlanders, she said, <No one touches her but me.>

A sound ripped the air behind him, a sharp-pitched yell that set his bones buzzing. He turned to see a Shadari slave standing straight as a rod with one fist upraised.

<Silence that slave!> Frea roared without even turning around, and a white-caped soldier swept over and clouted the slave over the head with the pommel of his sword. Then another shout sounded from the back of the crowd, and another answered it, and then, with a blaring screech of common intent, the Shadari riot erupted.

<I knew it,> Rho said to himself, drawing Fortune's Blight as Shadari rushed into the camp from all directions.

Many of the slaves were armed, most with mining implements but some had actual weapons, or at least the battered remains of actual weapons. The Norlanders' arms were more formidable but they were heavily outnumbered.

<Wait.> Frea's order yanked him back like a tug on a leash. <Stay with me, Rho. I need a witness when I kill her.>

The Mongrel was forging a path straight toward them through the confusion and he needed all of his self-control to keep from looking away from her. The scaly pink scar-tissue crawling over her right forearm brought the bile to his mouth. Her mangled face was far more intimidating than Frea's silver helmet.

The Mongrel halted a few paces off and said the last thing he expected. <I surrender.>

Blood's Pride twitched in Frea's hands. <You're the Mongrel. I know what you are. Your tricks won't work on me.>

<No tricks. I'm unarmed,> she answered, extending her bare arms. She spoke the Norlander language in its pure, unaccented form, but she was as emotionless as a corpse. <Arrest me.>

<Fight me, or I'll kill you where you stand,> Frea informed her.

<Kill me? In cold blood?> the Mongrel asked, as impassive as a puddle of water. <You know what Onfar does to murderers in the afterlife, don't you?>

Rho flipped his sword around and grasped the unhoned section of the blade just above the hilt. <Here,> he said, forcing himself to look into her disfigured face.

She glanced at the sword and then at him, and he felt a glimmer of some feeling from her, but it was too veiled for him to identify it. She made no movement to take the sword.

<Take it,> he insisted, and then tossed Fortune's Blight into the sand at her feet. With a flush of satisfaction, he watched her pick it up.

<Now you're armed. And the penalty for killing my guards is death,> Frea crowed, and charged.

Her first sweeping blow came down squarely on the Mongrel's parry with a shock that Rho felt thrilling up through his own arms. He circled back out of the way as Frea struck again, a blow to her opponent's right side, and again the Mongrel's block sent waves of sound thudding over the sand. They circled. Frea feinted and changed direction and again they circled. Then she tried a complicated move to her left, a lightning-fast change of grip followed by a thrust that Rho knew well from the vicious sparring matches that she preferred to more traditional foreplay. The Mongrel slid to the side and avoided the blow without contact. Frea was caught off-balance and needed a stuttering step forward to come back on guard, but instead of capitalizing on her opponent's mistake, the Mongrel stepped back.

<Fight me,> Frea demanded.

<I didn't kill your men,> said the Mongrel. <I want the Shadari to believe I'm helping them. For now.>

<I don't care.> Frea's rage was a cold white flame. <What are you waiting for?>

As if only to oblige her, the Mongrel struck out with a tremendous sweeping blow that would have taken Frea's arm off at the elbow if it had connected, but she twisted around just in time to block it and then scrambled to repel two more attacks. She answered with a series of cuts to alternating sides. The Mongrel paced back amenably, but continued to frustrate every offensive. Then she halted Frea's advance with a blinding series of swipes, driving her back and then flitting past her with a quickness like bats' wings. <Arrest me. Take me to the governor.>

Frea spun around to face her. <The governor doesn't want anything to do with you. I'm the one you need to worry about.>

Rho never even saw the blow that knocked Blood's Pride from Frea's hand and sent it bouncing across the sand. Frea lunged after her sword, rolling onto her shoulder to retrieve it and then vaulting back up again, but before she could assume a fighting stance the Mongrel had the point of Fortune's Blight aimed at her throat. He could hear the tip softly scraping against the lower edge of her helmet.

<Kill me, then,> Frea challenged the Mongrel, breathing hard. <I'm not afraid to die.>

The tip of the sword wavered. <That's not why I'm here.>

But she wanted to. It was the first and only thing he had felt from her: a thirst for killing squeezing out between the cracks of the tight-shut vault of her emotions. He watched Fortune's Blight tremble in her gray hands and saw the gleam of the blade that he had whet with his own hands to the keenness of a razor.

But instead of thrusting the point into Frea's throat, the Mongrel dropped the sword into the sand. Then she reached up and slowly tugged the eye-patch down around her neck.

Frea froze. <This is a trick— You're dead—*she's* dead,> she said, staring at the Mongrel through the unblinking eyes of her silver helmet. Rho felt Frea's consternation like a blinding light, too glaring to look into. Blood's

Pride drooped in her hand until its point hit the sand. <Who are you?>

<You already know that.>

Blood's Pride fell from Frea's limp hand as if every muscle in her body had suddenly liquefied.

<Stay away from the boy,> said the Mongrel as she replaced the eye-patch. <He'll destroy you.> Then without another word of explanation, or another look at Frea or at Rho, she turned and loped off toward the mountains.

<Frea.> He grabbed Fortune's Blight from the sand and seized her arm. <Frea, come on,> he urged, understanding little of what had just happened except that she was squandering the miraculous chance she'd been given. <Why are you standing there? We can catch her! Come on!>

Frea swung out with her gauntleted fist and struck him viciously across the side of his face. His neck snapped around with the force of her blow and he pitched sideways into the sand. He clutched at his ringing head and for a moment he could do nothing else but lie there, waiting for the blackness in front of his eyes to clear. He could taste blood in his mouth and he could feel his left eye already beginning to swell.

<Get up, Rho.> Frea was standing over him, waiting. She'd returned Blood's Pride to its sheath and had regained some control of her emotions. <Get up,> she said again.

Groggily he pushed himself up, blinking the glittery spots away from in front of his eyes. He noticed several of his fellow soldiers standing close by, unsuccessfully pretending that they hadn't seen what had just happened. Ongen was openly radiating satisfaction. The uprising was already over, its momentum having evaporated along with the Mongrel's departure. Some of the slaves had simply run away from the camp in the confusion while the rest were kneeling before the guards in quaking ranks, most with some kind of injury.

Frea stood in front of him. For one moment, he thought she was going to apologize, but instead she said, <I have to go back to the temple. You're coming with me.>

He looked at the distorted reflection of his face in her silver helmet. <Why?> he asked.

She said nothing, but he felt it: the encounter with the Mongrel had shaken her to the core and she didn't want to be alone. She had no one else she could turn to but him. And, mangy dog that he was, she knew he wouldn't refuse her.

<Go and check my harness,> she told him. He heard her giving more orders as he left for the paddock: <Get those slaves clearing that shaft. Haul those bodies out of here. Fix those huts. Come on, get moving!>

Over in the paddock the triffons were nervously butting their heads and twining their long tails together, restless after the two earthquakes. He could smell the reek of the beasts' anxiety as he passed through the gate and sought out Trakkar. He was surprised to find him in a corner by himself, lying contentedly with his head between his paws. Then he saw why.

"Get out of here," he said hurriedly to the little Shadari boy standing on the other side of Trakkar's head with his stubby fingers buried into the bristly brown fur between the triffon's ears. "You can't be here."

"He likes me," said the boy. His high, childish voice was as sharp as a needle. "What's his name?"

"Trakkar," Rho answered, dumbfounded. It was impossible for a child to be here at all, and insane for him not to run away the moment he was discovered, but the boy only pressed back a little closer to Trakkar's shoulder, as if he expected the triffon to protect him. *Something must be wrong with him.*

"Is he yours?"

"No," he answered; the boy's behavior was so odd he wasn't sure what else *to* do other than answer. "Guards don't get their own triffons."

"Who does he belong to?"

"Lady Frea."

"Oh." His eyes widened, but it still didn't look like fear. "I want to be a soldier when I grow up, but I want to have my own dereshadi."

"*You* want to be a soldier?"

"Yes, like you." He pointed a chubby finger at Fortune's Blight. "I like your sword. I want to learn how to fight, but there's no one to teach me. Maybe you could teach me some day?"

"Me? I don't know, maybe." He forced himself to focus. Frea could be coming into the paddock at any moment, and there were guards roaming all over the place. If they caught the boy he'd be lucky to escape with a bad beating. "You need to go home now. Go on—get out of here."

"Why are all those people crying?"

"The mine caved in," he said, but by now he was reaching under his tabard into his shirt pocket, remembering something he'd learned from dealing with his little cousins in Norland. "Here," he said, drawing out Daem's leaf-wrapped sweet, "I'll give you this if you go right now."

"Okay." The boy's arm shot out without hesitation, but as Rho dropped the treat into his hand, he heard the gate creak open behind him. He was too late. Frea had entered the paddock.

"Get down. Hide," he whispered, stepping aside and pretending to examine the buckles on Frea's harness. She passed him without a word and hooked her foot into Trakkar's stirrup.

"I can help."

A shudder quivered up Rho's spine. "Don't—" Rho whispered to him, but before he could finish his warning, the boy looked up at Frea and spoke again.

"I can help," he repeated. "Look, I'll show you." The boy reached out his right hand toward the mineshaft.

Rho looked over and saw the guards positioned in front of the mine's entrance suddenly hop into an odd little dance, mincing over the sand and shaking dirt out of their white hair. He stared harder. This time he clearly saw a wedge of dirt detach itself from the pile and sheet down to the ground, revealing a deeper cross-section of lifeless bodies and smashed equipment. Norlanders and slaves alike scrambled backward to avoid being swept off their feet.

He turned back to the boy. The child's hand was still stretched out and his small face was wrinkled up like an old fruit.

Then he heard a loud, muffled thump, like the sound of a cushion being punched, and an avalanche of dirt and rock swept out over the flat ground, followed by a rush of stale air. Scores of gasping slaves poured out from the depths, trampling over the bodies of the dead and dying in their frenzied need for air. The collapse had been confined to the entrance to the shaft: most of the slaves trapped behind it had been slowly suffocating, but were otherwise mostly unharmed.

"See?" crowed the boy.

Rho looked up at Frea, who was still sitting on Trakkar's back, watching the liberated slaves cavorting in front of the mine. Her emotions were a throbbing but inscrutable blur. <Rho,> she said slowly, without looking down at him, <ask this boy if he wants to go for a ride on Trakkar.>

A deep eddy of uneasiness rippled through him, but Frea was waiting for him to follow her command.

"Would you like to ride on the dereshadi?" At the same time, he was trying to remember what exactly the Mongrel had just said. She had mentioned a boy, hadn't she? His head was pounding . . .

"Really?" the boy cried out, jumping up and down with excitement. "Yes, please!" Rho put his hands on the boy's waist, glad that he had his heavy gloves to shield him from the heat, and hoisted him up onto the saddle behind Frea and strapped him in.

Stay away from the boy. That's what she'd said.

"Dramash—*Dramash!*" A wild cry cut through the noise of the camp as a disheveled Shadari woman in a blue patterned head-scarf flung herself toward them.

<Stop that woman,> Frea commanded, <but don't upset the boy. I want him cooperative.>

Rho stepped out to block the woman's progress. She cut around him, but he seized her arm by the wrist and pulled her back, grabbing her other wrist at the same time and holding her in front of him. Even with his gloves on, the heat was intense. She struggled, but she wasn't very strong and he had no difficulty holding on to her. But then she unexpectedly kicked back and her foot caught him painfully in the shin. Cursing, he transferred both of her thin wrists to his left hand and drew his dagger with his right. He held the point of the dagger warningly against the back of her neck, underneath her black hair where the boy wouldn't see it.

<Careful, Rho! You may need some help,> he heard Ongen snicker. <She looks like a dangerous rebel.> Ongen, Ingeld and Daem were all watching with thinly veiled curiosity.

"That's my mother!" the boy said to Frea as she snatched up Trakkar's reins. The triffon snorted and tossed his head and then stretched his wings out lazily. "Can she come, too?"

Rho glanced down at the Shadari woman's fear-bleached face and then back at the boy. Frea reached into her pocket and drew out a single imperial eagle. The child's eyes caught the shine of the gold and widened into two large, round mirrors: that was probably more money than his family had possessed in his entire lifetime.

<Rho.> Frea tossed the coin down. It glinted in the moonlight as it hit the sand in front of the woman's feet. <Give her this. I want her quiet.>

<After that, you can give her a bath,> Ongen interjected, leaning against the gate and enjoying the amusement he was providing for the others. <And then take her home to meet your mother.>

Rho tried to ignore him. The woman had calmed under the influence of his knife and he relaxed his grip on her wrists. Her shoulders sagged and she gestured her head downward toward the coin. He stepped back so that she could bend down to pick it up.

Frea snapped the reins impatiently and whistled to Trakkar. The creature tensed his stumpy back legs and sprang into the air.

The Shadari woman rushed forward. Rho lunged after her, grabbing her and pulling her back against him, though the heat radiating from her body was nearly unbearable. He raised his dagger again, this time holding it up against her throat.

"Dramash!" the woman screamed, the sound exploding from her throat with so much force that it felt as if it would rend the very air. The Norlanders recoiled in pain, pummeling Rho with their collective outrage. "Dramash! *Dramash!*"

<Shut her up!> Frea roared, and Rho pulled the blade of his knife across the Shadari woman's throat.

The silence was instantaneous.

The woman's body stiffened against him and blood streamed down from the gash across her throat, burning hot like molten metal as it steamed in the night air. Then she sagged against him and he quickly shifted his weight to keep her on her feet, cradling her body against him. He held her round the waist, like a lover. Her head lolled back against his chest and her black hair drifted across his neck and over his shoulder.

He looked up at the triffon rising higher and higher into the air and noticed a strange flicker of movement from the saddle behind Frea. Dramash was waving goodbye.

Chapter Eleven

Daryan moved swiftly through the same echoing corridors he'd paced as a child, remembering an odd little game he'd invented where he pretended that he was the only person left in the world. Even though the game had come from his own imagination, it had given him nightmares. Sometimes it still did.

Eofar had left the temple to look for Harotha, leaving Daryan alone to wade through the secrets his master had poured out to him. Now, with no way to help and nothing for him to do, all he wanted to do was drown himself in the oblivion of sleep until Eofar returned. *If* Eofar returned.

Harotha was alive.

He wanted to be happy. He wanted to be overjoyed; he wanted to spring into the air and dance and whoop for joy, but instead, he flung himself down the silent corridors feeling a poisonous brew of abandonment and hurt burning through him. Eofar and Harotha. Harotha, the insurrectionist for whom no sacrifice was too great, was carrying the child of a Dead One. Daryan hadn't even known that such a thing was possible—how could they *touch* each other? Let alone conceive a child? And how had they deceived him so completely?

But no, he had to admit to himself that he had noticed little things here and there—little clues that he had hastily brushed aside; now they piled up in front of him, mocking him with his own willful ignorance. He could have seen it, if he'd really wanted to know.

Throughout Eofar's tale, Daryan had nourished a dark little hope that what his master thought was a love story would turn out to be some sort of trick of Harotha's, or a ghastly mistake—but when Eofar told him that she had insisted they keep the truth from him, he knew without a doubt that the whole story was true. Nothing could be more real than Harotha not having enough faith in him to trust him with her secret.

He counted the empty brackets along the wall: two, three, four, five.

The corridor ended in a sharp turn to the left with a doorway in the wall directly up ahead, a low doorway even for the Shadari. He had spent more pointless hours than he cared to admit skulking outside that doorway and now he felt his steps slowing as he approached. She always went there when she was upset or hurt or lonely. He stopped beside the doorway where he could look in unobserved and a soft touch, like a gentle hand, moved the curls on his forehead: a breeze from the skylight in the room beyond.

She was there, standing just where he expected her to be, on the topmost of the three stone steps. Her back was toward the door and her white head was bent over the polished stone of the sarcophagus. Starlight filtered in from the skylight above her and both her hair and the stone gleamed with the same soft radiance. She was perfectly still, and the stillness was profound, both deeper and more resonant than ordinary silence. It was the stillness of a pause; of a breath, held, which must by necessity be breathed out again.

In an instant, the last twelve years vanished and he was ten years old. He had been in the temple exactly two days. The governor's family, the higher-ranking soldiers and the more favored servants had gathered in this room to witness the internment of the mangled body of the governor's wife, Eleana, in its hastily prepared tomb.

Shairav had clapped his hand in front of Daryan's eyes—he could still smell the oily reek—and he was trying to look through the old man's fingers. He didn't care about the dead body; he had seen his fair share of those already. He was trying to get a better look at the little white-haired girl pressed up against her brother's leg. She was watching the bearers shove a crude stone slab over her mother's crypt with unblinking silver-gray eyes. Whispers curled into his ears, floating down to him from the half-covered mouths of the slaves. *Her fault*, they were saying, shaking their heads at the little girl. *All her fault*.

The tomb had changed since then. The polished lid, grooved and etched with symbols and images, had been imported from Norland. Stone steps had been placed against the near side. But the pause that had begun that day still hung over them all. They were still waiting to breathe out.

She knew that he was watching her. She remained as still as ice, but he could feel it. She wouldn't turn around, not as long as he stood there, and he wouldn't go in to her, no matter how badly his loneliness urged him toward the open doorway. Such was their unspoken agreement, ironclad and irrevocable, reached silently and spontaneously one awkward, confounding day three years earlier. Now they lived by its prescripts: never to stay in the same room together longer than necessary, and never alone; never to look directly at each other; never to speak to one another, not even in private, except to issue or acknowledge a command. He had broken their agreement once already tonight in the stables, in a moment of unreasoning concern for her safety. Doing it again, now, when he had the time to consider the consequences, was unthinkable.

Daryan backed away from the doorway and walked on down the corridor. Empty brackets passed by: three, four, five. When he reached his room, he had no memory at all of anything he had seen since leaving the tomb. He stood looking down at his disheveled bed and knew that sleep would never come to him now. Instead he lit the lamp on the little table, then moved aside the bedclothes and burrowed down into the rushes. He drew out his treasure, untied the strings and folded back the flaps of protective cloth.

His history of the Shadar: twenty-seven pages, so far. He tossed the cloth onto the bed and brought the pages up close to his face, breathing in their special scent. Hours of rumination had gone into each meticulous line. Each page represented a meal not eaten, or a rest passed over, or a duty neglected. This was the one victory he could claim; the one thing he had been able to do for his people, even though most of them would have thrown his gift on the fire, and him after it. But that would change one day. He had already taught Harotha to read, and there would be others. The Shadari would have books and libraries just like the Dead Ones. The Shadar of his dreams was a serene place of learning, a place where the pursuit of knowledge was godly, and complacency and ignorance were sins.

He took the sheet of stolen paper from his pocket and fished underneath the table for the hidden shelf where his writing implements were stored, but just as his fingers brushed the smooth side of the inkpot he heard a noise from the hall. He blew out the lamp and listened into the darkness, heart thumping. Shairav wasn't above spying on him—he had done it before. He wormed the manuscript underneath his robe, and it was only then that he remembered Eofar's knife. He needed to return it to Eofar's room as soon as possible—he had been mad to accept it in the first place—but for now, he tied his sash as tightly as he could and pulled up the front of his robe to conceal the bulky objects. He moved silently to the doorway.

"Daimon?" a timid voice called to him from the hallway.

He jumped at the sound but at least he knew it wasn't Shairav spying on him. "Who's there?" he called back.

"It's Rahsa, Daimon."

"Rahsa," he breathed out. "You know you're not supposed to call me that." He stuck his head out of the door. The shutters had been opened for the evening and there was enough light for him to see her standing there, playing with a tendril of her reddish hair.

"I'm sorry to disturb you," she said, "but I heard that Lord Eofar had left the temple and I wanted to ask if you'd had a chance to speak to him about what happened."

He sighed and stepped out into the hall. "It's fine, Rahsa. Everyone's forgotten about it. You should, too. What are you even doing here? Isn't there something you're supposed to be doing?"

"It's just that Lady Isa frightens me, she's so odd," she whispered confidentially, as if any Dead One within a hundred paces wouldn't have been able to hear her no matter how softly she whispered. "Is it true that she was on the dereshadi when her mother fell off and died?"

"Yes."

"And the White Wolf, she was there, too?"

"It was a long time ago. They were just little girls."

"Ugh." Rahsa shuddered. "So it *was* her fault?"

"No one knows for sure. They think Isa wriggled out of the harness and her mother fell off trying to strap her back in. The sun was rising. If Frea hadn't taken the reins and flown the dereshadi back here, both girls might have burned to death."

"Oh!" she exhaled in excitement. "And that's why she's so odd? Why she doesn't ride the dereshadi and never leaves the temple like the other Dead Ones?"

"I guess so. Rahsa, don't you have some place you need to be?" he asked again. "I know you're new here, but if you just concentrate on your duties, you'll be fine. It's really not a good idea to stand around gossiping."

"I'm— I'm sorry," she stuttered, paling so suddenly that he stared at her in alarm. She looked as if she was trying not to cry. "I'll try to do better—I promise."

"It's okay," he reassured her guiltily, "I didn't mean—"

At that moment another Shadari turned the corner just ahead and caught sight of them with a little exclamation of relief. Daryan searched for his name.

"Oh, there you are! Thank goodness. Lady Isa wants you. She sent me to find you."

"Tebrin," Daryan greeted him in relief, before a chill slid across his skin. "Wait— *what* did you say?"

"Lady Isa. She wants to see you."

"No, that can't be right." He stepped further out into the hallway. He could still see the shine of Isa's hair in the starlight. "Are you sure? Why?"

"I don't know," Tebrin answered. "It seemed strange to me, too."

In the dim light, Daryan thought he detected an odd look on his face: not exactly fear, more like unease. "All right, I'll go. Where is she?"

Tebrin glanced at Rahsa, then wet his lips nervously. "She's— She's in the bath."

Chapter Twelve

Isa stared down through the water at the bumpy shapes of her knees, then pulled them up to her chest and circled her legs with her arms. She'd sent the servants away and the room was silent except for the gentle lapping of the water; the little lamp flickering on the other side of the cavern cast the only light. She lifted her chin and let her head loll back against the tub's polished stone rim. She'd had a thin notion that the bath would wash away some of the taint of failure she'd brought away with her from the stables. She'd been wrong.

A drop of water plunked down into the cistern in the corner.

She sat up again and flung her arms out with a splash. Little gleaming rivulets ran over her iridescent skin and pattered down onto the dry stone floor. Her arms looked odd, unfamiliar, like a pair of snakes lazing on the edge of a pool—like they didn't belong to her at all.

Brooding over her failures was a waste of time; she already had a new plan. Frea and her soldiers would not return from the mines until an hour or so before dawn, so when she went back to the stables there'd be no gawking Shadari or snickering Norlanders, and no taunting sister to jangle at her emotions and disrupt her concentration. She had sent someone to find Daryan; he knew how to saddle a triffon. Shairav was his uncle, after all, and he had practically grown up in the stables. No one else would know anything about it until she landed at the mines and gave Frea the surprise of her life. It would be easy this time, just her and Daryan, in the stables, alone—

Another drop of water fell into the pool and the sound broke into her thoughts like a rebuke. A guilty flush welled up from the pit of her stomach. She *had* to do this—she had to take action—bold, immediate action—before the last flimsy remnant of her Norlander soul burned up in the Shadari sun.

Unable to stand the inactivity any longer, she rocketed up with a great splash and floundered her way out of the tub—and just at that moment, Daryan came in through the doorway.

He instantly dropped his eyes to the ground, bending his head so low that the dark curls fell over his forehead and obscured his eyes completely. He appeared to be holding his breath. "Mistress," he murmured, "you sent for me."

Isa found herself watching Daryan's bowed head with irrational fury as she retrieved her robe from the back of a chair. With a sick feeling, she realized that she *wanted* him to look at her.

A slight whisper of movement caught her ears and she looked up past Daryan. Someone was lurking in the corridor outside the door, someone clearly too inexperienced to realize that Isa would be able to see her in the darkness. She dropped the robe over her shoulders and yanked the sash tight.

"You, out there," she called out, pitching her voice as far as she could. The girl in the hallway jumped with a little squeal.

"Rahsa, what—?" Daryan whispered through his teeth, clearly surprised to see her there.

Isa thought the girl was going to run away for a moment, but then she stepped meekly into the doorway. "You don't belong here," Isa told her. "Go."

The girl glanced at Daryan, who was still staring down at the ground. His shoulders were stiff as a board.

"Go!" she commanded again, and as the girl's large eyes swung back to her, Isa finally recognized the skittish creature who had accosted her in the hallway outside Daryan's room. For a startling moment she thought she saw something like defiance in the girl's face, but then the slave scuttled backward, taking her leave with an exaggerated subservience that Isa found distasteful. She watched until the girl was out of sight.

Now they were alone.

She opened her mouth to speak, but for a moment nothing came out. Another drop of water fell into the cistern.

"You sent for me, Mistress," Daryan reminded her.

"Aeda," she said finally, stumbling a little over the unfamiliar syllables. Her horrible, croaking voice sounded much louder than his. "Saddle her for me."

He made some kind of displeased exclamation. For a moment his eyes darted up to her face, but then just as quickly dropped back down again. "I'm sorry, Mistress. Your brother has taken Aeda. He might—" Daryan paused oddly. "He might not be back until morning."

So, here it was again. That all-too-familiar feeling of the thing she wanted—whatever it was—sliding away from her, just beyond her reach. She turned away from him and gripped the slick rim of the tub with both hands. The water was perfectly still, and without the glow of her skin beneath it, perfectly black. She was sure that Eofar had found out what had happened in the stables and had taken Aeda away on purpose. He knew full-well she had no chance at all of riding any of the less well-trained animals successfully.

She felt Daryan step closer. "Mistress?" She continued to stare into the dark water. "You don't have to do this tonight, do you?"

Another drop of water fell into the cistern.

She turned back around and saw his lips still slightly parted. "Yes," she answered, unequivocally. She ran her fingers through the wet ends of her hair, feeling the damp robe clinging to her shoulder blades. "I need to name my sword before the emperor's ship comes."

The expression on his face changed. His eyes grew darker and his mouth drooped. "Why?"

"I'm going back with them."

He stood very, very still, as if the air had grown too dense for him to move. She felt a drop of water slide down behind her ear and trace a path down her neck and between her breasts.

"What are you talking about?" His voice sounded different, tighter. And he had stopped calling her *mistress*. Isa felt the self-imposed distance between them beginning to shatter. "Your father wouldn't send you back now, not when he's so sick."

"He doesn't know," she told him. "No one knows."

He stepped back away from her, tugging at the curls on the back of his neck. "Then you're *choosing* to go?"

"Yes."

Very distinctly, he asked, "Why?"

"You know why."

His face changed again, this time to an expression she'd never seen before. He was tall for a Shadari, she realized. It had been so long since she'd stood this close to him that she hadn't noticed that her eyes were nearly level with his. Or that he still had the long eyelashes that had always made his eyes seem so large. He had a fresh scrape on his chin, and she remembered the way Frea had knocked him about in the stables. Her eyes came to rest on his mouth. It was always moving, as if he were struggling to hold something in.

"You were born here. You belong here," he told her.

"I am a Norlander."

"So is Eofar, and your sister, and your father," he pointed out. "They're not going anywhere."

"They have work here," she told him. She couldn't

hold his gaze any longer and found herself staring at his chest. "They have something to do here. Frea—she even has a Shadari name."

"The White Wolf?" He laughed in a way she had never heard before and it stung her. "Is that a joke? That name isn't meant as a compliment. Is that what you want, to be like her?" He kept on laughing in that ugly, brittle way. "To terrorize everyone in the Shadar until they hate and fear you? To make them despise you so much that they can't even stand to say your true name? Because I'll tell you a secret, you don't have to go to Norland for that."

She felt a dreadful ache in her chest. "You don't understand."

He abruptly stopped that dreadful laughing and passed his hand over his face in a gesture that she couldn't interpret. When he looked at her again his eyes had softened, and when he spoke his voice was so deep that she could feel its vibrations. "Yes, I do," he said. "You know I do." His eyes moved slowly over her face and he moved a little closer to her, as if he wanted to see her better. "And I have a Shadari name for you. I just thought of it," he told her. "It's 'Lahlil.' "

The lilting word filled the space between them. It shivered through her, resonating with something far below the surface, some deep place she had locked away. "Lahlil," she repeated, closing her mind to the shred of memory that flicked by, quick as a moth.

"It's a flower—a very rare flower. It grows in the desert, and it has to stay where it's taken root. If you take it out of the sand, it withers and dies." Another drop of water plinked down into the cistern. "I've never seen one, but I hear they're beautiful. They're the most beautiful things in the world."

He was closer now. Isa couldn't be sure whether he had moved closer to her or she had moved closer to him, but she could feel his warmth. She blinked, and something cool touched her cheek.

He reached out an unsteady hand and with his fingertip

radiating heat like a flame, he smoothed away the single icy tear. "I see the problem now, Mistress," he whispered to her. He let his finger remain where it was for a moment, not quite touching her cheek. "I think the Shadar is melting you."

With the languid, half-conscious volition of a dreamer, she leaned forward until her lips brushed against his. His warmth shot through her, deeply, and her breath stopped. But she didn't pull away and neither did he. There was something on the other side of that burning pain, and she wanted it. His fingers grazed her cheek, guiding her closer. Then with a surge of heat like a blast furnace, his lips pressed against hers.

A strangled, inarticulate cry broke from the doorway. Isa froze as Daryan jumped away, snatching his hand back to his chest. Then Rahsa emerged from the hall like a specter, pale and wild-eyed. One look at her face told them that she had seen and heard everything.

"Rahsa," Daryan cried out, but as he turned, he knocked into the chair that Isa had left sitting by the tub. He stumbled across the floor, trying to regain his balance, but as he twisted, an object dropped out of his robe and hit the ground with a clang. She watched it skid to a stop a few paces in front of Rahsa.

For one silent heartbeat, all three of them stared at the knife.

Rahsa lunged first, diving to the ground at the same time as Daryan darted forward. She scrambled up with the knife in her hand and thrust it out to him. "Take it!" she screamed, her shrill voice sending a jab of pain through Isa's head. "Quick! Kill her!"

"Kill her?" He turned to look at her over his shoulder. "What are you—?"

"She'll tell them! She could be calling them now!" Rahsa screamed at him. "Kill her! Do it now, or they'll kill both of us!"

He reached out and slapped the knife out of her hand. It slid across the floor, still in its scabbard, and disappeared into a dark corner on the far side of the room. "What's *wrong* with you?"

"What's wrong with *me*?" Rahsa yelled back at him. "You were—"

The air around them shuddered.

The floor tilted and slipped away from Isa, throwing her against the side of the tub. She tried to grab on to it for support but the polished stone slipped out from beneath her hands and she fell down, barking her hip painfully against the floor. Daryan was on his knees, trying unsuccessfully to stand. She couldn't see Rahsa, but she could hear what sounded like frantic prayers coming from somewhere near the door. Debris rained down from the cavern ceiling, stinging her eyes and snuffing out the lamp. The room was drowned in darkness.

"It's the gods!" Rahsa screamed out.

"It's an earthquake!" Daryan roared back at her.

This was nothing like the earlier tremor, or any of the other earthquakes that she could remember. A crash sounded just behind her and she threw her arms over her head and braced herself for a blow. She pictured the whole temple falling in around them, or sliding off into the sea.

"Rahsa! Stay in the doorway! Keep still!" Daryan called out.

"The gods have come to judge us!" she keened. "They're going to throw us into the sea, like the ashas!"

"Rahsa, come back!" he called to her, but from the sound of her screams she had fled out into the hall.

Isa kept her back up against the tub as the floor rocked sickeningly beneath her. One of her slippers had come off and her naked foot was the only thing she could see in the darkness. "Isa!" she heard Daryan call out, and an instant later his arm brushed against her. "Are you—?"

A loud cracking sounded from somewhere overhead and the next thing she knew, he had grabbed her bodily and was diving out of the way. She heard the crash as the tub shattered and a moment later a current of gritty water washed over them both.

They lay there, soaked to the skin, panting for breath, listening fearfully as the rumbling and grinding noises grew fainter. She drew in a breath and held it. The floor stopped moving and the room fell silent except for Daryan's soft panting near her ear. His hands were still clutching her arms and Isa realized that she had her palms pressed up against his chest. The heat was painful, but fell just short of being unbearable; she didn't feel it was harming her. His face was so close that she could count his long eyelashes by the light from her own skin.

Then he released her and pushed his wet hair out of his eyes. "Are you all right?" he asked unsteadily.

Isa moved back as well, tentatively moving her neck, her arms and legs. "I think so," she told him. "Just . . . wet."

"Wet?" Daryan repeated. Then she heard him patting his own soaked robes. "Wet," he repeated again, this time in an entirely different voice. "The lamp!" he cried out, startling her. "Where's the lamp!"

He sprang to his feet and while he was still splashing around in the darkness, Isa listened for the sound of the water dripping into the cistern to orient herself. At last she rose and picked her way carefully around the smashed tub, then followed the sound to the ledge where she soon found the lamp. It had been knocked on its side but still contained a few drops of oil. She righted it, drew out the flints and struck a spark.

Daryan held a sheaf of loose papers in his hands. As she drew closer she could see that the pages were covered with tiny characters—not Norland writing, nor any other language she had ever seen. But the paper was soaked and the characters were beginning to run into indistinct blobs. He peeled back the top page and looked at the one underneath, then the one beneath that, but there was nothing more than row upon row of smudges. He gave a tug and the paper came apart easily in his hands. With a blank stare he shredded the soggy sheets and dropped them onto the floor. She watched his chest rise and fall; she saw the way he pressed his lips hard together, and the tension hiking up his shoulders. The spoiled papers lay in the dirty puddles around his feet. She didn't know what it was all about, but she understood.

The lamplight retreated and then jumped back up again as the flame sucked up the last few drops of oil. In the unsteady light, the room still seemed to be tilting downward toward the sea.

"She was right," said Isa, "Rahsa was, about the gods—*my* gods. They hate me." She looked away. "That's why I have to leave, before it's too late." She focused her burning eyes on the ruined papers at his feet. "Before I make *your* gods hate *you*, too."

With a hiss, the last drop of oil in the lamp evaporated and the tiny light snuffed itself out.

Chapter Thirteen

Eofar turned Aeda back around. His eyes burned from staring into the darkness and seeing nothing. Acid gnawed at his empty stomach. Phantom sensations, some sort of lingering influence from the elixir, crawled along his spine. He had flown from one end of the city to the other, up above the mountains and along the other side and even out into the desert as far as he dared, but he'd found nothing that even resembled the place in his vision. Dawn was not far off; soon he'd have to give up the search. The thought of another day shut up inside the temple, at the mercy of his worst fears, filled him with desperation.

He found himself grasping for his memories of Harotha, as if by holding on to them he could somehow pull her toward him. Something had changed in him the very first time he saw her: for the space of one blink, he had felt as if he looked through the eyes of a god, straight through to the world's design, and it all made perfect sense. The feeling was gone an instant later, but after that, nothing had mattered except his need to be near her. Still, it wasn't until months later—he remembered it perfectly, she had just set a carafe of wine down on the table, he had thanked her and she had looked up at him—that he understood what it meant, and then only because he recognized it in her eyes. The first touch of her fingers still burned on the back of his hand; the first kiss still raced through him like liquid fire.

He looked beneath him at the broken walls and shattered towers of the old royal palace and guided Aeda down, but then with a frustrated snap brought her back up again. He had searched there already; and in any case, the Norlander soldiers had combed through those ruins decades ago. His father had never rid himself of the nagging suspicion that some of the royal family had survived the invasion and gone into hiding. Eofar himself had once teasingly accused Harotha of being a renegade Shadari princess on a secret mission to destroy the Norlanders. She had laughed her low, musical laugh, and it wasn't until she lay sleeping by his side that he realized he hadn't been joking.

As he flew westward toward the mountains he became more aware of the damage the second, more powerful earthquake had caused. The abandoned neighborhoods on the edge of the city had been completely destroyed; it looked as if part of the mountain had broken off and come crashing down.

An idea suddenly grabbed hold of him and he sat bolt upright in the saddle. He had been assuming the place in his vision was some sort of house or building, but all he had really seen was a doorway mostly blocked up with rocks. These mountains were riddled with caves: might he not have seen the entrance to one of those? With so many rocks jarred loose, some hidden place might have been revealed, somewhere not even Daryan knew about.

A rush of air whistled past his ears and the head of a triffon floated up out of the darkness. His heart flew into his mouth as Aeda, panicked, snapped in her wings and plummeted toward the ground to avoid the collision. His stomach dropped; he yanked hard on the reins and Aeda tossed her head and snorted, but she checked their descent only twenty feet or so from the ground. The thump of wings sounded behind him and he whirled in the saddle in time to see the other rider swing past just overhead.

<Rho?> he called out. <What are you doing? Where did you come from?>

Rho banked sharply and turned his triffon toward the temple. He didn't answer.

Eofar could feel the frantic thrum of his anxiety, but he didn't think the near-miss was the cause of Rho's distress. Something else had shaken Rho out of his usual patrician languor. But before Eofar could question him he was gone, heading back up toward the temple. Feeling even more anxious than before, he took up the reins and prepared to take Aeda up higher.

And there it was.

He sprang up in the stirrups, afraid his eyes were playing tricks on him, but no, the symbol was there, as tall as a man standing, and below it was the doorway—or at least the top of one, just like in his vision, with a pile of rocks almost completely blocking it.

Eofar snapped the reins down. When he whistled for Aeda to land she tilted her wings and dived into a tight spiral. His tired eyes lost focus for a moment and he shut them and pressed his hand to his forehead—

—and then, in the darkness, he was no longer in control.

The elixir's visions howled through him again, unwavering in their intensity, like the sustained scream of metal against a grinding wheel, refusing to be anchored to anything like reality. He swatted at the air, struggling frantically to breathe and trying to fend off the onslaught. The elixir boiled in his blood, and again he saw Harotha standing in front of the doorway, backing away from some danger, with an unfamiliar knife in her hand and an expression of such hatred and fear on her face that it rent at his heart, and then just a flash of the second vision, a single image of Daryan, grappling with an unidentifiable Norlander on a stone floor. It was why he had insisted Daryan take his knife.

The jolt of landing flung him up against the straps of the harness and he tugged blindly at the buckles until he found himself on his hands and knees in the sand, retching violently. A few moments later he rolled on to his side, breathless and trembling, wiping at his watering eyes. The elixir had left his skin crawling and his white hair and the back of his linen shirt were damp with cold sweat. Slowly, he sat up.

He looked back up to the temple to orient himself. He was still in the Shadar, not the desert, but a dune was there, rising to about twice his height and measuring about thirty paces to either end. In the sandy dirt all around him were footprints: smaller footprints than his own, and made by sandals, not boots. The first led south, toward the mines, while the deeper set wound around the dune and turned toward the mountains. Eofar lurched to his feet with his heart pounding in his chest. He followed the deeper set around the dune, and then swerved with them around the piles of fallen rocks, zigzagging as if he were running by the side of an invisible companion.

He cut around the jagged sides of a boulder, and there she was.

She had climbed a treacherous pile of rocks all the way up to the doorway and was leaning with her face close to the wall, tracing the line of the carving. Strands of her dark hair waved in the breeze. The moonlight was bright enough for his Norlander eyes to make out every change in her: her full lips were fuller than before; her round cheeks were a little rounder; her rich brown eyes were the same, but underneath were pink swells that told of fatigue and worry. But it was the baby, the baby that was enormous within her, that made Eofar feel the stirrings of an impossible joy.

He was trying to find a way of calling out to her without startling her when she suddenly turned to him. The expression on her face changed, her eyes opened wide and her lips parted. One hand fluttered to her mouth as she reached back with the other to brace herself against the rocks.

"Eofar!" she gasped. "I don't believe—" She began to

stand, and grit and pebbles skittered down around his feet.

"Careful!" he cautioned her, his flat voice reflecting none of the agony of his concern as he watched her climb down to him, but he was there the moment her foot touched the ground, and he swept her into his arms. She shuddered, either from emotion or the chill from his skin, he didn't know and he didn't care. For him, her heat was like a brushfire, burning away the misery and doubt that had infested him while they'd been apart. He was renewed, reborn. "You're all right—you're all right," he repeated, releasing her by necessity but kissing her searing lips, weak with relief. He couldn't stop staring at her firm, round belly.

"We can go, right now—tonight," he said finally, leaning back to look into her face and carefully tucking a strand of hair back under her scarf.

One of Harotha's fingers strayed up to stroke her bottom lip, a familiar gesture that enflamed his desire to kiss her again. "But how did you find me? And here, of all places?"

He reached into his shirt pocket and brought out the little bottle. "You told me about it," he reminded her as he held it up for her to see. He had not taken it all; the bottle was still almost a quarter-full. "We can sell the rest. The Nomas—"

"Elixir!" she cried, taking the little bottle from between his fingers and holding it up to the predawn sky. She tilted it and watched the dark liquid slide slowly down to the lower end. "And you took it?"

"Yes."

Her shoulders twitched excitedly. "So? What happened?"

"I saw you, here. Then I had to find you, and I did." He leaned in to kiss her again, but she evaded him.

"Is that all?" she asked. "Eofar, I need to know: is that *all* you saw?"

"That's all that matters." He watched her tuck the little bottle into the pocket she wore at her side. "The sun will be up soon. We must find some place to spend the day. Then we'll leave when the sun goes down. This cave, maybe? With Aeda's help I could move the rocks."

She didn't need to say anything; he had only been pretending not to know. He stared at her bowed head, a few locks of lustrous hair falling over her face, as their future together, his one and only dream, broke into bits.

"We're not leaving," he finally forced himself to say. He felt sick to his stomach again, but this time the elixir was not to blame. "You never sent the signal—I thought something had happened to you, but you just didn't want to go."

She winced as if in pain and clasped his arm for a moment, but still she didn't look at him. "Eofar, I'm so sorry."

"Is it your family? Is that why?"

"Not exactly. It's— Eofar, kiss me," she sobbed suddenly, but this time, he was the one to avoid the embrace.

"Tell me," he insisted.

She fell back from him, her eyes clouded over with the worry he'd already sensed. "People are scared and angry. Three years ago, when word got out that your father was ill, everyone assumed that you would take over the colony—but then, when the White Wolf—" Harotha wet her lips. "Eofar, they brought the *Mongrel* here. She's here in the Shadar, right now."

"The Mongrel?" he echoed, taken aback, suddenly remembering the girl in the desert, the girl who was not Nomas, nor Shadari. *The Mongrel?* That would certainly explain why Jachad had not wanted him to meet her, but it did nothing to explain Eofar's unsettling sense of recognition.

"You understand, then," she said, mistaking his reaction. "You see how serious it is. I'm afraid they're going to do something really reckless."

Eofar looked down at her belly. He reached out and held his palm up close enough to feel the warmth. "Even more reason to leave," he said.

"Eofar—"

"You said that being together was all that mattered, remember?" His throat burned. "You said that we can never change anything here."

"That was *then*—in the temple. Things are different now," Harotha told him. Her eyes flashed strangely. "I discovered something—something about the past. If I have the chance to tell people, I could save them from—"

"I don't care about *them*," he interrupted, "I care about you, and our baby. What will happen if he's born here? Do you think we'll be able to protect him?"

"I don't know," she said. She walked away from him, back toward the rocks, but her shawl slipped from her shoulders and fell to the ground. She bent down awkwardly to pick it up. "Running away, just to suit ourselves?" she said, twisting the dark fabric in her hands, still with her back to him. "How can that be right? Abandoning our families? Our friends?"

"Harotha." Every muscle in his body clenched. "Do you still love me?"

She stopped pulling at the shawl. "You know I do," she answered, but she did not turn around.

"Harotha?" he called faintly, walking toward her. "Harotha: look at me."

Now she did turn around, with her lips parted as if she was about to speak. But before she could, the expression on her face suddenly collapsed into shock. Her eyes fixed on a point over Eofar's shoulder. So softly that even his finely tuned Norlander hearing could barely make out the word, she murmured, "Faroth!"

He whirled. A group of Shadari men, roughly a dozen of them, had stopped on the near side of the dune about thirty yards away, as if they had just run around from behind it and drawn up short. Their leader took a couple of steps forward, dragging his left leg lamely behind him. Eofar knew him at once from Harotha's description.

"I recommend that everyone stay calm," a voice called out from the opposite direction, near the cliffs.

<Jachad?> Eofar called out in confusion, and he turned back toward the mountains in time to see Jachad emerge from behind one of the larger boulders. <What are you doing here?>

"Sorry, we haven't been introduced," Jachad said to Harotha, smiling and holding up his palms pacifically as he walked toward them. "I'm only here to—"

She lunged toward Jachad so unexpectedly that neither the Nomas king nor Eofar had time to react. She grabbed the thin, sharp knife from the scabbard at Jachad's waist and paced back, brandishing the knife at both of them until she bumped up against the rocks.

The world tilted for a moment. The elixir's vision hung before Eofar's eyes as if it had been etched on a piece of glass. This was the moment he had seen: it was the same, in every detail.

"Harotha!" he cried, lunging toward her.

"Stop! Stay away! Don't touch me!" she shouted, and he drew back, cringing. They were the very words he had dreaded hearing from the first moment he'd realized, with despair, that he'd fallen in love with her. Then she cried out to the Shadari, "Wait there!"

"Harotha," he said.

"I used you." Her voice sounded flat and hard, and totally unfamiliar: the voice of a stranger. "I want you to know that. Everything I told you was a lie. I needed to escape with my baby, and you were my way out."

She stepped forward, away from the rocks, and waved the knife to move them aside. Eofar and Jachad both backed up out of her way, clearing a path between her and the other Shadari. She walked past them, revolving as she went to keep them in sight, until she was backing across the sand toward the dune. The band of Shadari waited behind her, jostling restlessly around their leader.

"Harotha, please," he begged, his throat so raw that each word was little more than a cough.

"Did you really think I would carry your baby?" she spat at him, one arm crossed over her belly as if to shield the child even from his sight. "I would have thrown myself from the temple before I did that." In a voice less loud, but filled with more venom than he could possibly have imagined, Harotha delivered her final, crushing blow. "Daryan is my *real* husband. *Daryan* is the father of my baby."

She took another backward step, leaning awkwardly to balance the weight of the baby. He wanted to reach out to her, but his arms hung at his sides like leaden weights. She kept her head tilted so he could not see her eyes.

"Don't follow me," she commanded.

She turned and ran into her brother's arms.

<Eofar?> He heard Jachad calling to him from somewhere behind him. He had lost all ability to move. <Eofar? Come on. You shouldn't stay here. I know you have that wonderful sword, but there's a big gang of them over there. I don't think you want that. Not with her there.>

He could feel the elixir's poison twisting through his veins still as he gazed across the sand at the Shadari. <That's what I saw: that look on her face. That's why I was afraid for her.> Despair slid in front of his eyes like an oily film. <She was looking at *me*.>

<Come on, Eofar. Aeda's right over there. You should go back to the temple. There's nothing you can do here now.>

But he was thinking of the long, hot days that he had slept away, alone in his bed, and of Daryan and Harotha quietly talking, laughing, casually touching one another on the arm or the shoulder. The pair of them fluttered through his mind, eating away at his happy memories like moths.

<Should I congratulate you? Or is it too late for that?> someone asked from behind him—not Jachad. This was a different voice: an ageless, sexless, expressionless voice. <She was lying. You know that, don't you?> He turned and looked into a single silver-green eye, and now he was sure of one thing: the Mongrel was his sister.

Chapter Fourteen

Harotha clung to her brother's shoulder and rubbed her face against the coarse fabric of his robe. She wasn't weeping; she was trying to gouge from her memory the stricken look in Eofar's eyes. Faroth circled his left arm stiffly around her back and she could see his right arm stuck out awkwardly beside her, keeping the blade of his curved sword at a safe distance. "All right, it's over now. Get a hold of yourself," he said gruffly into her ear.

"Faroth!" Elthion cried out.

She lifted her head away from her brother's shoulder and saw the young Shadari dancing at his elbow. She recognized most of the same faces she'd seen at Faroth's house, plus a few others. Most of them were armed, of a sort, and many were bloodied. Their ragged clothes reeked with an unwashed funk that turned her stomach, but it was the hard expression on their faces that made the muscles in her throat constrict.

"Come on," Elthion shouted, "what are we waiting for? He's just standing there by himself—let's get him!"

"He's got an imperial sword," said Binit, sounding worried. "That Nomas is there, too. He's got that fire trick."

"Jachad works for the Mongrel, and she's working for us," Elthion reminded him impatiently. "He won't stop us."

"The Mongrel didn't say anything about killing Lord Eofar," Sami pointed out.

"But she did tell us to come here!" Elthion insisted.

"To get Harotha," said Sami.

"The *Mongrel*? That's how you knew I'd be here?" she asked, shocked. But then she bit her lip. Best to keep her other questions to herself for the moment.

"Come on, Faroth, Elthion's right. Let's kill him." Alkar flexed the only remaining digit on his maimed hand. "We can take him. This is a lucky chance for us: one less Dead One to worry about later on."

"We should take him hostage," she said, gripping Faroth's forearm. She filled her voice with loathing and gestured toward Eofar with Jachad's knife. "He's the governor's son—and he's weak. We can use him."

"Use him for what? Practice? We already know how to kill Dead Ones," snarled Alkar.

"Shut up, all of you," said Faroth, pulling his arm away. "Look! What's *she* doing there?"

She turned toward the mountain and saw a bare-armed woman standing next to Eofar and Jachad in front of the cave. The stranger looked remarkably similar to Eofar—his build, his height, even his stance—but her skin had a much darker cast, and her tangled hair was as black as Harotha's own.

A shrill whistle cut through the chilly dawn air: Eofar, calling to his dereshadi. He was going back to the temple, she realized, simultaneously relieved and panicked. In a few moments he would be gone, perhaps forever, carrying her ruinous lies along with him.

"The Mongrel is helping him!" Sami called out. "She's betrayed us!"

"Faroth!" Elthion shrieked, scooping a sharp rock up from the ground.

She heard the piercing whistle again. "Faroth, listen to me—don't—!"

"Come on!" Elthion shouted, ignoring Faroth's barked command to stop. As he halved the distance between the dune and the cave he hurled the stone with all of his might. The throw was true: the stone flew through the air, well-aimed, dangerous.

Elthion's comrades cheered and charged forward, washing past Harotha, who remained where she was, paralyzed with dread and her own helplessness.

Suddenly her hair was blown back from her face and the air before her shuddered. She heard her brother calling her name, screaming at her to get down, but she stood rigidly straight as the dereshadi flew toward her. It swooped overhead, near enough for her to touch its bristling gray belly. She could feel its breath on her face. The men around her scrambled backward, clawing at each other in a panic as the curtain of sand kicked up by the strokes of Aeda's wings blinded them.

She turned to watch the creature as it swung past and slid to a stop next to Eofar. The Mongrel pushed him into the saddle; then she vaulted up behind him and the dereshadi leaped back into the sky. They flew higher and higher into the graying sky until they blended into the dark walls of the temple and disappeared.

"You're pathetic." Faroth stalked among his bedraggled followers, pulling them back to their feet even as he berated them. "Look at yourselves! This is why they were able to overcome us at the mines: discipline. I expected as much from Elthion, but the rest of you should know better."

Harotha weighed the hilt of the Nomas knife in her hand and looked back at the cave. She didn't see where Jachad had gone, but he hadn't left on the dereshadi. She knew he and Eofar were friends, of a sort—but Elthion had said the Nomas king was working for the Mongrel . . .

"Faroth," Sami began, "if the Mongrel's betrayed us—"

"Shut up." Faroth's stormy eyes fixed on Harotha. He limped toward her, winding a rag around the blade of his sword before tucking it under his sash. "The Mongrel said we'd find you here. I didn't believe her, but here you are."

"Here I am." Harotha swallowed, and tried a wry smile. Both she and Faroth had always hated sentimentality, so she hadn't expected him to weep and catch her up in his arms, but this felt wrong. "Did you miss me?"

"We *mourned* you. Saria and me—and Dramash," Faroth said. His voice was hard, angry, but she could see the pain in his eyes, still raw after all this time. "Five months ago: that's when they told us you were dead. Not that I ever expected you to come back from the temple, dead or alive."

"I had no way to get word to you." The other Shadari were coalescing around them. She curled her arm across her belly, feeling their stares. Faroth's eyes roamed dispassionately over her body, almost as if she were a jug priced too cheaply and he was looking for the telltale flaw.

"The daimon, hm? Did we hear that right?"

She nodded as the others murmured to each other. "Once I knew about the baby, I had to do something before the Dead Ones found out. You know the rules for temple slaves—no marriages, no babies. I wasn't going to let them kill Daryan's child."

"Go on," Faroth urged, when she paused.

"Eofar had made it plain that he was . . . well, interested. It was an obvious choice."

"And so you talked him into thinking he was the father?" asked her brother.

"I did what I had to do." She let some of her discomfort show through. "It wasn't easy, but I convinced him that I was in love with him."

"You must have done a good job. Convincing him." Faroth shifted his weight from his good leg to his bad and then back again, and spat on the ground.

She looked steadily into his eyes. "I couldn't afford to be squeamish. I had to protect the baby."

"And you're sure that Daryan is the real father?"

"I should know, shouldn't I?" she retorted.

He rubbed the stubble on his chin with the heel of his hand. "So, then. Where have you been for the last five months?"

"Up there." She shuddered. "I thought Eofar would help me escape once I started to show; instead he locked me up where no one would see me. Until tonight." She dropped her head. "Five months. You can't imagine— I finally told him the baby was going to be born any day now; that someone would hear it cry—that's when he finally agreed to take me away."

This was a dangerous lie, but she couldn't think of any other way to explain why she'd been in the Shadar for five months without telling anyone. Now it was imperative she find Saria and get their stories straightened out before Faroth found out the truth.

"It's lucky we were here, then," said her brother, "or you might not have escaped from him so easily."

"I would have found a way."

"And what about your great plan to defeat the Dead Ones?" His voice lifted in mockery and his dark eyes shone as hard as glass. He'd been nurturing this anger a long time. "Did Shairav ordain you and teach you the magic? Did he tell you why our parents and the other ashas committed suicide just when they were needed? Did he show you the way into the temple? Give you anything useful? Anything at all?"

Harotha's mouth stiffened. "Shairav was uncooperative."

"I told you not to go," he reminded her, as if she could possibly have forgotten that terrible argument. "Three years—*three years*, wasted."

Harotha crossed her arms across her belly again, conscious of the proximity between her unborn child and the naked Nomas blade in her hand. "Not wasted."

Faroth came closer to her. "All right. Maybe you're not such a fool after all," he told her softly. "To most of these people, the daimon still means something. But you and I both know that ever since Shairav stole him from his mother, Daryan has been nothing more than the old man's lackey. If you think I'm going to—"

He was interrupted by the sound of a faint shout coming from the south, and everyone turned. In the distance, dereshadi were still circling over the mining camp, no doubt preparing to return to the temple with the dawn, but much closer at hand, a group of six or seven Shadari were advancing toward the rebels, juggling a large, awkward burden. Harotha saw the leader raise a hand to his mouth and a moment later heard his cry again.

"Faroth? Faroth with you?"

He checked the area around them cautiously, then he cupped his hands to his mouth and shouted back. "Here!"

She saw the leader turn for a moment to speak to his companions. Then they came on at a faster pace. A tense restlessness had fallen over the waiting company. Their failed attack on Eofar had left them somewhat sheepish, but not enough to quell their curiosity about Harotha, and she was conscious of the surreptitious glances and the murmured discussions she couldn't quite make out.

Faroth suddenly reached back and gripped her shoulder, hard.

"Ow! That hurts! What did you do that for?" she asked, moving out of his grasp.

"Harotha—you go— Go and see," Faroth urged her. He had gone pale, and a shiver of fear raced up her spine.

"All right," she told her brother, laying a hand on his arm before she walked forward to meet the approaching party. The sun had just crested the horizon and she had to shield her eyes from the glare as she made her way toward them. When they were only about twenty paces apart, the men paused briefly to reposition their burden, and as they lowered it for a moment, she saw a mass of long, dark hair tumble down and sweep the sand.

She drew in a long, painful gasp, but still she watched silently as the bearers came forward and lowered Saria's body to the ground. Her sister-in-law's lush hair was matted with blood. Her skin was the ghastly yellowish-gray of an old bruise. The cause of her death was all too clear: a great gash split her throat, partially hidden by her collar and the mess of dried blood caking her skin.

A sob too large to release wedged itself in Harotha's chest and swelled there, threatening to burst like an angry blister. Her head spun and she fell to her knees in the sand.

"We chased Dramash to the mines after he ran out of the tavern," she heard Sami say. "Saria must have gone there after him. It was the White Wolf— She— She took your boy. One of her men killed Saria when she tried to stop them." He looked down at the ground and added awkwardly, "I'm so sorry."

Faroth screamed in fury, and the cry ripped Harotha open like a jagged blade. She became headily aware of the hard wooden hilt of the Nomas knife still clutched in her palm, smooth as a bone, as she rose up from her knees on legs shaking with rage. The Dead Ones had been doing this all of her life: destroying, killing, taking away any chance that the Shadari might have at happiness. The rotten Norland Empire teetered on a foundation built from pain and fear, and she wouldn't let it stand a moment longer.

"Look! It's Jachad!" someone shouted, pointing to the robed figure hurrying over from the mountain.

Faroth shook off the friends trying to comfort him and rushed at the Nomas, with Harotha bolting after him.

"You! You've betrayed us—you and that *monster*!" Faroth's voice was hoarse with fury and grief. "You're working with the Dead Ones—you always have been! Why did the White Wolf take my son?" He reached out for Jachad's throat, crying, "Why did she kill my wife?"

"I'm sorry—believe me, I'm truly sorry, but I don't know!" protested Jachad, holding his hands up both in supplication and in warning: yellow flames snapped between his fingers.

Faroth's friends restrained him and Harotha felt hands on her own arms, pulling her back as well. "The Mongrel has not betrayed you, that much I swear. You've got your sister back, haven't you, just like she promised?" He turned his blue eyes on Harotha, and she could see both the compassion and the quick look he cast at the knife in her hand.

"Is the Mongrel on our side, or isn't she?" Elthion shoved his way forward through the crowd. "Why did she leave with the Dead One?"

"It's all part of the plan—" Jachad tried to explain.

"Why should we believe anything you say?" asked Faroth. He lunged forward again, but this time Harotha grabbed his arm and pulled him back.

"Wait, Faroth," she said, wishing that her hands weren't trembling so violently. "Listen to what the Nomas has to say. If the Mongrel is going to betray you, there's nothing you can do about it now. But I don't think this one," she nodded at Jachad, "would have come over here if that were true."

"That's right. Thank you," Jachad said to her. He spoke calmly, but she could see the angry flush on his cheeks behind his freckles. "Now, please listen: the Mongrel has gone back to the temple to distract the Dead Ones—"

"Distract them from what?" Elthion asked.

Jachad fixed him with a withering look. "If I could finish? The dereshadi being ridden by the two guards Faroth killed in the tavern—"

"Faroth, you killed two guards?" asked Harotha.

"—are still tied up near the old palace," Jachad continued patiently. "The Mongrel wants you to fly them back to the temple, find Shairav and Daryan and bring them down here to the city."

Outcries of dismay burst from the little company.

"That's suicide," Binit wailed. "We don't know how to fly the dereshadi!"

"You don't have to do much more than get on and strap yourself in," Jachad reassured them. "They don't like the sunlight any more than their masters. They'll be happy to get back to the stables. The Mongrel will make sure that no Dead Ones are around when you land."

"I wouldn't trade a one-legged dog for Shairav or the daimon," said Faroth. "If that's where Dramash is, I'm going to get him and bring him home. The others can rot up there for all I care."

"Think, Faroth," Harotha advised him, digging her fingers into his arm. "We need more men for this uprising—the more the better. If Shairav and the daimon are with us, every Shadari will see our cause as the will of the gods. We'll have an army. The Mongrel is right—it's a good plan."

Jachad turned to her with a searching look in his blue eyes, then he nodded. "Yes, that's it exactly."

"We don't want Daryan here, trying to take over, not after we've taken all the risks!" Elthion cried.

"That won't happen—Daryan isn't like that," she assured them.

"She's just thinking of herself, Faroth," Elthion insisted. He jabbed an accusing finger at her belly. "Do you think she's forgotten for one second about that baby's father?"

"Harotha? Are you all right?" The light had dimmed and Faroth's voice came from a long way away. Harotha realized she was fainting. She felt Faroth's hands, supporting her. "Harotha, what is it?"

"I'm all right," she finally managed to say. "Just a little dizzy." She forced herself to take a deep breath and reached up to massage the back of her neck. Faroth handed her the waterskin from his belt and she gulped down a tepid mouthful. “I’m all right,” she told her brother, handing the skin back to him. “I’m all right. And I’m going with you.”

“You can’t go back up there!” said Sami, backed up by a chorus of incredulous shouts.

“The temple is a maze,” she said, raising her voice above the clamor. “You’ll never find your way around without help. I can lead you straight to Shairav and Daryan. They can help us get Dramash away from the White Wolf.”

“And Eofar?” Faroth asked. “If he finds you again?”

She looked him in the eye. “I’ll deal with it.”

Faroth’s face puckered into a scowl. “I’m going to get my son,” he proclaimed ominously. “Elthion, Binit and Sami. You’re coming with me.” Then he turned back to Harotha. “You’re staying here.”

Harotha began to protest, but Faroth cut her off.

“Don’t argue with me. I’ll bring back Shairav and Daryan,” he assured her. Then he added, “Elthion is right: without the daimon, that’s just another Shadari bastard in your belly.”

Harotha could feel herself breathing hard, but this time she kept her mouth shut. She could see the naked suspicion on the faces of the other Shadari: this was no longer the courageous band of freedom fighters she had carefully gathered from the downtrodden citizenry; this was a gang, and it was Faroth’s gang, not hers.

“All right,” she agreed.

He ordered Saria’s body brought back to the city to be prepared for her funeral and Harotha taken back to his house, to wait there until his return. Then he struck out for the palace ruins with his three companions jostling nervously at his heels. The rest of the men stood awkwardly around the body for a moment until someone took the initiative, then more hurried to help lift her up.

Alkar came forward to her, holding out his good hand. “Come with me.” He reached out as if to take her by the elbow, but she jerked backward, repulsed at the thought of his sweaty hand touching her.

"No. I need to stay here, by the mountains." She needed time alone, to think. "The earthquake uncovered something over there that I want to investigate. I know Faroth's house. I'll come later."

"I can't allow that," Alkar told her. His eyes flashed dangerously. "Faroth said to take you with us."

"The sun's already up," she said. "I'll be perfectly safe."

"I have orders. So do you," said Alkar.

She flushed, remembering a time when Faroth's orders would never have countermanded her own. "All right."

He smiled unpleasantly and immediately turned his back on her. The bearers swung around and headed northeast, in the direction of Faroth's house, the rest drifting after them, in whispering twos and threes. She hung back, letting them get as far ahead of her as she dared. She wanted no more eyes on her.

"Can I have my knife back?" Jachad was standing behind her, holding out his hand. She had completely forgotten he was there. He flashed his disarming smile. "Please? It was a gift from my mother."

She handed him the knife.

"Thank you," he said pleasantly as he returned the knife to its sheath. He adjusted his robes and then, in an urgent voice completely at odds with his open smile and the casualness of his stance, said, "They don't trust you. You won't be able to fool them for long."

Something inside her chest fluttered. "What do you mean?"

"Stop." He cut her off immediately, fixing her with his arrestingly blue eyes. "I'm Nomas, remember? This game you're running wouldn't have fooled me when I was five years old. Don't worry; you're in no danger from me. But I wouldn't say the same about your sweaty friends over there."

Alkar, bringing up the rear of the ragtag procession marching away across the sand, looked back suspiciously.

"I don't know what you mean," she said. "They're waiting for me. I have to go."

"Get away from them as soon as you can," Jachad pressed. "Come to us in the desert. We Nomas have the blood of a dozen different races in our veins. No one will judge you there. You have my word."

She looked into his eyes and saw the blue skies of a beautiful dream: roaming with the Nomas, no attachments, no obligations, no one to disappoint or to betray, beholden to no one and to nothing. Tears of exhaustion sprang to her eyes, but they refused to fall.

"Harotha!" Alkar called out. With an annoyed shake of his head, he began stalking back toward her.

"I can't," she whispered.

Jachad shrugged and turned away.

"Wait! Where are you going?" she called after him.

Jachad continued walking as he called back, "To pray."

Chapter Fifteen

Jachad stood up and brushed the sand from the front of his robes. Once again he had said his prayers alone, and once again, without his people around him, the familiar ritual had failed to comfort him. He was sick to death of the Shadar. As he shivered in the temple's shadow, Shof, spilling his light extravagantly over the sea, had never felt more distant. He looked up at the temple's blank, uncommunicative windows. Meiran was in there somewhere, and up to Shof knew what.

He squinted up at the spot where he had seen Nisha's pre-arranged signal fire burning the night before. She was waiting on the mountain to accompany him down to the gathering place, and he was already late.

In his haste to reach her Jachad chose a path better suited to goats than people. By the time his shadow had shrunk down to a stout little dwarf, he was using hands as well as feet to climb. Loose rocks, gnarled roots and other hazards kept him occupied, but not even the physical demands of the climb could stop the thoughts churning in his head. They were driving him mad, repeating themselves, round and round, like the first phrases of a tune with a forgotten ending.

Midday had passed by the time he finally crested the narrow, flat ridge that Nisha had chosen for her camp. She had erected her tent of sailcloth—dyed a silvery blue and conjuring the *Argent*, the ship of which she was captain—on a patch bare of the scrubby vegetation. Nisha herself was sitting on a carpet in front of her tent, tending to a small fire with a kettle swinging over it. The silver medallion of Amai, the token of her office as high priestess to the moon goddess and queen of the Nomas, hung against her breast, flashing in the afternoon sun.

"Have you eaten?" she asked.

He stared at his mother for a moment and then laughed heartily, diving onto the carpet beside her. He touched his forehead to hers in greeting and inhaled from her hair the fresh, blustery essence of the sea. "Oh, I've been away too long, Mother," he said, still chuckling, falling back on his elbows. "That's just what I needed: some good old hard-headed Nomas practicality. No, I haven't eaten."

"Or slept either, hmm? You look terrible, Jachi."

"I know," he said, rubbing at his aching eyes. "Smells good. What is it, fish soup?"

"Want some?"

"I could stick my head right in the pot."

She dipped a bowl into the pot and handed it to him. He sat up, took a sip, grimaced as it burned his tongue and then sat back on his heels to blow on it.

"So, how was the bargaining?" she asked.

"Good. Profitable. Here's the fee for bringing Meiran. That's all going into the treasury." He untied Faroth's purse with one hand and tossed it down on the carpet. "But the elixir—now that was a pretty piece of bargaining. I sold it to Eofar for thirty-one eagles, even though the bottle was only half-full. How's that for a result?"

"That's wonderful, son."

"Although," he mused, scratching thoughtfully at the wiry growth of beard he was now sporting, "if I had known he was really going to use it on himself, I might not have sold it to him."

"Yes, you would have," she said.

"Yes, I would have," he conceded with a grin and playfully grabbed at his mother's legs. She swatted him away.

"Stop it, Jachi. Eat your soup."

He obeyed, and they sat in silence, kept company by the gentle rustlings of the tent flaps in the mountain breeze. Eventually Nisha's lashes fell lower over her blue eyes—eyes the color of a shallow sea in sunshine—and she gazed pensively down at the city below.

"All right, old lady. Out with it," he prodded.

She waited a moment and then without looking at him, asked, "So, how is she?"

He considered the question. "Complicated," he answered finally.

"Did she tell you why she left us?" she asked. Her eyes were shining.

"Come on, Mother. We already know that: she was sick and we were arguing over her. She must have thought that what happened in the temple was starting all over again."

"But it was all so long ago, and she was so young. Maybe she doesn't even remember what happened."

"Oh, I think she remembers," he assured her. "Otherwise she wouldn't have come back here."

Nisha sat up. A worried frown creased her forehead. "Does she understand now why she's ill?"

Jachad pushed the empty wooden bowl aside and stood up. "No, I don't think so—not the real reason, at least. She's not interested in us Nomas at all, as far as I can tell. She's more concerned with this ridiculous Shadari rebellion—though for the life of me I can't figure out which side she's really on." He began pacing the ridge, knotting his fingers together as he walked. "I did try, but you know Meiran: you can't really ask her anything. I gave her the full Nomas charm, but got nothing. It's like trying to charm an oyster."

She watched him pace, and finally told him sternly,

"What's wrong here was not your doing. What's done is done. No one said it was up to you to make it right. You take too much on yourself."

"I don't know," he mused. "I've been praying to Shof for guidance. He hasn't seen fit to give me any."

"Shof?" She gave a little snort. "It's his fault—and old King Tobias's—that we're in this mess in the first place."

"Mother," he said wearily, "I don't want to have this argument again. It's just as much Amai's fault as it is Shof's—more, even, if you'd just admit it. Meiran was dedicated to Shof first, and you know it."

"She was a female child. The old king had no right to keep Meiran, no right to consecrate her to Shof," Nisha retorted with her lips pursed.

"She wasn't Nomas, Mother! What right did you and your women have to steal her from our camp and consecrate her to Amai? Behind our backs?" he demanded.

"We did not *steal* Meiran!" Nisha insisted, rising to her feet. "She came wandering into our midst that gathering like a lost soul, searching our faces as if she were looking for someone. Our hearts went out to her. We thought she needed us. We wanted to help her."

"She didn't need you. She was already consecrated to Shof."

"There! That's what I'm talking about," she crowed, gesturing triumphantly. "Why didn't the old king tell anyone about her? Why did he consecrate her to Shof in secret? Why did he deliberately try to hide her from us at that gathering? Unless he knew he was doing something wrong, hmm? He should have discussed it with us first and we could have decided together what was best for her. Meiran would never have been harmed."

He folded his arms over his chest and pressed his knuckles against his lips, saying with dark reflection, "Maybe he just couldn't face the risk of being parted from her."

She took a deep breath as if gathering strength for another volley, but instead she let it out again in a long sigh. Her lips curled into a rueful smile. "He did have a big heart, old Tobias. As big as the desert, we used to say. And he loved Meiran, didn't he? He was never the same after she left, poor man."

Jachad's eyes lost their focus and the ridge, his mother and the Shadar below all disappeared. "Yes, he loved her—it was impossible not to love her. That day she crawled into our camp, burned, bleeding, hungry, speechless from thirst—she was nearly dead, and we never did find out how long she'd been out there on her own. The old king himself nursed her back to health like she was an infant. He put her in my tent and treated her as if she were my sister. She'd wake up in the night, Mother, screaming like you never heard, and nothing would make her stop, not until he came in to comfort her. Some days she would just sit by his side, silent as a mute, watching him, those mismatched eyes never leaving his face. Other days she was just another kid, like the rest of us, laughing and playing, fighting and making up and fighting some more—until you lot got hold of her and consecrated her to Amai and the attacks started coming." Jachad looked at his mother. "And then one morning I woke up and she was gone." He rubbed his eyes and looked down on the Shadar. "What did we do?"

"We blessed her twice, Jachi. Worse things have been done in this world, believe me."

"But there must be something we can do to help her."

"Is it very painful for her?" she asked, coming to him and squeezing his shoulder with her rope-callused hand.

He nodded. "The attacks still come at sunrise and sunset, but it looks like the pain is much worse than I remember. I've seen Amai and Shof push her almost all the way to death, squabbling over her. And I've noticed other things—I think they've taken different bits of her over the years, like she was a map and they were generals claiming territories. They've taken an eye each—she can't see properly out of both of them at once any more, that's why she has to wear that patch. And she drinks with her left hand at night and her right hand during the day, things like that." He narrowed his eyes, looking at the sky. "That's how they show their love for her: they torture her. They're driving her mad."

"Amai and Shof are gods," Nisha reminded him. "The war they fight stalemated at the dawn of time. If they both want her, what can we do about it? I've prayed to Amai to release her claim; you have prayed to Shof, but it's no use: we're a stubborn people and we have stubborn gods."

He circled his arm around her waist and hugged her to him. "Mother, I'm not coming to the gathering with you," he told her. "I can't leave things the way they are. I have to go back—I have to know what she's trying to do. I may have to stop her from doing it."

He felt her stiffen in his embrace. "Are you going to tell her the truth?"

"How can I?" he demanded bitterly, releasing her. "I'm the king of the tribe of Shof, the king of the Nomas. I don't know what she'll do if she finds out the truth. My first duty is to my tribe. I haven't forgotten that."

She put her hands on his shoulders and looked at him through a blur of tears. "You are a king, Jachi, and you do have a duty to your people, and that's all well and good. But you're afraid to tell her the truth, for the same reason I am: you're afraid she'll hate you for it." Her tears spilled over and he hugged her, burying his face in her sea-swept hair.

"There," she said finally, disentangling herself and plunking a motherly kiss down on his cheek. "You don't need to worry about the gathering. Come here," she commanded, holding out her hand to him. Her rings flashed in the sun. "Come!"

He took her hand suspiciously and allowed her to lead him past her tent, over to the other side of the ridge toward the desert, away from the temple and the Shadar. The undulating dunes, tinged red and yellow and white, stretched to the horizon. He felt a sharp pang of homesickness at the sight of them. Somewhere out there his tribe was getting ready to see the wives and daughters and sisters and mothers and lovers who had not set foot on land in the rising and setting of six moons. Even now he could see the dust cloud on the horizon that was probably his tribe, journeying toward the traditional meeting-ground, eight long days' journey from the Shadar.

She pulled him right toward the edge of the ridge. "Look!" she said, putting a hand on the back of his neck and tilting his head downward.

A patchwork of riotous color, a small city of brightly hued sailcloth tents crouched in the shadow of the mountain: the tribe of Amai. The camp swarmed with activity. The shrill voices of children floated up on the breeze and a hundred fires danced. Jachad glanced back out at the dust cloud on the horizon. It was hard to tell, but now he could see that they were moving toward the Shadar, rather than away from it as he had first thought.

"There's no law that says the tribes have to meet at that old place in the desert. We're tired of lugging our tents through the sand," Nisha informed him with a touch of defiance. "We beached the boats in the usual place and just came here instead. I sent word of the change to your caravan twelve days ago. I knew that with you away, no one would dare contradict me. The men will be here by tomorrow. Besides, I think a change of scenery will do everyone some good."

For once Jachad was at a complete loss for words.

She smiled. "There, you see, Jachi? Simple. You come to us when you're ready. And if you need us, we're your people, and we're here for you." Then she caught at his hand and held it tightly, holding it to her cheek. "Bring her back to us, if you can."

He nodded, took her hand and kissed it.

Chapter Sixteen

As Isa reached the top of the stairs she could see the heat rippling the air in front of her. Greasy cooking smells came in waves and she paused, waiting for a sudden surge of nausea to pass. From the refectory doorway just up ahead she could hear knives clattering on clay plates, and every now and then a strained word of command to the slaves. Occasional bursts of light flared out through the open archway as fat dripped down onto the cooking fires.

Frea wasn't in the refectory. Isa didn't have to look inside; no wall in the temple could conceal the frigid intensity of her sister's presence.

She shut her eyes. Sweat sheeted down underneath the stiff new leather of her fighting clothes. She could feel the heat pulling her back toward the darkness of her room, the softness of her bed, the filminess of the gown she'd left lying in a heap on the floor, pulling her back toward sleep and the greedy way it devoured the long, pointless hours of her life.

But no, not this time. Now she was made of ice. No amount of heat could thaw her. She was frozen as solid as the statues in the emperor's palace at Ravindal. Her fingers were icicles. Her breast was a snowdrift. Her heart was a glacier.

<Isa.>

Her eyes flew open. Rho was standing in the shadows

at the far end of the hall. All she could see of him was a long face and two indistinct hands hovering in the darkness.

She greeted him coolly, keenly aware of the shiny newness of her leather suit. The sleeveless jacket was supposed to be worn with a shirt underneath, but it was just too hot here. She tugged at the buckle across her chest to make sure it was still fastened.

<Well. Look at you,> Rho said noncommittally. She expected him to continue down the hallway toward her, but he didn't move. <You look just like her. Except for your hair.>

<I didn't have time to braid it,> she said. She didn't want him to know that after she'd left Daryan alone in the bathing room, she'd wasted the rest of the night away sitting half-dressed on the edge of her bed, lost in a miasma of feelings she couldn't even name. She had left herself only enough time to put on her clothes and tie her hair back like a boy's. <You were right about the triffons. It shouldn't matter, and I'm not going to wait any more. I'm going to Frea's room to challenge her.>

<She's not in her room.>

<Beorun's room, then,> she amended bluntly, hoping to shock him. She was not as innocent as he thought: she knew all about Frea and Beorun, just as she had known all about Frea and Rho. <Frea's disgusting. I don't know how she can lower herself like that. It's not just that Beorun's from such a low clan—he's got a neck like the hind leg of a triffon.>

<Strange, then, that someone managed to cut through it anyway. Beorun's dead.>

<That's not funny, Rho.>

<No?> he asked. <Good. Because I wasn't joking.>

For a moment, all of the breathable air disappeared from the corridor. Nothing was left but the lung-searing heat.

Ice, she reminded herself. <Beorun's really dead?>

<Oh, he's dead all right. Unless you know a cure for decapitation.>

Made of ice, like a Norlander. Like Frea. Like Rho. <Well, that was stupid of him, getting himself killed.>

<Yes, wasn't it?> he agreed.

Something was different about him—she should have noticed it right away. The aristocratic disdain that was the mainstay of his personality felt forced. And why was he standing so far away from her? She started down the hallway toward him.

<Don't!> he warned her, shrinking back, but not before she had seen what he hadn't wanted her to see.

<Onraka's eyes! What happened to you? You look awful!> she cried out, both in alarm and disgust. Some dark stuff was splattered all over the front of his tunic and messy streaks of it trailed down his arms and hands. A grayish-blue bruise swelled under his right eye, distorting his handsome, quintessentially Norlander features.

<Nothing. Trouble at the mines,> he answered, pushing away her concern with the finality of a slammed door.

<What are you playing at, walking around like that?> she chided him. <You can't do much about the bruises, but you could at least clean yourself up. What if someone sees you?>

The dark pupils in his silver eyes roamed up and down her frame. <And here I thought you only looked the part.>

She didn't understand the comment, but she felt the criticism. <What do you mean by that?>

<Eofar didn't want me to train you,> he went on, <and he was right. I should have listened to him.>

Isa felt him as oddly distant, as if he were talking to himself, without quite realizing she was there. <Eofar was right?> she asked incredulously. <Why would you say something like that?>

<Because it's true,> he replied.

<True?> Ice. She was made of ice. <You've spent

months helping me train. You said I had a gift—you said I was the best natural swordsman you'd ever seen. You're the one who told me I could beat her.>

<You can.>

<What's the problem, then?> Isa demanded helplessly, feeling the brittle wall of her composure beginning to splinter.

<I wanted you to defeat her. Not *become* her.>

She tossed her head and took a step back from him. <Why? What happened? Did she give you a hard time tonight, Rho? Maybe you thought that with Beorun dead, she'd take you back? Is that it?>

<Don't, Isa.> His warning came at her, glinting and sharp, like the edge of a blade catching the sun.

<You're such a hypocrite. You're the one who said Frea was the perfect Norlander—the ideal. And we both know the only reason you helped me was to irritate her.>

<That's right. She is the perfect Norlander. Do you really think you know what that means? Do you really think you understand what it means to be one of us?>

Now, even through the buzz of her own anger, Isa could feel some dark emotion churning up beneath his genteel posing. <Of course I do. That's what you trained me for,> she reminded him.

<Well, I wish I hadn't,> he said again.

<That's fine, then. You're not as special as you think you are,> she tossed back to him. <If you hadn't done it, someone else would have.>

<Yes, I know. I know that.> His emotions suddenly rolled to the surface, striking out at her with the force of a blunt fist, and as she reeled back he reached out with both hands and grabbed her wrists. She could feel the blood pulsing wildly through his fingertips, and for the first time she noticed the heavy scent of wine clinging to him and realized that he was drunk. <That's what I keep telling myself. But it doesn't make it any better.>

<Let go!> she cried—but he'd already released her and as she watched in revulsion, he lurched and fell

against the wall. He tried to tamp down his emotions, but the best he could do was reduce them to a dark smolder. She reminded herself sternly that she didn't have time for compassion, or pity, or curiosity—she didn't even have time to be angry.

<You won't get what you want from her,> he called after her as she walked away from him. <You'll win the sword, but that's all. You'll never get her approval.>

She turned back to him. <I don't need her approval.>

He didn't bother to contradict what they both knew was a lie. <Listen to me, Isa. Frea loves only one thing: perfection. Nothing less.> He was calmer now, but still intense, in a way that she had never known him to be before. <If you fight her, you'll have to be perfect. And that can end only one way.>

<And what way is that?>

His silver eyes flashed in the dark hallway. <You'll have to kill her.>

<Don't be ridiculous.>

<Is it so ridiculous?> He had straightened up against the wall, but his shoulders were still slightly hunched, as if something were pressing down on him from above. <Soldiers. Warriors. Norlanders. That's what we train for, isn't it? The swords we're all so proud of—that's what they're for, isn't it? To kill?>

<Not our own families. Not our own kind.>

<Onfar's balls, Isa, are you really that naïve?>

She was too furious to respond. She stalked off down the corridor, hands trembling with rage.

<Wait—don't go.> She felt him behind her just as her foot touched the first stair. <There's no point going that way. Frea's with your father. They won't let you in there.>

<Then I'll wait for her in her room.>

<You can't. She left Jeder there with . . . > He trailed off, but then said with a new eagerness, <I have a better idea. I know what to do.>

She stopped halfway down the stairs and turned back to him warily.

<Frea will fight you if you make it a matter of honor—her honor, your family's honor. Challenge her in the refectory, in front of her men.>

Isa regarded him suspiciously. <Why should I take advice from you? You're drunk.>

<Not as much as you think I am, and I'm right.>

She considered his proposal. <If she hasn't gone to the refectory by now, she isn't going at all.>

<That's just it—I just thought of the perfect way to get her there.> A shadow of the same bleak emotion that had overwhelmed him earlier hovered between them, but this time he had it under control. <Go back there and wait. Frea will be there soon, I promise you.>

She looked past him, toward the doorway. All of those bodies. All of that heat. <No. I'm going to do it the way I planned. I'll find her.>

<That won't work, Isa. You know it won't.>

He was right. She'd fail again, just as she had before.

<Just wait in there. That's all I ask,> he assured her. He moved past her down the stairs, leaving the sweet, rotten-fruit scent of wine in his wake as the darkness closed over his head. She remained there for a long time, halfway up and halfway down the stairs, staring at nothing. Finally she ran her tongue slowly over her dry lips, turned and walked back up to the refectory.

Chapter Seventeen

Daryan stopped at the junction of two passages, his momentum gone. He told himself that he should keep going, but he felt incapable of propeling himself any further. Isa had played with a wooden toy when she was little, a Norland animal—he had never known what it was called—on rackety wheels; no matter how hard you pushed it, it never traveled more than a few feet across the stone floor before stuttering to a halt. That's what he felt like now.

He didn't know where she'd gone after she'd left him alone in the bathing room. That had been hours ago. He should have been helping to restore order in the wake of the earthquake, and Shairav was looking for him. He couldn't just stand here brooding, going nowhere, doing nothing. People were hurt; they were afraid. He was the daimon. He had responsibilities. He wasn't a child any more.

But neither was Isa.

Finally he heard footsteps, light and quick, too light for a man, too quick for a woman, and only a soft pattering, not the percussive strike of boots or the slap of sandals. And as the source of the footsteps solidified out of the gray darkness at the far end of the hall, he understood quite plainly that his mind had snapped—temple sickness, his people called it, from living too long in the dark. He had gone mad.

Because it was a child: a little curly-haired Shadari

child, just like Daryan himself had been when he first came to the temple. It was a likeness, an echo, conjured up from his own memories. The apparition walked toward him without slowing, and he would have not been at all surprised if it had passed through him as easily as if he were made of smoke. But the child stopped in front of him and looked up into his face.

"Hello," said the boy.

Daryan bent down. The warm, fresh smell of the boy's hair and clothes—a mixture of bleached sand and hearth fires and sea-salt—made his head swim with longing and loss. "Who are you?" he asked faintly. "Where did you come from?"

"I'm Dramash. From the Shadar."

"But how did you—?"

"I'm going to live here now and help take care of the dereshadi."

"Who told you that?"

"The White Wolf. One of the soldiers said he'd teach me how to fight, too. I don't know his name. What's your name?"

"Daryan."

The whites of the boy's eyes widened. "Oh! I've heard of you! I know all about you."

"Do you?" he asked, smiling, but he was not really listening. He heard more footsteps coming their way.

"My father told me," said Dramash. "He says you're a coward."

Daryan's stomach muscles screwed up tight. He was careful to keep his face turned away from the boy. "Does he?" he asked, struggling to keep his voice level. "Why does he say that?"

"He says if you didn't like it here you would have done something by now. He says you get to lie around here while other people are dying in the mines," the child continued blithely.

He was just repeating what he'd heard, Daryan reminded himself. He was just a little boy.

"He says that you don't really care about the Shadari at all. He says that if we wait around for you to do something, we'll be waiting forever."

Now Daryan did hear the scrape of boot-nails and he recognized that long, confident stride. "That's the White Wolf—come here, quickly!" He grabbed the child by the hand—a small, moist hand—and yanked him down the hallway to their right.

"Hey!" the boy protested, pulling his hand from Daryan's grasp. He skipped away before Daryan could grab him again. Frea's silver helmet gleamed as she passed and he waited in the shadows with his heart in his mouth for her to notice the boy. She never even broke her stride, but the boy—Dramash—fell into step behind her heels and padded after her like an obedient puppy.

He watched, dumbfounded, until he lost them in the darkness.

"Oh, Daryan! I'm glad I found you," a voice called out from behind him, and he started, nearly knocking his head against the wall. He turned around and found another slave advancing down the corridor toward him.

"Shairav wants me. I know," Daryan said tightly. As usual, he had to search frantically for a name. "You can tell him I'm on my way, Veshar."

"I'm sorry," said Veshar, "but Shairav didn't send me. Lord Eofar has come back. Aeda's just landing now. I thought you'd want to know."

"Are you sure it's Lord Eofar?" Daryan asked, not sure whether he was glad that Eofar hadn't left the Shadar, or sorry that he hadn't found Harotha.

"Well, we weren't at first, actually," said Veshar, eyeing him quizzically, "because he's brought someone back with him."

"He has?" He grabbed the startled man by the shoulders. "Who?"

"I couldn't really tell," Veshar answered, "but it looked like a woman. A woman with dark hair."

He released Veshar and ran toward the stables. The scene he rushed into was even more chaotic than usual, with dereshadi everywhere: circling in the gray sky above, diving in to land, trundling along on the ground, flopping heavily into their berths. Shairav's brown-robed assistants were ubiquitous, unsaddling, feeding and watering the creatures before bedding them down for the day. Dead Ones crowded near the walls, wary of the dawn, shrugging out of cloaks and peeling off gloves smeared with all kinds of grime and effluvia. And as Daryan waded in among the crowd, he kept hearing the same phrase, whispered over and over again by the Shadari.

Trouble at the mines.

He touched the arm of the first slave he recognized. "Rasabal, is Lord Eofar here?"

"I think he just landed over there somewhere," she answered, pointing.

He wove through the confusion, craning his neck this way and that, trying to spot Eofar or Harotha. Just as he caught sight of a tangle of black hair, someone grabbed his arm from behind and jerked him back sharply.

"Run," Shairav hissed into his ear.

"What?" Daryan cried out, recoiling from his uncle's touch.

"Run! Get away from here!" he insisted again, circling in front of Daryan and staring into his face. The old man's skin was slick with perspiration and his eyes bulged with fear.

"Run? From Harotha?"

"That," Shairav growled, "is not Harotha."

Just then the crowd parted and he saw her. In the first instant he could do nothing but stare at the black eye-patch. Then he saw that her other eye was fixed on him, staring at him with a strangely intimate intensity. He couldn't look away. Even in the uncertain light he could see the smoothly shining scars written across her face like a cipher. He thought at first that she was smiling—a mocking, half-smile—but then he noticed the scar pulling up one corner of her mouth.

"Who is that? I've seen her before," he told his uncle, adding in a low voice, "haven't I?"

A stablehand paused his vigorous saddle-scrubbing long enough to lean toward them. "That's the Mongrel."

"The Mongrel? No, it can't be." Daryan stepped around Shairav to get a better look.

Eofar trudged along behind her with his head down, unaware or uninterested in the sensation his companion was causing. They disappeared behind a stack of hay-bales and as they emerged on the other side, Daryan saw the woman stumble and fall heavily against the bales. She fumbled in her clothes for a moment and brought out a flat silver flask, but as she tried to unscrew the stopper the flask clattered to the floor. Eofar retrieved it for her and she gulped down a few swallows. Then she stowed the flask away again beneath her vest and took another moment to adjust her eye-patch before straightening up.

"Run!" Shairav cried out again, clutching his shoulder as the strange woman started toward them once more, but Daryan couldn't have obeyed if he wanted to. His legs had turned to stone.

He *knew* her. He didn't know how, or what it meant, but he knew her: she was part of something he had forgotten; something he'd been *meant* to forget. And she wasn't supposed to be here. He didn't need his uncle's histrionics to tell him that; he could feel it with every step she took toward him: like an alarm bell, ringing louder, and louder, and louder.

She stopped in front of Daryan but she aimed her gaze over his shoulder, at Shairav.

"No welcome home, Uncle?" she asked in Shadari.

Before Daryan could react, the Mongrel reached out and raked the tips of her fingers under his chin. Her touch, delicate as an insect's wing, shot through his limbs and raised every hair on his body.

"He's pretty," she murmured, and then bent her head down next to his. She whispered into his ear.

When she lifted her head, Daryan stared desperately into her scarred face. "I don't understand," he whispered back.

The Mongrel focused her flat brown eye on Shairav once more. "What do you think, Uncle?" she asked, in that same soft drawl. "Was he worth it?"

Then she stepped back and walked past them both, through the doorway just behind them and out into the corridor. Shairav made a strangled cry and lurched after her. Daryan followed, but as soon as Shairav entered the corridor the old man crumpled against the wall, clutching his heart.

"Lahlil!" he cried out into the darkness after her. "Lahlil!"

Lahlil.

That name again. The echo of it boomed in Daryan's head, thumping like a drumbeat. A name he'd completely forgotten until Isa had brought it to his mind tonight; and now, in defiance of any kind of probability, here it was again. So he really did know her; he even knew her name.

"Uncle," he breathed, turning to the old man, but Shairav buried his face in his hands and fled back out into the stables. Daryan thought he heard him sobbing as he passed by.

He was about to run after him when a rasping voice beside him spoke his name.

"My Lord," Daryan exclaimed. He hadn't noticed that Eofar had let the Mongrel go on ahead of him. "Who is that woman? What's happening here?"

Eofar said nothing for a moment. Daryan thought he looked even sicker than he had earlier. "Tell me the truth," he choked out. "You, and Harotha."

"The truth?" he repeated, confused. "My Lord, you're ill. Let me take you to your room—"

His master broke into a wracking cough. "Tell me," he insisted again. His shoulders were hunched and he stared dully down at the ground. "Were you in love with her?"

"No, my Lord," he answered with complete candor, despite the fact that his heart was pounding wildly. "I could have been, I think, but she made it clear from the beginning that she didn't want that." He braced himself. "She's dead, isn't she?"

"No. She's alive." Eofar leaned back against the wall, ignoring the sword still in its scabbard across his back, and shut his eyes. "I found her—everything was just as it had been, and we talked about leaving together. Then her brother and his friends came and she ran from me. She told everyone that you were the father of her baby. Not me. *You*."

"Her brother was there?" Daryan asked, thinking quickly. "Then she was protecting herself—and your baby." He chuckled appreciatively; he knew exactly how Harotha's mind would work in that situation. "Clever. They won't dare touch her now, no matter how much they might suspect her."

"Why not?"

With a start, he realized what he had just opened up.

"Daryan, what do you mean? Why won't they dare harm *your* baby?"

This was what she had always wanted from him, wasn't it? She had brought him to it at last. How many times had she told him to stop listening to Shairav, to stop waiting for something to change and to *make* change happen? Well, if not now, when?

He could still feel the frost on his lips from Isa's kiss.

He stepped closer to Eofar and looked into his eyes. "Because of me. I'm the daimon."

Eofar's shoulders rolled back and he straightened up. "You're the *what*?"

"I'm the daimon," Daryan told him again. "That's

why Harotha told her brother that lie. You can believe me when I tell you, Harotha and I were never together."

Eofar was too shocked to speak. He looked at Daryan as if he had never seen him before.

"My Lord, who is that woman you brought here? I feel like I've seen her—"

But before Daryan could finish speaking, Eofar started violently and cried, "I have to go," and was already heading off down the corridor in the direction the Mongrel had gone. "Wait in my room. I'll come to you," he called back, as he sped off after her.

Daryan was still staring after him when Majid, Shairav's assistant, rounded a corner just up ahead. "Oh, Daimon, there you are! Shairav has been looking for you all night."

"I know. And please don't call me—" Daryan began. But then he stopped.

"Daryan?" Uncertainty shifted behind the man's eyes. "Daryan? Are you all right?"

With a thin smile Daryan said, "You can tell him I'm on my way."

Chapter Eighteen

<Lady Isa!> The soldier sprang up as Isa emerged from beneath the narrow portico shading the refectory doorway and quickly poured out the traditional welcoming cup of wine. He proffered it to her. She walked forward, feeling herself watched by everyone in the room. They saw how she was dressed, they saw the sword, and they knew exactly why she was there. Trickles of sweat ran down her back and thighs and tickled her already twitching nerves.

She stepped down from the portico, took the cup from the soldier—Falkar, Frea's lieutenant—and drained it in one swallow, stifling a shudder as the alcohol burned her throat.

<Thank you,> she said, handing the cup back to him. She brought her hand up to wipe her mouth in a nonchalant gesture and took the opportunity to assess her surroundings.

Four dozen or so bare-chested guards were sprawled around the large room. Through an aperture on the far wall adjoining the kitchens she could see cooking fires, and red-faced slaves swam out of the heat-haze at intervals carrying platters of meat, fish and bread to the long wooden tables. Threads of morning sunshine scored the floor just underneath the windows as the sun found a way through the shutters' slats. Originally this room had only been used for cooking; the benches and tables had been appropriated from the windowless dining hall several levels down, where Isa's father had presided over their meals before he fell ill. No one ate there any more.

She was still deciding whether to sit down or remain standing when she felt the attention suddenly shift away from her and focus on something behind her. She turned around.

A young Shadari child was standing on the step, looking around him with wide, dark eyes.

<Rho,> Falkar called out, half-amused, half-annoyed, to the figure lingering in the doorway behind the boy, <what are you playing at now? What's this child doing here?>

Rho was nicely hidden by the portico's wide columns, so no one could see the mess on his clothes or his bruised face. He leaned back against the wall, as if he were too weary or too indifferent to come any closer, and said laconically, <I asked him if he was hungry. He said yes.>

The boy trotted down from the step, past Falkar and Isa and over to one of the tables, returning the stares of the Norlanders with startling aplomb. He sniffed at the meat heaped onto the platter in front of him. "Can I have this?" he asked Rho.

"Help yourself."

Before Rho had even finished speaking, the boy was shoveling food into his mouth until his cheeks bulged.

<Rho, have you lost your mind? Where did he *come* from?> asked Daem, rising from a bench in the far corner of the room. Everyone wanted to know the same thing.

<Frea's room. Jeder was supposed to be minding him, but he was glad to have me take him off his hands.>

<That's not what I meant.>

<Oh. She picked him up near the mines. If you want to know why, you'll have to ask her,> answered Rho. He never once looked at Isa, or gave any indication that he was aware of her standing there. He was acting even more intoxicated than he had out in the hallway, but

this time she could see through the ruse. <She should be here soon, anyway. I left her a message.>

Moments before the ringing sound of Frea's boots ricocheted up the steps, around the corner and into the refectory, Isa felt her sister's anger heralding her arrival. The Norlanders nearest to the boy jumped away from him as if he were on fire.

<Where is he, Rho?> Frea's dark figure swelled in the doorframe. She had removed her helmet, but she was still wearing her riding clothes, and with a hectic spasm of anticipation Isa saw the burnished hilt of Blood's Pride gleaming behind her shoulder. She also carried a folded sheet of paper, yellowed with age and crumbling at the edges, but she tucked this into her jacket even as her hard stare swept over the company. Her gaze passed straight through Isa without a jot of interest or surprise.

A piercing cry sounded from the Shadari boy, who flew across the room and vaulted up to the portico by Frea's side. "Are we going now? To see Shairav and the dereshadi?" he demanded, hopping up and down in his excitement. "Can I really be his apprentice? Did you ask him?"

Isa tensed, waiting for Frea to silence the boy with a slap, or worse.

Instead, Frea turned to Rho. <Jeder gave me your message, and it will be the last thing he does for a long time. Go to your quarters. I'll decide what to do with you later.>

Rho half-walked, half-stumbled toward the door, but just before he disappeared into the corridor Isa felt him in her mind: a little push, a little urge.

She stepped forward. <Frea.>

Her sister barely glanced at her. <Take off those ridiculous clothes and go to bed.>

Isa drew her sword. The scraping sound echoed off the stone walls. Ice crystalized in her veins; her eyes were as cold as hailstones. <I challenge you, Frea of the ancient and noble clan Eotan, champion of our bloodline,

for the right to name this sword I hold in my hand according to the custom of our people; to pledge my loyalty to the Norland Empire on its blade; to honor the great Lord Onfar with its service; and through it to carry the strength of our bloodline to the generations to come.>

No one moved.

Frea's silver-green eyes looked over Isa, down and then up again. <Grow up,> she said, turning to go.

Make it a matter of family honor. That's what Rho had said. <Fine,> she said complacently, <then I name this sword—>

Frea whirled. <What do you think you're doing?>

This time Isa wasn't pretending. This time she could really feel the ice hardening to the strength of diamonds under her skin. <Naming my sword,> she told her sister as the anticipation of the soldiers crackled all around her. <You forfeit. I win.>

<Forfeit?> Frea cried.

<I have fifty witnesses who saw you turn your back on the challenge. That should be good enough for the emperor and the rest of the clans at court.>

<Court?> Frea echoed hollowly. <Kharl,> she called out to one of her more loyal and dim-witted followers, <take the boy back to my chambers and stay there with him.>

Kharl leaped up from the table where he'd been sitting. He circled the boy as warily as if he were a poisonous snake before shooing him through the doorway.

Frea stepped down off the dais and stalked toward Isa, who felt a sudden flush of panic. Rho's strategy had worked. The moment of her redemption was finally here. Now all she had to do was see it through. Now she had to *win*.

Frea reached back over her shoulder and drew Blood's Pride with an impatient jerk. The other guards jumped up from the tables and formed up in a ring around the room, snatching up benches and pushing the heavy tables out of the way. <A clever trick, trying to make this

about my honor. I can guess who put you up to it. Too bad neither of you knows the first thing about honor.>

Isa slid into her guard stance, but Frea walked right past her and past the soldiers who hurriedly cleared the way. With her free hand she drew the black-bladed imperial knife and flicked it toward the windows. The blade, unerringly guided by her thoughts, came down precisely on the latch of one of the shutters and split it apart. For a stunned moment nothing happened; the knife itself, wedged into the wood, kept the shutter closed. But then the knife gave a wriggle and yanked free, and a wall of deadly sunlight bisected the room, sending the Norlanders stampeding into the shadows.

The light was so bright that Isa saw only flares of hectic color, searing rainbows that moved with her wherever she looked. Then she felt her sister grab her arm and haul her over to the open window.

She blinked her eyes frantically, trying to focus. Frea shoved her up against the wall. The angle of the sun kept her safe from burning, but she could feel the heat crawling over her flesh like a swarm of insects. Far down below, the Shadar's white rooftops blazed like beacons. A weight dropped in her stomach and she felt insubstantial, as if her feet were no longer anchored to the ground and nothing was preventing her from spinning off into space.

<Look,> Frea commanded, seizing the hair on the back of her head with a grip like a vice. <Look down there. You can't, can you? Do you think I would dishonor myself and my sword by fighting a coward like you? Do you think I would let you name her sword when every day that you live you shame her memory?> The words drove into her mind, each syllable like a shove between her shoulder blades, pushing her over the edge. <I should have let you drop and done us all a favor.>

Frea's other hand was still on her arm and she could feel the cold. She focused her eyes on the Shadar, feeling every inch of the distance between her and the ground.

With imaginary fingers as cold and merciless as the ones that gripped her arm, she grabbed hold of the fear dancing in her chest and squeezed it as hard as she could.

<Can you still feel her scream?> Frea was saying. <Do you remember how she screamed when she fell? Do you remember how she clung to the saddle with one hand, knowing that she couldn't hold on, but still trying to tie you back in with the other? Do you *remember*?>

Isa looked down. She felt the screams in her sore and swollen heart and she squeezed that, too, burying the treacherous organ under layer after layer of ice so strong that it choked off every pulse; she kept piling it on, letting all of her senses slide away into numbness, and still the ice spread outward, encasing her, so that nothing—not the soldiers' embarrassment, not Frea's disdain, not the sunlight's piercing rays, not the memory of her mother's screams, not the deadly pull of the city below—could get near her.

This is what I've always wanted, she realized. *This is what it feels like to be Frea.*

<Lady Frea!> Three of the governor's bodyguards, part of the select circle of people who were still allowed to see him, were standing in the portico. Arnaf, the tallest of them, rarely left his side.

Frea released Isa's arm and pushed the broken shutter back into place, though it didn't close completely. <What is it?> she demanded.

<Lady Frea,> Arnaf said again, hesitating awkwardly. His eyes were fixed straight ahead. <The governor—>

<He's dead, is that what you're trying to tell me?>

Arnaf had no need to respond in words. A tangle of emotions snaked up from the guards as they took in the news.

Her father was dead.

<The physic said the governor said some things, a message for you—> Arnaf began, but Frea cut him off.

<I already heard what he had to say.> She turned to a nearby table and picked up a jug of wine and a cup. Isa

watched her sister pour herself a cupful and drink it down, then pour another.

Her father was dead, and she didn't know what she felt. When her mother died she had ached with missing her—the feel of her arms, her scent, her presence like a soft mantle, the way she'd lift her into her lap to brush her hair. What would she miss about her father? Judgment had been the only thing he had to give, and Isa had been found wanting. There would be no appeal now, except maybe in Onfar's Hall—though if her father was right, that was a place she would never see.

She walked past the gaping soldiers and their uncertain mess of feelings, past the plates of half-eaten food and splashes of spilled wine, past Frea, past Arnaf, toward the door. She didn't know where she was going; she just wanted to move. She wanted to surround herself with a blankness that was as still and empty as her heart and she wanted to merge with it, to disappear into nothingness.

<Where do you think you're going with that?>

Isa turned back and saw Frea pointing to the sword that she still held, unsheathed, in her right hand.

<Put it down,> Frea demanded.

The air in the room became perfectly still. Isa's measured steps rang out on the stone floor as she walked up to her sister and looked into her silver-green eyes. She slapped the cup out of Frea's hand. <Make me.>

Chapter Nineteen

For as long as he could remember, Daryan had suffered a recurring dream—it always started well enough, with him waking up in his own bed, in his own dark room. Nothing would be out of place—the outlines of his few simple possessions were familiar and unthreatening—yet a deep sense of dread would begin to creep over him, as if something evil were massing in the shadows, just out of sight. He would reach for the lamp, but when he tried to strike the flints, the stones would crumble into dust in his hands, and at that moment, his vague fears would crystalize into terror.

He felt something like that now, standing in the hallway in the doorway of Shairav's unlit room, staring at a sliver of light running mysteriously from the floor to the ceiling in the far corner of the chamber. The outlines of his uncle's rather opulent collection of furniture—the tables and chairs, the little ornaments, the bed heaped with cushions, all purchased from the Nomas with the governor's gold—were all familiar, but something about that light in the corner evoked the nightmarish feeling of nefarious forces gathering strength around him.

He crossed the room slowly, moving toward the light. On the way he had to pass by the heavy chair in which his Aunt Meena had spent her final days. He remembered her sitting there, day after day, her frail body pinned down under a blanket, staring past him with rheumy eyes.

Most of the time she was oblivious to his presence, but every now and then he would catch her looking at him. The expression in her dull eyes would barely change, but he had the uneasy feeling that she hated him. She had already been ill when he had first arrived in the temple and she'd died soon after. No one had ever explained to him what was wrong with her. She had terrified him.

The light was shining through a fissure in the wall no wider than the edge of the coin—or actually, he quickly realized, it was *exactly* the width of a coin, for a single Shadari sudra was wedged in the opening near the floor. He put his eye to the crack. He had the sense of a room on the other side of the wall, but he couldn't make out anything specific. He heard nothing but silence.

He put his shoulder to the wall and shoved.

With a soft scraping sound, the entire wall pivoted from the center, widening the opening to the width of a hand-span. The sudra rolled free.

"What the—?" he began, backing away until he knocked into the back of a chair. Through the gap he could see the shapes of furniture, and the glimmer of a lamp burning on a small table. But he saw and heard no one who might have been responsible for lighting the lamp and leaving it there.

With a cautious look back at Shairav's dark room, he turned sideways and slid through.

"Huh!" The air rushed out of his lungs as if something heavy had hit him in the chest. He found himself standing in a child's bedroom. In addition to the bed there was a child-sized table and a couple of stools, baskets spilling over with painted balls and wooden swords and crude carvings of animals, and a cradle from which a heap of dolls regarded eternity with unblinking eyes. An inch of reddish dust gave everything the soft, mottled texture of rotten fruit. No one was there, but a track of smeary footprints led across the room and then disappeared behind a high pile of furniture covered with old rugs. He started forward, but on the third step his foot came down on something soft and he hopped backward in alarm.

He bent down slowly and picked up the Shadari doll. Sand sifted through rips in its cloth body and leaked out between his fingers. Someone had gone through the trouble of altering it: the brown threads of the left eye had been picked out and replaced with a splotch of green; the doll's right arm was a mess of fat red stitches, crisscrossing over each other in no particular pattern. He glanced over at the other dolls in the cradle. They were all the same.

"I remember you," he whispered to the doll, squeezing its lumpy body tightly. "Now I remember you."

He remembered twilight in the desert, and his mother holding his hand so tightly that she was hurting him, but he wasn't trying to pull away. His mother was crying—she wouldn't say why, but he blamed Uncle Shairav—Mama called him Shairav'Asha. He was afraid of his mysterious uncle, and he refused to be impressed by the fact that Shairav'Asha could pilot a dereshadi just like a Dead One. His mother had shooed him away so that she and Uncle Shairav could talk about grown-up things.

He was throwing stones at a dead snake when he saw her. Her red Shadari cloak dragged behind her through the sand and she had the hood pulled up over her head. Her hair was black, like a Shadari, but her skin was very pale. She was probably a year or two older than Daryan and quite a bit taller. As she came closer, he saw that there was something wrong with her left eye.

She stood a little way off and watched him throw the remaining stones in his hand. When he bent down to look for more, she asked, "Do you like living here?"

"It's all right." He looked up at her. "Why? Where do you live?"

When she pointed up to the temple her cloak swung

open. He caught his breath in wonder: enflamed red and pink scars crawled over her right forearm, like a cluster of engorged worms.

"Wow!" he exclaimed appreciatively. "What happened to your arm?"

"It burned—a long time ago, when I was a baby," she said. Her voice sounded funny, as if she had a sore throat.

"Does it hurt? Can I touch it?" he asked.

"No," answered the girl, apparently to both questions, and tucked the arm away again under her cloak.

"Lahlil!" Uncle Shairav's harsh voice cut through the air as he ran toward the two children. Daryan noticed with cheerful malice how funny he looked with his robes flapping out behind him. "I told you not to get down," he reminded the girl sternly. "We're going now. Come on." Then he called to Daryan's mother, "Until midnight, then, but that's all. Have him ready this time."

"Who? Me?" He watched his uncle and the girl climb back on the dereshadi and fly away. "What am I getting ready for, Mama?" he asked, as she flung her arms around him and pulled him into a smothering embrace. She was crying too hard to answer his questions. A few hours later his uncle had returned, alone this time, and taken him to the temple. Less than a year later, Daryan received word that his mother was dead. He never saw her or the girl again after that day.

"Daryan."

He looked up from the doll. Shairav was standing in front of him.

"It was her." His body felt as heavy as stone. "That girl in the desert—the girl with the burned arm—you called her Lahlil. That was the Mongrel."

His uncle nodded. The small sack he carried in his right hand jingled and Daryan realized that the old man was shaking. He thought of the lone sudra stuck in the doorway. "She's coming to kill us."

"Why?" he asked faintly. "What did we do to her?"

Shairav circled past him and moved toward the secret door. "Later. First, we must get to the stables—"

"No." He squeezed the doll a little harder, but he didn't move from the spot where he was standing. "Tell me now."

The old man turned back. "She knows about this place. She'll come here."

"All right, then talk fast."

Shairav stared at him for a moment with his lips pursed. "Very well. What do you want to know?"

"Who is she, really? She was just a girl when I saw her with you in the Shadar."

"Lahlil is the governor's daughter. His eldest daughter."

"His daughter?" Daryan repeated, finding himself not as surprised as he might have been. Eofar's older sister. He remembered the cowed way Eofar had shuffled behind her in the stables. "Go on. What else?"

"The burns on her arm, that happened when she was just a few months old. It was an accident—a shutter with a bad latch." Shairav glared at Daryan. "Do you know what the Dead Ones do with their injured and deformed?"

"They abandon them in the wilderness," he answered stonily. "They think they're cursed."

"Well, the governor's wife, Eleana, she was different. She pretended to everyone—even Eonar—that the baby had died from the burns. Then she found Meena in the Shadar and brought her here to nurse the baby. She thought Meena's milk might keep her alive."

"Aunt Meena?" Daryan asked, confused. "But wasn't she here already? I mean, wasn't she your wife?"

"Temple servants aren't allowed to marry," his uncle reminded him impatiently. "Meena was nobody important, just a penniless woman whose own baby was dead."

"Oh." He blinked at this new fact, but then he forced himself to return to the story. "And then what happened?"

Shairav smiled grimly. "Lahlil got better. She grew

strong on Meena's milk. Her arm healed, but it was obvious that the scars would never go away. And soon her hair began to grow in dark, and then her eye . . . Well, you've seen her. You know how she looks. It must also have made her able to withstand the sunlight, but of course none of us knew that then."

"But that's impossible," Daryan interjected. "Just from having a Shadari nurse? Shadari milk couldn't have done all that—"

"That's what happened," the old man snapped. "Who are you to say what's possible or impossible?"

Daryan drew his elbows in tighter against his sides, holding in his impatience. "No, you're right. I'm sorry. Go on."

The creases around Shairav's mouth deepened. "Meena became frightened that the governor would find out what she and Eleana had done and punish her, so she came to me for help."

"You helped them hide her—that's right, isn't it?" he interrupted. "You hid Lahlil here—this was her room. For how long?" He was afraid that he already knew the answer. He remembered Lahlil in the desert, pointing up to the temple with the scarred arm that had made her an outcast. She had looked older than him then, but Norlanders were taller . . .

"Nine years."

Daryan shut his eyes. He could feel the walls of the chamber pushing toward him, boxing him in. "Nine years," he whispered to himself.

"Meena was there for her, always, and Eleana gave us money—she wanted for nothing. And Eleana came often; she even brought the other children with her—"

"The other children—do you mean they all knew about her? Frea? Even Isa?"

"Of course."

"But then why didn't I ever see her, except for that day? She couldn't have been here when I came, I would have—" A chill of fear pulsed through Daryan and he stopped abruptly. Another idea had just occurred to him, this one too terrible to be true.

"The governor found out about Lahlil," Shairav went on. "I still don't know how it happened. He sent for me, told me he knew what we'd done, but instead of punishing me, he asked for my help."

"Your help." His mouth had gone dry.

"He told me to name my reward—I expect he thought I'd ask for gold, or my freedom, but there was something more important to me than that." He fixed his eyes on Daryan.

"Me?" he asked numbly. He shut his eyes again. "Please tell me you didn't—"

"I told him I had a nephew that meant everything to me. I told him my only wish was to save this boy from the mines," Shairav informed him. "You see, then: I traded her for you."

His stomach cramped and he thought he was going to be sick. "No—you couldn't have—"

"I did." The old man's eyes were as hard as stones, but his mouth twisted for a moment. "I did what I had to do. I took her into the desert that night and I left her there, and then I brought you to the temple."

Daryan opened his eyes and stared down at the doll in his hand. It was damp with his sweat. "Was I worth it?" he whispered to the doll. "That's what she wanted to know: was I worth it? How could I be? How could *anyone*?"

"Perhaps you'll take your responsibilities more seriously now that you know the sacrifices that have been made for you."

"Aunt Meena—she hated me. It wasn't my imagination," he muttered. "Of course she hated me. She lost her child because of me."

"Come, we must—"

"The next day—the day after I came here—no one knew why Eleana took the girls out on the dereshadi that day, but you had just taken Lahlil. She was looking for the daughter you stole from her—that's what she was doing when she fell, looking for Lahlil!"

"Of course!" his uncle bellowed. He gestured toward the door. "Now do you finally understand? None of us realized Lahlil would survive in the sunlight, but she did, and now nothing will stop her from having her revenge. Our only hope is to escape!"

But Daryan didn't move. Somehow the insanity of everything he had just learned had synthesized into a moment of searing clarity. As if she was standing right beside him, the Mongrel's whispered words repeated themselves in his mind, only this time they made perfect sense. And he knew what she wanted him to do.

He turned around and followed the trail of footprints—Shairav's footprints—away from the door toward the dark end of the room.

"Daryan!" Shairav called wildly behind him, but Daryan ignored him. He picked the lamp up from the table and kept going, around the pile of furniture. There was a heavy tapestry hanging on the wall, and when he held the light close he found exactly what he'd expected to find: a smeary handprint, just where someone would grip the material to push it aside. He matched his own hand to the handprint and lifted the tapestry.

"Stop!" Shairav shouted.

He blew out the lamp as he crossed the threshold and set it down on the floor. He didn't need it any more.

The tiny round chamber was bright with morning sunshine. The room was barely five paces across in either direction, and open to the seamless blue sky. It was entirely empty. The only reason for the room to exist was the hole that took up most of the floor. He peered over the edge. The sides of the shaft disappeared into blackness and he couldn't tell how deep the hole went. But the walls weren't entirely sheer, like those of a well; triangular shapes were recessed into the sides. They looked as if they'd been designed to slide in and out.

It was a staircase, or would be, with the steps in the right position.

Of course he had also noticed the sand strewn over the floor around the hole. With a pained smile, he read the prayers that had been scratched there just as easily as he read the splatter where a fist had pounded the floor in frustration.

"He never had the power," he said softly, repeating Lahlil's words aloud. The sun felt warm on his face. "He never did. That's why they let him live."

He heard Shairav's heavy breathing behind him in the doorway. "Come away!" the old man insisted, wheezing in distress.

"This is the way out—the ashas' way out," he said, pointing to the secret staircase. After all these years, all of the people imprisoned in the temple with no hope of escape, it had been right here all the time.

"We can't go this way—I would need to use my powers to make the steps slide out and my vow—"

Daryan looked into the old man's eyes. "You were trying to open it. Just now."

"I was doing no such thing!" he shot back as he pressed a hand over his heart. His skin had an unpleasant, waxy sheen.

"It's true," Daryan told him, "you can't make it work. You never could."

"I'm an asha." His voice sounded thin and unsteady. "An ordained asha. The last one."

Daryan waited, watching curiously as Shairav's face flushed, turned pale and then flushed again.

"Smug, self-important—" Shairav finally blurted out, "all of them. They hated me—your precious Harotha's parents, they were the worst. It was all your father's fault; he insisted they take me after I failed the initiation. He said it would be too embarrassing for the king's brother to fail, but I know he really just wanted me out of the city—out of the way."

"You were here when the ashas died—so why did they jump?"

"Hah! Do you think they told me? Me who they treated like a servant, or worse? When the Dead Ones came, they locked themselves away and took the elixir. They didn't tell me what they were doing. Then they jumped—not a word why! And they never even thought to open the staircase so that I could escape to the city. They just left me here . . . I had to hide when the Dead Ones came and it was weeks before they started bringing servants up from the city and I was able to mix in with the others."

Daryan wet his lips. "Shairav'Asha," he whispered to himself, and chuckled darkly—but the laughter was too close to a sob and he clamped his mouth shut over it.

"She's coming for us," his uncle promised. "She's going to kill us."

Daryan shook his head. "Not me, I think. When someone stabs you, you don't blame the knife."

The old man stepped backward until the doorframe checked his progress. "You're going to let her kill me." The bag dropped out of his hand and fell to the floor with a musical crash. A few coins slid out; one rolled to the hole and went pinging down into the darkness.

"You used us—all of us," he told his uncle, "Meena, Eleana. You used Lahlil to make your own little privileged world here, and after you couldn't use her any more, you traded her for me—so that you could use me and all of us Shadari to keep yourself nice and comfortable right here. You didn't bring me here to *protect* me—you brought me here to make sure that nothing changed for you. You never wanted me to be a leader, like the one Harotha always thought I could be. You wanted me to feel worthless, so that you could control me—so that I'd never see what a fraud you are."

The hard lines around Shairav's mouth went slack and he suddenly looked years older. "That's not true."

"Yes, it is," Daryan said, unmoved, and walked past his uncle and across Lahlil's bedchamber.

A shaft of dusty sunlight pierced the blackness as the old man followed behind him. "You're leaving me—you're going to let her kill me," he moaned. "You can't leave me! After all I've done for you—"

Daryan kept walking, but just before he slid through the secret door, he turned to his uncle and said, "Let me go, or I might just kill you myself." He stumbled through the doorway and out into the hall, taking deep breaths like a diver coming up for air, but the dank atmosphere of the temple gave him no relief. After a few pointless turns, he threw himself into a corner with his face against the wall and broke down.

He couldn't have said how much time had passed when he heard the voice behind him. He'd finished his angry sobbing, but he'd remained in the corner with his forehead pressed against the cool stone and his eyes closed, too drained to move.

"Daryan."

He blinked his sore eyes open reluctantly. "I wondered what happened to you," he said, but he didn't turn around to face her. He was embarrassed at having been caught weeping in the corner like a child. "You'd better stay out of sight for now—that business with the knife was bad. I'll try to straighten things out for you later, if I can. It won't be easy."

"You don't need to worry about me," said Rahsa. He felt the tips of her fingers touch his shoulder, then dart away again like a timid little mouse. "Won't you tell me what's wrong?"

"It's complicated."

"I want to help you."

"All right then, can you tell me what I'm supposed to do now?" he asked, with a grim laugh. He looked briefly over his shoulder at her and caught a glimpse of dark eyes staring intently at him and what looked like a nasty gash on her forehead.

"That's not hard. You're our daimon," Rahsa said calmly. It was hard to believe she was the same girl who had behaved so wildly in the bathing room. "You're our king—our leader. You're supposed to *lead* us."

"Lead?" he asked derisively. "The only thing I know how to do is follow. I do what Eofar tells me to do, or Shairav, or Harotha. I'm a slave, Rahsa, just like the rest of you; that's all I've ever been."

"That's not true. You're much more than that."

"Well then, that just makes it worse, doesn't it?" he countered. "Because if I'm capable of more, that must mean that I *chose* this. I *chose* not to see what Shairav really was, or what he was doing. I guess it was easier to blame him for this mess than try to do something about it on my own and fail. I'm worthless; I've always known that. Even my own mother knew it or she wouldn't have let Shairav take me away in the first place."

"Stop, please! I won't let you talk like that," said Rahsa. "You're the daimon! You may have lost your way, but—"

"Leave me alone, Rahsa!" he shouted, slapping his palm angrily against the wall. The girl's quivering body and wide-eyed stare fueled his sudden rage. "You don't *know* me—you don't know anything about me. There's only one thing in the world I care about, and tonight I let her go forever because I don't have a single thing to offer her. I'm in love with a Dead One, Rahsa: how do you like that? Is that the daimon you want to lead you? I don't care about the Shadari, and I don't care about you! For the gods' sake, find someone else to worship—I can't help you, don't you understand?"

The sight of Rahsa's stricken face after he delivered this cruel speech was more than he could stand and he turned back and pressed himself against the stone walls again, wishing that the rock would swallow him up.

After a moment Rahsa spoke again, her voice soft, sympathetic, almost soothing, as if she were speaking to an overwrought child. "My father was a healer. Did you know that?"

"No," Daryan answered miserably, "I didn't know that."

"He's dead now," Rahsa said. "He worked near the mines—the Dead Ones used to bring the mining accidents to him. Father would tell the miners that if they wanted to live, he'd have to take their arm, or their leg, or the wound would drain the life out of them." She paused and moved a little closer. "The men would scream and cry. When I was a little girl, I thought my father was a very cruel man, but when I got older, I understood that he knew how to save them."

"I'm sure he was a good man," he responded vaguely. He didn't know what response was expected of him. "Rahsa, I'm sorry, I didn't mean all that—I just heard some things that . . ." He trailed off as a thought occurred to him. "All these years, I did what Shairav wanted me to do because I was afraid to be on my own with no one looking out for me. I was afraid to make decisions for myself. But the truth was that I was on my own anyway; I just didn't know it." He straightened up with a deep sigh. "Maybe you're right: maybe I am more than that. I have to be, don't I? I couldn't very well be less." He rushed on, trying to express himself before the idea slipped from his grasp. He fixed his eyes on the solidity of the red rock wall. "And so the things I've wanted, for myself—for all of us—don't have to be wrong, do they? Nothing Shairav told me means anything at all; I have to decide for myself, don't I?"

He turned back hopefully to Rahsa, but she was gone.

Chapter Twenty

Eofar ran down the corridor after Lahlil, leaving the startled Daryan behind; under the circumstances, even Daryan's incredible revelation would have to wait. He kept his sister in sight and caught up with her a moment after she turned the corner, but when he tried to fall into step beside her, she quickened her pace and left him trailing in her wake.

The ragged Shadari robe over her shoulders and the tangle of black hair almost made him feel as if he was chasing a slave, but her height, her rod-straight shoulders and the self-assured swing of her arms said otherwise.

<Wait, Lahlil!> He had to force himself to use her name. After all the years of silence, all the careful self-censoring of his memories, to say her name now felt like a betrayal. Just whom he was betraying, and how, he couldn't explain even to himself.

She stopped but didn't turn, sending the message that she would not allow him to delay her for long. Eofar was well aware that he was frightened of her, in the irrational and all-consuming way that only a small child can be frightened. This made him angry, but his anger hit the blank wall of her presence and slammed right back into him. He had the urge to provoke her into some emotional response, to slap her into wakefulness as he might a fainting victim.

<Why are you here?> he demanded. <If you've come

back for revenge, you're wasting your time. Father's ill—he's been ill for a long time. There's nothing you can do to him now. You're too late.>

<Why are *you* here?> asked Lahlil, echoing his question but not his churlishness. <Why didn't you stay in the Shadar with your wife?>

<You don't know anything about that.> He wished he could believe it; she seemed to know everything somehow. <Bloody Onfar, what was I supposed to do? Fight her brother? Fight *her*? Chasing after her would have only made things worse.>

<Poor Eofar.> Reflected torchlight licked out of the center of her wide, black pupil. <Left behind again.>

He had never given himself permission to hate her for tearing their family apart while their mother was still alive—but Mother was dead and gone now. <I know why you're here. It wasn't me. I wasn't the one who told Father about you.>

Lahlil remained so still, and so blank, that he wasn't even sure that his words had reached her.

<All right,> she said finally, accepting his unsolicited denial with equanimity. She continued up the corridor ahead of him. <And you're wrong. Eonar's not sick. He's already dead.>

She turned the corner up ahead and disappeared. The moment she was gone, the bulky figure of Arnaf, Eonar's personal bodyguard, emerged from a crossing a few yards ahead leading two other guards.

<Lord Eofar!> Arnaf said in surprise. <I need to—Oh!> he broke off quickly as he sensed the grief that Eofar wasn't even aware of feeling. <You've already heard. I'm very sorry, my Lord.>

Dead. He'd been expecting it for so long, he would have thought it had no power to shock him. He'd been wrong. His knees suddenly felt weak, and for no practical reason he reached up and grabbed the hilt of Strife's Bane, holding on tight: his father's gift to him, so long ago, before everything went wrong.

<Are you all right, my Lord?>

<No. I mean, yes.>

<Any orders?> The guard exchanged something with his two comrades. <You are the governor now, my Lord.>

<No, no orders. Thank you, Arnaf,> Eofar replied, and left the startled guards behind. He needed to be with his sisters. He raced blindly down the corridor and was taken aback when he nearly ran into Lahlil, who had stopped in the refectory doorway: he'd forgotten about her.

<What are you—?> Then he heard the clang of swords. <Oh, no,> he groaned, suddenly remembering Isa's ridiculous determination to fight Frea. He shot past Lahlil, not caring for the moment what she did with herself, only to find the inner portico crowded with Norlander soldiers in various states of undress, as if they'd been hauled from their beds.

<Make way!> He shoved his way through the crowd, breaking through the ring of spectators. In the first instant he couldn't tell his two sisters apart. They were both clad in dark leather, they both had tendrils of damp hair plastered to their skin, and they were both nearly at the end of their strength.

Eofar arched his arm over his shoulder, ready to charge between the two girls. Strife's Bane leaped a few inches from its scabbard into his palm; but then, like the soldiers around him, he stopped and stared.

He couldn't take his eyes off Isa.

In the last few hours she had somehow throttled back the volatile emotions that had always been her greatest obstacle and become the Norlander she had always aspired to be: cold, efficient, ruthless—and she was obviously out for blood. This was no ritualized sparring match, nor the kind of short-lived fit of passion that he had come to expect from her. The very real possibility of death whined in every swing of her sword. Frea was stronger, and far more practiced, but once she had cycled through her repertoire of moves she had no recourse except to repeat herself. Isa was relying on some preternatural skill; it was flowing through the lean lines of her body, her unconventional style throwing Frea off-balance, making her incapable of anticipating Isa's next move or finding an unguarded spot at which to strike.

Even as he watched, Frea aimed a swipe at Isa's body that had a good chance of hitting the mark. Isa was in the wrong position to block. He could see her only chance lay in diving backward, out of the way, but instead she dived forward underneath Frea's sword, slapping her palm on the ground to catch herself at the last moment. As a defensive move it was dreadful, leaving her nearly prone and vulnerable to a downward thrust—but it wasn't a defensive move. She swept her blade up behind her, slicing just inches above the ground at Frea's ankles. Frea had to jump to avoid the sword, and already off balance from her swing, fell heavily onto one knee. Isa used the momentum of her own strike to roll onto her feet and a heartbeat later she was lunging for Frea.

Sick with the fear that he was about to see one of his sisters killed right in front of him, Eofar finally drew Strife's Bane. The black blade twitched with eagerness in response to his distress.

<Stop!> he cried out, charging forward between his sisters. Their mutual outrage leaped out at him: a pair of lionesses robbed of their prey, and he could feel an angry undercurrent of disappointment and resentment buzzing out from the crowd. He swung around and addressed the assembly at large. <Everyone return to their quarters. Now!>

<You can't order my soldiers—> objected Frea, lurching back to her feet, but before she could finish, Isa, capitalizing on her momentary loss of concentration, charged around Eofar and launched a new attack.

<I can, and I will. Our father— Governor Eonar is dead.> The violence of his emotion thudded out like a

shockwave through the room. <I am the eldest. It doesn't matter what arrangements were made while my father was sick, I am in charge now. Everyone to quarters! Now!>

Reluctantly, the soldiers began to jostle their way out of the room. Eofar kept one anxious eye on their departure and the other on his sisters, listening to them still hammering at each other while he tried to work out what to do next.

It wasn't until after the last soldier departed that Lahlil emerged onto the portico from whatever niche she had found to conceal herself. His sisters didn't notice her right away, but he wasn't surprised about that. It wasn't just the dark cloak; she had a trick of shrouding her presence so completely when she wanted that even staring straight at her, he had a hard time believing she was really there.

He turned back to Isa and Frea and watched in frustration as they continued their battle. As soon as he saw an opportunity he jumped between them, beating back their blades with two quick strokes. <That's enough! Stop it, both of you. Isa, sheath that sword—you too, Frea.>

<Forget it,> Frea told him, using the respite to wipe a sheet of sweat from her face with her free hand. This time she kept her guard up. <She started it; now it doesn't end until somebody bleeds.>

<Until *you* bleed, Frea!> Isa's words slammed into the back of Eofar's head like a hurled brick. She, too, was still at the ready, glaring at Frea over his shoulder. A raw welt was rising on her neck where the stiff collar of her new jacket had chafed her.

<I'm not going to let you two kill each other,> Eofar thundered at them. <Isa, I want you to stop this. This is—> He stopped abruptly, but the word he had so hastily held back was supplied by another source.

<Pointless?> Frea finished for him.

He had been so struck by the change in Isa that he'd

barely had time to notice Frea, but something was different about her as well. Something was moving beneath the rock-hard slab of her anger: a thin trickle of despair, the kind that eroded everything in its path, drop by drop. Then he noticed the corner of paper—just a corner—between the folds of her jacket. It could have been anything . . .

Except that it wasn't.

He averted his eyes too late. She'd seen him looking and she knew that he'd recognized the letter.

<Why don't you tell her?> Frea asked cruelly.

He would have asked her for mercy, except that he didn't deserve any.

<You know what I think?> she asked, each word a little snap of hatred. <You remember four years ago, when they caught you trying to stow away on the ship to Norland? I think Father told you then. That's why you left me to run the colony by myself—you've known for years that none of it mattered.>

<Don't do this,> he implored her.

<Get out of the way!> Isa demanded, and without waiting for him to comply, she jammed her shoulder into his back and shoved him, hard.

He stumbled forward. Strife's Bane struck the floor and was wrenched from his stinging hand, then skidded out of reach under one of the refectory tables. He hastily focused his mind on recalling it, feeling naked without its weight to ground him, though he had to admit to himself that a sword—even this sword—wasn't going to help him now. The shiny triffons on the hilt rattled against the stone floor and slid a few inches toward him, but not far enough. The bond eroded over distance, but he was only a few feet away; he wasn't concentrating. Again he turned his will to the task, bearing down hard, and this time the blade skidded out from under the table and flew up, hilt first, toward his waiting hand.

Lahlil plucked the sword out of the air before it reached him. <That's a nice trick,> she said, holding it out to him. She'd shed her cloak and the scars on her forearm squirmed in the firelight. As he took the sword from her, he realized the clash of metal on metal had finally stopped. He turned to see Isa and Frea staring at her.

Frea was the first to put words to the question that was already pulsating through the silence, snarling, <What is *she* doing here?>

<I know her,> said Isa, examining Lahlil's disjointed face intently.

Eofar tried to walk away, but the tables blocked his path; there was nowhere to go. The four of them stood equidistant from each other: the four points of a square.

<She's supposed to be dead,> said Frea.

<All right, let's talk.> Eofar looked slowly around at his three sisters. <I'm not forgetting the past, but we should talk about what happens now. Mother is gone, and now Father is, too. It's just us.>

<Not her,> Frea countered instantly. <She's not one of us.>

<You can't say that,> he said.

<No, she's right,> said Isa. He looked over at his baby sister in surprise and found her still fixated on Lahlil. Isa confused him. She had both aged and regressed in the same moment: she was both grown woman and five-year-old child all at once. <She's not one of us. She *is* "us." Everything we are, all that we've become—it's all because of her.>

Frea charged, just as Eofar had expected. He knew Lahlil was unarmed and that he should intervene, but still Strife's Bane never twitched in his hand—not that it mattered, because Isa was there. She stepped in front of Lahlil as if she, too, had anticipated Frea's lunge.

His bones shook with the impact of Isa's sword against Blood's Pride. She and Frea circled and he stepped back out of the way, but Lahlil stayed behind Isa like a shadow, hovering dangerously close to her back swing.

<Isa,> said Lahlil, <can I ask you something?>

Isa's eyes flicked back to her for a fleeting moment. <What?>

<Where was Mother taking you that day? You remember, don't you?>

Eofar could feel Lahlil's intensity snaking out toward his little sister, like vines. <Stop,> he begged her as Frea aimed a thrust at Isa's heart. Isa parried neatly and slid out of the way. Frea lost her balance for a moment and Isa charged, scraping sparks from the two swords as she pressed Frea backward.

<Do you remember?> Lahlil asked again, ignoring him completely.

<I remember.>

<Do you remember looking down and seeing someone below? Someone looking up at you?>

Frea lunged with a soundless snarl, but again Isa stepped fluidly out of range. Lahlil moved in tandem with her and now, when Isa's arm came up to block the blow, it was as if Lahlil had pulled it on a string.

<Isa, don't—> he began, but she was already answering.

<Yes, I do remember: we all looked down. There was a girl there, down in the desert, and she was waiting for us. Mother was happy.> Isa paused and then in that same calm way she said with certainty, <It was you. Mother was looking for you. That's why we had gone out, to find you.>

Eofar shut his eyes, as if by doing so he could block out the image of his mother and sisters on the back of that triffon, flying away from him.

<The sun was coming up.>

<Yes.>

<And there was a flash. I saw something flash.>

<I'll kill you! I'll kill you all!> Frea screamed, and she threw herself forward like a rabid animal. She hacked at Isa with all of her strength, all technique abandoned in her rush of frantic rage.

Strife's Bane trembled in Eofar's hand and he tightened

his grip sympathetically on the hilt, that same desperate urgency to stop what was happening shooting through his veins. He didn't *want* to know—he had never wanted to know.

<I remember the flash,> said Isa. Her arms and legs were quaking with the force of Frea's blows, and her shoulders were beginning to sag with the effort. Still, she held her ground. Frea, her strength squandered, changed to a two-handed grip and fell back, and Isa immediately went on the offensive. Eofar watched her blade slicing and darting. <I remember it.>

<What was it? What was it that flashed?> Lahlil pressed.

<It was a knife.>

Isa twisted her wrist to change her grip. The hilt of the sword leaped from her hand and hung in the air for an elastic moment. Then it dropped back into her palm with a slap and she swept her arm around in a long, lovely arc, turning with the blade as smoothly as a fish in an ocean current and sliced a gash along Frea's unprotected side.

Blood's Pride fell to the ground with a clang.

Eofar watched numbly as Frea—invulnerable Frea—clutched her bleeding abdomen and doubled over. Isa stood over her and ended the story with the finality of an executioner's axe.

<Frea cut the harness.>

Eofar's thudding pulse went suddenly quiet. It was all so obvious: of course Frea had cut the harness. With the harness broken, Mother would have had to turn back; there was no room on the back of that triffon for another little girl. And if Lahlil *had* come back, she would have shoved the rest of them out of Mother's life, just as she had always done. He would have done the same—no, he admitted to himself; he would have *wanted* to—only he would never have had the courage.

Blue blood welled through Frea's fingers and spattered the dirty floor. With her other hand, she reached into her jacket and brought out the letter.

<Congratulations, Isa. You win.> Frea was frothing with bitter triumph as she tossed the letter down at Isa's feet. <Happy Naming Day.>

<No!> Eofar cried, diving forward. He scooped the letter up from the ground, scraping his knuckles bloody with cuts that he never felt. Clutching the letter to his chest, he backed away from all of them toward the door until his heel caught the bottom of the portico step and tripped him up.

<Eofar, what is that paper?> asked Isa.

<It's nothing, it's not—>

<Eofar.> Isa advanced with her sword pointed at him. The blade was still slick with Frea's blood.

He could feel Frea's fervid anticipation as she sat on the ground, bleeding. She had won before she'd even drawn her sword.

<Tell me,> Isa insisted.

<It's a letter> he said wretchedly. <A letter Mother wrote to Father before she left.>

<Give it to me. I want to read it.> She started to sheath her sword before remembering the blood still sliding down the blade. She looked around and found a cleaning cloth on a table nearby, but as she wiped down the blade, Lahlil swept by and plucked the letter out of his hand.

Lahlil sat down on the step and unfolded it with her long gray fingers.

<What does it say?> Isa asked, still addressing herself to Eofar. <How did you know about it before now?>

He forced himself to look at her. <Father showed it to me a few years ago. It— It's about our family.> Frea's maliciousness swirled around him. He had no choice but to tell her the truth. <It says that our family's bloodline is tainted, something to do with our great-grandfather. The Shadar was never just a posting for Father; it was the

emperor's way of banishing him without causing a scandal. That's why we've never been recalled. The emperor himself told Mother, and she was the only one who knew, until she wrote Father this letter.> He forced himself to come to the point. <We're all impure. We can never return to Norland—not any of us. Not ever.>

A curious sound rumbled through the room. He turned in alarm and saw Lahlil, still sprawled on the step, waving the letter gently in her hand. Her shoulders were shaking and the sound was coming from somewhere deep in her throat.

She was laughing.

<That's why he didn't want you to fight me,> Frea trumpeted, climbing awkwardly to her feet. <He knew it didn't matter. You see how he lied to us?>

<Shut up, Frea,> said Isa.

<Maybe I should have told you,> Eofar said, <but you were still so young when I found out, and I thought that—>

<You shut up, too,> Isa commanded, and he did. Her sword was clean now, gleaming in the firelight, reflecting fragments of the room and the people in it. <I know why you didn't tell me—it's the same reason Mother never told, isn't it? You wanted to keep pretending that nothing was wrong. You thought if you acted as if everything was all right, somehow you'd be able to believe it.>

<Isa,> he beseeched her, knowing full well that he was losing her, <it doesn't matter now. Father is dead. We don't need to worry about the colony, or Norland, any more. We'll figure out what to do together.> He seized on the one positive thing he could find. <And now you know about Mother: it wasn't your fault. The accident had nothing to do with you. You don't need to blame yourself. You don't need to be afraid. We can leave. We can go somewhere else.>

Isa sheathed her sword and looked around at her siblings incredulously. <Bloody Onfar, are you all really that stupid? Did you really think that I just suddenly

remembered, just now, what happened that day?> To Eofar, she said, <I always knew that Frea had lied about how Mother died. I let her. She was right to blame me, even if she didn't know it. It was my fault.>

Her eyes were glittering as she walked over to Lahlil. <I'm the one who told Father about you. It was me.>

Eofar recoiled in shock. <No, it couldn't have been you—you were only—what, five years old? It had to have been—>

<It wasn't Frea,> said Isa, whirling back to him. <You always assumed she was the one, I know. Did you know that Mother and Frea both thought that *you* did it? I think that's why Mother left you behind. Well, it wasn't either of you. It was me.>

<All right, then,> he interjected, trying to rationalize it for himself, <but you can't blame yourself for that. You were just a kid—hardly more than a baby. It was too much to ask you to keep a secret like that. You couldn't have known what—>

<I knew exactly what I was doing.> She was firm and immovable, but the icy veneer she'd had earlier had burned away, revealing something very different underneath. He felt like he was seeing the real Isa for the first time. <I've spent every moment since that day living with the shame of it. But you're right, Eofar. It doesn't matter, not any more.>

His own buried truths churned inside of him. <I understand, really I do. I know that Mother thought she was doing the right thing, but she should never have put us in that situation. It wasn't fair—>

Isa didn't have to tell him to shut up this time: her wordless contempt for his ignorance was more than enough to stifle him.

<I wasn't trying to get rid of Lahlil. That's what a real Norlander would have done—that's what you and Frea wanted to do. I needn't have been ashamed of that. I thought Mother was wrong—not because she saved Lahlil, but because she lied about it. She kept Lahlil shut

up in that awful room, even though she didn't seem to be different from us in any way that was important. I told Father the truth because I wanted Lahlil to come and live with us. I wanted us all to be together.>

Lahlil stood up, still holding Eleana's letter in her hand.

<*That* is what I'm ashamed of. No real Norlander would ever want such a thing. I knew it meant that I'm not what I'm supposed to—that there's something wrong with me. I didn't need an old letter to tell me that. I've known it all my life.> Isa turned and walked to the steps.

<Wait!> Eofar and Lahlil called to her simultaneously.

She turned to Eofar first, but he found he had nothing to say.

Lahlil held out the letter. <You should read this.>

Isa's reply throbbed with pain. <I know what it says.>

<No, you don't,> said Lahlil, still holding the paper out to her. <You know what they told you it says. That's not the same thing.>

Isa took the letter and left the room.

Eofar felt a chill as Frea walked in front of him, her hand pressed against the still-bleeding wound. He felt closer to her than he ever had before, even as she turned her wrath and disdain on him.

<So you just swallowed that story about our tainted bloodline without question?> Frea asked incredulously. <Rumors—tricks. That's what they do at court. Don't you know anything about Norland? It's all politics. I don't believe a word of it.>

<It doesn't matter whether you believe it or not,> he answered. <You can't go back.>

<The emperor won't send for me,> Frea told him. <That doesn't mean I can't go back.>

<What are you—?> Eofar began, but suddenly the room went black and he could no longer feel the floor beneath his feet. His first thought was another earthquake, but then the nightmarish visions grabbed hold of

him again. He heard the crash of Strife's Bane striking the floor, but now the images of Daryan returned, sharper this time: again he saw him wrestling with a Norlander, and someone else was lying on the ground beside him. It was Isa, wearing the same clothes she had been wearing a moment ago; bloodied, perhaps even dead. Eofar couldn't feel himself falling; he could only feel the blackness pulling him in, until his head hit the stone floor with a crack and splintered the vision into a thousand bloody shards.

He opened his eyes to find Frea gone and a sticky trail of blue blood leading out of the door.

Lahlil was still sitting on the step, her chin in her hands, watching him. <You should have left that stuff alone,> she told him. <It won't do you any good. You can't change anything.>

He clawed his way to his feet. His head spun dreadfully and he felt like he was going to be sick again. At least he finally understood one thing. <You took it yourself—the elixir. That's how you knew that Father was already dead.> He looked toward the door. <Frea's gone?>

<She went to announce to her men that the rest of us are traitors, to be killed on sight.> Even now, she showed no sign of any emotion.

<How long was I out?>

<Long enough for some to obey it.>

It wasn't until one of them moaned that he noticed the two soldiers tumbled together in a heap near the doorway. The other one moved his legs weakly, trying to get up; she had left them alive, at any rate. He had more urgent matters to worry about. <The last time I got sick like that was right before my vision came true. We have to find Isa—I need to get her away from here before something terrible happens. She always goes to Mother's tomb when she's upset. We'll start there.>

<I told you—whatever you saw is going to happen. You can't change any of it.>

He staggered over to her, grabbed her by the arm and hauled her to her feet. The tight compartment of resentment he had banked down inside him for so many years had finally burst open and his anger overpowered his fear of her, at least for the moment. <I'm going to find Isa and keep her safe, and you're going to help me.> He gave her arm a shake. <Do you want to know why? Because somehow, in spite of everything, Isa cared about you enough to want to help you. I'm betting that she's the only one who ever did. And I think you owe her for that.>

Eofar felt a crack zigzag through Lahlil's emotions and hastily dropped her arm just as a searing flash of red burned into him. He was sucked into a nightmare landscape, an endless battlefield in a chasm lit only by the flash of bloody blades. She hadn't meant to let him in—she didn't want him there—but she was too late. Though her will slammed into him, pushing him out, he had seen what churned behind her disconcerting blankness, and the strength of will it required to maintain her façade staggered him.

<All right,> Lahlil said, <let's go.>

Chapter Twenty-One

Rho rolled over and buried his face in his pillow. <Daem, douse that lamp, will you? Can't you see I'm trying to sleep?>

<You've got no blood in you,> his friend commented lightly. <How can you even think about sleeping? We haven't had this much excitement in years.>

<You've been in this dump too long,> Rho informed him, jamming his face into the limp cushion. Sleep was the refuge he wanted. Asleep, he could dream up a better ending to the evening's débâcle. He let his bruised body sink into the mattress, and his racing thoughts drifted into a pleasant fantasy: Isa stabbing Frea through the heart; Isa coming to thank him for helping her; Isa taking his hand, leading him some place dark and private. She looked so much like Frea, gazing up at him coolly as he undid the clasps on her jacket—

<Hey! Have any of you been watching the slaves?> Kharl poked his square-jawed head in through the doorway just as Rho reluctantly opened his eyes.

<That's all we do around here, Kharl—watch slaves,> Ingeld replied, smacking his lips loudly and throwing a chewed bone down onto the table.

Rho shut his eyes again. <You're drunk. Go to bed.>

<Slaves acting strangely, you assholes,> Kharl elaborated. <I saw a few of them poking around down by the armory. One of them had a limp—I'm sure I've

never seen him before. You don't think they're getting *ideas*, do you? After what happened at the mines? You don't think they have some way of getting into the temple?>

<Do you know where Frea is?> Rho asked without sitting up.

<Yeah, in her room—she kicked me out the moment she came back,> Kharl answered, expecting him to commiserate. He walked over to the table and helped himself to the heel of a loaf of bread. <I know the kid was there and she was bleeding, but I still thought—>

<Bleeding?> He sat up quickly, and then wished he had not. His stomach fluttered and his mouth felt as if it had been stuffed with sand. The wine had been a mistake.

<Didn't you hear? Isa finally got to her—after we all left. Can you believe that? I would have let Ingeld here kick me in the balls to have seen it—> Kharl cast a quick glance toward the door and then added, <Don't tell anyone I said so.>

<Well, that is interesting,> Daem remarked mischievously. He leaned back against the wall and folded his arms across his bare chest. <Lord Eonar's dead. Little Isa fights Lady Frea and wins. Things change, as my mother was fond of saying. We may even get to go home one of these days. I'll wager Lord Eofar won't make us wait five years for a transfer like his father.>

<Lord Eofar? Please,> Ingeld interjected, jamming the point of his knife into the table.

<What was that, Ingeld?> Daem asked.

<Wise up, Daem; you know exactly what I mean,> he sneered, wiping grease from his mouth with the back of his hand.

<No, I'm sure I don't,> said Daem, <because even though I know how much you like the taste of Frea's boots, I know you would never question the rightful transition of leadership as set out by our Great Lord Onfar and inscribed in *The Book of the Hall*. Hmm?>

Rho poked his head out of his shirt and found his friend staring at him.

<What's wrong? Are you cold?>

<Onraka's holy tits!> swore Ongen lustily, taking a look at Rho's battered face. <Look at you! You're a disgrace to the empire.> He tossed the remains of the rib he was gnawing down onto the table. <I've lost my appetite.>

<They're just bruises,> Rho fumed, as he adjusted the shirt over his shoulders. <They'll be gone in a few days.> The fabric was still damp with his own sweat, but had escaped most of the blood; unlike his tabard, which was now soaking in a tub in the laundry.

<If I'd been laid-out by a few half-starved slaves, I'd be too ashamed to show my face.> Ongen leaned back and scratched at the wiry white hairs sprouting beneath his lower lip. <But then, I don't have your breeding.>

<The slaves didn't do that to him,> Ingeld announced, relishing every word. <Lady Frea did. I saw the whole thing.>

Rho tugged on his boots.

<Lord Eofar ordered us to quarters,> Daem reminded him.

<I know, but I have to see Frea.>

<I wouldn't, if I were you,> his friend advised. <This hasn't been her best day, and at the moment you're about as attractive as a triffon's turd.> He came over and sat down on the bed. <Come on, she can't be that good a lover, can she? To keep you still hanging off her titties?>

Rho stood up stiffly. <That's why you're still stuck here in the Shadar, Daem. Not everything is a joke.>

<This is about the boy's mother, isn't it?> Daem asked as he followed Rho out into the hall. <I want to tell you something—as your friend.> For once, he was completely serious. <Get over it. Frea may be a crazy bitch, but she was in charge tonight, and she gave you a direct order, which you obeyed. No one would have acted differently.>

<That's what I keep telling myself.>

<Then start listening. Go back in there and sleep it off.>

Rho looked back through the doorway at his invitingly rumpled bed. <Having your throat cut—it's quick. They say it's almost painless.>

<Sure—I've heard that, too. But the only people who would know for sure are dead.> If it was a joke, it was too grim, even for Rho.

<I have to see Frea,> he said again.

<Then what?> Daem asked. <Kiss her, or kill her?>

<If I get the chance to do either, then Onfar and Onraka love me more than I deserve.> He clapped Daem briefly on the shoulder and then turned away and headed down the corridor toward Frea's chambers. He didn't want Daem to know it was the boy he was going after; he would have wanted to know the plan, then he would have had to admit that he didn't have one. He didn't want anyone else figuring out the boy's significance before he had deposited him safely back in the Shadar, where he'd be just another dirty little urchin playing in the streets.

Doorways flicked by, each framing the same scenes of guards and lamps and cold meat and hot tempers, until Rho caught sight of Falkar coming out of one of the chambers up ahead.

<Rho!> he called out, coming down the hall to meet him. He glanced at Rho's bruises and then looked away uncomfortably. <Did you get the orders?>

<What orders?>

<Lady Frea wants everyone to assemble in the training rooms right away.>

<Lady Frea? I thought Lord Eofar was in charge.>

<Lord Eofar and Lady Isa are traitors. They're plotting with the Mongrel to hand the colony over to the Shadari. Their lives are forfeit, according to Lady Frea.> Falkar hailed from a minor but very proud military clan, and a dark swell of uneasiness rolled through his words.

<I don't like this—I was afraid something like this might happen when Governor Eonar died, but I thought it would be handled with more,> he looked for the word, <subtlety.>

<Subtlety? You mean, like Eofar falling down a flight of stairs? Or maybe getting hit on the head with a big rock?>

Falkar winced at his bluntness and changed the subject. <Can you help me tell the others about the new orders?>

<Sorry.> Rho improvised. <Frea summoned me to her chambers.>

Falkar's silvery eyes flashed over him, skirting the bruises and puffy eye with repugnance. <Well, good luck,> he said hastily, and then ducked into the next room to continue his task.

Soldiers were already beginning to emerge from the rooms up ahead, pulling on their uniforms as they walked. Rho ducked his head and moved through them as quickly as possible, buffeted by their heightened emotions, until he was able to turn away from the barracks and into some of the less frequented corridors.

He wound his way toward the stables until he reached Frea's chamber. All was quiet. A torch burned in the bracket outside the red-curtained doorway, and by its light Rho could see a trail of dark spots leading into the room. He knelt down and touched the stain at his feet. It was blue Norlander blood, and it was still wet. He moved closer to the curtain, and now he could hear Frea moving about inside. Suddenly the stupidity of his vague plan became apparent to him. He had no way of rescuing the boy short of asking her to release him, and that was never going to happen. He thought of reminding her of the Mongrel's ominous warning, but she was so stubborn this was more likely to make her tighten her hold.

No; he had nothing. Disgusted with himself, he continued pacing on down the corridor, trying to think of something. He was so lost in his own thoughts that by the time he heard the soft sounds from the crossing he had just passed it was too late. The point of a blade pricked him between his shoulder blades, covered hands jerked his arms behind his back and he felt his wrists being lashed together.

"Call for help and you're dead," someone hissed, his hot breath tickling Rho's ear. There were six or seven of them, by the sounds of their feet scuffling on the floor. He struggled experimentally, but the bonds held fast and the hand that held the knife at his back stayed steady.

"Have him go in there and bring Dramash out," someone whispered.

"Why would he come back out, you idiot?" the man holding him answered, and spittle flecked his face. "You don't let a hostage go; you trade him. This Dead One for my boy."

"She'll never do it."

"There are six of us, Omir, and we're armed. We don't need her to cooperate."

"You've only been here two hours, Faroth—"

"And you've been here two years, Omir: *two years*! I remember you swearing that if they ever came for you, you'd kill as many as you could before they cut you down, but here I find you, alive and well. How many of them have you killed so far? Fifty? A hundred? Or is it none?"

"Wait," Rho interjected, "if it's the boy you want, I—"

"Shut up!" the man whispered.

They began pushing him back down the hall toward the red curtain. As he was shoved forward his foot caught the bottom and set it gently swinging; he caught a glimpse of Frea's bed, with the boy curled up in the luxuriant furs at the foot, apparently asleep. Then he saw Frea herself, clutching a blood-soaked cloth to her side while she turned the blade of her sword over the the flame of a lamp on an iron stand. Rho could just make out the round curve of her breast in the soft lamplight and in defiance of every ounce of reason he possessed, his desire for her was aroused all over again.

He knew he should call out to her, but he couldn't make himself do it. He couldn't bear for her to see him like this.

In one smooth motion Frea drew back the blade, lifted the cloth and pressed the heated metal against the open wound. The terrible hiss of burning skin and an acrid smell filled the room.

Rho's captors shoved him through the doorway, shouting, "Let the boy go!"

Frea lunged for something on the bed beside her—at first Rho thought she was reaching for the leather jacket, to cover her nakedness, but instead she grabbed the silver helmet and jammed it over her head; only then did she pick up the jacket and sling it over her shoulders. She didn't bother with the clasps, and the hollow place between her breasts and her taut stomach gleamed between the folds of dark leather.

"Papa!" cried the boy, jumping off the bed.

"Come here, Dramash! We're getting out of here." Rho's captor stepped out to the side, and now Rho could see he was lame, his left leg dragging. He held a curved sword, the edge none too clean, and notched from rough use. The boy looked at Frea and then back again at the man with the sword. He did not move.

"I don't *want* to go," he announced. "I want to stay here. Mama's going to—"

"Dramash! Come here!" roared the man, and he lunged out to grab the boy, but Dramash deftly ducked out of his way and ran around behind Frea's legs.

Frea's imperial knife flew into her hand from its scabbard. The slaves leaped back as one, pulling Rho with them, until Dramash's father cut off their retreat with a savage shout. The lame man pressed the edge of his weapon against Rho's stomach. "Give me my son, or I'll gut your man," he said.

The silver helmet moved and through the slits Rho saw Frea's black pupils fix on him. He felt nothing from her: not concern, nor anger, not even disappointment. The only thing he saw in the silver mask was his own reflection.

"She doesn't care if you kill me," Rho told the Shadari. "She's not going to give you the boy."

He jammed his shoulder into his captor's chest and threw his body sideways, hoping to get clear of the sword; that was as much of a plan as he'd worked out so far. He heard the ripping sound of his shirt tearing, and hands reached out to grab him, but they recoiled from the chill of his skin. He tried to turn around, but his head swam and it wasn't until then that he saw the blood welling up and dripping from the fresh cut across his side and stomach—the wound he hadn't felt—and he realized that he was falling. He grasped with his bound hands for something to keep himself upright and managed to clutch the door covering, but the rings tore away from the rod with a series of stuttering pops and he and the red curtain tumbled down together in the doorway.

Frea charged at the Shadari, her knife and Blood's Pride screaming in her hands, and they panicked and scrambled back out into the hallway with Frea right behind them.

He kicked ineffectually at the curtain tangled around his legs while blood seeped from his wound and soaked into his shirt.

"You're bleeding. He hurt you." Rho looked up and saw the round eyes of the little boy looking down at him. His small head was cocked to one side and his forehead was furrowed. He looked like he was trying to find the solution to a difficult riddle. "Are you a bad man? You don't seem like one."

"Dramash," Rho implored him, "you should—"

But before he could say anything more, a pair of cold hands slipped under Rho's arms and pulled him back through the doorway and into the hall. He saw Frea fending off the Shadari—it was six against one, and Frea was wounded, but even as he watched one of the slaves collapsed in a heap against the wall. They wouldn't be able to stand against her for long.

<You followed me,> he remarked to Daem in surprise as his friend pulled him back away from the fighting and propped him up against the corridor wall.

<I figured you were going to do something incredibly stupid and I wanted to watch. You're forgetting how little entertainment we get around here.>

<The boy—> Rho began, but then a spasm tore through him, and he fought for breath.

Daem grabbed up a long knife dropped by one of the Shadari and started on the knot binding his wrists.

A shriek sliced through the air and both men looked up to see the largest of the Shadari men carrying Dramash over his shoulder like a sack of meal—except that the boy was kicking and beating the man with his fists and yelling something about the dereshadi. The others were trying to hold Frea at bay so the man could make his escape down the corridor.

<They have the boy. I'm guessing that's what you want,> Daem said reassuringly as the knot finally gave way and Rho's arms snapped forward, adding a new dimension to his pain. But he wasn't concerned with that, not yet. He lurched to his feet and threw himself forward, reaching out to grab Frea's arm, but his head swam and his legs wouldn't hold him; he collapsed in front of her.

<Frea, let him go,> he implored her raggedly, gasping with pain: begging at her feet like a mangy dog. <Let him go—>

She kicked him away in disgust, and as he went sprawling, a second shriek careened off the corridor walls and the Shadari holding Dramash cried out in pain and anger and dropped the boy, who streaked back to Frea.

"Dramash!" the lame man bellowed, "*get back here!*"

Rho heard a strange splitting sound, like a board being torn in two, and the rock beneath him trembled. He looked dizzily up at the ceiling. Another earthquake.

A black fissure wormed its way down through the red rock, and dust and small rocks pattered down onto his head and shoulder. He tasted chalk on his lips. The crack widened and extended down the wall and across the floor, snaking toward him—no, this was no earthquake. He looked at the boy standing rigidly behind Frea's legs. The look on his face was just the same as it had been at the mines.

Daem grabbed Rho and jerked him to safety just as the floor spread open beside him, a crack several feet wide, running from one wall to the other. The Norlanders were all on one side of the rift and the Shadari—except for the boy—were on the other. Rho looked down into the fissure. He could see the flicker of torches on the level below, and even as he looked, more of the edge on either side crumbled away, widening the breach.

"Dramash!" the lame man shouted, and thrust out his hand to the boy. He hobbled toward the crack. "Jump, Dramash—come on!"

"I want to stay here," said the boy. "I'm going to be a soldier. I'm going to have a dereshadi. Mama's going to come here and live with me."

"Come here, you little brat! I'll teach you to defy me!" He shook his sword, but it was an idle threat; he couldn't leap across the gap, not with that lame leg. Rho saw the other Shadari arguing now, and finally, after one last long look at Frea, they fled. Doubtless they were planning to come around and cut Frea off from the other side, but of course she'd be long gone by then.

In fact, when Rho looked back, she was gone already, and the boy with her.

<Daem, listen—we have to do something. That boy—>

<Move your hands, will you? How am I supposed to help you?> Daem complained.

<I know why Frea wants him. We can't let—>

<Oh, sweet stinking crap, Rho!> Daem broke in, sputtering. Moving Rho's arms had brought a fresh stream of blood welling from the gash. <All right, all right: don't panic,> he rattled on, <it's long but—hold *still*!—it doesn't look too deep. If I can get this closed up, you should be on your feet again in a few hours.> He darted into Frea's chambers.

Rho's eyelids felt heavy and he wanted to sleep, but Daem finally returned carrying one of Frea's spare swords. <It hurts,> he complained feebly as Daem grabbed a torch off the wall.

<You're joking, right?> He began fumbling around Rho's waist. Rho couldn't tell what he was doing; that part of his body had drifted off somewhere very far away. The need to sleep was overpowering, but he knew he mustn't give in, not yet. <Stop thrashing around! Do you want me save your useless aristocratic backside or not?> Daem snapped.

<The boy—>

<Shut up about that boy and let me finish this, will you? When I'm done you can tell him bedtime stories, give him piggy-back rides, I don't care— Rho? *Rho!* You have to stay here. Do you understand? Stay here with me.>

<I'm sorry— I'm sorry.>

<I know you are. Don't worry about it now.> Daem's hand rested for a moment on his forehead; it felt wonderfully cool. He forced his eyes open again and saw Daem holding the blade of the sword in the torch's flame. <All right: if you were planning on passing out again—now might be a good time.>

Chapter Twenty-Two

"You can't be serious?" Daryan asked wearily. His head was still pounding from his confrontation with Shairav and that strange conversation with Rahsa in the hallway, and now Omir had cornered him with news of Faroth's astounding and preposterous rescue plan. He wouldn't have believed a word of it if Omir hadn't hastily introduced him to Binit—a thick-waisted, nervous man whom Daryan had never laid eyes on before—and the short, tarnished sword he clutched to his side. Two others, Hakim, and Daryan's friend, Tal, kept a nervous watch over both ends of the corridor. "Omir, you don't really believe Faroth wants me back in the city, do you?"

"That's what he says," Omir replied. "And as for him being serious, I just saw him slice a guard open right in front of the White Wolf."

"But Faroth has no use for me—or Shairav," he protested. He wished they weren't crowding around him so closely. "Harotha made that clear enough: it was one of the things they argued about before she came here. Why would Faroth do something like this? Why now?"

"I don't know, but the longer he's here, the more trouble he's going to stir up. That's why I came to find you."

"Well, let me talk to Lord Eofar first, then we can—"

"Lord Eofar can't even help himself now," Omir broke in. "I thought you'd heard: Governor Eonar is dead and the White Wolf is using her soldiers to take control of the colony. She's declared Lord Eofar and Lady Isa traitors to the empire—they're to be killed on sight, along with anyone caught helping them."

Daryan clenched his fists. "I knew something like this would happen. I tried to warn him—"

"Daimon!" Tal said in an urgent undertone, and Daryan looked up to see someone staring at them from a dozen paces away.

Rahsa still had that nasty gash on her forehead, and under the dirt, her cheeks were bright red from exertion. Her robe was torn at the shoulder and bloody scratches marked the soft flesh above her breast. She blinked too often and she breathed in sharp, shallow gasps. Even as Daryan watched in horror, she raked her nails across her chest, bringing up lines of fresh blood.

"Oh, no," he breathed to the others. "Wait here—let me talk to her. And don't move, please," he implored them as he pushed past.

The girl's face broke into a shy smile as he came toward her, but the smile was an ill match for the eager look in her eyes and did little to reassure him. "Is everything all right, Rahsa?" he asked her, trying to sound as casual as possible. "You look like you want to tell me something."

She giggled, a horrifying sound that chilled him to the bone. "No. I don't want to tell you. That would spoil it. I want to show you. Everything's going to be all right now."

"That's good." He tried to smile back. He could see that she was holding something behind her back, hiding it like a child with a stolen sweet. "You can show it to me later, okay? I have to talk to these people now. You look tired. Why don't you go lie down and I'll come and find you?"

The expectant smile on her lips crumbled away, making the intensity in her eyes even more alarming. "But you have to come with me," she sang out softly. "I did it for *you*. I have to show you—you have to see it for yourself."

"I really can't, Rahsa," he said, holding up his hands in a helpless gesture. "Not right now. I'm sorry." He turned away and began to walk back to the others, but he could feel her staring at him. He turned back and said, "Really, Rahsa: go and get some sleep. I mean it."

Something like anger flashed across her face, but so quickly that he thought he must have imagined it. Then she smiled at him again, even more broadly this time. "You just don't understand yet," she said, nodding to herself. She walked toward him. "Don't worry. It will be all right. I'm going to help you. I'll always help you. That's all I've ever wanted to do."

Before he realized what was happening, she had grabbed his shoulder and thrust her lips violently against his. He struggled, trying to push her away, but no sooner had he loosened her grip than she shoved him, so hard that he fell backward onto the ground, winded.

"I won't *touch* you!" she shrieked, her shrill voice almost belonging to a different person. "Her stink is on you—traitor! Traitor!"

"Rahsa, what—?" he gasped as he struggled back to his feet. He heard voices raised in alarm and as the others rushed forward, her own dreadful scream ripped through the air and she covered her ears with her hands. And now Daryan saw what she had in her right hand: Eofar's knife, the same one he had so carelessly left in the bathing room after he'd knocked it away from her; he'd never had the presence of mind to go back and retrieve it.

She shrieked again and lunged for him, and as he stared at the point of the blade, with the suddenness of a thunderclap he became acutely aware of the precarious collection of bones and soft tissues that made up his body, the flesh that offered no more resistance than the skin of a fruit. He was not so amazed that he was about to die as he was confounded that a creature so fragile could have survived as long as he had.

A heavy arm shoved him out of the way and he crashed into Binit as Rahsa's scream suddenly choked off: Omir had grabbed Binit's sword and plunged it straight through her chest.

"No!" Daryan screamed, as Omir tugged the blade out and Rahsa crumpled to the ground. He scrambled over to her on his hands and knees. The front of her robe was already soaked with blood. She was still alive, but each breath was a gasp of pain, and her eyes were rolling heavily in their sockets. "Why did you do that?" he demanded frantically of Omir, who stood over them with the bloody sword clutched in his hand. "You didn't have to kill her!" He tried to lift her up, but the jostling made her cry out in pain.

"What do you mean? She tried to kill you!" exclaimed Binit, circling around next to Omir and staring in consternation at the blood dripping from the point of his sword. "Omir just saved your life!"

"He knows that," the tall Shadari told Binit. He was looking down at Daryan, frowning thoughtfully. "She was going to kill you," he told Daryan, "but your first thought was for her. Not yourself."

"I just—" began Daryan, but then he saw Rahsa's eyes fix on him. Her lips moved and dark blood bubbled up at the corners of her mouth—he bent his head closer to hear what she was trying to tell him.

"I did it . . . for you," she gasped out.

"I know," he said, trying to reassure her, though he still had no idea what she meant. "I know you did."

Tal picked up Eofar's knife from the floor. "There's blood on this!" he announced, holding it up in the torchlight.

"Daryan, are you hurt?" Omir asked.

"No, no," he answered, watching Rahsa's face as she struggled to form more words.

"She's burning now," she whispered. "I wanted us to watch together."

"We will," Daryan assured her, then he realized what she'd said. "Burning? *Who's* burning? Rahsa?"

"The blood's on the handle, not the blade," said Tal,

running his fingertip over the hilt of the knife and then holding it close to his eyes. "It's all right, it's not Shadari blood."

Daryan looked down at Rahsa's right hand, which was resting on his chest. Her fingers had left a bloody handprint on the front of his robe: a *blue* handprint.

"*Who's* burning?" He pulled her closer to him. "Rahsa!" he cried as her eyelids fluttered, "*Rahsa!* Who's burning?"

As suddenly as if a string had been cut, her body went limp and heavy in his arms. Her head smacked down on the stone floor: she was dead.

"Poor girl," Hakim said, staring at her. "Temple madness, I guess. I've seen it before. And now with Shairav leaving she won't even get a real funeral. She'll have to stay shut up in the Dead One's tombs—"

Daryan rocketed to his feet, crying, "That's it—the tomb! She said 'burning'—the sun—the sun shines on the tomb. She's there—she's *burning*—"

"I don't—" Hakim started, but Daryan had turned to Omir and was clutching his robe.

"Find Shairav—get to the stables; I'll meet you there. Go!" He grabbed Eofar's knife out of Tal's hand.

"Daryan, what—?" Omir called out after him.

"*Go!*" he yelled back, running as hard as he could for Eleana's tomb.

Isa was burning.

Chapter Twenty-Three

She had to move—but the body that she inhabited no longer belonged to her. She couldn't feel her heart beating. She couldn't feel the stone beneath her. Her eyes were open, but looking through them was like looking through a window; she could only guess that the wheezing gasps that occasionally broke the silence were the sounds of her own breathing; if she still had lungs, she couldn't feel them.

Her mother's letter lay open on the tomb a few inches from her face, shifting gently back and forth in the breeze from the skylight above. There was a bright light near her knee which might have been the sunlight glancing off her sword. She thought she could remember putting it down there just before she'd perched on the edge of the tomb to read the letter. But mostly she could see her left arm. She didn't want to look at it, but she couldn't turn her head away, and she was afraid that if she closed her eyes, she would never open them again.

She had to move: she knew that. But she knew the reason she couldn't move was because she couldn't feel, and the reason she couldn't feel was because she didn't want to, not since she'd woken up screaming, convinced that someone was pounding her hand over and over again with a hot poker.

The sun had been blazing down on her hand and forearm. It had taken just a few frantic heartbeats for her to realize that the pounding was the rhythm of her pulse. Then the pain had stopped; it hadn't gone away—she wasn't stupid. She knew it was waiting for her, daring her to acknowledge that the mangled thing connected to her shoulder still belonged to her. And as unbearable as the pain had been then, by now it would be far worse, for all this time the sun had been beating down, it had also been steadily creeping over the tomb, and by now it was past her elbow. The skin on her forearm was bubbling with inky-black blisters; shortly, the flesh would begin to char away and poisoned blood would seep out, as it was already doing on her wrist and the back of her hand.

She had to move, and soon, if she wanted to survive this. She didn't want to die—not like this, not facing an afterlife as pointless and insignificant as her mortal one had been. Only warriors who died by the sword were admitted to Onfar's celestial hall. *The Book of the Hall* relegated the murdered—and she was being murdered; she knew that—to the same shabby realm as accident victims, children and others of marginal status. Even worse, she had been killed by a slave, some scrawny creature who had snuck up behind her and smashed her in the head with something and then left her lying in the sun to burn without her having lifted even a finger in her own defense. The shame of it would haunt her through eternity.

But to live—that meant to feel the pain, and this pain terrified her. She'd never known such fear. Whatever courage and fortitude she'd built up over her lifetime were laughable, mewling little things in the face of this. Was a little more life worth so much suffering? Death would find her, sooner or later; right now it would be so easy to close her eyes, just drift away. Already she could feel gravity's hold over her lessening, and lightness filling her, pulling her upward, like a glistening soap bubble . . .

Her reverie was interrupted by a sharp cry, then her vision blurred as she was lifted up. There was a babble of unintelligible words, and a crash, followed by another shout, and finally cool shade poured over her like balm. Away from the hateful sun, her eyes were able to focus again: she could see the doorway of the chamber, and her sword, teetering on the edge of the step next to the oozing lump of flesh that had once been her left hand. The crash had been the sound of the sword, falling from the tomb.

She didn't see him until he ran to the doorway, and then ran back to her. She wanted to say his name, to tell him that she was glad he'd found her. She wanted him to hold her—that most of all.

"Can you walk, Isa? Do you think you can walk, if I help you?" His face was close to hers, though she couldn't feel his warmth. She saw her right wrist in his hand—he was feeling her pulse—but she couldn't feel his fingers. "You're so warm. We have to get you out of here. Frea's soldiers, they're—"

They're here, she thought. She could sense them in the hallway, a moment before they entered the chamber, both talking at once.

<—saw him go this way, if we follow him—>

<—sure it was him? They all look alike to me. I don't—>

<—he'll lead us to Eofar—>

<—care about Eofar! We should be looking for the Mongrel. If we—>

Daryan leaped up as they entered and placed himself between her and the two men. He had a knife—Eofar's knife—but even in her present state, she could tell by the way he held it that he had no idea how to use it.

"Stay away from her!" he shouted to them, his voice breaking in the middle with a kind of squeal. But the soldiers weren't looking at him; they were looking at her.

<Somebody *burned* her,> said one of the soldiers after a pause in which Isa could feel the full brunt of their horror.

<One of *them*,> the other replied in disgust. <None of us would do something like that.>

<This one's got a knife—that'll count as a battle kill.>

<All right, but let's make it quick,> his companion replied, and they stepped toward Daryan with their swords drawn.

Air sliced into Isa's lungs and feeling tingled back into her limbs—but not the pain, not yet, though she could feel it pushing, ready to explode. She had just a few heartbeats before her brain awoke to the truth. She reached across her body and closed her right hand around the hilt of her sword. She felt the coldness of the metal: it was the clearest, most vibrant sensation she'd ever felt in her life.

She tried to stand up, but her legs weren't ready and instead she found herself sliding down the steps until her feet hit the floor. She used the momentum to rock herself upright. The left side of her body felt ridiculously heavy, as if it were weighted down by sandbags. Her right arm was too weak to lift her sword any higher than her knees, but she staggered forward. She could feel the pain beginning to claw its way over the barrier.

<Leave him alone!> she demanded as she pulled herself across the room toward the two guards. She knew them: the shorter one was Finlas, the taller one Varnat. Daryan turned to her and called out her name. Somewhere she found the strength to lift her sword up. She pointed it at her adversaries.

Either one of them could have taken her down; together, they could have done it with laughable ease—but instead, they backed toward the doorway.

<Stay away!> stammered Finlas as he crashed into his companion. <Stay back!>

They were afraid of her, Isa realized with a sick kind of relief. Afraid of *her*. And she thought of what she must look like to them, with her burned arm, and black blood, viscous as paint, dripping down and spattering the dusty floor. She was a monster, a thing out of their nightmares—an affront to the gods. She was an abomination.

<Get out!> she roared, and the two men fled from the room.

And then the pain, as if knowing the battle was over, finally broke free.

"Dar—" she gasped, expending the last ounce of her strength. She didn't feel herself falling, but she did feel his arms as they came around her and she felt his warmth—no longer burning—as he pressed his cheek against hers. In her head she was screaming, but he couldn't hear her and she was glad of that, because then he might have stopped telling her that everything was going to be all right, that he loved her, that he had always loved her, that he wasn't going to let her go.

But there was something she needed him to know. "Rahsa," she coughed; all she could manage, but it would have to suffice.

"She's dead," Daryan reassured her, without understanding that the danger she feared was for him, not herself. "She was mad; I should have known. I should have made sure—"

Now she wanted to reassure him, but she had no more strength for words. She could feel the pain beginning to ease again, but this time, instead of embracing the numbness, she fought it. She tried to feel the coarse cloth of Daryan's robe under her fingers, his arm beneath her, holding her up. She tried to feel the ache in her head where she'd been struck, but it was all slipping away. She heard the sound of swordplay, sounding very far away, and the last thing she saw before the room went dark again was her brother's face swimming in the doorway.

Moments passed, or hours; she couldn't know. The pain existed outside of time. But she knew when she felt the pain again that she was coming back, moving closer to reality. She heard the sound of voices, but the words were garbled, as if she were under water. She focused all of her efforts on dragging her eyelids upward.

She found herself looking up through a dark gray haze at the point of a sword. The sword was suspended over her heart, like a stake, and the white-knuckled hands that held it belonged to her brother. Then something streaked by the corner of her vision and slammed into Eofar, knocking him and his sword against the side of the tomb.

"No! No!" she heard Daryan grunting.

She could no longer see either of them, but she could hear them grappling somewhere behind her. "I won't let you do it!"

"There is no other choice!" Eofar's voice sounded flat, but emotions too complicated for Isa to parse were cascading from him.

"There is! Find it!"

"Tell him!" Eofar pleaded to someone Isa couldn't see. "Tell him the burns are poison—it's too late for her. Tell him she's *dying*!"

The person he was addressing didn't answer, but a moment later Daryan made a funny choking sound and cried, "*Wait!* I know what to do—Rahsa—her father—" Then in a different tone entirely, he said, "I know what we have to do. We cut off her arm, just like they do with the mining accidents."

"No—*No!*" Eofar barked. There was a long pause and she knew he was talking to someone in Norlander, but she couldn't quite follow it—

"Speak Shadari, damn you!" she heard Daryan demand. "I've had enough secrets for one day."

With a shock, Isa heard Lahlil's voice coming from the other side of the room. Her emotions were so suppressed that Isa would have never known she was there if she hadn't spoken. "He was reminding me what that will make her: an outsider. An outcast. He said that of all people, I should understand."

"Your arm didn't make you an outcast," Daryan told her pointedly. "Your mother did that when she shut you up in a room."

"How dare you!" Eofar rasped.

"No—listen to me," Daryan said, "you're not worrying about Isa; you're worrying about how people will treat her, and that's not the same thing. All of my life, people have treated me like I'm useless, and a coward—but that wasn't the problem. The problem was that I believed them." His voice broke. "Isa isn't like that. She's better than me—better than any of us. The only one who's going to decide whether she lives or dies is her. We're not going to stand here and make that decision for her."

"Taking her arm won't save her," Eofar argued. "She's not Shadari, she—"

"It might," said Lahlil quietly, "if we do it now."

"You don't know that. You couldn't—"

"Did you see that?" Daryan asked sharply. "Her eyes just opened. Isa!" She felt his hands on her right wrist and she managed to open her eyes again. The blurry face bobbing in front of her eyes said, "There, look! Isa? *Isa!* Can you hear me?"

She couldn't answer him—she didn't have the strength, not even to speak her own language. The pain was draining everything, and soon there'd be nothing left.

"Here—give her this." Lahlil's voice was much closer now.

Isa heard a metallic scraping sound. Then a pause.

"How much?" asked Daryan.

"All of it."

"This won't hurt her, will it? You wouldn't—"

"It won't hurt her. It won't save her, either, but she'll be able to decide for herself. That's what you want, isn't it?"

"What about you? Don't you need this?"

She didn't hear an answer, but a moment later something hard pressed against her lips and a warm liquid dripped into her mouth. Her throat convulsed, but she forced herself to swallow. She could feel the liquid, whatever it was, spreading through her—first hot, then very cold, pushing back the pain. Isa pushed, too, half-hallucinating that she was pushing her shoulder against a door, holding it against an angry mob trying to shove their way through from the other side. Her sight began to clear and now she could see Daryan, kneeling beside her with a metal flask in his hand. Lahlil was standing next to him, and on the other side she could see Eofar's dark boots.

She tried to speak, but her lips were too dry. She wet them, and croaked, "Cut it off."

Daryan jerked up. "You heard that! You heard what she said?"

"No," Eofar said again, "I can't—"

She didn't have the strength to explain, and she wanted them to understand, in case . . . "Paper," she whispered.

Daryan leaned closer. "What did you say? Paper?"

"I think she means that," said Lahlil, pointing at the letter lying ignored on the tomb.

Daryan disappeared from Isa's sight for a moment and then reappeared with the letter in his hand. "This is Norlander," he said after a moment. "I can't read this."

<Read it to him,> Isa told Eofar.

<Isa, don't.>

<Do it.>

She knew that only Lahlil's medicine was making the pain bearable, and she wondered how long it would last. The room was already darker than it had been a moment before. Was the sun going down already, or was lucidity slipping away from her again?

Then she heard Eofar. It was strange, how hearing her mother's words spoken aloud in Shadari brought the memory of her back to Isa more vividly than anything else that had happened today.

Eonar,

I am going to find her. I am taking the girls with me. Our son I leave with you, but I fear he will be of no consolation to you when you learn what I must tell you now.

You can never return to Norland. Not you, nor I, nor any of our children. Your bloodline is tainted. The emperor has received proof that your real grandfather was a servant on the Eotan estates, a man of the very lowest clan. To save you the humiliation and the court from scandal, he sent you here and agreed never to make it known, provided we never left the Shadar. He made me his conspirator on our wedding day. He made me pledge to keep you here.

I kept the secret, believing I was protecting you. I thought that by hiding Lahlil I was protecting her, too. Now I see that in both cases, I was only protecting myself. I was afraid to do what I knew in my heart to be right. I was afraid of what I would lose. Now I can see that what I had was not worth keeping. I should thank you for that.

I'm glad this happened. I'm going to find a place where I can make up these wasted years to Lahlil and the girls. No more secrets. No more hiding.

For the love I once felt for you, I will try to understand what you have done. Someday, I may find a way to forgive you. As for now, Onraka forgive me, I want you to suffer.

Do not try to find us.

Eleana

Eofar slowly folded the letter and laid it back down on the tomb.

"You see," Daryan said hoarsely, "she saw it, too. What's the point of trying to hold on to a life that doesn't want you, that has nothing to give you? Because you're too frightened to look for something else? What are you afraid of?"

"This is about Isa, not me," Eofar replied. "And I am *not* afraid."

"No?" asked Daryan, standing up and facing Eofar. "Then why haven't you and Harotha left the Shadar? Why are you still up here while Harotha's down there?"

There was a long moment of silence, and then Isa felt herself being lifted again, this time in her brother's strong arms. She noticed for the first time that he was no longer wearing a shirt, and then realized it was wrapped around her wounded arm, the fabric streaked with dark blood. When had that happened? She caught a glimpse of Lahlil, standing near the door, guarding against intruders.

"It's not safe here," Daryan said, following her eyes. "I know you people heal fast, but how long will it be before she can be moved?"

"Not long—an hour, maybe less," said Lahlil.

Eofar laid her on the tomb again, only now the sun had moved off. She could see the skylight up above her, but it looked very, very far away, and the sky itself looked flat, like a splash of paint on the ceiling.

"We'll have to leave the temple—we can't do that until sunset," said Eofar.

<Eofar?> Isa called to her brother. She felt the touch of his cool fingers on her cheek. <I'm sorry. I'm sorry she left you behind.>

He wanted to hide his sorrow from her, but he could not. She entwined herself in it, trying to reach him, to comfort him. She knew now why Eofar had never told her about the letter, and she could forgive him. It didn't have anything to do with her or Frea, or Norland; their mother's abandonment had cut him so deeply, made him feel so utterly worthless, that he couldn't bear the thought of anyone else knowing about it.

Isa let her eyes fall closed. She'd done all she could for now. It was up to the others to work out the rest.

"Getting out through the stables is going to be hard," Daryan was saying. "We'll have to distract—"

"Not you," said Lahlil. "You're going with Faroth."

"I'm not leaving Isa."

"The Shadari want their daimon: they're killing and being killed in your name. Is that what you want?"

There was a pause. "I never wanted that." Another pause. "All right, I'll talk to Faroth. But I'm not leaving here until I know that Isa's safe." Then more sharply, "She's unconscious again. Is that bad?"

From the other side, Eofar said, "Would you rather have her awake for this?"

But I am awake, Isa worried. She was too far away for them to hear her. She heard the scrape of metal, the crackling of a torch.

"No. Use this one." Lahlil's voice again. "She told me its name." Had she? She didn't remember. "She's called it Truth's Might."

Yes. Yes, that was the name she had chosen for her mother's sword—her sword, now. *Truth's Might*.

"Do it in one stroke," Daryan advised. "And then seal the wound, or she'll bleed to death. You can't hesitate."

Wait, Isa tried to cry out to them. *Wait, I'm awake. I'm not ready—don't—*

There was the sharp strike of metal against stone, then a hiss and the bright smell of smoke. And that was all. This time Isa ran from the pain and before it could catch her, she plunged into the darkness.

Chapter Twenty-Four

Daryan paused by the window on his way to meet Faroth at the stables and stared at the broken slats lying on the ground. All of the windows he had passed had been uncovered; it looked as if someone had run through the corridors, giddily denuding the windows as they went. The sight of the bright sunshine piercing through the temple's gloom brought home the fact that nothing in his life would ever be the same again. He tried to breathe deeply, waiting for the tightness in his chest to ease.

Then he passed through the archway to the stables and a Shadari sentinel turned around and hissed, "Here he is!"

There were no Dead Ones in the stables—Frea would never have left them unguarded, so the soldiers had either been lured away, or otherwise dispatched by Faroth's gang. Two saddled and skittish dereshadi were being held by half a dozen slaves, while scores of others watched over the many entrances. Omir stood out among them, and Daryan recognized Binit, too. His uncle was standing between the two dereshadi, stroking their bristly snouts, trying to soothe them.

One of the Shadari took a few limping steps toward Daryan and he stared in astonishment. He'd always known that Harotha and her brother were twins, but he had never imagined the resemblance between them would be so striking.

Without preamble, Faroth asked, "You're Daryan?"

"Yes."

He saw Faroth cock his arm and he knew he was about to be hit, but it happened too fast for him even to flinch, let alone defend himself. He stumbled backward under the weight of the punch, but he didn't fall. Through watering eyes he saw Omir charging over.

"That was for letting that Dead One touch my sister," Faroth informed him, and then spat on the ground.

"Stop!" he called out hoarsely to Omir, who was about to grab Faroth. His face hurt and he could taste blood on his lip, but his mind was too busy with the problem of keeping on the right side of Harotha's tangle of lies to worry about the pain. "You're her brother. I'd expect you to do that," he said, wiping the blood from his mouth. "But you know her. And you know that once she's made up her mind to do something, there isn't anything anyone can do to stop her."

Faroth eyed Daryan suspiciously, but he didn't seem inclined toward further violence. "I was sent here to take you back to the Shadar," said Faroth. "You can go if you want to, but I'm not leaving without my son."

Shairav left the dereshadi. "Daryan, we must go at once," he said. His shoulders were straight, his grim mouth and heavy brows were set in their usual uncompromising lines, but to Daryan the old man looked like a shadow of his former self. His eyes had a strange bulging look to them, as if something were pressing on them from behind, and his skin still had that unhealthy waxy sheen.

"I'm not leaving either," Daryan told all of them at once. "That's what I came here to tell you."

"It's not safe here," Omir advised. "You should go with them. It might be your only chance."

"No one's safe anywhere," he replied, "and I'm not going to hide any more. The White Wolf is planning something—we have to find out what she's going to do, and if she's threatening the Shadar, we have to stop her.

There aren't many of us, but we have a better chance of stopping her here than down in the city."

"Fine," Faroth agreed, "we all stay then. That suits me."

"Sorry, but you're going back—you and the others you came with, and my uncle."

Faroth's eyes widened incredulously. "Are you giving me orders?"

"Yes, I am," said Daryan.

"You wouldn't dare without Omir here to protect you," Faroth said.

"But I am here," Omir reminded him.

"All right, stop it," Daryan told them both. "Look, Faroth, you have an organization down in the city—Harotha told me all about it. You can get the people in the Shadar ready to fight back, if it comes to that. They need you there to defend the city—you're the only one who can." He glanced back toward the door. Who knew how much time they had before more guards arrived? "We'll get your son away from the White Wolf; that I swear to you. But you'll never get to him now, and we're running out of time."

"You can't stay," Shairav told Daryan. His usual stentorian voice sounded gruff, its force blunted. "You must come with me, to the Shadar. You must—"

"I know what you're going to say, Uncle, but I'm not that important to the Shadari, not really. They don't need me; it's you they need. You're the last of the ashas." Daryan emphasized the last few words, well aware of their mocking cruelty. He was enjoying being able to remind Shairav of his perfidy in front of the others, even if no one else understood. They would, soon enough. "You're the most important person in the Shadar; I'm nothing compared to you. It's vital that you survive."

"Yes, yes. I must survive," agreed the old man vaguely. His eyes had taken on a vacant look during Daryan's verbal onslaught, and now he turned and walked, a little unsteadily, back to the dereshadi.

"Daryan is right," said Omir quietly, in his deep voice.

"You're needed in the city, Faroth, and we need Shairav alive. You must go now, while there's still time."

"You swear to me that you'll stop at nothing to get Dramash back from the White Wolf?" Faroth demanded. Daryan knew that he had won the argument. He wondered which of his appeals had worked: those aimed at Faroth's sense of duty to his people, or those at his vanity.

"We'll get him," he promised, "I—"

Binit called Faroth's name, but Faroth ordered him to wait and turned back to Daryan and Omir. "You could be trapped here. There's no way out except the dereshadi. We should make Shairav show us the ashas' secret entrance before we take him."

Daryan was startled, but he quickly realized that as angry as he was at Shairav, he didn't want Faroth finding out the truth; not yet, anyway. "There really isn't time," he started, "not when the guards could come back any moment."

"All right; he can do it from the Shadar, then," Faroth amended, waving off another summons from Binit. "The ashas could come and go when they pleased, so there must be a way up from the beach. I—"

Binit appeared by Faroth's side, looking white-faced. "Faroth," Binit said, swallowing, "we need you. Right now."

"What is it?" Faroth growled, frowning, but he followed Binit over to the others.

As soon as they were out of earshot, Omir said, "There's something you're not telling him."

Daryan looked up quickly into Omir's grave, intelligent eyes. "Yes, you're right," he admitted. Harotha's first rule for telling a successful lie: stay as close to the truth as possible. "It's Eofar and Isa—if they're still alive, I want to help them escape. I want them to join with us against the White Wolf."

Omir was surprised, but not shocked; Daryan, watching his face closely, saw it take him only a moment to grasp the sense of this plan. "You don't believe that all of the soldiers are loyal to Lady Frea."

"I do not," he said. "The Dead Ones take their honor and traditions very seriously. What Frea's done—turning on Eofar, the eldest son, the heir—goes against both. They'll follow her if they've no other choice, but if Eofar steps forward and asserts himself as the rightful governor, I bet more than a few Dead Ones will be happy to switch sides."

"But we don't even know where he is. He's disappeared."

"I know where he is," Daryan assured him. He thought of the plan he and Eofar had made, sitting next to Isa but not looking at her, listening to her labored breathing, while Eofar pretended not to notice that Daryan was trying not to be sick, and Daryan pretended not to notice that Eofar was sitting on his hands to stop them from shaking. They were still in the funeral chamber—they had considered Lahlil's old room, but Frea knew about that, too—waiting until the sun was low enough for them to fly safely. Lahlil had assured them that Isa would be awake by then. She had some plan to clear the way for them to escape, but she hadn't given them any details; all he knew was that Eofar would take Isa to the cave he and Harotha had discovered after the earthquake, and Daryan would find Harotha and bring her there after his own escape. He hadn't told Eofar that he had no intention of leaving the temple until he knew that Isa was already safely away.

"You know Lord Eofar better than I do," said Omir. "If you think we should help him, that's good enough for me."

"I think I have an idea about how to keep the White Wolf here in the temple, too. We should get out of here as soon as Shairav and Faroth are gone and find some place safe to talk about it."

"I have a few friends who—"

But Daryan was growing worried. "Maybe we'd better

see what's going on over there," he suggested as he noticed the other Shadari converging on Faroth and Binit. Omir fell into step by his side, but Daryan's steps slowed as he saw the looks on the faces of those who turned aside to make way for them.

Shairav was lying on the ground, his eyes closed and creased with pain, and one hand lay over his chest, fingers curled.

"He's dead," Faroth told him unnecessarily.

Omir's heavy hand gripped his shoulder. "I'm sorry, Daimon. I'm truly sorry."

"Yes," Daryan replied. "So am I."

Chapter Twenty-Five

"Is she still asleep?"

"Shhhhh!"

"Do you think we should do it now?"

"We have to do it before Faroth gets back."

Harotha heard the curtain rings rattle softly against the rod. She kept her eyes closed and her breathing regular, not sure whether they could see her in the darkness. Pretending she needed sleep had got her away from the excited prying of the Shadari women Alkar had handed her on to, but despite the hours she'd spent anxiously ruminating in the dark, she was no closer to knowing what was happening in the temple. The separate lies she had told Faroth, Eofar and Daryan were going to collide up there, and nothing in her power could prevent it.

More whispering sounded from the other side of the curtain, and then someone sang out, "Okay, we're ready!"

The curtain rings rattled again and she heard the same faintly familiar jingling sound she'd been hearing from time to time all morning. She yawned and said sleepily, "Is someone there?"

The jingling came closer, and in the dim light she could see a slim Shadari woman creeping toward her. "Who's there?" she called out, struggling up out of the cushions.

"Now don't spoil it!" the intruder cried out, clapping a scented hand over Harotha's eyes and urging her toward the doorway. She felt the rough fabric of the curtain, then saw the glow of daylight around her captor's fingers.

"Surprise!" a voice yelled in her ear, the hands fell away and the room exploded with sound. She stood blinking in the bright light with a shrill chorus of congratulations ringing in her ears. Faroth's house was jammed full of women, all watching her with eager, shining faces. A huge pot of tea simmered over the hearth in the center of the room. Next to it was a well-worn cradle, surrounded by a jumble of baskets overflowing with linens and other, less instantly recognizable implements.

"Did we surprise you?" asked an eager voice at her elbow and she turned to see a very young woman, not much more than a girl, looking up at her with keen excitement. Both of her forearms were covered up to the elbow with wedding bracelets; that was the jingling sound that Harotha had recognized but couldn't place. "We figured, coming from the temple and all, that you wouldn't have anything for the little daimon." She giggled.

The rest of the women in the room had fallen silent and now they all turned to her expectantly.

"Thank you," she said faintly. "This is really—"

"Oh, let her sit down!" cried a woman from across the room. "Look at the poor thing—she's going to faint!"

Far more people than were necessary sprang forward to help Harotha down into a comfortable seat. A cup of cooled tea found its way into her hand and once again the room filled with the noise of thirty chattering voices. She took a sip of tea and looked around, starting to recognize some of the individual faces of the women surrounding her.

"I know it probably doesn't feel right," said a low voice in her ear. Elthion's mother, Trini, was sitting next to her. She had much more gray in her hair than the last time Harotha had seen her, and her eyes were red-rimmed from crying. She patted Harotha's knee. "But I think it's what Saria would have wanted. She would have been so proud of you, you know. To think, she missed knowing about this by just a few hours."

Harotha gasped at a sudden flutter of panic in her chest.

"Oh, my!" cried Trini. "Was that a contraction?"

"No, no," Harotha reassured her, trying to smile. "He just kicked me, that's all."

"So it's a boy?" someone cried out.

She shrugged, still smiling tightly. "I think so." She raised her voice to be heard over the celebratory shouting. "At least the signs say so—but they're not always right, you know."

"I knew it! She's carrying high. Boys are always like that," someone announced.

"Were you dizzy a lot at the beginning? I was dizzy with both my boys, but then when I had my girl, I wasn't dizzy at all."

The babble of conversation quickly rose in volume as everyone presented their own theories for determining the sex of an unborn baby.

A young woman she didn't know came over to refill her tea. As the liquid trickled into the cup, she asked shyly, "So what's the daimon like? Is he very handsome?"

Those guests close enough to hear the question immediately fell silent to listen to the answer. Harotha smiled with relief. Here was one question that she could answer with perfect honesty. "Yes, he is. Very handsome."

Her interrogator sighed happily and swung the teapot around to offer it to someone else.

"I'm so glad you finally came to your senses and decided to leave the fighting to the men," Trini told her. "What the men don't understand is how much braver we women have to be. It's much harder for me to sit here and worry about Elthion, up to the gods know what out there with your brother, than it is for him to fight. And you"—she leaned closer, whispering in her ear—"these others don't know, but Elthion told me what you had to do to get away. I can't imagine how horrible it must have been for you, with that Dead One, all those months. You were very brave to endure it—most girls I know would have given up the baby, daimon or not, or even done themselves in. At least now you know that monster will never be able to touch you again. It is too bad they didn't kill him when they had the chance, though. Oh, well—maybe they'll get him now, in the temple. My dear, are you feeling all right? You look very pale."

"There are so many people here," she explained. "I'm feeling a little light-headed—I think I need some air." She put down her teacup and stood up.

"Do you want someone to come with you?"

"No, no, I'll only be a moment."

Trini turned around to respond to a question about her sister's health and Harotha took the opportunity to slip away through the crowd, all the while feeling as if her flesh were tightening and turning transparent under their scrutiny, like a jellyfish on the beach. She noted a fair amount of dark looks coming her way, too, and comments whispered behind fingers and received with grave nods. Trini never could keep a secret.

By the time she reached the door, her hands were tingling unpleasantly and she realized that she had forgotten to breathe. A few people saw her heading outside and asked where she was going, but mercifully, no one insisted on accompanying her when she said she just wanted a little air.

The midday sun was blazing as she lurched to a large flat rock under a spreading palm tree. She sat down, rubbing her forehead with her hand as the baby wiggled inside her. She shut her eyes and circled her arms around her belly, trying to feel the soothing coolness that she had to admit was probably only a product of her imagination. For the moment, the politics of rebellion felt as unimportant as the revelers' gossip. The only thing that she knew clearly was that she wanted to feel Eofar's touch, more than the secrets of the ashas, more than a free Shadar, more than living another lonely day.

But longing was an indulgence she couldn't afford, and time was running out. She had to make a choice. If Faroth's mission to the temple met with success, Daryan was almost sure to expose her lies with his usual feckless candor; if not, and she ran now, she would be abandoning her people just when they needed her leadership most. She had to have more information.

The little bottle of elixir she'd taken from Eofar felt warm in her hand. She had no time for indecision; at any moment the women from the party would come looking for her. The time, the place, the circumstances were all wrong, but she'd be the worst kind of fool if she squandered her only chance by waiting for the perfect moment. With a steady hand, she wormed out the stopper and drank the liquid down in one swallow. If history judged Harotha, daughter of Ramesh'Asha, it would not be for a fool.

Chapter Twenty-Six

Undoubtedly the ashas had elaborate rules and caveats for the elixir's use, but as Harotha knew none of them, she just focused her mind on what she wanted to know and waited for something to happen. She was anxious, of course, but she needed to know what to do and she would not allow fear to ruin her only chance to learn what the future had to tell her.

The visions, when they came, were not at all the vague, static images she'd been expecting. Instead, they were whirling, furious things that surrounded and buffeted her. The bright daylight saturated into a storm-driven red as the townscape around her faded into smoky outlines. Hurriedly she slid down from the rock until she felt the relative safety of solid ground beneath her.

Ashen faces streamed past her, shouting, eyes filled with anger and terror. The vision whisked her to a red rock wall set with a small rectangular window, through which she could see ships with storm-torn sails listing in the harbor and a city burning: a city invaded.

"No!" She clenched her fists. "This is wrong—this is the past. This isn't—"

But the vision spun her round into the midst of a furious argument: the ashas, the last ashas. She didn't want to look at their faces, in case her father or mother were among them; it was better not to remember them at all than to remember them like this, on this day—

They were arguing about what to do, she realized. She couldn't hear them properly—their voices sounded thin, far away—but she could read their gestures well enough. Some wanted to go down and fight; others were afraid that their powers over the sands would be useless against the dereshadi.

Then Harotha saw one old priestess take a vial like the one she was still holding and put it to her lips. *The future*, she thought eagerly; they would see it together.

Then she felt herself yanked backward, the scene around her retreated to a speck in a fraction of a heartbeat and she flew backward through time at an impossible speed, years rushing past in an indistinguishable blur. She clenched her teeth and shut her eyes, but it made no difference. The eons screamed by, pulling at her limbs, squashing the breath from her body.

"No!" She forced the word from her lips, fighting against the vision, trying to use her physical reality to swim against the current of time. "This is the wrong way. I need to—"

But as if in answer, she was suddenly struck by the unmistakable feeling of being watched. She opened her eyes. The visions overlaid her reality with their own, but she could see that the street was empty. She understood now that she had no control over what was happening; someone else was deciding what she would be shown. The gods? Were they speaking to her at last? But why would they want to take her so far back?

She shut her eyes again, this time surrendering to the dizzying spectacle. Time slowed and then stopped, and she found herself looking into the mouth of a cave. Her pulse quickened because she recognized the place: it was the cave she had discovered only hours earlier, there was no mistaking it—only now the doorway was wide and tall and open. The vision pulled her inside to a great cavern with a smooth, domed roof painted all over with stars of the night sky: the gods. The beauty of it brought tears to her eyes, but she blinked them away as quickly as she could, because covering the spaces between the stars was writing, actual *writing*. This was not a picture or a map, it was some kind of— She didn't even know what to call it, but her heart faltered in greedy wonder at all of the secrets that were there to be read. When she was finally able to tear her eyes from the ceiling she saw that all around the vast cavern were tables and cases and boxes spilling over with scrolls and papers and pens and ink. It was just like the places Eofar had told her about in Norland, where scholars met to study and debate and write down what they knew for others to read. She had never imagined such a thing had once existed in the Shadar. With a deep pang of regret she wished that Daryan could have been with her to see it, too.

Time jumped again; the scene changed, but not the location. A crowd had gathered in the cavern, but no one was reading or writing now. Grim-faced men and women, even some children, stood in anxious clusters. Some were frightened, or angry; some were weeping. They were ashas, but they weren't like the ashas of Harotha's era: they wore no ceremonial robes, and obviously they did not shut themselves up in the temple, for they were here with their families close around them. She understood intuitively that their powers had not been granted to them in a secret ceremony—they had come by them naturally, just as she had.

She could follow enough of their bitter talk to learn that they had been betrayed by one of their own. They spoke no name, but it was clear that her powers far outstripped their own.

Time began to dash forward again, this time in jerky little jumps through a series of confusing tableaux, but she recognized a war when she saw one. The ashas were battling their betrayer—conspiring, planning and attacking—but each time they were beaten down, their numbers dwindled and their enemy's wrath grew, and harsher punishments were meted out on the despairing cityfolk.

And then she was transported from the beleaguered city to a magnificent, shining palace where she flitted through rooms glowing with color. She was dazzled by gilded and jeweled ornaments, beguiled with richly carved images. She thought she must be in some other country, some place far from the Shadar, until she came to a cavernous rotunda open to the sky and realized with a shock that this palace was the temple. *This is what it was like when it was first built*, she thought. She couldn't conceive of the magnificence and power of the being for whom a citadel like this would be required.

And it was here that the ashas tasted victory at last. The vision coyly refused to show her how they had finally brought it about, but as she followed the ashas out onto the roof the cost of that victory was clear: the city below them lay in ruins. The people limping to the base of the temple were shattered and broken and as they looked up she could see the exhaustion and hopelessness in their faces. They felt no joy at their liberation; only a cringing relief, and they watched their oppressor thrown down from the cliff with dull eyes.

Harotha winced and felt her stomach drop as the figure, indistinct in the bright sun, tumbled through the air, but before the body shattered on the rocks the vision changed and time cranked forward once more.

And now she witnessed the great, impossible lie: the ashas—the few that were left—had only one purpose now, and that was to prevent this horror from ever happening again. Their battle-scars ran so deep that they were unable to stop fighting a war that had already ended, or to see that the real enemy was now their own fear.

From the depth of this fear came the decision to protect the future by erasing the past. Harotha watched with a deep, howling loss as they threw their books and scrolls onto the bonfires, consigning all their knowledge, all the Shadari's history, to the flames. She saw the cave blocked up and the sumptuous walls of the palace blasted bare, until what had once been a mansion become a prison—one without doors or locks—where the inmates thought incarceration the highest of honors. And over the people they set a secular king, to deal with the city's terrestrial affairs.

All this was preparation for the conspiracy of an entire generation to deceive their own descendants: a new initiation rite was invented, ostensibly to confer the power of the gods on those they favored, but whose real purpose was to cull those already so endowed from the rest of the population. These initiates—the ashas—were then schooled in the use of their powers in a manner so ritualized it guaranteed they would never discover their full potential, nor dare to use their powers in any way except in the pre-sanctioned service of the gods. No one person would ever again develop the capability to throttle the nation.

It had all worked perfectly: no one had questioned it, not in all of the generations of Shadari and ashas who came after—until Harotha.

Time wrenched her forward again, moving with bone-crushing force, this time to her parents' time. There was the old priestess, still with the vial to her lips. She drank, and Harotha's vision merged with hers . . .

They saw the city blackened, destroyed, drowning in ash. The temple had been obliterated, nothing left but a pile of rubble. The people were homeless, dying of disease and hunger, and still they were fighting and murdering each other. It was the end of the Shadar and the Shadari—and it was not the Dead Ones who had brought about this terrible future; the damage had been done by one of their own, someone whose power was virtually limitless.

This was precisely what those ancient ashas had tried so hard to prevent: someone rising with power so strong that it could not be contained. Harotha remembered that bright figure, falling in the sun.

As the old priestess spoke, Harotha saw a young man

step forward—and all of her thoughts dried up and blew away.

This man was her father.

He was telling the ashas they had a sacred duty to make sure that not one of their company was left alive with the power to do this terrible thing. The elixir must have shown them this future for this reason: the gods were demanding that they sacrifice themselves.

The ashas listened to him gravely, silently, as Harotha wept furious tears. "No, no," she cried, "they *lied* to us! It's pointless for you to die—you can't stop it that way. I know why you think it has to be one of you here, but you're *wrong*. You're still not the last ones who will have the power. It could be *anyone*! Don't, please, don't do it—!"

And now she was pleading with both the elixir and the ashas as she was forced to watch her father embrace the woman who was her mother. She could hear them beat the drums to summon the people of the city to bear witness. With streaming eyes she watched them all climb out onto the roof and stand on the edge of the cliff, their hair and robes blowing in the cold evening wind.

"Please," she whispered uselessly as the first body fell and the vision shattered into a thousand fragments, then drifted away like embers on the breeze. She sat in the empty street with her back hard against the rock, staring in frantic relief at the dusty houses, the scrubby trees, the pitted road.

"They did it for nothing," she said through clenched teeth. She had watched her parents act nobly, bravely, but that was no comfort. She had always tended a little flame of hope: that if one day she could understand why her parents had killed themselves, she might find some meaning in their deaths. The vision had snuffed out that flame forever. "They died for nothing—because of a lie. They didn't end anything; they didn't change anything. It's still going to happen. It could be anyone." She blanched.

"It's not me—it can't be me," she muttered. She remembered the dune she'd conjured to save Saria and herself from the landslide. She hadn't known she'd had so much power—was it enough to destroy the temple? "I *couldn't*. There has to be another explanation. There has to be someone else."

The baby kicked, and she reflexively crossed her arms over her belly, her eyes fixed on the heat-baked earth. Then she stood up, carefully composed the expression on her face and went back to the party.

Chapter Twenty-Seven

As soon as they heard the shouting outside everyone crowded into the street, and the news tore its way through the throng: Faroth and his men had returned from the temple. Harotha followed along with the rest, painfully aware that she still had not decided whether or not to tell her brother about the elixir and the visions.

There was a shriek of joy and Elthion's mother rushed forward to embrace the tall, skinny man. He pushed her away with a scowl. Harotha could hear the dereshadi snorting and stomping up ahead, and she could hear Faroth's bellowing voice, but her way to him was blocked. Then Sami came pushing toward her through the crowd, his head down.

She caught his arm as he went past. "Sami!"

"Let go," he said dully and tried to pull away, but Harotha held on until he looked at her. When he recognized her, the dark look on his face sagged into something like relief. "Harotha," he confided to her in a low voice, "we didn't get any of them—not one. We couldn't get Dramash away from the White Wolf. We almost had him—I think we could have got him out, if it hadn't been for that last earthquake."

"What earthquake?" she asked. "There haven't been any more since you left for the temple."

But Sami went on as if he hadn't heard her. "Then Daryan refused to come back with us, and just as we were getting ready to leave, Shairav—" He stopped for a moment and swallowed, then whispered, "Harotha, he just *died*. His heart gave out, they said. Dead—just like that. It wasn't Faroth's fault—he did everything he could—but where does this leave us with the Mongrel?" He scowled and shook his head wordlessly, then pulled away from her and disappeared into the crowd.

She pushed her way toward Faroth, a cold knot of anger in the pit of her stomach. "What happened?" she asked. "You couldn't get *any* of them? Not even Daryan?"

"Daryan!" Faroth burst out. "He refused to come. He doesn't give a damn about you, by the way." He was upset and he was trying to make her angry, she knew that. She could see the dark circles under his eyes and the lines of exhaustion around his mouth.

"He knows I can take care of myself," she told him, refusing to take the bait, "but why did he stay behind?"

Someone pressed a jug into Faroth's hands and while he paused to drink deeply, Binit answered for him. "He wants to stop the White Wolf in the temple. No one knows what's going on up there—the governor is dead and the White Wolf has taken over. We think she's already killed Lord Eofar—at least you'll be happy to hear that. She's organizing the soldiers for something, so Daryan stayed behind to try to figure out what they're up to."

"Lord Eofar is dead?" she asked, keeping her voice as steady as she could. "Who said so? Why do you think that?"

"Well," said Binit, sympathetic for all the wrong reasons, "I can't say for sure, but he was supposed to be the next governor, wasn't he? So, how can the White Wolf take over if he's still alive?"

"I never wanted Daryan here in the first place," Faroth said, staring into the distance with smoldering eyes, "but Shairav—it figures he would decide to die just when he might have made himself useful. And he took everything he knew with him."

"Harotha, you don't look well," said Binit. "Maybe you should sit down somewhere?"

"I'm all right," she muttered. They all moved aside to make way for the two nervous dereshadi, who were being led away to a quieter, shady spot. "And Dramash? What happened there?" she asked, unable to keep the harshness from her voice.

"I'll tell you this," Faroth vowed, to no one in particular, "if Daryan comes back here without my son, I don't care who he is—I'll kill him myself."

Alkar came trudging toward them, his maimed hand tucked fastidiously under his opposite arm. "I just talked to Sami," he said to Faroth as he reached them. "He's right about one thing, anyway. They must be planning something up there. There's not a single patrol left anywhere in the Shadar, and no guards at the mines. We've been keeping watch the whole time."

"Maybe the Dead Ones really are going to leave the Shadar," Harotha mused, stroking her bottom lip with the tip of her finger, "just like Saria said."

She became aware of a change in the level of noise around her, a sudden silence, and she looked up to find Faroth staring at her intently. Even before he asked the question, she realized the horrible mistake she had made.

"How did you know Saria said that?"

She twisted her mouth into a derisive grimace. "Oh, these women! They never stop gossiping. I know more than I care to about the last two years—it's no wonder I have a splitting headache."

"Faroth!" a voice cried out from behind them and Elthion came forward, pushing Jachad in front of him. "I found him hanging around—spying."

"Didn't you go back to the desert? Aren't we done with you yet?" snapped Faroth.

"I came back to help, if you want to call that spying," Jachad explained, his breezy manner unaltered by Elthion's rough treatment. "I saw you land. Where is Meiran?"

"Who?"

"The Mongrel."

"Her?" Elthion burst out. "She sent us up there for nothing! It was a trap—I knew it would be. Daryan wouldn't come with us, the White Wolf still has Dramash and Shairav is dead. And she's still up there—she's probably telling the White Wolf everything she wants to know about us."

"Shairav is dead?" Jachad asked. Tension pulled at the Nomas king's usually engaging smile. "How?"

"His heart. It gave out just as we were leaving," Binit repeated, clearly relishing his role as the bearer of bad news.

"Oh, how sad. I'm sorry to hear that," Jachad answered, but Harotha wasn't fooled by his attempt to sound sympathetic. She could tell he was relieved.

"You're the one who told us to go up there," Faroth said to Jachad. "Well, we failed—so now what? What does the Mongrel expect us to do? If this has all been some kind of trick, we'll kill you, even if you burn us all alive while we do it."

"Faroth," she broke in, taking his arm. She tried to draw him aside, but there was no place to go; the crowd had been steadily gathering around them and now people pushed in on all sides, waiting to hear what Faroth had to say. "I think we're missing something. Why did the White Wolf take Dramash? She's never done anything like that before. There has to be a reason."

"It's obvious," said Elthion, with a haughty wave of his hand. "The White Wolf knows about the rebellion now, and she knows Faroth is our leader. She took Dramash to get at him. She knows she's losing her grip. She's desperate."

Harotha stared hard at Elthion and then looked at her brother. "That makes no sense. It's ridiculous."

"It's true!" Alkar said, daring her to challenge him. He raised his voice to address the crowd at large. "The White Wolf killed Faroth's wife and took his child! It's true, the White Wolf is afraid of Faroth!" A murmur of excitement, of pride, swept through the crowd.

She pressed her fingers to her throbbing temples and asked her brother in an incredulous whisper, "You don't really believe that, do you?"

Sharp fingers gripped her shoulder: Trini was standing next to her, frowning, with a basket of bread under her arm. "Come with me, girl, and let the men have their talk," the older woman insisted, none too gently. "There's better things—"

"Take your hands off me!" Harotha exploded in frustration, jerking away. She spun back to her brother. "Faroth, don't be a fool! The White Wolf didn't take Dramash because of *you*. To her, you're nothing more than another worthless Shadari cripple."

Even as the words left her mouth Harotha knew she'd made another dreadful mistake.

Faroth stared at her with a terrible look on his face as a deadly silence swept over the crowd.

"Bread! Thank goodness. I'm starving!" Jachad cried. He scooped the basket of bread away from Trini with one hand and with the other he took Harotha's elbow and turned her smoothly around. A moment later, she found herself strolling with the Nomas king toward the same large flat rock that had offered her refuge earlier in the day. She was sickeningly aware of the way the other Shadari subtly retreated before them.

"Bread?" he asked, pushing her gently down onto the rock, then sitting down next to her. He proffered the piece he'd just torn from one of the loaves.

She took the bread without a word and looked at it. The thought of eating turned her stomach.

"I don't suppose I'm doing you any great favor, sitting here with you," he said as his shrewd eyes took in every hostile glance cast in their direction, "but I didn't like the way that conversation was tending and I thought it might be prudent to end it."

"Thank you," she said, matching his tone. He was

right, of course, on both counts. He had rescued her when her own presence of mind had failed, but now his companionship was arousing more suspicion, even among those who hadn't heard what she'd said to Faroth. She should go, find some way to repair the damage she'd done, but she didn't have the energy. The teetering structure of pretense she had built for herself was ready to topple over, and she was afraid that she no longer had the strength to keep it up.

She looked over at the redheaded king sitting beside her, contentedly chewing his bread. She had a feeling that pretense was useless with him; she felt like he could see straight through her. She had been raised to believe that the Nomas never gave away anything for free, but she had a hard time believing that he expected anything from her in return for his friendship. And so they sat together in silence, idly watching people bustling in and out of the houses or moving purposefully up and down the street.

Eventually she forced herself to take a bite of the bread in her hand. The sun would be setting soon and she couldn't remember the last time she'd eaten. She squinted up at the fiery orange disk hanging over the mountains. "Do you really believe the sun is your father?" she asked, breaking the silence.

He turned to her. "That's not the kind of question I'd expect from a Shadari," he said, arching his eyebrows. "Do you really want to know?"

"Yes, I really want to know."

"Then, yes, I do."

She thought for a moment. "And does he answer your prayers? Does he tell you what he wants from you?"

"Ah, now that," he said sagely, "is exactly the kind of question I'd expect from a Shadari. You have a very complicated relationship with your gods, you know that? Ours is much simpler. Our gods don't want anything in particular from us, and we don't expect them to pay us any special attention."

"You don't believe that your gods have some purpose for your life?"

"If they do, that's their business. We're a practical people, and most of us feel that trying to know the unknowable is pretty much a waste of time. We'd rather try to solve the problems nearer at hand."

"But you pray."

"Oh, yes," he agreed. "Shof gives us light and warmth; that's reason enough to be grateful, isn't it? But we don't believe that he requires our worship to climb into the sky each morning. That would be tremendously arrogant, don't you think? And as you can see, he shines just as brightly on those who don't pray to him at all. Frankly, I don't have too much respect for gods who love only one group of people and let the others go hang."

"So, do you think that the gods can be cruel?" she asked, keeping her tone light. She took another bite of bread.

He surprised her by considering her question with absolute seriousness, frowning in a thoughtful way that changed his face completely. His eyes took on a distant look. "Yes, I do. By mortal standards, anyway."

She forced the bread down her dry throat. "So what are we supposed to do then?"

"Well, I think the worst thing you can do to gods is to stop believing in them." He peered up at the sky, then he grinned at her, and the clouds left his eyes. "But I wouldn't be too hasty. It's not so easy to tell the difference between what the gods have done, and what has simply been blamed on them. I've met a lot of people in a lot of places who claim to speak for the gods. Personally, I've never understood why people believe them, but many do."

She thought about the elixir. What did she really know about it? How could she be sure the visions came from the gods when everything else she had ever been told about her religion had turned out to be a lie?

"Are you married, King Jachad?"

He gave a rueful little laugh. "Now you sound like a Nomas—like my mother, to be precise. No, I'm not married."

"Is it because of her—the Mongrel?"

The Nomas king turned sharply to her, and she could see that her question had both surprised and disarmed him. "Yes. I suppose you could say that," he answered. His eyes held a curious intensity. "You are an extraordinary woman, do you know that? You certainly don't miss much."

"It's in your voice, when you speak of her. The way you say her name," she explained, uncomfortable with the compliment, if it had been one. A breeze, the first harbinger of evening, rustled the hair around her face. "You're bound to her somehow."

"That's one way to put it—though it's probably not in the way you think."

Apparently he was not inclined to explain further, and the companionable silence returned. She let her mind drift, not thinking about anything in particular. She could feel herself on the edge of some crucial understanding; instinct told her that if she pursued it too vigorously, it would slip away.

A dove's mournful cry sounded from a drooping palm tree nearby. Its mate fluttered over in a whir of wings.

"There were two earthquakes," she said. "Not three."

Jachad looked over at her. "That's right."

"You're sure?"

"Quite sure. A smallish one, and then the big one just after sunset last night. I'm not likely to forget either of them any time soon, believe me."

"But nothing after that. Nothing at all—no aftershocks, even."

"That's right," he agreed again. There was curiosity in his voice, but it wasn't his way to question her. "I heard about what happened at the mines after the second earthquake," he offered a few moments later. "It sounds quite extraordinary: hundreds of miners were trapped in the collapse, and then the shaft just suddenly opened up. No one knows how." His blue eyes fixed on her. "They're calling it a miracle. And it happened just before Frea took off with Dramash."

Harotha reached up and rubbed her cheek. Suddenly she could feel the imprint of Saria's fingers there as if her sister-in-law had slapped her no more than a moment ago. But Saria was dead. *Maybe when you're a mother, you'll understand*: Saria's last words to her before she ran after Dramash—her son. *Faroth's* son. The last in a line of ashas stretching as far back in time as the elixir's stream had carried her.

Jachad stood up from the rock and stretched languorously. "I'm not used to sitting for so long. I think I'll go for a walk."

The street had emptied out again as Faroth and his friends had moved inside his house, pointedly excluding Harotha from the meeting. Smoke wound up from the chimneys and the familiar scents of homely cooking drifted by on the steadily cooling air.

She stood up as well. "I'll go with you."

By mutual accord they turned right, walking away from Faroth's house, and when they came to a crossing, they turned left, again by unspoken agreement.

"Careful," Jachad murmured as he steered her around a trench in the road that looked as if it might have been dug out by a large, clawed foot.

"Just to be clear," she began. She glanced at her companion as they walked along in the fading light. Both of them had subtly quickened their pace. "We're going to find those two dereshadi Faroth brought back, take one and fly it back to the temple, yes?"

Again she found herself caught in his deep blue eyes; at this moment she could truly believe that his father was the sun. He had warmth banked down inside of him, an unending and limitless supply, and it radiated out from his gently conspiratorial smile. "Of course we are," he agreed. "Isn't that what we've been talking about?"

Chapter Twenty-Eight

A voice ordered Rho to wake up, and nothing would have given him greater pleasure than to obey—he tried to say this, but the voice had already become just another random detail in the jumbled landscape of his nightmare. He was in a forest with a little curly-haired Shadari boy, and they climbed a tree, only now the boy was his brother, Trey.

<You're not Trey,> Rho told the boy. <Trey's dead. He died hunting, a month after I left Norland.>

<Isn't this Norland?> asked the boy. They were sitting side by side on a broad branch, and when Rho looked down he saw not a forest floor but a mountainside sloping away from him, all jagged rocks under a blanket of new snow. The boy who was and wasn't Trey stood up and began jumping up and down on the branch. Rho wanted him to stop—he was afraid, but he found that he could neither speak nor move; all the while the boy was laughing out loud and jumping, jumping and laughing. He heard the cracking sound as the branch began to break, but it wasn't the branch that was cracking, it was the dark Norland sky, slicing open to reveal a zigzag of blinding light—

<Rho. Wake up.> The voice had returned, and it was hard and cold. Gratefully, he grabbed on to it and rode it back to consciousness. He became aware of his limbs, of the dampness of sweat on his skin. The familiar

lumpiness of the mattress underneath him told him that he was back in his own room. He blinked his scratchy eyes until he could see again.

He turned his head and saw a black-gloved fist dart out and flick up his shirt to expose his wound. The warm air hit his sore flesh like a handful of sand.

<That sword was a piece of junk. It's not healing right. You may have a scar.> Frea's finger traced the long line of the gash. He could not feel her touch in any one place; the whole wound pulsed and throbbed as one. She was right: the cut had not closed cleanly, despite Daem's efforts. Where was Daem, anyway? And Ingeld and Ongen, where were they? <Lucky for you I'm past caring about that sort of thing. I came to ask you something.> He felt the pressure of her hand where it had come to rest on his hip. <Do you want to go back to Norland?>

He dragged his eyes up to her face and saw that she was wearing the silver helmet. If he'd had the strength, he would have ripped the thing off her head. <What I wanted never mattered to you before,> he reminded her.

She withdrew her hand and paced around his bed. He forced himself to sit up, clenching his teeth against the pain screaming from his side. The room was empty except for the two of them, but he had no doubt the Shadari boy was somewhere close by.

<You don't belong here,> she said. <You're an Arregador; you were a palace guard at Ravindal. Your clan ranks almost as high as the Eotan. How did you end up here?>

A scrap of memory floated through his mind: walking Ravindal's battlements on a seamless Norland night, listening to the wolves howl, breathing in the cozy scent of wood fires on the sharp air, watching the lights from the town of Ravinsur twinkling far below. He had been alone then, but not lonely, not like now. <I got bored watching my brothers kill each other,> he told her.

<They let me name my father's sword. And I'm still alive. I suppose I should be grateful.>

<And are you? Grateful?>

He noticed the jug of wine she had presumably brought for him left out on the table. Beads of sweat rolled lazily down its side. <No. No, I'm not grateful.> He pushed himself away from the bed and let momentum carry him to the table. He fell heavily onto the nearest chair. The jug was cool against his palms as he lifted it up and drank greedily.

Frea circled around to the opposite side of the table and jerked another chair underneath her. <I've ordered the men to assemble in the armory. I'm going there now, to address them.> She paused for a moment, watching him drink, and then flicked her white braids back across her shoulder. <I sent a patrol out over the ocean with our best spyglass—the emperor's ship will be here tomorrow. I'm going back to Norland, Rho, and I want you with me. I want you by my side.>

<*Me?*> he asked. He looked over the rim of the jug at his reflection in her helmet. <You've got Ingeld to lick your boots now—why would you want me?>

<Because you're smart,> she said.

Rho wasn't flattered; intelligence was a quality she neither liked nor admired. At the same time, he couldn't help but notice the way her left hand rested on the table, with her white wrist visible between the top of her gloves and the sleeve of her shirt, and he found himself staring fixedly at that sliver of naked flesh.

<You know things I need to know,> she was saying, <like the layout of Ravindal. Defenses. Defenders. And you know about the boy.>

<What boy?> he asked.

Her warning slapped into his mind, but he didn't flinch. Whatever she was planning, it had put her in a position he had never believed possible: Frea needed him.

<How many of the palace guards have imperial swords?> she asked.

<By the time I left, nearly everyone from the higher clans—even my little cousin Uhlen had one when he came up to court. It was bigger than he was. I remember Prince Clovis complaining that family swords were starting to go unnamed.>

<That magician—the one who brought the ore to the empire, all those years ago. Where did he come from? What happened to him?>

There was a sour taste in the back of Rho's mouth and he took another swig of wine. <He must be dead by now.>

<Before that.>

<The story I heard, he showed up in Ravinsur, just a street performer. He was sprinkling black dust on things and making them move around. The emperor—well, I suppose he was only king then, not emperor—heard about it. He had the man brought to Ravindal.>

<But he was a Shadari, wasn't he? A priest—an exile?>

<He must have been, although until then we barely knew the Shadar existed. I don't know how the emperor figured out about the blood and the swords, but we attacked right after that.> Rho reached across the table and ran his fingers lightly over Frea's wrist. To his surprise, she didn't pull away. Slowly, he pushed the sleeve of her shirt further up her forearm. <I heard the emperor kept him alive in the dungeons with some kind of magic, but I don't know why he would do that once he knew about the ore. I don't know how true any of it is—we're not supposed to talk about it. I don't think the emperor wants people remembering that we have one starving street magician to thank for our great and glorious empire.>

He was stroking her forearm, lightly but insistently, and he saw her fingers move, responding to his touch. Then she stood up suddenly, knocking the table, and he caught the jug just before it fell. Wine sloshed over his hands and ran onto the table and the floor.

Frea looked down at him. Her words fell softly into his mind: the stillness of a frozen lake, a moonless winter night. <Are you with me, Rho?>

And then she told him her plan, and he marveled at how badly he'd underestimated her ambition. He had thought only of the damage the boy's power could do in the Shadar, but Frea had seen beyond that: she had seen a weapon that could turn other weapons against those who wielded them. Her genius for mayhem took his breath away.

<It wouldn't be very smart of me to say no, would it, my Lady?> He held the jug of wine out to her, keeping his hand steady even though a red mist swam up in front of his eyes from the pain jabbing at his side.

Frea took the jug and drained it to the bottom.

Chapter Twenty-Nine

They landed on the roof instead of in the stables: Harotha's idea. Jachad had never driven a triffon before—if that was even the right term—but he followed the same advice he had given the Shadari and tried to do as little as possible. To keep himself from thinking about the ground far below them, he'd told Harotha a tall tale about how his third cousin's wife had given birth to her son in a crow's nest in the middle of a gale, with a gull for a midwife and the ship's flag for swaddling. Harotha had laughed and then in her calm, competent manner pointed the way to a well-concealed trapdoor and a staircase that, judging by the dust, hadn't been used in decades. She didn't tell him how she had found out about it, and he didn't ask.

He should have asked her to stay with him a little longer—at least until he had his bearings—but she'd gone her own way as soon as they breached the temple without giving any indication of her destination or her intentions. So now she was gone and he was lost—and he badly needed to find Meiran, because the moment he'd heard of Shairav's death, he'd known something had gone very wrong.

He turned another corner to find corridors branching out on both sides, blank walls vanishing into darkness. He looked back the way he had come: nothing but darkness. The air was stifling, making it hard for him to think clearly, but he took a deep breath and tried to dispel the panic that was beginning to prick at him. He'd always hated the temple, and never more than at this moment.

As he hesitated, he heard a rustling sound from somewhere behind him and he slipped back into the shadows, pressing his back up against the wall. A few moments later a Shadari woman passed by, moving quickly and keeping close to the wall. She was cradling a largish jar protectively against her chest. For lack of a better plan, he decided to follow her; wherever she was headed, she meant to get there fast and that was good enough for him.

He followed her carefully, waiting for her to turn each corner before dashing forward, peering ahead and then waiting again, all the while looking for some familiar object or mark. All of the walls and doorways looked the same—so it came as a shock when the next corner revealed the woman not six feet away, speaking furtively to a group of four or five Shadari men. Just beyond them loomed one of the entrances to the stables. If the rest of the temple felt empty, it was because everyone appeared to be there; he could see the great cavern ablaze with light and swarming with activity.

"I think it's all right," he heard one of the Shadari say. "So many soldiers came in at once they never noticed the place was unguarded. Good thing you thought to move the bodies of those guards when you did, Omir."

"How close are they to flying out?" asked someone else.

"We have some time. The dereshadi are still being fed and watered, and the saddles haven't even been brought down yet—it must be hard to get so many ready without Shairav. He would have—" The speaker broke off abruptly. "I'm sorry. I—"

"No, no—it's all right," said the other speaker. "That big pile on the other side, that's the one. It's nice and dry. If we get enough oil on that, it'll go up fast."

"Will the fire be enough to make the dereshadi bolt?"

"I think so—there's no way to know for sure, but we've been over this already and no one's come up with a better idea, have they? The White Wolf is planning something big and we've got to stop her, or at least slow her down. All right, give me the jar, I'll do it."

"No, Daryan—one of those soldiers might recognize you as Lord Eofar's servant. I'll take it."

Jachad heard the other man laugh warmly. "Omir, you're a lot of things, but inconspicuous isn't one of them."

Daryan? Startled, he took a closer look. He had seen Daryan many times during his previous trips to the temple, and he would never have guessed that confident voice had come from Eofar's unassuming, spiritless servant. Here was another change—and changes were crowding in thick and fast, every place he looked, affecting everyone he met. He suddenly remembered a play he'd seen once at Prol Irat: with no warning, and for no apparent reason, the principal actor had abruptly left the stage. The other actors, completely at a loss, had stayed in their places, marking time: the scribe kept on writing his letter, his head bent low over his desk; the young girl with a heap of sewing in her lap stitched, and stitched, and stitched, her cheeks burning with embarrassment; the stony-eyed servant stood mutely beside his master's empty chair, awaiting his command. Ever since Meiran had left the Nomas, his life had been trapped in that same tense, endless pause, and now he realized for the first time that he was not the only one. The actor had returned to the stage at last, and now the play rushed on.

"I stole the oil. I'll do the rest, too," the woman offered. There were protests, more volunteers, but Jachad turned his attention away: he was now fairly certain he knew where he was, and he was just about to go when he heard something that shifted his attention back to the Shadari.

"When is the Mongrel supposed to be here?"

"She said before sundown, so she should have been here already," Daryan said anxiously. "Isa and Eofar should have been here by now, too. The Mongrel's supposed to draw the guards away so they can escape without being seen. If she doesn't come, we'll have to think of something else."

"The White Wolf may have already have found them. They may already be dead."

"No, they're not. I don't know about the Mongrel, but Eofar and Isa are on their way, I know it. You'll just have to trust me."

Jachad didn't wait to hear the rest. The Shadari had confirmed his misgivings: all was not going according to Meiran's plan. He went quickly, sure of the route now. A few moments later he was standing in Shairav's chambers, staring down at the corpse laid out on the bed.

The old man had been arranged with the utmost decorum: hands folded, eyes closed, brow smooth and composed. Even in death his mouth had set in its typical self-satisfied line. Jachad had been in this chamber many times before, taking orders from Shairav for rugs, cushions, urns, ornaments; he'd stand in the doorway making small-talk while the old man counted out his payment. He remembered the effort it took to keep his broad smile from slipping as he imagined the coins tossed so carelessly into his hand steeped in Meiran's blood. He remembered how badly he had wanted to clasp his burning hands around the old priest's throat and make him beg for the mercy he'd never offered her.

With a disgusted breath, he puffed out the flame in his hand. He had already noted the bar of light in the corner and he knew what it signified. He made his way to the opening and slid through—and stopped short.

He let out a low whistle. The chamber looked as if it had been torn apart by wild dogs. Every object had been smashed, crushed or pulled to bits, every scrap of cloth ripped to shreds. Dolls' heads, bodies, arms and legs were bleeding out their sandy innards among the broken furniture. A puddle of flaming oil from an overturned lamp was slowly spreading outward across the floor. He hurried to stomp out the wayward flames.

"Don't do that." Her low voice came from just behind him, but when he spun around, he couldn't see anyone. "Doesn't Shof love fire? Wouldn't he like to see it all burn?"

Finally he found her sitting with her back up against the wall, surrounded by the wreckage. She'd pushed the patch up onto her forehead and her mismatched eyes were swollen and bloodshot. He stamped out the last few flames, then carefully righted the still-burning lamp and sat down on the bed. He watched her in silence for a long moment. Her face looked strangely naked in the low light; the gentle flickering smoothed over her scars and it was if the years had been wound back, as if everything that had happened to her, everything she'd done, had been erased. And he was surprised to find he didn't like it—he had come to see the scars as a part of her; without them, she seemed incomplete. He found the realization disturbing, and wondered which of them it said more about.

Suddenly a memory whisked him away to the desert nights of his youth, to the tent he and Meiran had shared, to the stillness that descended after the voices and music of the Nomas had been replaced by the lonely sound of the tent-ropes singing in the cold wind, and to the memory of pretending to sleep so that he might watch her staring up at the brightly-striped cloth rippling above their heads. Her face, her expression—they had been just the same all those years ago, and just like then, he wished he could go to her and stroke her dark hair and lie with her until those depthless, mismatched eyes finally found sleep.

He picked up a wooden sword and toyed with it aimlessly, until at last he asked, "Are you all right?"

Her eyes lost focus. "I'm tired, Jachi."

He rubbed his forehead and huffed out a long sigh. "Why don't you go home, then?" he suggested.

"Isn't that what I've done?"

"Not here." He stood up and hurled the wooden sword across the room. It made a satisfying crash as it banged into the wall and rattled to the floor. "I mean *home*—with me. In the desert." He clasped his fingers behind his neck and shut his eyes, trying not to sound pleading as he said, "Leave it, Meiran. Whatever it is, whatever you came here for, just leave it. Come home with me—tonight. Mother is there. She's crazy to see you, you know."

"Nisha?" she asked, with just the hint of a plaintive look in her eyes.

"She's waiting with the others, just on the other side of those mountains. Meiran, let's get out of this—this damned tomb."

She stood up to meet him, but it was a lurching movement, starkly at odds with her usual grace.

"Are you all right?" he asked again, and this time the question was not rhetorical; as she reached up and pulled the eye-patch down over the Norlander eye he caught sight of her bloody knuckles and the fresh scrapes on her forearms. But the cuts weren't the cause of her shallow breathing, or the tension throbbing in her neck and shoulders; she was in pain.

His eyes searched for the bulge of the flask under her vest. "Where's your medicine?"

"Gone."

"Is there more somewhere?"

She gasped out a ragged laugh. "No."

"Meiran." His hand just brushed her arm. "Come on. Let's go."

"All right," she said, then added, "to the Shadar. Not the desert."

"The Shadar? Why?" he demanded. "What for?"

She stared mutely back at him, unblinking, as silent as a stone.

"Oh, for Shof's sake," he cried, "Eonar is dead. Shairav is dead. That's enough death, isn't it, even for you?"

A hostile spark flashed in her brown eye and she moved her arm away from him. He flushed and felt the warmth of flames tickling over his palms. He was angry with her—and angry with himself, too, though he didn't know why. "You don't even seem surprised to see me here, after you left me behind. Aren't you at all interested in how I got here?"

"Isn't that what you do?" she asked, as she moved away from the wall. She kicked a broken chair out of her way. "Follow me around?"

Fury burned in his chest like acid. He tried to control himself as she disappeared through the doorway, but a moment later he went charging after her. He needed to confront her, to make her tell him what she wanted here, or he'd force her hand one way or the other. If she meant to hurt someone, anyone, he would stop her.

But when he came through the doorway, he found her collapsed over a chair, convulsing, fighting for air.

"I can't breathe," she choked out. She was shivering violently, but when he gathered her into his arms, her skin was as dry as paper and much too hot. He settled her down in the chair and looked around for water, but he couldn't see a jug or waterskin anywhere. The sight of the impassive corpse infuriated him, setting flames dancing in his hands. He snuffed out the fire with a clench of his fists and grabbed a blanket from a nearby chest.

"Here," he said, wrapping her up. She had stopped convulsing, but her stillness was more like paralysis than ease. In the faint light shining in from the other room he could see that her eyes were squeezed shut and her mouth was open. Each breath was a tiny moan of pain.

He found her sudden and total vulnerability unbearable. "Some interesting things are happening up here," he babbled, trying to overlay the sound of her torment with his gossipy chatter, as if the two of them were lounging in a tavern over a carafe of wine. He wanted to rid himself of the image of her tortured face, but it hung there in the darkness in front of him, full of reproach. "The Shadari are determined to keep Frea in the temple, at least for tonight—sounded to me like they're planning to light a fire in the stables and frighten the triffons into bolting before she can leave, which is not a bad idea. But they're going to help Eofar and Isa escape first, isn't that odd? I suppose that's Daryan's doing. I'm surprised he's so loyal to Eofar, but maybe that was Harotha's idea. It was certainly brave of her, flying back here with me, but I think she may be too courageous for her own good. I hope she gets out with Eofar—I don't like to think of her trapped up here—but I'm afraid she might not leave without Dramash. You remember him, don't you, from the tavern? Cute little thing; a little precocious, maybe. I sort of had an idea that he might—" He stopped as he felt a tug at his waist.

He turned to see Meiran, patch down over her brown eye now, pulling his long Nomas knife from its scabbard.

"Oh, *come on*, I just got that back from Harotha—can't you women get your own knives?" he complained, but his forced humor was nothing but bravado. Her silver-green eye held a wild urgency that he'd never seen before, and it terrified him.

"She won't take him away from me," she vowed. "He's *mine*. No one will take him from me." With his knife clutched in her hand she ran from the chamber and out into the hallway.

Jachad shut his gaping mouth with a snap and scrambled after her.

Chapter Thirty

"We can't wait any longer."

"I know."

"You've done all you can. Lord Eofar's dereshadi is saddled and waiting. There's still a chance they could get out. Or maybe they found some other way—"

"I know," Daryan repeated wretchedly. Omir was watching him. After a few moments, he finally forced himself to nod. "All right," he said, swallowing against the lump in his throat. "Does everyone know the signal?"

"I think so."

"I hope so," he murmured. He narrowed his eyes and looked through the doorway into the stables. "We've only got one chance at this; we all have to move at the same time." He turned to the slaves huddled together in the hallway, just a handful of the men and women Omir had mobilized in their cause; dozens more waited outside the other entrances to the stables. He looked at their solemn, scared faces, at the sad collection of tools and equipment they'd scrounged in place of weapons, and prayed that he wouldn't let them down. He was no leader. They deserved someone much better, but he couldn't tell them that. He had already learned that Shairav had been right about one thing, at least: the Shadari did need their daimon. If he could make up for a lifetime of failures and missed opportunities by claiming a confidence he didn't really feel, then so be it.

He straightened up and took a deep breath—

"Wait!" a voice called out behind him, and Daryan spun around. Someone was coming from the other end of the dark hallway, and he craned his neck to see over the heads of the Shadari. The voice called out again, "I know what you're about to do, but you need to wait."

"Who is that?" he called back, wondering why his heart was suddenly thudding in his chest. He started toward the speaker, pushing his way through the crowd, his palms clammy. Even before he'd really seen her, he'd broken into a run.

He'd had this dream before: it's all a mistake, she isn't dead, she's right there and he runs to embrace her—but even as he holds her, the flesh rots and drops from her bones, the bones turn to dust and the dust chokes him until he wakes up alone on his hard pallet with his pulse racing and his body sheeted with sweat.

But not this time: he felt the weight of her body against him, warm and solid and undeniably real. "Harotha," he cried, breathing in the scent of her hair, a scent that he had forgotten until this very moment, but one that instantly evoked a hundred different memories of her.

An alarm went off inside him: something important, something he needed to remember, and as her arms came around him and returned his embrace, he remembered what it was.

"I'm so angry at you, I could kill you," he whispered into her ear. He leaned back and gazed for a moment at her round-cheeked face, then he bent down and kissed her deeply.

She tensed in his embrace, then she, too, remembered and returned his kiss with equally feigned ardour. Around them, people were repeating her name with varying degrees of surprise, until Omir succinctly recounted the story Faroth had told him earlier: how Harotha and Daryan had been married in secret some months ago, and how she had been hiding in the temple until yesterday.

With a tremendous effort of will Daryan broke off the kiss, putting aside the heady sensations of the softness of her lips, the warmth of her skin. "I'll explain everything later," he told his followers. His voice sounded husky, strange. "Just give us a moment alone, will you?"

The Shadari murmured knowingly before moving along the corridor.

He guided Harotha back into the shadows. "What are you doing here? How the hell did you get here?" He felt like his nerves would snap at any moment.

"The same way Faroth did, on a stolen dereshadi," she told him in her low, steady voice, "only I landed on the roof instead of in the stables."

"The roof?" he repeated, blinking in confusion. "The roof—all right then. You can go back the way you came. How do you get up there? I'll take you."

But she was shaking her head. "It's too late. The dereshadi got away from us while we were trying to tie her up. She's probably back in her berth in the stables by now."

"*Us?*"

"King Jachad came with me—but never mind that, I don't have time to explain any of it right now. We have to—"

"But why are you here?" he demanded again. *Did she really think she wouldn't need to explain?* "Do you have any idea what's been happening up here?"

Her mouth hardened; he knew that impatient frown all too well. "That's what I'm trying to tell you—if you'll let me finish."

He stared at her in disbelief: here she was, the same old Harotha, not softened one bit by her pregnancy. The resentment that had been stewing inside him ever since he'd learned of her deception began to boil up. "I don't know why I'm surprised," he said, "because this is just like you. You couldn't just stay in the Shadar and let me handle things up here, could you? Haven't you put Eofar through enough misery already? Do you have any idea how upset he'll be if he finds out you're here?"

"Eofar is all right then?" She tried to keep her voice low, but when she grabbed his hand he felt her pulse thudding through her fingers. "He's still alive?"

He looked down into her glistening eyes. "You know, I don't think I really believed it, not until just now. You and Eofar—after everything you said about them. The way you acted when I told you that Eofar was my friend—"

"I'm not going to explain myself to you." Her face flushed, but she was as composed and uncompromising as always: the Harotha who made him feel small. "I can understand why you're angry, but I can't do anything about that right now. Do you want to stop the White Wolf or don't you?"

"You know I do."

"Then listen to me, I've been spying on her for the last hour: her men have cleaned out the armory and raided the storerooms. She's rounded up anyone who might still challenge her authority, even Eonar's physics, and locked them in the lower levels. What we need to do is—"

"I know all that. We already have a plan. Everyone's already in position."

"That doesn't matter. The only way—"

"Yes, it does matter." He backed away from her as he realized that she expected him to do whatever she wanted—to do as he was told—without questioning her. Worse, she expected him to be grateful that she was here to take charge of the situation. He swallowed his anger—this was neither the time nor the place for a confrontation—and repeated, "We have a plan, Harotha, a good one. It might not be perfect, but we're going through with it. You can't just turn up here and—"

"Daimon!" Omir called out from the end of the hall.

"Daryan," Harotha started, and as he looked at her he realized he had nothing more to say.

He reached out to stroke her hair, years of gnarled, unspoken feelings contained in that one awkward gesture. "Hide," he told her. "Go and hide. If you care anything about Eofar or that baby, hide until we can find some way to get you out."

Then he pelted over to Omir and the others waiting near the doorway. Even in the torchlight, he could see that Omir's face had gone pale.

"I'm sorry, Daimon, but she's here. It has to be now."

He clenched his jaw tight, even as fear squeezed his chest. Harotha would do just as she pleased; he knew that. There was nothing more he could do for her now. He lifted the nearest torch from its bracket in the wall.

"All right, then," he told his comrades, taking a moment to look at each resolute face. "Here we go."

Harotha felt a cold lump of shame hardening in her chest as she watched him hurry back to Omir and the others. She could still feel the unexpected touch of his hand on her head, but the tenderness of the gesture did nothing to soften the truth: the puppyish adoration he'd once had for her was gone. Somehow he'd become aware of his role as a toy or a tool, something to be picked up when she needed and discarded when she did not. Though she'd always urged him to defy Shairav, to make a stand, she had never really believed that he could amount to anything more than the puppet king he had always been. And now, somehow, he knew that.

She ran her thumb along her bottom lip. There was no help for it. She'd have to rescue Dramash on her own. Her nephew was the key; she was certain of it, and she had to get him back before the White Wolf forced him to carry out the horrors she had seen in her visions. If she could stop this, then the sacrifice of the ashas would still count for something. They wouldn't have died in vain, because their deaths would have led her to this.

She had only a few moments to come up with a plan before Daryan and his friends began their attack. Once they lit that fire, the White Wolf would be on her guard and getting to Dramash then would be impossible. But the fire itself—that would be the perfect distraction. As soon as they lit it, she could dart out and grab him. She still didn't know how she was going to get him out of the temple, but if she could find the location of the ashas' secret door, with what she knew now . . .

She forced her heavy body into a run. Her hands were trembling and she was feeling dizzy. She knew she'd been foolish not to eat and sleep when she'd had the chance; it was too late now. *Too late, too late*: her footsteps beat out the rhythm as she ran. There was a small, easily overlooked doorway leading in to the eastern end of the stables which should put her quite close to Frea, who was bound to be keeping Dramash close.

She concentrated on the turns: left, round some rubble from a wall damaged in the earthquakes, past a basket of laundry dumped out on the floor. Now to the right. The geography of the temple hadn't changed and yet everything felt odd and unfamiliar, like a place she'd heard about in a story or seen in a dream. She slipped down a hallway so narrow that she could touch the walls on either side. The stench of the dereshadi rolled over her and her stomach muscles heaved at the assault; she steeled her nerves and looked out into the stables.

She saw Dramash at once, less than a dozen paces away. He was standing at the White Wolf's side, balancing impatiently first on one foot, then the other. She could see no signs of injury. He wasn't tied up or restrained in any way—he didn't even look frightened. She had heard him say he wanted to be a soldier when he grew up, and now here he was: the White Wolf's protégé. At least Saria wasn't alive to see it.

Suddenly a wave of nausea hit her with such intensity that she had to lean against the rough wall behind her for support. A dreadful clammy feeling crawled over her skin, and once again her hands tingled numbly. An image of Saria lying on the ground, her hair matted with blood, flew into her mind, and she shut her eyes tightly against the image. She couldn't give in to grief or fear now. Saria had died trying to protect her son and Harotha had failed her sister-in-law then. She mustn't fail her now.

Once she had slowed her racing heart she looked out into stables again. Whatever Frea had in mind apparently required the support of the entire garrison; it looked like most of the soldiers were here, and they were far more heavily armed than usual. Most were wearing their white cloaks, even though the night was only a few hours old, so they obviously expected to be out for a long time. Many of the soldiers carried filled sacks—supplies, maybe. Almost all of the dereshadi had been coaxed down and were shambling sleepily among the stacked bales of fodder, wagging their massive heads, leaving barely enough space for the slaves to walk between them. It looked like the Dead Ones were preparing for a journey—except for the obvious fact that there was no place for them to go except the desert or the sea.

She couldn't see Daryan, so she moved to the other side of the hallway to get a broader view. Something must have delayed him. She peered across the cavern, looking for a finger of smoke, the glow of fire.

One of the soldiers had been talking to Frea; now he walked up to a slave no more than a few paces from her hiding-place. As she shrank back against the wall, the Dead One said out loud, "Find Shairav. Lady Frea wants him. These triffons should have been saddled and ready by now."

"Yes, sir," the slave agreed rapidly, and then melted into the crowd. As the soldier turned back to the White Wolf, Harotha saw his face. She recognized him at once despite the colorful bruises: Rho was one of the few Dead Ones who spoke Shadari. He was also Frea's lover.

Dramash walked up to Rho as casually as if the two of them were old friends. "Are we going soon?" he asked.

"Soon," said Rho.

"Are we coming right back after we get Mama?"

The soldier hesitated. "I don't know."

"Can I ride with you this time? Will you let me hold the reins?"

Rho hesitated even longer this time. "I'll ask."

Harotha's hands tightened into fists. *Now*, she thought, as loudly as she could, hoping Daryan could hear her somehow. *Send them now—please! He's so close . . .*

For one heady moment she thought that her plea had been answered. There was a definite change inside the stables, a sudden hush, and she caught the flare of a torch moving among the dereshadi and the hay-bales. A heartbeat later, she saw the torch-bearer emerge from the crowd.

It was Daryan himself.

She bit her lip angrily. How careless of him, to expose himself like this. He should have lit the fire from the other side, where the Dead Ones wouldn't have seen him—

But as she watched, stupefied, he passed by the pile of hay-bales and walked straight up to Frea. He stopped little more than a sword's-length away from her and said, "Shairav isn't coming." He held his head high and he spoke using his full voice, not with the whispers of a slave. "Shairav is dead."

Now the other armed Shadari melted out of the crowd and ranged themselves in a ragged line before the Dead Ones. Daryan backed up a few paces—purposefully, not cringingly—putting himself closer to the bales piled up behind him. Harotha watched, sick with apprehension. Certainly the gesture was brave enough, but was he trying to get himself killed?

"This hay is soaked with oil," he called out, speaking slowly and clearly to ensure that Frea understood every word. "If I light it, none of you will be leaving the temple tonight."

Frea drew her sword.

The armed Shadari leaned forward. "Stay back!" Daryan roared out to them. "Everyone! Stay back!"

Why was he doing this? Harotha thought frantically. They were going to kill him; he had to know that. What did he hope to accomplish by throwing his life away?

But then she realized that while she'd been staring at Daryan, she had forgotten all about Dramash—and so had Frea. The boy stood only three paces away, and all of the Dead Ones, Frea included, were facing the opposite direction. She leaned forward, readying herself to lunge.

Then she saw Rho looking at her. He could see her, even within the darkness of her hiding-place. His reflective silver eyes told her nothing. She couldn't move, couldn't breathe—

His eyes moved toward Dramash and then back to her face and he shook his head, slightly, just once. Her eyebrows shot up. He shook his head again: *No*, he was telling her, *I see you. I know what you're going to do. Don't.*

"Tell us what you're going to do," Daryan was saying. "If you're leaving the Shadar, go, and good riddance. I will take your word. I know how much you value your honor."

There was another pause, and then the White Wolf looked at Rho. Harotha caught her breath in a gasp and pressed her back against the wall. She wanted to run, but her legs wouldn't move.

Rho drew his sword and walked toward Daryan, leaving Dramash behind.

Harotha felt the air rush back into her lungs. Rho had not apparently given her away, but she had no time to wonder why not, or what he had meant by his warning. It didn't matter; she wasn't going to give up now. She would grab Dramash the moment she was sure that the White Wolf was looking the other way.

In his flat Norlander accent Rho told Daryan, "Lady Frea says that any slave who stands in her way will die."

"Does she?" he replied, ignoring Rho and looking straight at Frea. "Well, that's all right, then, because I'm not a slave. I am the daimon." Rho looked back at Frea, as if listening to her response, but Daryan went on without waiting for him to translate, "I am the humble servant of the gods. I am the nephew of Shairav'Asha. I am the son of the father whose name I bear—" His voice broke, but after a moment he continued, "and the protector of the Shadari. And the Shadari, my Lady," he added in a voice that welled up from somewhere below the very roots of the great stone temple, "have had all they're going to take from *you*."

Harotha's chest tightened with pride and pain. She didn't know why he'd taken such a chance, but it didn't matter: he really was the daimon now, and no one could ever take that away from him. The White Wolf would command his death now. Rho would thrust his sword, and Daryan—beautiful, suddenly brave Daryan—would be dead. This was her last and only chance to get Dramash, to make good on his sacrifice and the sacrifices of every other person who had died to bring about this moment. She took a deep breath—

—but before she could move, someone rushed past her, knocking her into the wall. As she struggled to regain her balance, she saw the person run into the stables, straight to Dramash, and hoist him off the ground as if he weighed nothing at all. Just as she remembered where she'd seen that mane of black hair, its owner turned around to face Frea, easily managing the bucking, kicking child she was holding. Harotha saw a long Nomas knife—the same knife she'd held in her own hand—shining against the boy's throat.

The Mongrel had Dramash.

<No, no, no, Isa! You can't sleep now!> she heard Eofar say as he rushed back to her from scouting ahead to determine the situation in the stables. <We've got to go now—right now!>

<I'm not sleeping,> she told her brother. It was true, but it was also true that she didn't want to open her eyes, or give up the cool, steady support of the corridor wall. The weight of Truth's Might, strapped across her back despite Eofar's exasperated protests, pulled like a lodestone. <Did you see Lahlil?>

<What do you think?> he muttered as he tried to lift her right arm around his shoulder without unbalancing her. Her head swung down as he pulled her gently against him and she found herself staring at the knotted sleeve of the clean shirt he'd found for her, watching it inscribe little circles in the air where her left elbow should have been.

Lahlil had left them in the funeral room, supposedly to gather more supplies, but she had never returned, and now Isa was convinced that something had happened to her. Eofar was equally convinced that she had abandoned them. They had waited long past the time when they should have gone, until finally he refused to wait any longer. For her part, Isa would have been quite content to lie in that chamber indefinitely, looking up at the stars through the open ceiling while she slowly emerged from the cocoon of Lahlil's drugs, listening to Eofar tell her about Harotha, and Daryan, and all of the other things she'd missed. A strange odor had filled that room, not at all unpleasant, a soft mixture of perfume and ash and sand. Isa thought she would remember that scent for the rest of her life.

<All right, put your weight on me.>

Together they continued on to the stables, staggering awkwardly. The numbness had given way to spasms of fiery pain, and when those finally abated they'd been replaced by a relentless, teeth-grinding ache. She felt so weak that she could barely lift her head.

At last they made it into the stables, but the room was so crowded with triffons, slaves, bales of hay, paraphernalia of all kinds, that she could see only a few feet in front of her in any direction. The Shadari subtly moved out of their way, and though no one spoke to them or looked at them directly, Isa thought they exchanged glances as they passed.

<What's that shouting?> she asked her brother. There was a raised voice somewhere on the other side, but she couldn't make out the words over the sound of her own pulse pounding in her ears.

<Nothing to do with us,> he said. <Aeda's about a dozen paces away, hidden behind some hay-bales. If we're quick and quiet we can be aboard and in the air before anyone notices us.>

She tried to pay attention to him, but most of her mind was preoccupied with the impossible task of lifting her feet and putting them down again. She vowed that she would never again take her strength for granted, now that she knew what it felt like to be without it. She never wanted to feel this helpless again.

As they approached Aeda, the triffon responded to Eofar's scent with a nervous, welcoming snort. Isa stopped beside the creature's massive head, breathless and exhausted.

<Are you sure you can do this?> he asked her.

She looked into Aeda's great dark eyes and felt nothing. Her nightmarish fear of flying had vanished completely in the face of the real nightmare she was living—but then, how could anything be like it was before? She had pushed up against the membrane that separated life from death and nearly passed through it. She had lost a part of herself that she would never get back and she had found something that, if she lost it now, would be worse than losing her life.

<You're sure Daryan will meet us at the cave?> she asked her brother.

<I told you, yes,> he answered shortly, as he tried to lift her up onto Aeda's back without jarring her. <Can you grab the pommel? Stay low. There, good, now slide

back and find the stirrup with your other foot— I told you, Daryan and Shairav left the temple hours ago. I told him exactly where to go. He'll be there.>

Eofar climbed up in front of her and began fastening the buckles. Aeda's tail thumped the ground in expectation.

<We're leaving here, maybe forever.> She had to say it to believe it; it felt so unreal.

<If we're lucky,> Eofar answered darkly, and took up the reins.

Jachad seized Harotha's arms and pulled her further back into the tunnel. "For Shof's sake, stay here!" he pleaded as her stunned face stared into his. "Let me handle this," he insisted a little more gently. He released her and charged into the stables after Meiran, skidding to a halt almost immediately as he stared at the naked blade of Frea's sword. He tried to ignore the choking stench of the triffons as he flicked his fingers over his palms. Fire blazed up from his hands.

<Don't move!> he warned the Norlanders boldly, but he wasn't fooling them. They could feel his uncertainty and *he* could feel them feel it.

<This is not your business, Nomas! Don't interfere,> Frea warned him. Her fury was like a wall of ice, slamming into him. The fire in his hands dipped.

"Meiran. Let the boy go," he said in Nomas, bringing the flames back up again, but he couldn't look at her; he was too afraid he'd see this betrayal written across her scars. He reminded himself that this wasn't his fault; she had left him no choice. He couldn't stand by and allow her to harm an innocent child. He would never be able to live with himself. "Let him go. Now."

"Jachi." Meiran's expressionless voice was as keen as the edge of the knife in her hand. "You don't understand."

"You're right: I don't," he agreed. He still couldn't look at her. He wanted to go back to the desert; he wanted to see his mother; he wanted to feel the sun on his face. "Put the boy down and you can explain it to me."

"You can't stop me," she told him. It was a statement of fact, not a warning. "You can't change it. No one can."

"Let him go!" he heard himself roar.

Frea's silver helmet flashed; she was looking up at something. He looked up as well, and watched a solitary triffon rise into the air on the opposite side of the cavern. There were two passengers, a man and a woman: Isa and Eofar. He heard an odd, jagged shout, and with a start he realized that it had come from Daryan; the Shadari king's face was alight with some unknown triumph. Jachad saw him stretch his arm back, ready to fling the lit torch in his hand at the bale of hay behind him.

But in a flash Rho was there, bringing his right elbow down hard on Daryan's forearm and knocking the torch out of his hand. It bounced on the ground, spattering the floor with droplets of hissing oil and sending up a shower of sparks; before the fire could take, Rho had grabbed a bucket of slops and dumped its stinking contents over the flames. The repulsive smell rolled past Jachad, gagging him.

<What are you doing? Just kill him!> Frea commanded Rho.

The fireball had already formed in Jachad's hand long before his sluggish thoughts had put words to his intentions. He flung the flames upward with all of his strength, feeling the fire leech the strength out of him. It traced a brilliant arc over the heads of the Norlanders and Shadari, and he watched as two decades of Nomas neutrality came to an abrupt and decisive end. Jachad's arm fell heavily to his side, weak and tingling all over.

The flames struck the hay-bale. For a moment, nothing happened—then the sparks caught the oil, there was a sucking noise and a muffled thump, and the fire rolled upward and greedily swallowed up the dry straw. A column of winking cinders swirled upward, caught in the updraft from the open roof.

The triffons bellowed in fear and launched themselves into the air, colliding dangerously with each other in their haste to reach the open sky. Their heavy bodies blotted out the moonlight, and in the deeper darkness the fire glowed more brightly still, sending shadows dancing over the rock walls.

With whoops and screams, the Shadari rushed forward to attack.

A hand gripped Jachad's arm and he turned in alarm, but it was Harotha, her face streaked with color from the firelight, her eyes wide with fervent gratitude but burning with intent.

"Look out!" he cried, hooking his arm around her thick waist and swinging her around just in time to avoid a Shadari armed with what appeared to be a roasting spit.

She grabbed his shoulder. "Where's Dramash? We have to—"

But she stopped abruptly as they both saw the boy at the same time, running through the confusion.

Jachad looked for Meiran, but he didn't see her. He didn't know how the child had managed to get away from her.

"Dramash!" Harotha called out over the noise of the fighting and the fires. She pushed past Jachad and moved toward the boy with her arms outstretched. He turned at the sound of his name and Jachad saw the child's dark eyes rest for a moment on her face. He saw a tiny spark of recognition—perhaps the resemblance she bore to his father?—but instead of changing course toward his aunt, he ran even faster and threw himself headlong at the unsuspecting Rho.

Rho couldn't take his eyes away from Daryan's face. He could feel the Shadari's scalding blood splattering his neck, soaking into his tabard. His gauntlets dripped with it. He could even taste it, a metallic taint at the back of his throat. The fire roared around them, but he was oblivious to the heat and the danger. Triffons swarmed overhead, beating waves of searing air back down into the cavern, but he hardly noticed; all that mattered was the blood.

<Wake up!> Daem's voice came crashing into Rho's head. <Don't just stand there, man!>

He looked down at his sword hand. The gauntlet was clean and white; the blade shone, pristine, in the firelight. His new tabard, with its embroidered imperial signet, was immaculate. Daryan stood waiting, quietly watching the tip of his sword.

<Rho!> Daem shouted again, struggling against an ill-armed but frantic group of Shadari trying to go to their daimon's aid, but before Rho could even think about helping him, Ingeld came swooping in from the other side.

<Lady Frea told you to kill him,> he hollered, charging forward toward Daryan with his sword already drawn. <What are you waiting for? Just get out of my way, I'll do it—>

Rho turned smoothly, and Fortune's Blight crashed against Ingeld's blade.

<What—?> Ingeld trailed off, speechless.

Rho was nearly as surprised as Ingeld, but he understood something now. He regarded Ingeld over their crossed swords and said, simply, <I don't want to kill any more Shadari.>

Ingeld stared back at him, laboring to catch up, but it wasn't long before Rho felt the acid burn of the big Norlander's pleasure as he took in Rho's meaning and tightened his grip on his sword. <I've been wanting to do this for a long time,> he growled.

Rho heard voices shouting aloud behind him and a heartbeat later he felt a rush of air as a host of dark shadows streaked past him. The Shadari who had been struggling against Daem tackled Ingeld to the ground.

Daem grabbed Rho from behind and swung him around. <What's happening—what are you doing?> he demanded. His chin was bleeding, his cape was gone and the left sleeve of his shirt was hanging by a thread.

<I don't—> he started to say when something slammed into his stomach, his legs gave out and he dropped to his knees. Pain snatched his breath away. He looked up into Dramash's wide, dark eyes.

The boy's hands, hot as blacksmith's tongs, squeezed his arm before flinching away. "I'm scared," Dramash confided to him in a tight little whisper. A pair of large tears rolled down his cheeks.

"How did you get away from the Mongrel?"

"She let me go."

"Did she hurt you?"

"No. She said she wouldn't if I stayed still."

Rho lurched back to his feet.

<Good! Hold him there!> Frea commanded. She was tracing the same path as the boy and was not far behind, but now Shadari were throwing themselves upon her with suicidal abandon. She cut them down, barely looking at them, slicing at them with Blood's Pride, then elbowing or kicking them out of her way. Rho saw Dramash's eyes following the faceless silver helmet, the white cape spattered with gore.

"Don't let her get me!" The boy shrank back in terror, pressing his scorching body hard against Rho's leg. Rho pushed him off with his gauntleted hand.

Was he imagining it, or was the floor trembling under his feet?

"I won't," he said hastily, moving the boy around behind him. "I won't let anyone hurt you. Everything will be all right, I promise."

"I want my mama," Dramash whimpered behind him.

Frea stopped in her tracks and Rho saw the black eye-slits fix on his face. Hollow: that was what he would become if he joined her. Each time he obeyed an order, each time he followed a command, that emptiness would swallow him, piece by piece, until he was a just a shell, as lifeless as the figurehead on the silver helmet.

But Frea really did care for him, as much as she had ever cared for anyone; he knew that now. As she began to understand his betrayal, he felt it stab into her heart, wounding her far more deeply than he could have imagined possible.

<I'm sorry,> he told her.

Daem, by his side, looked from him to Frea, then back again. <Well. All right, then,> he said. He heaved his sword above his head and cried out, <Lord Eofar! The emperor! *The emperor!*>

A strange tension sang in the air, a silence completely separate from the cacophony of the room.

<For the emperor!> From within the ranks of the Norlanders, Rho saw Falkar raise his sword above his head. His battle cry throbbed with a kind of wild relief. <For Lord Eofar!>

<Lady Frea!> Ongen shouted, standing right next to Falkar. <Lady Frea!> he roared again, pumping his sword in the air, and the next moment the competing battle cries of the Norlanders crashed down over Rho's head like an avalanche. Over the shouting of the Shadari and the noise of the fire rose the heavy clang of swords and he watched, aghast. Somehow he had started all of this.

He looked back at Frea, but the Shadari rebels had surged between them and he could no longer see her. The fighting was completely chaotic now, with the Norlanders fighting each other, the Shadari attacking them indiscriminately and smoke, ash and knee-buckling heat everywhere.

Daem stepped out in front of him. <Take the boy, if he's so important. Get him out of here.>

Rho gingerly touched the boy on the shoulder. The wound in his side raged hotter than the fire, and he felt weak and lightheaded. He wondered in a vague way if he was going to die, but that wasn't something to think about now. He had a task to complete, and it deserved his full attention.

After that, he didn't care what happened.

<I'm sorry, I'm sorry, I'm sorry,> Eofar apologized over and over again, repeating it a hundred times, and still Isa would not stop screaming at him, or pounding his back with her fist. <Isa, please, save your strength—>

<How could you?> she broke out savagely. <How could you leave him down there?> Finally he felt her sag down against the saddle behind him.

He took a deep breath of the cool night air. Riderless triffons wheeled about them in the sky. It was strange to see them like this, flying free, rolling and diving as they could never do with a rider strapped to their backs. He patted Aeda's neck gratefully: She had brought them safely through the stampede when he was sure they would be killed, and all the time, Isa had been screaming for him to go back for Daryan.

<Isa?> he called back to her, but she didn't answer him. A strange kind of tension was pulling at her; he could feel it. It felt as if a cord was wrapped around her waist, and each beat of Aeda's wings drew the cord a little bit tighter.

<He wanted you to be safe—he said this was the only way. He insisted that we go,> he tried to explain to her again. He wished with all his heart that she hadn't spotted him, or that he'd made Daryan explain it to her himself. <Believe me, I didn't know anything about it until we got to the stables and I found him still there. Shairav had some kind of attack and died just as they were about to leave. He was afraid to leave the other slaves behind until he knew what Frea was up to, but we were so late getting to the stables that she was already there—it was sheer luck that she didn't see us. We *couldn't* wait—there was no time to argue, or come up with a better plan.>

<She'll kill him,> she said, dredging the words up

from somewhere deep and dark. <Frea will kill him. He's probably dead already.>

<No—don't say that. You don't know that,> he told her sharply. <He has friends; he's not alone. There are a lot more slaves in the temple than soldiers: they're going to take the temple back. You'll see: Daryan will meet us at the cave, just like we planned, only a little later. It's going to be all right.>

<I hope you're right, for your sake,> she said. Her words were calmer now and quieter, but they slid into his mind like the blade of a well-honed knife. <Because I think I saw Harotha down there, too.>

Chapter Thirty-One

Rho lurched through the crowd herding Dramash in front of him, trying to shield the boy from sight with his sun-proof cape. He felt naked without Fortune's Blight in his hand, but the child had been too scared to move until he'd sheathed it; the boy was still shivering, from fear or from Rho's chill, or both. The shifting firelight and the smoke added to the confusion, but made it easier for him to avoid both Shadari and Norlanders as he made his way to where he'd seen her last, in front of the little doorway. She was still there, and the Nomas king was with her, but there was no one else close by. At first he thought Jachad was protecting her from some danger, but as he got closer he realized they were arguing. It sounded like he was trying to force her out of the stables.

Her eyes widened when she caught sight of Rho coming toward her.

"I remember you. You're Harotha—" he started, but a rasping cough took hold of him and he half-shoved Dramash toward her. "Take him," he choked out. He waved his hand meaningfully at her belly. "You must know some place to hide if you've been here all this time—a safe place. Take him there, now!"

"Wait," said Jachad. Little yellow flames wound around his fingers and whisked up his arms, singeing the sleeves of his robe. "What's this all about?"

Dramash's eyes were shut tight and his shoulders

were hunched over protectively, but relief broke over Rho as he watched Harotha grab the boy by the hand and pull him toward the doorway—until the child dug his heels into the ground and raised his shrill voice over the rest of the din, screaming, "Rho! Rho!" Harotha pulled him back against her and clapped her hand over his mouth.

Rho ran forward. "Dramash, stop—" he began, but the boy burst from Harotha's restraining embrace and clamped his arms around Rho's leg. Rho rocked back with a gasp of pain but Dramash gritted his teeth against the cold and held on. "No, no! You must go with them!" he pleaded, trying to push the child away without hurting him. "Go to your family!"

The light dimmed as a cloud of smoke rolled over them. Rho covered his mouth with his sleeve and wiped at his burning eyes. The others were gasping and coughing around him, but out of the smoke two Shadari rushed up to them: Daryan, with another, much taller man just behind him.

"You! I've been trying to find you. You saved my life. Why?" Daryan demanded of him. His face was patched with soot now, and the knuckles of both of his hands glistened with fresh blood. *Blue* blood. "Why are the Dead Ones fighting each other? What's going on?"

Rho coughed again as he started to answer, but this time he couldn't stop. Every convulsion pulled at the wound across his abdomen; he pressed his forearm hard against it as if he could somehow keep in the pain. At last, eyes streaming and doubled over, he managed to gasp, "Frea's gone too far. She plans to burn your city to the ground. Take the imperial ship, attack Norland. Attack the emperor himself."

Daryan looked back at his companion and laughed; to Rho's ears it had a strained, panicked sound. "You're saying you've turned against her—that you're on our side now?"

"Some of us."

"Well, which ones? How are my people supposed to tell which ones to fight and which one to help?"

"I don't know—they can't!" he shouted hoarsely. He shoved Dramash away from him with both hands and drew Fortune's Blight, desperate for the feel of the cold metal in his hand. He began backing away from the Shadari and the Nomas. "I don't know anything—I don't know what I'm doing. Just take the boy and go! I have to help my friends."

Harotha knelt behind Dramash and circled her arms around his chest. "It's all right," she said, "You don't remember me, but I'm your aunt. I'll take you some place safe. You'll—" But then she stopped, and Rho noticed two things simultaneously: first, Dramash was standing as straight and rigid as a stake instead of struggling in her embrace or trying to run back to Rho; second, a soft shower of dust was raining down onto Harotha's brown scarf.

"No!" he screamed wildly. He charged forward and grabbed Dramash's arm. "Stop!" he ordered, shaking the boy fiercely. "Stop—you'll kill us all!"

The boy looked up at him with an indecipherable expression on his face, but the tension in his arm melted away. He had been trying to get Rho's attention and he had succeeded.

Rho glanced at Harotha. Her lack of surprise was enough to tell him that she already knew what Dramash could do.

"I have to get him out of here," she said, her voice low, but her dark eyes blazing with meaning. "You'll have to come with us."

"Yes," Rho capitulated heavily. He sheathed his sword again. "Where?"

"Someone tell me what is—" Daryan interrupted, but Harotha cut him off.

"Dramash was born with the power of the ashas and the White Wolf knows about it," she said. The expression on Daryan's face changed dramatically, as did that of his companion. "We need to get him as far away from Frea as possible."

"But then the ashas . . ." Daryan's face changed again and he rushed forward and seized her by the shoulders. "The way out—I know where it is. I was there, just a little while ago."

She drew in a sharp breath. "By the gods—then we can get him out—we can get *everyone* out."

Daryan turned back to the tall Shadari. "Omir, tell everyone to meet at Shairav's rooms—but they mustn't all go at once. The Dead Ones mustn't find out—especially the White Wolf. Find a way to get word to everyone who's not here. We don't want anyone left behind."

The tall man—Omir—nodded curtly and disappeared into the smoke.

Jachad had left the odd little company at some point without Rho noticing, but now he returned with news. "It's chaos in there: Meiran and Frea are both caught up in the fighting. I'll stay and do anything I can to keep Frea from following you."

"But you should come with us," Harotha said.

Jachad shook his head. "No, I need to wait for the triffons to come back. I need get to my people in the desert and I'll never be able to walk there in time. This time the Nomas are going to take sides."

"Jachad." She reached out and clasped the Nomas' hand. "Thank you."

"Thank me later. I'll let you buy me a drink." He flashed them a quick smile and then he too disappeared into the smoke.

"Come on, then, quickly!" Daryan ducked into the little passageway as Harotha gestured for Rho and Dramash to go before her. He stooped down through the dark opening with Dramash skipping along behind him. The space was cramped, and he sucked in a deep breath of relief when they emerged at the other end.

Daryan ignored the quickest way to Shairav's chamber

and took a route that would keep them further away from the stables and Frea. The night was well advanced and the hallways were dark. Harotha took up a position by Daryan's side; Rho saw their heads tilted toward each other and caught a few words of their conversation. "I have an idea about that. Let me handle it," he heard Daryan say before the daimon looked back at him, his brow furrowed.

As they neared Shairav's quarters they met more glassy-eyed, wheezing Shadari. One woman caught sight of Rho and screeched in terror until Daryan rushed forward to quiet her. "He's all right, he's with us—he won't hurt you."

Dramash brought his scorching body nearer to Rho's side as the two groups merged and he began to feel faint again. Then they rounded the last corner and found a much larger crowd bottled up in the hallway.

"Make way, make way, please," Daryan called, elbowing his way through, but now it was Dramash leading them all forward, wanting to be at the front for whatever was about to happen. Daryan continued burbling reassurances to the crowd as they entered the chamber, while Rho kept his eyes on Harotha's back and tried not to think of all those hostile Shadari eyes fixed on him.

"Daimon!" a rich voice boomed out of the darkness.

"Omir?" Daryan called toward the faint light coming from the far end of the room.

"This way, Daimon, over here. We've found it."

They passed through a narrow doorway and made their way slowly across a floor littered with debris of some kind, then ducked through yet another doorway. This last room was round, hardly large enough to be called a room at all. A black hole in the middle of the floor took up most of the space. A dozen Shadari hung back against the walls, their expressions hard, nervously fingering their weapons. Rho felt the unmistakable movement of fresh air over his face and looked up to see the star-lit sky. He shut his eyes for a moment and breathed in the clean, cool air.

Dramash stretched toward the hole as they shuffled carefully into the room. "What's that? It doesn't look like a well. How deep is it?" he asked excitedly. Instinctively Rho tugged the boy back against the wall.

"There it is—and the sand's there already, just like I told you," Daryan said to Harotha; to Rho it sounded like the continuation of their secret conversation in the hallway. "Do you really think you can do this? Why don't we ask—?"

"I can do it," she said firmly, and slowly lowered her heavy body to the floor. She began sweeping up the scattered sand into a pile.

"What are you doing?" asked Dramash. He was almost dancing with impatience, shifting his weight from one foot to the other. Rho was careful to stay between the boy and the hole.

Daryan turned to Dramash. "There are steps there," he explained, watching as Harotha smoothed the pile of sand out into a crude rectangle, like a tablet. "They were made to slide into the wall, like they are now—that's why we can't see them. We need to get them to slide out again, then we'll all be able to go down the steps and escape."

"What's she doing?" Dramash asked, pointing to Harotha with his free hand.

"Praying," said Daryan as she began to write in the sand with her finger. Every other Shadari in the room hastily turned against the wall, or covered their eyes with their hands.

Dramash snorted. "You don't need that. Here—" And before Rho could stop him, he darted toward the gaping hole. For a dizzying moment Rho thought he actually saw him hurtling over the edge, disappearing into the bottomless darkness while he stood there, paralyzed with dread—but the boy had just flopped down onto his stomach next to his aunt. He peered into the chasm.

"Look, like this," he said, extending his hand over the opening.

There was no tremor, just a gentle little click, echoing down into the darkness. Even the grinding sound was soft and innocuous. And then the scent of the sea came wafting up to them.

"Light," Daryan cried, "we need light—someone bring a torch."

Moments later someone placed a torch into Daryan's hand and he stepped toward the hole. Dramash was now sitting on the edge with his legs dangling over the side. Rho looked around: every Shadari face displayed the same stunned expression.

"Gods," Daryan breathed. There were the steps, spiraling down, and in the center was a gap about the length of Rho's forearm. Daryan gingerly extended the torch over the gap and released it, letting it fall down through the aperture. A dozen heads bent forward, watching the sparks fly as the torch bumped against the sides of the chasm on its way down. The light grew dimmer and dimmer, but then, noiselessly, it hit the bottom and then vanished completely for a moment, then flared back up again. It was just a far-away glow, but it was vastly significant: there was no water at the bottom, and enough air to keep the torch alight.

"Omir," said Daryan. He spoke quietly, but the silence he broke was so profound that he might as well have screamed. He moved over to help Harotha up. "You go down first with Harotha. The rest of you, get back into the hallway and try to organize this somehow. We need to move quickly, but it's a long way down and we can't have people pushing each other or someone's going to get hurt. We'll have to stagger them somehow. Groups of ten or twelve, maybe . . ." He trailed off, but those in the room had already roused themselves to obey. Everyone except Omir, Harotha, Daryan, Rho and the boy left the chamber. Rho saw the looks as they went out; in a few moments every Shadari in the temple would know what Dramash had done.

"Daryan," Harotha said—and then she, too, looked at Dramash. Her face had gone very pale. "I'll take him with me."

Daryan shook his head. "I said I would handle it, and I will, I promise. But you must go, please. I'll be with you soon. Then I'll explain everything."

She hesitated, but Omir started down the steps immediately and stood waiting for her at the point where the turning would take him out of sight. She frowned, but started down after him. A moment later both were out of sight.

Rho looked at Dramash, still sitting on the edge of the stairwell, kicking his heels into the wall. One of the Shadari returned with the first disconcerted party of escapees and began ushering them down the steps.

With the noise and movement as cover, Rho beckoned Daryan over and whispered, "I must get back. My friends need me. You'll take him back to his family and make sure Frea can't find him?"

"I need to talk to you about that." Daryan flicked his tongue over his dry, cracked lips. "You see, I have this idea."

Chapter Thirty-Two

Harotha squirmed, struggling to loosen the burly arms that held her, and when the squirming failed to produce a result, she jammed her shoulder pointedly into the man's chest. The stranger released her at last, but he gave her an affronted look before he turned to grab a more willing partner out of the crowd.

"You were crushing the baby," she explained, but it was too late; he'd gone. She swallowed against the dryness in her throat, feeling a burn deep in her chest from the smoke she'd inhaled in the temple. A sharp elbow poked her in the small of the back and someone else trod on her foot. She felt like she had just landed on some alien shore. She didn't understand how word of their escape could have spread to the city so quickly—the beach had been deserted when she and Omir had groped their way out of the caves at the bottom of the steps, splashed across the little hidden cove and climbed around the rocks to the shore. But now jubilant Shadari were cavorting on the beach in droves, and everywhere she looked she could see joyful faces and tearful reunions. People had unearthed drums from some dusty hiding-place—their ceremonial drums had been forbidden by the Dead Ones long ago as an affront to their sensitive ears—and unpracticed hands were taking turns reviving the half-remembered rhythms. The uneven beats jarred against her pounding pulse, shaking her half-formed thoughts loose before she could grab hold of them and examine them properly.

She had wanted to bring this moment about—this *exact* moment—for as long as she could remember, and now here it was, all around her, and yet she could not surrender to it. She watched strangers embrace, lovers kiss, old enemies shake hands or clap each other on the back, while she remained detached and unfeeling. She accepted the thanks and congratulations of those around her, but behind her smiles she knew that she deserved neither. Daryan had been the one to rally the temple slaves and start the uprising—against her advice. Rho, a Dead One, had been the one to free Dramash from the White Wolf. And Dramash—was it the effortlessness of what he had done that galled her so, or his innocent, unabashed pride? Or was it just the fact that he had done it and she had not?

A strong hand clamped down on her shoulder and spun her around.

"Where's my son?" Faroth demanded. His face was pinched and pale, in sharp contrast to the flushed faces of the revelers, and his eyes were as hard as stones.

Harotha's heart thumped. "He's with Daryan," she answered. "I've been trying to—"

"No, he isn't," Faroth said coldly. He kept his tight grip on her shoulder. "And no one saw him leave the temple."

"What?" She looked back over her shoulder toward the little cove, but the crowd was too dense for her to see very far. "No, that's not possible. He—"

"How could you let my son out of your sight?" he asked in a low, tight voice, thrusting his face close to hers. "I've heard what happened up there—everyone is talking about it. Can't you see what this means to us? For the gods' sake, just how stupid are you?"

"*Me?*" She straightened up and stepped away from

him with a derisive laugh. "You're blaming *me*? You're his father—would you care to explain to me how the White Wolf found out about Dramash before you did?"

He shot out his hand and grabbed her around the throat, pressing his thumb down on her windpipe. She gagged as he squeezed, too surprised and terrified to fight back. Her vision blurred, and through the fog she realized she was looking into the face of an absolute stranger.

"I know you and Daryan are trying to keep him from me, but it won't work," he snarled. "The daimon means *nothing* to the Shadari. He's a bootlicker, and soon all those who helped the Dead Ones will pay for it. Soon only my favor—only *mine*—will keep this mob from tearing you both apart."

She fell to her knees when he released her, breathing in great choking gasps. His thumbprint burned her neck like a hot brand and some nameless feeling pressed down on her chest. And now, humiliatingly, she found herself convulsed, not with tears—she never cried—but with noiseless, heaving sobs that came from someplace outside of her control. She crossed her arms over her belly and tucked her head down into them, not sure whether she was trying to comfort the baby, or whether she hoped to draw comfort from him.

It wasn't until her brother's attention shifted away from her that she realized that the drumming had stopped and people were calling out all around her. She struggled awkwardly to her feet, fighting to regain her equanimity. A figure stood on top of a tall cluster of rocks at the surf's edge: Daryan, his dark hair wet with spray and curling romantically over his forehead. The moon, setting across the sea to his left, lit a sparkling path to him over the water. He had already begun to speak, and Harotha, far up the beach, had to strain to hear him.

"—the bravest ones, died tonight," Daryan was saying. His voice was hoarse, but it sounded deeper, older than it had just a few hours ago. "Don't let it be for nothing. There will be a time to celebrate, believe me, but it isn't now. Go home, sleep if you can. Eat. Be with your families. We're going to need everyone's help. We've got to be ready to defend our city from whatever's coming next." He paused. She saw him tug at the back of his hair and even now she smiled a little to herself: that old, familiar gesture. "Okay. Well, that's all for now, I guess," he finished awkwardly. He looked around at the rapt crowd and then repeated, "Everybody go home." She lost sight of him as he climbed down from the rock, but the crowd around her began to move, breaking up into groups, murmuring earnestly among themselves.

"Come on." Faroth grabbed her hand and pulled her down the beach with him, but they had not gone far before Binit appeared, shouldering his way toward them. As soon as he saw Faroth he announced, "Here he is, Faroth! We've got him!" Just behind Binit came Daryan, flanked by the rest of Faroth's crew, with Omir and some of the others from the temple following closely at their heels. But Dramash was not with them.

"Harotha! Here you are, thank the gods! I was looking all over for you!" Daryan cried out the moment he saw her. He brushed past Faroth and rushed toward her with his arms outstretched.

Faroth stepped out in front of her. "Where's my son?"

"Safe," he answered, dropping his arms. "He's safe. We got him away from the White Wolf. But he's not here."

She groaned. Faroth was right: she should have never trusted Daryan; she never should have let Dramash out of her sight. She'd been such a fool.

"Then where is he?" Faroth snarled.

Daryan's eyes hardened. "I can't tell you that."

"Give me my son!" Faroth screamed, and lunged at Daryan in pure blind rage. Omir caught his fist in one of his huge hands and cocked his other arm menacingly. Faroth's friends tried to pull him back, but he kept on shouting, "Curse you, you have no right—he's *my* son! I know what you're trying to do—I see what you are!"

"That's enough." Daryan's smoke-darkened voice roared out over the sound of the surf and the murmuring crowd hushed instantly. Faroth's wrathful glare did not change, but behind it Harotha saw that same strange, dangerous look she had seen a few moments ago.

"Let him go, Omir," Daryan commanded, without taking his eyes from Faroth. Omir hesitated a moment, but then let go of Faroth's hand. Faroth dropped his arms to his sides and she found herself staring at her brother's hands, reliving the memory of them pressed around her throat. "For the gods' sake, Faroth, is the White Wolf not enough of an enemy for you that you have to fight me, too?" he asked. He turned a reproachful eye on the rest of the company. "Dramash is safe; that's all I'm going to tell you right now. Now, I have good information that the White Wolf won't do anything else until sundown tomorrow—we've bought ourselves one day. I'm going to get some rest; my head feels like there's a swarm of bees living in it. Faroth, you keep charge of your own people in the city. Omir, I want you to look after the temple slaves. We'll all meet at midday, at the palace, and I'll explain everything. All right? Now, go!"

Faroth held Daryan's gaze for another moment, his lips pressed together in a thin, hard line. Then he turned without a word and joined the others as they headed back up the beach toward the city. His followers went with him, as silent and stone-faced as their leader.

"He's not going to leave it at that," said Omir.

"I know," Daryan sighed. "Well, we'll deal with him when we need to. You should get some rest, too, Omir. You must be exhausted." He turned to Harotha. "What about you, are you all right? You look terrible."

She didn't trust her voice enough to speak, but she nodded.

"Come on, *dear*," he said, putting his arm around her shoulders and turning her toward the water.

"Daimon, you should have something to eat. We'll bring you—" began Omir, but Daryan waved him away.

"Thanks, Omir, but I'll take care of that. Don't let anyone disturb us, all right? I want some time alone with my wife. I'm sure you understand." She felt a little pinch on her arm as he made that last remark, and with a shock she realized he was actually teasing her.

A few others among the crowd had hung back, eager for a chance to see or speak to their daimon, but Omir shooed them away.

Daryan led her down toward the water, and in a few moments they were alone. She could see the long white crests of the waves as they crashed down and then ran foaming up the smooth stretch of wet sand toward them. The tide was high, but it had already turned. He brought her around to a little dry hollow on the far side of the rocks, protected from the spray by a jutting outcrop.

"Holy hells, what a night." He exhaled deeply, then dropped down onto the sand and let his back fall against the rock. He stared up at the dark sky. "There's so much space out here. It feels strange, like my eyes don't quite know how to focus." He reached up and ran his fingers along the stone beside him. "Odd to think I used to play here with my friends when I was a little boy. I don't remember it, really. Only the smell. Isn't it strange how sometimes you can remember a scent more clearly than anything else?"

"Daryan," said Harotha, "where is Dramash?"

The moon was behind the rock, shadowing his face. She could not read his expression. "You won't like it, but it's too late now, anyway. There's nothing either of us can do about it."

"Daryan!"

He sighed. "All right. Dramash is still with Rho—in the temple."

She felt the blood drain from her face. "You—"

"Listen," he interrupted, "we need allies. We can't

fight Frea alone, or we won't fare any better against the Dead Ones than our parents did. Rho and I came up with a plan. He's going to lure Frea and her men out of the stables. Wait—" He held up his hand as she tried to interrupt. "He's going to let Frea find out that we're escaping. He's sure she'll abandon the stables to chase after Dramash."

"But then she can follow us down the stairs."

"No, no, I was the last one down. Dramash has already closed them. And Rho shut the secret door, so Frea won't even know we were ever there." He paused to yawn. "She knows about the secret room, but Shairav always kept the steps hidden. She won't even know where to start looking."

"You can't be sure of that."

He frowned at her comment, but continued without addressing it. "It will take hours for her to search the temple, and when she finally gives up and goes back to the stables, she won't be able to get in. All of the entrances will be blocked."

"Because Dramash will have caved them in."

"That's right. As soon as the triffons come back, Rho, Dramash and the rest of them will leave. They'll be long gone before Frea digs her way back in."

"What about the Mongrel? Where is she in all this?"

"I don't know. I can't worry about her right now."

"That's your plan?" she asked, making no attempt to hide her consternation. "Not only do you give Dramash to the Dead Ones, but you make it possible for them to get him out of the temple?"

"To join us at the cave, the one you found," he insisted. "We're to meet Eofar and Isa and Rho there, and then go to the palace together. Rho will make a show of returning Dramash to his family—that should be enough to convince everyone that we can trust him."

"Listen to what you're saying! You've put our fate in the hands of Frea's *lover*! Daryan, you can't possibly be this naïve. Can't you see how he's tricked you? Who knows what he's really going to do with Dramash, or what he might force him to do?"

"No, you're wrong. Rho is on our side. He saved my life—I trust him."

"He's a Dead One!"

"So is Eofar."

He said it quite calmly, but it hit her with the blunt force of a fist. "That's different."

"No, it's not," he said, "it's exactly the same, and I think you know it."

"What is that supposed to mean?"

"Come on, Harotha. Why aren't you with Eofar right now, somewhere very far away from here?" He sat forward and his dark eyes, black in the shadows, held an unexpected challenge. "It's because you don't really trust him. Hell, I don't think you've ever trusted anyone in your life except yourself. I know you've never trusted me." He sat back again. "Eofar really loves you, Harotha. Believe me, I'm lucky he didn't murder me after you told him that lie about us. He may be a Dead One, but he's a good man, and he's my friend. All he wants is to be with you, but you keep pushing him away. I wish you wouldn't do that to him. He deserves better."

When she didn't respond, he stood up and came slowly toward her, but she shrank back.

"Gods, are you crying? I never thought— I've never seen you cry before."

"No. I don't cry." Ashamed, she scrubbed at her cheeks with both hands, but he caught her wrists.

"No, no, don't do that. Go ahead and cry. Come over here and sit down." She allowed him to lead her over to the little hollow in the rock, where there was just enough room for the two of them to sit together side by side. The sand was soft and deep, but it was cool and she shivered.

He put his arm around her shoulders. "Let's get some sleep," he suggested, and then he yawned long and loud. "It's a long walk to that cave. Someday you'll have to tell me how you found it in the first place."

She leaned forward and reached around her belly, drawing her knees up so that she could massage her swollen ankles. His head nestled against her shoulder. "Listen, don't fall asleep yet," she told him. To her surprise she realized she had unconsciously made a decision she had not even known she was considering. "There's more you need to know. I took the elixir, Daryan—the things I saw . . ."

She wove through the narrative of her visions, censoring nothing, and he listened without interrupting.

When she finally finished, he said thoughtfully, "Then you were right, getting Dramash back was more important than fighting Frea. I'm glad you ignored me. Thank the gods my stupid stunt with the fire actually helped you. I just couldn't think of any other way to distract her so that Isa and Eofar could get out. So you and the ashas did stop it, in the end. They didn't die for nothing."

"It's not over yet. We still have to keep Dramash away from the White Wolf. We can only hope that Rho lives up to the trust you've placed in him."

"Yes, well, let's leave that for tomorrow. I'll die if I don't get some sleep. And we've got that long walk in the morning." He nestled more comfortably against her, and she found herself taking a surprising amount of comfort in the solid feel of his body and the rhythm of his slow, sleepy breathing. Just before they both fell asleep, he added drowsily, "I have a lot more to tell you on the way."

Chapter Thirty-Three

Once he was certain no one in the stables could see him, Rho leaned against the wall of the blocked tunnel and reached gingerly underneath his shirt, clenching his stomach muscles tight against the anticipated pain. As soon as he touched the swollen ridge he wanted to pull his hand back, but he forced himself to trace the whole length of the wound. The moisture he felt could have been perspiration—the cavern was still ridiculously hot, even with the fires out—but the throbbing and the feverish heat were harder to dismiss.

Dramash slid down against the opposite wall and laid his dirty cheek down against his knee. "I'm tired."

"Only one more," Rho reassured him, "but we have to wait."

"Why?"

"We said we'd leave the last one open for King Jachad—" He cut that explanation short; Dramash wasn't likely to have forgotten the feel of the Mongrel's knife at his throat, even if she *had* let him go without hurting him. "Some of our friends aren't back yet," he said instead.

An alliance with the Mongrel was the last thing Rho wanted, but Falkar had dismissed his objections: the mercenary had aligned herself against Frea, and under the circumstances that was enough to make her an ally. Now she and Jachad were keeping Frea and her rebels busy in the tunnels while the loyalists, as Daem had facetiously dubbed them, secured the stables. When they returned, Jachad planned to take one of the triffons and rally his desert people to their cause.

"And then we're going home?"

"When the triffons come back down."

"Are they back now?"

"If they were—" he began, but again he checked himself. "I'll see. Stay right here."

He hurried back out into the main cavern to assess the situation. Daem was keeping watch over the last open tunnel and Falkar was overseeing the furious effort to clear the stable floor and dissipate the remaining smoke.

<Rho,> Daem called, <I want to talk to you.>

<Have to wait,> he replied. Daem had already expressed the opinion that he should have given Dramash back to his own people and had nothing more to do with him, and Rho had no intention of arguing the point again. He found Falkar flapping a blanket in the air, trying to drive more of the smoke up through the aperture. It didn't appear to be doing any good, but Rho thought it best not to comment. As many as thirty men, many with as-yet untreated wounds, were trying to sweep aside the ash and dragging or tossing the bigger pieces of rubbish strewn across the floor into the blocked tunnels. Frea would not have an easy time digging her way back in.

<Any sign of the triffons yet?> he asked Falkar.

<They're up there. They'll start coming down if we can get enough of this damned floor clear.> The lieutenant balled up the blanket impatiently. <Anyway, I'm not leaving without the rest of our men. Why didn't you tell me what you were planning *before* you started that outcry about the slaves escaping?>

<It was Daryan's idea—I didn't really have time to think it through.>

<Onfar's eyes, if I'd known it was a damned trick to lure Lady Frea out of the stables, I wouldn't have sent our men after her.>

<Jachad said he'd bring them back.>

<While we wait here and sweep up rubbish. We can't even take our dead down to the tombs and give them a proper burial.> Falkar didn't look behind him at the dozens of blanket-wrapped forms lined up by the wall, but Rho did. Eleven of them were Norlanders: Norlander killing Norlander, like the clan-wars of old.

He wanted to tell Falkar that one day this would all be over, that everything would go back to normal, but the wound in his side was sapping all of the energy he needed to lie. He headed back over to Dramash instead.

<Rho, come over here,> Daem called again.

<I have to stay with Dramash.>

The ugly yellow flashes around Daem's words were not a good sign. <Rho, curse it: I *need* you to listen to me.>

<Stop talking and watch that tunnel,> Falkar commanded. <You two high clansmen can compare your bloodlines later.>

Rho thought Dramash had fallen asleep, but when he got a little closer he saw the boy was watching him through bloodshot eyes.

"You're going to take me home?" he asked again.

"Yes."

"To my mama?"

The hilt of Fortune's Blight scraped against the stone as Rho leaned against the wall. "To your father, after we meet some other people first."

"Maybe I shouldn't go." Tears welled up suddenly in his round eyes. Rho didn't really understand crying, but now he wondered if it was strange that the boy hadn't cried before this. "He's mad at me because I wanted to stay here. Can you take me to Mama instead?"

Rho could feel Daem's presence sneaking in the background and he strained to keep his panic at bay; he could handle this, just keep talking about his father instead. "Your father's not angry at you—he's your father, he loves you and he wants you to come home."

"Why can't I stay here and take care of the dereshadi like the White Wolf promised? She said Mama could come here and live with me."

"She was never really going to let you do that." He didn't want to upset the boy any further, but he had to get him out of the temple. "She brought you here to do things for her."

"Bad things?" he whispered.

"Yes, bad things."

Dramash put his head down again and said in a muffled voice, "Papa says all the Dead Ones are bad. He wants to hurt all of them, just like he hurt you."

"He has his reasons." *What was taking that cursed Nomas so long?*

"Mama says it's wrong to hurt people."

"Sometimes you don't have a choice," Rho ventured, but he knew that wasn't the right answer. He tried again. "Sometimes people make mistakes."

"Are you going to punish him?"

"No."

"But you're a soldier."

"I would never hurt your father."

"Why not?"

For a moment he was at a loss, but then the answer came to him, and it was simpler than he had imagined. "Because I know you wouldn't like it."

A rush of air warmed his skin as the first triffon spiraled down from above and Dramash sprang up and ran toward it. At the same moment Daem called out, and Jachad, the Mongrel and a string of Norland soldiers came clattering down the narrow tunnel.

<Rho!> Falkar called out as he led the first triffon out of the way to make room for the others now circling in the sky above.

"Come on, Dramash," Rho said. "Time to go."

Chapter Thirty-Four

No one came forward as Jachad landed the triffon at the edge of the Nomas camp; an onlooker might have assumed that no one had noticed them, but he knew better. His people were watching, but keeping their distance, at least for the moment. He struggled out of the harness and slid down the triffon's shoulder onto the cold sand. *Ah, the sand*: he could have dropped to his knees and kissed the ground.

He waited by the beast's foreleg while Meiran undid the buckles, one by one. They had not spoken a word to each other during the journey, or in the temple. She had acquiesced to Rho's plan with a few terse affirmatives; that was it. He had not asked her to come with him to the desert, but she had vaulted up into the saddle behind him without a word.

And now here they were.

He scanned the vast tent city, the whole Nomas nation in a thousand or more bright dwellings, gathered here from every part of the world. It was past midnight and the children were long abed, no doubt exhausted from a giddy day of chasing each other around the site. The married couples had retired as well, eager to make up for the months they'd spent apart. The fires remaining were mostly tended by young people: girls lounging around one, boys at another, both groups coolly pretending not to notice each other. Jachad smiled nostalgically.

Soon one of the girls would stand up and announce that she needed to stretch her legs; then one of the boys would do the same. And in a little while, in some dark spot, that boy would be drowning in the sea-scent of that girl's hair, and the touch of her hands, and the warmth and softness of her body. How he envied such beautiful simplicity.

Meiran walked past him into the camp, making her way toward the spot where Nisha's blue silk tent shimmered in silver ripples in the last of the moonlight. He trailed after her, letting the distance between them widen. The soft voices of the teenagers around the fires rose self-consciously as they passed, trying too hard to pretend that Jachad and Meiran's movements did not concern them.

He stopped when he saw the tent flap move. A pool of lamplight spilled out onto the sand and his mother's silhouette appeared. She slipped outside, letting the silk fall shut behind her. She looked at Meiran, and Meiran stopped.

Nisha's hand reached up to clutch the silver medallion at her breast and Jachad saw her lips move in what was surely a prayer to Amai.

Expectant sparks wound around his fingers. It wasn't too late: if Meiran ran into Nisha's embrace now, everything would be all right. Wrongs would be redressed; wounds would heal.

But Meiran walked toward Nisha like a general on the battlefield marching out to parley with the enemy, her boots striking the sand with military rigor.

"I need to speak to you," she said, "alone."

Nisha nodded and led Meiran into her tent. The sudden splash of lamplight as she held back the flap dazzled Jachad's tired eyes, but a moment later the two women had disappeared inside and the light was gone.

As if by mere coincidence, men and women began emerging from their tents and milling sociably around the dying campfires. Jachad steeled himself for their inevitable questions. He had not realized how much he had been counting on Nisha and Meiran's reunion to change the situation; now that it was clear that it would not, he just wanted to be alone to nurse the pain of his disappointment in private.

"Well, here you are finally, King Jachad!" cried a clear voice, and while others hung back out of a mixture of sensitivity and apprehension, pretty little Dannika, second mate on the *Veruna*, skipped up to welcome him. "I've been keeping a seat for you by my fire for the last two days, you know." She swept her light hair back from her bright-cheeked face, the tiny bells on her bracelets tinkling invitingly.

"That was kind of you, Danni," he told her. "I'm sorry I disappointed you."

She regarded him searchingly for a moment, and then frowned. "Not sorry enough to make it up to me now, I'm guessing."

"No, I'm afraid not. A lot has happened since the last gathering. Things are different now."

She shrugged, a gesture so quintessentially Nomas that he couldn't help but smile. "Why wait for the wind when there's oars a-plenty?" she said with a saucy wink. "That's what our captain always says."

"Captain—?" he repeated, reminded of the original purpose of his visit. "Danni, can I ask a favor? I need to speak with all of the chiefs and captains, right away—can you round them up for me? Tell them to meet by those rocks over there on the south side of camp."

"Now?" Her eyes widened. "It's only the third night, and it's late—you know what they're all doing."

"I'm sorry, but yes, all of them," he insisted. "And right away."

"If you say so," she agreed reluctantly. "At least I won't be the only one going unsatisfied tonight." Despite the grousing, she sauntered off on her errand with no ill will, leaving others pressing forward to welcome him in turn. He responded vaguely to those who asked what had delayed him, promising that they would all know more soon enough. As he listened to a trio of young men recounting the tale of a particularly profitable trip to the spice markets of Chervong, the crowd around him suddenly fell silent and he turned to find that his mother had joined them. She was alone.

Jachad excused himself and he and Nisha began strolling along the makeshift streets, heading for the edge of camp where the emptied wagons had been put to use as paddocks for their animals.

"Where is she now?" he asked in a low voice. A large brown dog raised his head at their approach, sniffed once and then settled back down to sleep.

"Still in my tent. I convinced her to get some rest."

"You've been crying."

"Of course I have." She stopped beside one of the paddocks and regarded the sleeping goats huddled together in one corner. Her shadowed face was hard to read.

"Are you going to tell me what she said to you?"

"No."

"Did she tell you not to tell me?"

"Listen to yourself, Jachi—you sound like a child. What she told me is not mine to tell. If you want to know, you must ask her. Leave it at that."

"So what am I supposed to do?" he demanded. "Trust her? Not trust her? Stay with her? Leave her?"

"Those are choices you must make for yourself."

"Oh, thanks, I hadn't thought of that." A fireball roared into life in his right hand and he spiked it into the sand. The goats sprang up, bleating, and skittered to the other side of the paddock with a raucous clanking of bells.

"Feel better now?" said his mother.

He met her eyes, and then looked away again sheepishly. "No."

"And here I almost forgot to tell you," she announced

briskly, very clearly changing the subject, "I have news for you."

"What kind of news?"

"The best kind. Amai and Shof have blessed us."

"Really?" He was genuinely surprised. "Here? Now? Who is it?"

"Callia."

"Callia of the *Dawn Gazer*?"

"That's right—and she's already four months gone. She wanted to wait for the gathering before she told anyone."

Jachad laughed. "Really? Callia? That little flirt!" He shook his head. "You'll have your task cut out for you, turning that chit into a queen. So that's what catches Shof's eye these days, is it? And a vainer, sillier girl he couldn't have found if he'd tried."

"She's a nice girl, Jachi—she's young, that's all. And Shof has nothing to do with the choosing. Amai chooses her own handmaiden to lay with Shof on her behalf."

"Well, Shof is still the one doing the laying."

"You go too far, Jachad," said Nisha. "The conception of a new king is a sacred and very private rite, not the bargainings of a procuress in the back of some tavern in Prol Irat."

"Well, I wouldn't know. Every procuress in Prol Irat takes a holiday when my caravan comes to town."

"I'm glad to hear that, at least."

"There's no point, you see: the girls are so eager they'd happily pay *us* if we'd let them."

She narrowed her eyes at him, but he was glad to see that his jesting had smoothed away some of her worries. His anger at Meiran warmed again as he looked at his mother's sad, lovely face. Nisha wanted nothing more than to be allowed to love her, and Meiran couldn't even give her that. Did she have any purpose here other than to torment them?

"So we're to have a new princeling," he said, scratching

his chin. "It's about time, I suppose, but it makes me feel old."

Nisha gave a soft snort. "How do you think it makes me feel?"

They watched the goats settle back down to sleep. Behind them, they could hear the effect that Jachad's demand for a council was having, rousing the Nomas nation out of their comfortable, well-populated beds. He would have to face his people in a few moments, and he still wasn't sure what he was going to say to them.

"What are you going to tell them?" asked his mother, following his train of thought.

"I'm going to ask for their help—I have to explain why we need to stop Frea."

"And why is that?"

He shrugged. "Because it's the right thing to do."

She nodded and put her arm around his shoulder. "Well, then, that should be easy, shouldn't it?"

Chapter Thirty-Five

Isa set her feet and then rocked back, searching for the fulcrum: the resting, ready stance that was more important in a fight than any thrust or cut or parry. She still had sand in her clothes from sleeping outside while Eofar—with Aeda's help—had cleared enough rocks from the cave's entrance for them to enter, and the grains scraped against her skin when she moved. The air in the cave was cool, but the sun was well up and Eofar had insisted she wear her cape in case they had to leave quickly. He had gone outside already; to check on Aeda, he'd said, but she didn't believe him. It was funny how they were both pretending they weren't waiting, as if pretending would somehow make the waiting more bearable. As if anything could.

The glove on her right hand was damp and slippery as she began the long series of drills over again, and on the sixth move she felt a flutter of panic as she lunged and stumbled yet again. The point of Truth's Might stuttered over the floor and the hilt kicked out of her stinging hand. She stood still for a moment, listening to the echo of the fallen sword ringing in the blackness of the cave. Then the pain came, great aching waves of it that swept up her shoulder and set her jaw trembling.

No. She must drill, and keep drilling: she must relearn what she had already spent so many years mastering. In a sudden fit of fury she let out a sound no Norlander had ever made before her. She listened, stunned, as it blared through the cavern.

"Isa?"

She shut her eyes tight. She knew that she had imagined the voice because he wasn't standing there behind her. He was dead. She knew he was dead.

"Isa? Are you—?"

"Daryan?" His name dropped from her lips but she still didn't want to turn around. If this was a dream—and it had to be—she needed it to continue. Life didn't give; life took—her mother, her sister, her arm . . . And it would take Daryan, too, just because she needed him.

She heard his footsteps behind her. How many times had she held her breath and listened to those same footsteps, wondering how long it would be before they went away again?

"Isa! Please . . ."

Then his fingers brushed her shoulder and she nearly went senseless with relief.

He pulled her into his arms; her back arched and her breath stopped as the heat seared into her skin like a hot iron. She heard his soft cry in her ear and felt him shudder even as his arms tightened around her. Then the first shock passed and she was no longer just withstanding the blaze but hungering for it, melting as his mouth finally pressed urgently against hers. It was like drowning in a lake of fire. Now it was her fingers tangled in his black hair and she was pulling him ever closer, engulfed but not consumed, gloriously tempered by the flames.

They drew back when they couldn't bear it any more, and he stroked the damp hair away from her face, saying, "I knew you'd be all right. I knew you wouldn't leave me. Not now—" She could see his eyes shining in her reflected glow and he kissed her again, short and hard, like a lightning strike.

It took another moment for her to find her voice. "When I saw you with Frea, I was sure— What happened? How did you get away?"

"No, I need to hear about you first." The corners of his mouth turned down and deep furrows sprang up on his brow. "How bad is the pain?"

She didn't answer; there was no point, he would know if she were lying to him. He lifted aside the fold of her cape and looked down at the knotted sleeve. Her stomach jumped and she felt horribly naked, more than she had ever felt from the mere absence of clothing. She saw his teeth grind together.

"If I'd got there sooner . . . if I'd—"

"Don't," she pleaded. "I can't— I have to think about *now*."

He let the cape fall back again. "You know Eofar wants you to leave? He wants to take you and Harotha away to some place safe before things here get worse."

"I won't go—I've told him that."

He touched her hair again. "Are you sure?"

"This is my home—*our* home." She ran her gloved finger over his bottom lip. "Eofar told me who you really are."

He laughed, but not happily. "Who I really am? I wish he'd tell me." He told her everything that had happened in the temple after she'd left. "What do you think my people would do if they found out I did it all for you?" he murmured at the end. "Do you think they'd still want me for their daimon then?"

She was saved from having to respond by the entrance of her brother and Harotha into the cave. She heard Harotha catch her breath, and the sound prompted Daryan to look around him, as if he'd seen nothing but Isa until that moment. As she retrieved Truth's Might and returned it to its sheath, Eofar went to the long stone table and relit the lamp they had brought along as part of their few supplies.

The cavern was one vast room, with tunnels leading out far beyond the reach of the lamplight. The cave itself might have been natural, but the floor was leveled and the massive domed ceiling was far too regular in shape not to have been worked. In the center of the room, heavy furniture carved out of stone sat under a layer of dust. Some of the chairs had been overturned, and the tops of the tables were streaked with black scorch marks.

Harotha followed a shaft of daylight to a little patch of wall not far from the entrance. As they gathered curiously around her, she wiped her sleeve along the wall.

Dust billowed out into the shaft of sunlight, glittering so brilliantly that Isa had to shield her eyes. When she was able to look again, she saw twinkling gold-painted stars surrounded by characters whose curving lines and dots reminded her of the cramped squiggles she had glimpsed on the pages of Daryan's manuscript before the water from her broken bathtub had destroyed them.

"Your vision," Daryan said in a low voice to Harotha. "It was real. This was the place."

"Vision?" Eofar repeated, and Isa felt her brother's sudden flash of anger—and the stark terror beneath it. "Harotha, tell me you didn't take that elixir."

Harotha and Daryan exchanged a look and some secret passed between them, something he hadn't told her yet. Isa felt a stab of jealousy.

"Don't worry, I'm fine," Harotha assured Eofar. "Of course I took it—what did you think I was going to do with it?"

"I bought it so that I could find out what happened to *you*," he reminded her. "What did *you* need it for?"

Daryan touched Harotha's arm. "I think you should tell them everything."

"Yes," Eofar agreed, "and right now."

Harotha launched into the tale, speaking too quickly for Isa to follow every word. The ancient history went by in a blur, but she focused her attention on the part involving the little boy she had seen with Rho in the refectory, and how Frea planned to use him to destroy the Shadar and attack the heart of the Norland empire. She had a dozen questions for Harotha by the time she finished, but Eofar drew the Shadari woman back into the darkness of the cave and Isa heard them arguing in strained voices.

Daryan turned back to the wall and traced the curve of a figure with his hand. "I never thought I'd ever see anything like this."

She moved closer to him, wanting to feel his touch again, craving the heat. She pushed aside the curls from the back of his neck and kissed him there. He shuddered and she drew back, afraid she'd hurt him, but then he turned and kissed her again with the passion of an inferno.

"Stop!" she hissed suddenly, drawing back from him. She had heard a sound like the scrape of a shoe against the floor and she shifted her eyes toward the doorway without turning her head. A shadow moved against the wall and then froze. Daryan's eyebrows were arched in question, but he kept still. She took a slow step to her left.

With a yelp that echoed through the cave, the figure broke for the entranceway and streaked outside.

As Isa sprang after the fleeing spy she was thankful that her brother had insisted she keep her cape on. She hooked the last clasp and flicked the cowl up over her head just before she plunged out into the blinding sunshine, drawing her sword as she ran. Daryan called to Eofar and then pounded after her.

The spy ran at a breakneck pace, but with her long legs and fluid strides she closed the gap until he was almost within her grasp. She lunged, but the brightness impaired her vision and he twisted just out of her reach. She stumbled past him and whirled back to find the man kneeling on the sand, waving his arms protectively in front of his face. She could see Daryan huffing over the sand toward them. The stump of her left arm felt like it was splitting apart, and she pressed her fist against it.

"Please don't kill me!" the spy wailed. "I was just

walking by and saw the cave—please, I have a family—I have five children. I've done nothing wrong, I swear. Please, please, don't kill me, please!" he begged, sobbing and scrabbling on his belly in the sand. She stared at the man with distaste and lowered her sword.

"Isa!" Daryan cried out to her as he ran. "Don't!"

Too late, she saw the Shadari's hand twitch and a fistful of sand hit her full in the face. She dropped to one knee and dug her streaming eyes into the crook of her arm. Before she could bring her sword up to defend herself, the Shadari aimed a vicious kick at the stump of her left arm and she fell back helplessly onto the sand, pain exploding through her entire body, seeing nothing but a purple darkness empty of stars.

Then she heard a wet smacking sound and a thud. She blinked her eyes until her vision cleared and saw the Shadari spy stretched out a few feet away. His eyes were closed and red blood oozed from his nose.

<Don't try to move yet.> She felt a cool hand gripping her shoulder and she looked up to see Rho bending over her. Spasms of pain were still ripping through her. <Easy, Isa. Breathe. That's it. It's all right. I can't believe that little prick threw sand at you.>

She tried to stand up, but the ground swung beneath her again and she felt Rho's hands catch her as she listed forward. <I'll be all right. Let me go,> she insisted, fully aware of how ridiculous she was being: if he obeyed her, she'd fall on her face. Instead he knelt down, angling himself so his shadow stretched out to cover her. He said nothing, just waited.

As the pain began to subside, she looked up and saw that Daryan had stopped a little distance away and was looking out over the sands. Suddenly she understood why he was hanging back; he wanted to give her a chance to tell Rho what had happened to her.

She could feel Rho's weariness, but his silver eyes were bright and clear in the shadows beneath the cowl. The bruises on his face had nearly healed and he looked almost like himself again, only stripped of his normal sardonic veneer. Except for her brother he was the only Norlander in the temple she had ever trusted, or who had ever shown any interest in her.

She reached up and unhooked the clasp nearest her throat, holding the folds of the cape together with her hand. <I need to show you something.>

Rho, bemused, watched as she pulled the cloak open just enough for him to see. Instantly his eyes darted away—then he forced himself to look back again at the knotted sleeve swinging beneath her shoulder.

She heard his breathing, quick and ragged over the stillness of the desert, as she did up the clasp.

<How did it happen?> His emotions were so thick and heavy she could hardly understand him. Most of all she felt his fury; it swarmed inside her, matching its pulse to her throbbing nerves.

<It burned. It had to be cut off.> She had to stop: the memory was too new, too strong; she couldn't tell him without reliving it, and she could still feel the burning. It wasn't fair, to have all the memories, all the pain, but not the arm. *It wasn't fair.*

<Don't, Isa. It's all right, you don't have to tell me.> He put his arm around her shoulders and she wondered why, until she realized that she was shaking. <Just tell me one thing: was this your choice, or did someone choose this for you?>

She began to feel calmer. The pain was becoming bearable again. <I didn't want to die. It was my choice, no one else's.>

He released her and stood up. <All right—then you'll have to live with it.>

<But we're Norlanders,> she said. <You're supposed to—>

He kicked his boot into the sand, hard, and the grains scattered around him. <Look around, Isa! Does this look like Norland to you?> She could feel him trying to control himself. <*The Book of the Hall* doesn't say anything about life in the desert. There's no forest here to leave you in. Your arm is gone; it's done. Just don't expect any pity from me.>

<I don't want any.> She started to stand up.

<Wait, I'm not finished.> She looked up, but the halo around his cowled head was too much for her eyes. <I may not think much of that religious stuff, but the others on our side—except maybe Daem—they do. I don't know if they'd hurt you, but they certainly won't accept you, and they won't fight alongside you. We need them, Isa. Do you understand what I'm telling you?>

She glared down at Truth's Might shining in the sand. <You're telling me to stay out of the way.>

<I am.>

She got to her feet, half-expecting him to offer her a hand, which he did not. She picked up her sword and returned it to its sheath. <All right. I can do that.>

Daryan was still standing in the same spot, glancing over at her uncomfortably from time to time, and now Harotha and Eofar were coming toward them, flanking Dramash. The little boy looked just the same as when Isa had last seen him in the refectory; she had a very hard time believing a child that size could topple a castle of blocks much less destroy a whole city. He called out Rho's name.

Suddenly she felt Rho's cold lips brush her forehead. <You did the right thing,> he said; then, before striding off to intercept the boy, he added like an echo of better times, <At least this way, you'll still have the chance to regret it.>

Daryan was instantly at her side. "You told him."

"It's all right," she said, feeling like a burden had lifted. "He doesn't think I should tell the others, but he said I made the right choice."

"Do *you* still think so?"

She swallowed against the dryness in her throat. "I'm alive. That's enough for now."

Eofar and Harotha walked up and they all gathered

next to the fallen spy; Eofar had a coil of spare reins from Aeda's saddle.

"Everything go as planned?" Daryan asked Rho.

"Yes."

"What about the White Wolf?" asked Harotha. Isa noticed how her voice sounded harder when she spoke to Rho. "Is she trapped in the temple?"

"For now."

Isa asked, "And Lahlil? Did anyone see her?"

"Who's Lahlil?"

"The Mongrel," said Daryan.

"Oh. She and King Jachad went to ask the Nomas for help. They said they would meet us at the palace." Rho kicked the spy's leg. "What are we going to do with him?"

"His name is Elthion," said Harotha. "He's one of my brother's men. He must have followed Daryan and me from the beach."

Isa looked at Harotha closely for the first time. She hadn't changed much despite the pregnancy: full cheeks; smooth skin; brown eyes flecked with gold and just a bit lighter than Daryan's; lips a deep coral pink. She was very beautiful, but Isa had known that already.

"We'll have to leave him in the cave," said Daryan.

They couldn't be sure they'd ever be able to return and release him. They might be sentencing him to death.

"We don't have a choice," agreed Eofar.

"All right, let's get him inside. At least he'll have shelter, and we'll leave him whatever water we can spare."

Eofar moved forward with the reins, but Harotha put her hand on his arm. "I think Daryan and I should leave for the palace now, alone," she said. "If my brother is sending people to spy on us, it means he's already suspicious. It's too dangerous for us all to be seen together."

"If you think that's best," said Eofar. Harotha couldn't feel how deeply it pained him to be parted from her again, but Isa could.

Daryan's eyes swept over all of them. "No, no, no,"

he said suddenly, his mobile mouth moving in distress. "No, this is all wrong—I shouldn't have— You, Harotha and Isa should leave, right now. None of you should be here." He looked at Harotha. "Go somewhere and have your baby—be happy, *please*. Forget about the Shadar, forget about this alliance. It was all a mistake." He blinked away the tears welling up in his eyes and growled at Eofar, "Take them away! Don't you understand what's going to happen?"

"Daryan, listen to me," said Harotha, even as Isa was still struggling to make sense of what he was saying, "we've all made our own choices; you're not forcing us to do anything. Tonight there will be a battle, and some of us will get hurt. Some of us will die. You're going to have to accept responsibility for that and still be able to live with yourself. That's what it means to be a leader."

"I'm not a leader. You're—"

"That's what it means to be a leader," she repeated. "That's what you are. You were right about Rho, and you were right about this alliance. This *is* the only way to stop the White Wolf."

He looked back at her for a long time without saying a word. At last he said to Eofar, "You told me you wanted to take Isa and Harotha away."

"I know. I was wrong," Eofar replied. "I have to make sure Frea doesn't get the chance to do the things Harotha saw in her vision. Isa and I are the only family she has; that makes her our responsibility."

Daryan turned around to face Isa. "You won't go either," he asked her, "not even if I beg you?"

"Not without you."

They both understood that their brief moment together, that tiny glimpse at happiness, was all they were going to get for now. It wasn't enough that they belonged to each other: he was a king, whether she liked it or not—and she was afraid she was already losing him.

Chapter Thirty-Six

Rho leaned his shoulder against the empty doorframe in the ruined, roofless hall of the abandoned palace—a doorway leading from nothing, to nowhere—and wondered when all of this would be over. Here they all were, the partners in this weird alliance: the Shadari, more than a hundred of them, ranged along one side, baking in the sun; the Norlanders huddling dispiritedly on the other side, hiding in the shadows of the broken walls, and the Mongrel in the middle, her every move scrutinized by the Nomas king. Rho's only certainty was that they all hated and feared Frea just a little more than they hated and feared each other.

He straightened up uncomfortably; every time he moved the fabric of his shirt tugged at his wound. He pressed his forearm hard against his side and tried to dull the throbbing, while his eyes kept returning to the curved sword stuck through Faroth's white sash. Reunite Dramash with his people: that had been his goal. Get the boy away from Frea and back where he belonged; that would make everything all right again.

When did I become such an utter fool? he wondered.

One look at Dramash asleep on the ground with his head in Harotha's lap, flanked by Faroth on one side and Daryan on the other, was enough to tell anyone with half a brain that reuniting Dramash with the Shadari had solved nothing. In fact, everything was certainly *not* all right, and he was beginning to doubt that it ever would be.

"He's the only real weapon we have," Faroth was saying to Harotha, "and you want him to *hide*? You'd make him watch his city burn around him, knowing that he might have stopped it?"

"Do *you* want him to kill people?" She spoke softly so as not to awaken Dramash, but Rho couldn't miss the ferocious look she aimed at her brother. The likeness between them was startling. "How is that any different from what the White Wolf wants to do with him?"

"Of course it's different—he's a Shadari. He should do whatever is necessary to defend his home, like *all* Shadari."

"He's a little boy. You can't ask him to—"

<But if Frea needs that boy to go through with her attack against the emperor,> Falkar interjected, speaking only to the Norlanders, <then we should just kill him ourselves. It's obvious, isn't it?>

<No,> Eofar answered, and Rho felt Falkar's frustration. *Just a few days ago I might have made that same suggestion myself*, he thought. *No—a few days ago I would still have been in the temple, hanging on to Frea's sleeve.*

<But why?> Falkar asked.

<We're not going to kill a child,> Eofar said, <no matter who he is, or what he can do.> He walked over to the Mongrel. As he moved out of the shade the sun caught the gaudy triffons adorning the hilt of Strife's Bane and the Norlanders winced against the glare.

Rho looked at his countrymen: no more than fifty of them, while Frea had nearly twice that number at her disposal. Many of those, like Ingeld and Ongen, were fanatically loyal to her, while most of the men sweating in this ruin were supporting Eofar as the lesser of two evils.

<He looks so ordinary,> Isa said, looking at Dra-

mash. She was sitting on a step near Rho's feet—a step that led up to nothing and down from nowhere—with her cape fastened tightly at her throat. She'd kept her distance from the other Norlanders as he had insisted, and since she had always been aloof, no one found anything unusual or suspicious in her behavior. Isa herself had shown no interest in anything except the Shadari; even now she was staring across at them from beneath her cowl with a fixedness that Rho found unsettling.

Just as Eofar started to speak, Dramash stirred on the rug beside Harotha, and every other sound and movement in the ruined hall ceased. The boy murmured something unintelligible and kicked at the dirt. Harotha swiftly laid her hand on the boy's back and began rubbing it in soft circles. He made a tiny grunting sound and for a moment it looked like he was settling back into sleep—but then he stretched his arms out over his head and opened his eyes.

"Is she back yet?"

"Who, Dramash?" Harotha asked, smiling down at him, but Rho noticed that she'd stopped patting his back so that he wouldn't feel the obvious trembling of her hand.

"Mama," he said, yawning. "Is she back from the mountains? Did she find the lost goat?"

Daryan leaned forward and gripped Harotha's shoulder. She bit her lip.

"Not yet," Faroth answered smoothly before Harotha could say anything. "She's still looking. She'll be back soon."

Rho closed his eyes. The ground beneath him felt unsteady and he was glad for the support of the doorframe.

<Rho?> He could feel Daem watching him.

<I'm fine.>

"I want her to come home," said Dramash, and then

yawned again before snuggling up against his aunt and closing his eyes.

No one else moved.

After a long moment, Harotha looked down at the boy, then nodded.

Rho, like everyone else, exhaled the breath he'd not realized he'd been holding.

<All right,> Eofar said to the Mongrel, first in Norlander, then in Shadari, <so we'll take the triffons and form a line over the city. I don't have a problem with that. But you should know that I intend to challenge Frea to single combat.>

<She'll refuse,> replied the Mongrel.

<Maybe her honor still means something to her,> Eofar countered, but clearly even he didn't believe it. <Even if she refuses, it should distract her for a while.>

<If you want, then.> Unconcerned, she turned back to the Shadari. "Any of Frea's men who get through Eofar's line will fly in low; their goal will be to set the city on fire in as many places as possible, to create as much chaos as they can. Your task is to stop them. Those who aren't armed should be ready to fight the fires. The Nomas have agreed to help—they'll be here by sundown."

"Here to pick our bones, I'll bet," one of the Shadari muttered.

"Why would she bother setting fire to the city?" Daryan asked. "You said she was going to attack Norland, so why would she waste her time here?"

"She needs Dramash and she doesn't have enough men to search the whole city," the mercenary explained. "She'll try to force him out into the open—make you use him against her."

The Shadari daimon looked down at Dramash. "So Harotha's right: we do need to hide him. But he can't stay by himself—someone will have to watch him. Someone he trusts. I think it should be her."

Harotha looked up at Daryan, and then they both looked at the Mongrel.

"Agreed," she said.

"I'll leave some of my men with them," offered Faroth, "to protect them."

"No." The Mongrel's tone brooked no further discussion. "No one goes near them. *No one*—Shadari or Norlander—is to know where they are."

Faroth glared at her. "No one but you, you mean?"

This was Rho's opportunity. He straightened up again and stepped forward. <Why don't *I* stay with them?> he offered, trying to appear disinterested. <The boy's used to me. Besides, he might try to run away from Harotha, and she's hardly in any condition to chase after him.>

He was again struck by the strange impression that somehow the Mongrel knew more about him than he did about her. <No,> she said.

He was about to press his point further when Daem jumped up from the broken column on which he'd been sitting and asked, <What about the temple?>

<Daem,> he said, <you—>

<Shut up, Rho. I'll talk to you later.> He addressed the Mongrel again. <You do remember the temple, don't you? That big, square thing up there?> Rho's dismay at his interruption curdled into anger: Daem was deliberately shifting the conversation away from Dramash. <Frea will leave reinforcements. I think we should circle behind her and take it from her when she attacks, cut off her retreat.>

The Mongrel waited for Eofar to translate Daem's suggestion to the Shadari—minus the sarcasm—then replied, "Frea won't retreat and she won't leave reinforcements. Tonight the imperial ship will drop anchor in the harbor. If they notice anything wrong, if no one comes from the temple to escort the emperor's ministers ashore, they'll sail on the next tide for the nearest port. Frea has to overtake that ship before it's out of range of the triffons. She has only one chance to strike and she knows it."

"But Daem has a point," said Eofar. "If the ship doesn't

arrive for some reason, or if she doesn't find Dramash in time, she'll have to return to the temple. There's nowhere else for her to go. And we still have people trapped there—my father's clerks and physics, for a start."

"And some of the slaves," put in Daryan. "They must have been hiding when the rest of us escaped."

Rho felt something new in the Mongrel's hesitation, an uncertainty that went deeper than just the weighing of the facts; it worried him. Finally she told Daem, "If you want to go to the temple, I won't stop you."

He racked his mind for some subtle way of bringing up the subject of Dramash's escort again, but to no avail. He could have strangled Daem.

Then Isa called over, <Rho, look. I don't trust him. What do you think he's up to?> She gestured toward Faroth, who was threading his way through the crowd toward the doorway in the eastern wall. One of his white-sashed followers was waiting there with the dirtiest, most bedraggled person Rho had ever laid eyes on. The man's garments hung in tatters to the point of indecency, and every inch of him was smeared with black dust. His cheeks were hollow, but the sinews in his arms were as taut as wire. There was no softness about him anywhere. Labor had whittled his body down to a skeleton of iron.

<A miner,> he said, keeping his eyes on the two men. The miner was speaking and Faroth was listening intently. <I don't know—they're too far away. I can't hear what they're saying.>

<Rho?> Isa stood up from the step and moved to stand beside him. He felt the light touch of her hand on his elbow. <Are you all right? What's wrong?>

He didn't answer her. He was watching the miner place something into Faroth's hand, something small enough to disappear when Faroth squeezed his fingers shut around it.

<What was that? What did he just give to him?> Isa asked.

<I don't know,> he answered, his eyes still glued to Faroth.

<A coin, maybe? But the color was wrong—gold doesn't rust, does it?>

The interview appeared to be over. Faroth made his way back through the roofless hall and walked up to the Mongrel. "All right, we've had enough talk," he said. "We know what we have to do. The sun will be down in a few hours, and we need to get ready."

The Mongrel looked around at everyone. "If you do as you've been told, you will defeat Frea, that I promise you."

The crowd began to break up and Eofar walked up to them. <I want you to stay with Daryan,> he told Isa. <The two of you can take Aeda and help the Shadari spot fires. They'll need help from the air.>

Isa said nothing.

Rho knew better than anyone how hard she had worked learning to fight, and better than Isa herself the extraordinary extent of her natural talents. *It wasn't fair.* <Isa, I know you want to fight, but—>

<You don't know anything,> she broke in, cutting short his attempt at compassion. <I'll do what needs to be done—*whatever* needs to be done. You just stop Frea's men from getting through.> She walked over to where Daryan was waiting and Eofar hurried after her.

Daem sauntered over as soon as the others had gone.

<Why did you interrupt me like that?> Rho asked him. <I was going to—>

<I know exactly what you were going to do,> said Daem, <and you can forget it. You're coming to the temple with me. Eonar's physics are still there. You're going to have them take care of that wound.>

<I don't need—>

<Oh, stop it, Rho!> Daem's anger flickered out at

him. He was about to say more, but then he abruptly turned to walk away.

Rho, taken aback, grabbed his cloak. <What's the matter with you? Why are you acting like this?>

<*Me?*> Turning around, he said, <Do you think I can't see that you can barely stand? Onfar damn this filthy place—I didn't close the wound up properly, did I? It's gone sour, hasn't it? It's infected.>

<I don't know—I haven't looked,> he answered truthfully, <but it doesn't matter. It's not your fault.>

<Believe me, I know it's not *my* fault: it's *your* fault, you stupid shit, for not staying where you belonged. Look over there.> He pointed at the Shadari, at Dramash, asleep in his aunt's lap. <He's back with his own kind now, and they'll take care of him. There's nothing more to be done. Do you understand? He doesn't need you, or your help—if you want to call it that—any more. It's *over*. If you interfere now you'll only make more trouble for him. Can't you see that?>

Everything around Rho slowed suddenly and he drew in a long breath of the warm, sand-scented air. A glimmer of hope danced around Daem's words: the faintest possibility of escape. <Do you really believe that? You really think the best thing I can do for him is to leave him alone?>

<Without a doubt.>

Rho pressed his forearm against his side as another twinge of pain shot through him. <All right, then. I'll go with you to the temple.>

<Then say it's over. I want you to *say* it.>

<It's over.>

He felt Daem relax. <Good. Then let's go and get ready. I have to say, I'm looking forward to paying Lady Frea back for all those day-patrols.>

<Daem—>

<Rho, for Onfar's sake, just don't say anything else.>

Rho clapped Daem's shoulder gratefully and followed him into the shadows of the broken palace wall. But as they joined the others he couldn't help looking back over his shoulder at the Shadari, and he couldn't help noticing that Faroth still held the miner's gift in his clenched fist: a coin, maybe. The color of rust.

Chapter Thirty-Seven

Jachad followed Meiran out of the ruined hall into a labyrinth of crumbling foundations scarred by wind-worn Norlander graffiti. The ruins were silent except for the occasional scratching of a lizard scuttling over the stonework. Wherever a fragment of wall cast a large enough shadow, a triffon lay in morose repose and watched them pass with dull eyes.

Once they had left the others well behind, Meiran stopped to take a drink from the wineskin she'd acquired during their brief visit with the Nomas, and he seized the moment. "When I was convincing my people to fight against Frea, I had the idea that you actually wanted to *win* this battle." He tugged the scarf from around his head and wound the colorful silk—a gift from his mother—around his neck. "And then I heard your battle plan, if you can call it that. I expected you to come up with something brilliant, something infallible. You can't possibly expect to defeat Frea like that—Eofar and a few dozen triffons have no chance against her."

"I don't care about Frea, or the battle," she informed him, wiping the excess wine from her mouth. Her Shadari eye sparkled with that same wild, greedy look he remembered from Shairav's room in the temple.

"But you told the Shadari they're going to defeat her."

"They are."

"Of course—you took the elixir, so you know that

already," he observed. He rubbed at the bristly stubble on his chin. "I've met a lot of fortune-tellers, seers, diviners, whatever. They all have one thing in common: they all make their living telling people what they want to hear."

"It's all happening just like it's supposed to," she continued as if he'd never spoken. "I was right, Jachi. It's all happening." She walked over to the wall, yanked a loose stone free and tossed it aside.

"And what will you be doing while the rest of us are out fighting Frea? I noticed you left yourself out of the battle plan. Faroth noticed, too."

"Faroth is a moron. He thinks I want his son."

"Can you blame him? Everyone else wants him."

"If I wanted him I'd have kept him when I had him," she said pointedly.

A dry, dusty breeze skittered through the ruins. He swallowed. "I didn't think you had forgotten about that, but you can't blame me—you had a knife to his throat. What was I supposed to think?"

In a flash her gray cheeks lost their brief color and the energy animating her gestures drained away. "The same as everyone else," she answered. She took another drink of wine and an uncomfortable silence settled in between them.

Into this silence he finally said, "I asked my mother what you spoke to her about."

The expression on her face could have been dread or expectation, or some bastard mix of the two. "And?"

"And she told me to ask you."

She exhaled and turned back to the crumbling wall. Laying the wineskin down on top, she put both her hands on the dusty stones and stretched her arms out straight.

"So," he said, realizing with a sinking heart that he had brought them to the very moment he'd been dreading, "you're still not going to tell me what you're doing here?"

"No," she replied, still looking down at the ground.

He moved behind her. "All right. I'm through playing this game with you." He brushed some of the tangled black hair back away from her ear, as if he wanted to be sure that she wouldn't miss a word of what he had to say. She flinched at his touch—only just, but he saw it. "I've pretended to follow you around; I've played the unwanted suitor, the bothersome child. I've let you pretend that you'd just as soon be rid of me. But we both know that isn't true. The Shadari may have hired me to bring you, but we both know *you* brought *me* here and not the other way around. Merciful Shof, I still don't know why, but you wanted me here."

Into the pause that followed, Meiran said in a voice that plunged straight into his heart, "I still do."

He steeled himself. "Then tell me why you're here."

She shut her eyes. "No."

"All right, then you give me no choice. I'm leaving you." He spoke louder than he meant to, but he couldn't help himself. "I convinced my people to join this fight, and fight is what I'm going to do. Omir and his crew are going to defend the north edge of the city, by the temple, and I'm going with them. You can do whatever you came here to do—it's of no interest to me. I know which side I'm on."

The afternoon sun glanced off the gray skin of her shoulder, warming it to bronze. "It doesn't matter," she said. Her voice was no louder than the whisper of the hot, dry wind. "You can't change anything—no one can."

"You keep saying that, but which one of us are you trying to convince?" He flexed his hands as sparks danced around them. "Well. We'll see." He turned away from her and started back toward the city.

"Jachi."

The sun had begun to slip behind the mountains. Long shadows stretched over the ruins as the warm light faded; the battle was near at hand. The stones around him still pulsed with the day's heat but the air was suddenly cool. He could see Meiran clearly—he felt like he was seeing her clearly for the first time since she'd come back into his life.

After a moment she dropped her head. Whatever impulse had made her speak had passed.

"The great Mongrel. The undefeated warrior," he said, smiling through the pain raking his heart. Before he walked away, he added, "Well, don't take it too hard. No one wins them all."

Chapter Thirty-Eight

Harotha woke with no idea where she was; the darkness was impenetrable. She couldn't remember where she'd fallen asleep, or what she'd been doing just before. Had they been flying? She was so tired, and nothing felt quite real, not even her own body. As she looked around she could see the faint glow of Eofar's skin, so he was with her—but the void robbed her of all sense of distance.

"Where are we?" she asked, but he didn't respond. "Eofar?" she said again, and then sighed. "You're still angry with me for wanting to stay, aren't you? Or is it because I went back to the temple to find Dramash? Or because I took the elixir?"

"None of that matters now," he said.

"No. No, you're right," she agreed, sweet relief flooding through her. "It doesn't matter; we left all of that behind us. It's just *us* now." She could still see the glow of him, but she wished he would come nearer. She remembered how wonderful it felt to be near him, the way the rest of the world disappeared when they touched. She wanted to feel that now. She walked toward him—had she been standing all along?—but he must have been much further away than she assumed because when she reached out for him there was nothing there.

"Eofar?" she called to him across the darkness. Her voice echoed strangely. Were they back in the cave? The last thing she remembered was the old palace, getting ready for the battle. "Where are you? Can you see me?"

"I'm here by the window."

"What window?" she asked, confused. But she turned, and then she did see a little rectangular window—she had seen a window just like that before. Where was that? The reddish-gold light flooding in was very beautiful, suffused with the rich colors of sunset. She went toward it, eager for a closer look, but her feet were heavy and slow, and with each step she grew more and more uneasy. Eofar offered no reassurance; his eyes were turned away from her, focused on whatever he was seeing through the window.

"I'm sorry about the Shadar," he said to her.

She looked down at the burning city spread out below her and caught her breath. "No," she cried. "No!" Dereshadi with ragged wings swept low over the little domed houses. She could hear people screaming, and bodies, bloody and dying, were lying in the streets. "What's happening?" She reached out for Eofar, but her hands jerked oddly and touched only air.

"The Dead Ones are attacking, see? Those are their ships in the harbor, over there. Come on, you remember all of this," said Eofar, only now he spoke with Daryan's voice. "This is what happened when you were a baby."

Baby.

Her hands flew down to her stomach. It was flat, taut. "Eofar, where's the baby?" she shrieked in terror.

"Don't you remember? We gave him to my sister. It was your idea."

"I don't remember anything! I would never give away our baby," she shouted. She was shaking him now, but he remained as impassive as a statue. "Where is he? We have to find him!"

"Oh, it's too late for that," he remarked, still unperturbed. He turned his attention back to the window. "Almost time. We'd better go up now."

"Up where?"

His silver eyes blinked at her. "Up to the roof, of course. It's time to jump."

Harotha awoke with a jerk of horror. The room was pitch-black, and for a moment she was afraid that she was still trapped in that terrible nightmare. But her hands flew to her stomach and with dizzying relief she felt the familiar heavy bulge. She hadn't meant to fall asleep, but at least now she remembered where she was—an ordinary sleeping chamber, in an ordinary house, on an ordinary street: worn cushions on the floor, fire-pit in the center, a cistern of water by the door. It had its very ordinariness to recommend it as a hiding-place. The Mongrel hadn't offered any explanation for her choice when she'd deposited her there with Dramash, and Harotha hadn't asked for one. As long as the Mongrel wanted to keep Dramash out of the fighting and away from the White Wolf, Harotha would do as she asked. And right now, that meant doing absolutely nothing.

She tried to take a deep breath, but a heavy ache sat on her heart, and she felt trapped, suffocated. She looked down at Dramash sleeping deeply beside her.

Moving quietly, she slipped into the main room and saw she'd foolishly left the lamp burning. She snuffed it out and the room plunged into darkness. It took just a few moments for her eyes to adjust and she made her way over to the cold fire-pit and looked up. The bit of sky she could see through the chimney-hole had turned from hazy lavender to deep indigo and the stars winked brightly. She took a deep breath and pressed her hand against her chest to ease the ache.

It was night: the White Wolf would have begun her attack by now. Somewhere up there, Eofar was already fighting for the Shadari—for *her*. He had been trained to fight since childhood, like all the Dead Ones, and he and Aeda had routinely triumphed in the aerial tournaments the governor had enjoyed prior to his illness. He was older than Frea, bigger and stronger, he had an imperial sword and she had an ordinary one—but he had never taken a life. And now they were expecting him to kill his own sister.

She found herself staring at the curtain separating her from the street outside. She'd tied the fastenings herself after the Mongrel had deposited the still-sleeping Dramash in the inner chamber and departed. Now she walked over to the curtain and ran her fingers experimentally over the rough, heavy cloth. She thought she smelled smoke, but it was hard to tell; she herself still reeked from the fire in the stables. Muffled sounds reached her ears from the street outside: shouts, and running feet.

Surely it wouldn't matter if she just glanced outside—?

"Aunt Harotha? Is that you? Where are you going?"

Her heart leaped into her mouth and she turned to see Dramash standing in the doorway of the sleeping chamber, blinking his eyes.

"Dramash! You startled me. I thought you were still asleep," she said, laughing to cover her consternation. She walked over and knelt down in front of him. The baby rolled heavily to one side and she wondered if she was going to be able to get back up again. "Don't worry, I'm not going anywhere. Why don't you go back to sleep? It's not nearly morning yet."

"Oh, I'm not tired any more," he informed her, and marched past her into the room. "Why is it so dark in here?"

Her heart still pounding, she picked up the flints and methodically re-lit the lamp. Her mind raced furiously. The night had only just begun, and if he wouldn't go back to sleep, how was she going to keep him inside until the battle was over? "You must be thirsty. Would you like some water?"

"No." He looked around. "Where are we? This isn't my house. Why are we here all alone? What—?"

"Dramash," she started, holding up her hand. She tried to mimic Saria's motherly tone. "You and I are going to stay here until morning, remember? Then we'll go meet your father and the others."

"And Mama?"

"Yes," she answered, with barely a pause.

"And Rho?"

Something was going to have to be done about his unreasoning attachment to that soldier. "And Rho."

"Why can't we go now?"

"Well, we just can't," she told him. "They're very busy right now. They have important things to do, and we'd only be in their way." She pulled a cushion over and patted the space beside her. "Now, come over here. You know, the night will pass much faster if you go back to sleep."

He looked down at her, pouting. "I think I'll go outside and look for them," he announced, and sauntered past her.

She struggled back to her feet. "Dramash! Stop!" He paused in front of the curtain and turned back to her. "Listen to me: you and I are going to stay here tonight. We are not to go outside. Do you understand?"

"Why not?"

She tried to stifle her anger. It had not occurred to her when she agreed to this that she knew nothing about children, but she had never imagined that leading a rebellion would involve handling the moods of a precocious nephew. In a sober voice, she explained, "Your father, Daryan, and all of our friends—"

"And Rho!"

"And Rho," she added with careful patience, "have a lot to do tonight. They're protecting the Shadar from very bad people."

"The White Wolf," he whispered, looking back at her with wide eyes. "I thought she was my friend, but she's not. She's *bad*. I saw her hurt people."

"That's right." She nodded approvingly. "Now it's

very important that you and I don't give the others anything else to worry about, or distract them in any way, do you see? By staying here, we're really helping them."

He beckoned her closer and a shy smile danced on his lips. "I can help better than that," he told her confidentially. "I did it before—I did it at the mines, and in the temple, too. Lots of times! I can do it whenever I want to."

She swallowed, feeling ill. "I know you can. It's a very special gift you've been given, Dramash. Maybe we should talk about—"

"I saw him move!" he announced, pointing at her belly. "There's a *baby* in there, isn't there?"

"That's right." She smiled and lurched back up to her feet, though her back ached fiercely. She moved further into the room, hoping he would follow her away from the door. "He's your cousin, you know—he'll be born in just a few weeks. Come over here and sit down with me and I'll let you feel him kick, if you like."

"I had a baby sister, but she wasn't alive when she was born," he told her, strangely boastful. Then he lowered his voice to a dramatic whisper. "I'm not supposed to talk about that."

"Oh, I'm sorry—I didn't know that," she said faintly. So Saria and Faroth had lost a baby, and Saria had never said a word about it. She stroked her stomach protectively. A stillbirth—how awful. And then for Saria to take care of her, all those months, watching her get bigger and bigger—

"Is Mama back yet?"

"Mama? No—no, I don't think she's back yet," she said, feeling the numbness tingling in her hands again. She had to remember to breathe.

"But I told Papa that she shouldn't have to look after the goats any more," said Dramash. "She should buy a new goat with the money I got for her."

"What money?"

"The White Wolf gave her a gold eagle when she took

me away—I saw it. It was *this* big!" He drew a circle in the air the size of a dinner plate, and she would have laughed had the circumstances been different. Then his face clouded over with anger. "Someone should tell her to come home. I want her to come home *now*."

She looked back at him helplessly, feeling her control of the situation sliding away. She didn't want to embroider the lies Faroth had already told the boy, but this hardly seemed the time or place to tell him the truth about his mother . . . Or maybe she was just too much of a coward. "I'm sure she wants to come home, Dramash, but—"

"I'm going to find Rho. He'll take me up on his dereshadi. We'll find her and bring her back."

"Dramash, I told you, they're very busy. You can't—"

"Rho will help me. He's my friend," he assured her. "I'll just go and get him. You can stay here if you want to."

"Dramash!" she shouted, close to losing her temper. "Dramash, you come back here and sit down, right this minute! You are not going anywhere: do you hear me?"

"I don't want to stay here!" he whined. "I hate it here!"

She seized his arm. "That's enough! You will stay here until your father comes to get you! I will have no more nonsense!"

He stiffened under her grasp, and his dark eyes widened and then narrowed. At the sound of a crash she spun around to find the cistern lying on the ground, cracked and gushing precious water. She dropped Dramash's arm as the lamp on the table trembled, throwing up shadows around the room, and the dishes began to rattle and skitter.

"I don't have to do what you say," he told her, a triumphant light kindling in his eyes. "I can do *anything* I want to and you can't stop me." He turned from her and ran back to the door.

She struggled up from the floor, calling, "Dramash,

wait!" but he dived underneath the curtain and disappeared. Harotha, now desperate, didn't bother with the knots either, but tore the curtains aside with a strength born of absolute panic and ran out into the street. Dramash was nowhere to be seen. She smelled smoke now for certain, and there were shouts and screams coming from all directions.

She guessed Dramash would head toward the dereshadi. She looked up, at first seeing only the glitter of lights darting around the sky, until her eyes adjusted to the darkness and she could make out the bulky shapes of the dereshadi and their slender riders. Just at that moment a torch fell from one, tumbling down until it disappeared behind the houses in front of her. She shut her eyes.

"*Don't,*" she muttered furiously to herself as a wave of dizziness and nausea swept over her. "Don't do this!" A deep pain grabbed her in the gut and squeezed like a fist, sending cramps pulsing through her, sucking the strength from her body. She clutched her stomach and fell to her knees in the dirt. "No! Not now—not *now,*" she chanted, praying for the pain to stop.

After a few moments she was able to pull herself back to her feet and drag herself to the side of the street, but she hadn't gone far before the next contraction hit. She stumbled over to the wall of the nearest house and pressed her forehead hard against the rough clay, leaning on it for support as she waited for the cramping to pass.

Without warning a hand grabbed her by the shoulder and turned her around. "What are you doing here?" the Mongrel demanded.

Looking into her scarred face, Harotha realized—quite suddenly, and with complete conviction—that the Mongrel hated her.

"Why are you here?" the mercenary asked again. "Why aren't you back there at the house?"

"Dramash ran off," she panted, still trying to catch her breath. "I couldn't stop him. We have to—"

"Are the Nomas there yet?"

"The Nomas?" she echoed in confusion. "No, no one is there—no one knows where we are. Dramash—"

"Forget about him—I don't care about him."

"But I was supposed to be protecting him! That's why you left him with me!"

"*He* was supposed to be protecting *you*!" the Mongrel shouted back.

Harotha stared at her, completely taken aback, but someone shouted her name and she saw Alkar rushing toward them, followed by others of Faroth's gang.

"What's going on?" he demanded, waving his maimed hand in her face. "Dramash is out there running loose—what have you done? What happened to your plan?"

"You saw Dramash? Where is he?" she cried.

"We have him and he's being taken to Faroth, of course," Alkar told her.

"Yes, I—" she began, but another contraction hit her before she could finish. Involuntarily she snatched at the Mongrel's arm and dug her fingers into her wrist.

"What's wrong with her?" Alkar asked, hurriedly backing away.

Over the pulse pounding in her ears, she heard the Mongrel say, "What do you think?"

"She's not having that baby now?"

"Not now," she gasped out, "no, not yet—it's too soon. It's just the first pains." She let go of the Mongrel's arm and cringed at the deep marks her fingernails had left in her skin, but the mercenary appeared not even to have noticed. "Take me to Faroth," she told Alkar, "quickly, please! There's something I must tell him!"

Alkar regarded her suspiciously for a moment, but then he said, "All right, come on then," and led the way down the street. The Shadari closed ranks around her, hemming her in, and though she couldn't see the Mongrel, she knew that she was following, too. The houses they passed were dark and quiet, but not peaceful; the whole city was holding its breath, and though she saw no fire, the air was riddled with the sharp smell of smoke. Every few moments a voice punctured the dark: a shout, or a scream, or a cheer. Shadari ran to and fro, waving torches, brandishing weapons.

She was hurried through a square where a crowd had gathered around the exploded remains of a downed dereshadi. The mob was cheering on the strong-stomached man who had taken it upon himself to drag the Dead One's corpse from the saddle. She snatched a quick look, just enough to be certain it wasn't Eofar, before she had to turn away. In another square they found piles of stones and Shadari ready to hurl them upward at any rider within reach. But the real battle was taking place high above their heads.

She touched Alkar's shoulder. "Are we winning?"

"Most of the Dead Ones are still alive."

"On whose side?"

"Both," Alkar answered, "and that's not winning, not as far as I'm concerned."

She soon realized she was being taken back to the ruined palace. She comforted herself with the thought that Dramash would be safe with Faroth by now, and once she'd told her brother about the visions, she was certain he would help her to protect him. *He hasn't changed so much that he will ignore a sign from the gods themselves, surely?*

They reached the walled courtyard at last. Torches reeking strongly of fish oil danced on spikes stuck into the dirt, making the air feel greasy as she drew it into her lungs. As Alkar hustled her past the sentries at the doorway with a curt word she saw Dramash dancing atop a pile of rubble. He was gazing up, open-mouthed, at the lights bobbing in the dark sky above. She sighed in deep relief.

She didn't see Faroth at all until he was right in front of her. "I knew you'd come," he told her, smiling in a way that raised the hairs on the back of her neck. "You were right after all, about the gods. They have given us a sign. I was wrong to doubt them."

"Faroth, that's why I need to—"

"I wasn't sure, not until Dramash came back to me, but now I have no doubts, none at all." He held up his hand and pushed something in front of her eyes. It appeared to be a coin, but as soon as she leaned forward for a closer look, he snapped his hand shut around it. "I know what I have to do, Harotha. I'm glad you're here to see it. We've waited all of our lives for this."

"Faroth, wait!" she called after him as he turned and walked away.

"Dramash." Faroth stepped up to the little hillock of broken stone. "Come down here. I need to talk to you."

"I can't see him. It's too dark," he told his father disappointedly, turning away from the dereshadi with a frown.

"I said come down here!"

He scrambled down and Harotha looked at the two of them standing together, her brother and Saria's little boy. The presentiment that had been pushing in at the corner of her mind suddenly crystalized, and the blood in her veins turned to salt water.

"No!" she wanted to scream, but the syllable came out no louder than a croaking whisper.

Faroth squatted down in front of Dramash and held out the coin he had shown her. "Take it," he told his son, who obeyed. "Do you recognize it?"

"Wait, Faroth, *listen* to me," Harotha begged him. "I'm your sister—your *twin*. We've always done everything together—"

"It's an eagle," the boy declared, holding the coin up in front of his eyes. He rubbed his fingers over its surface. "It's got dirt all over it."

"Blood," said someone else, and a man in rags stepped forward. He'd been standing unnoticed behind Faroth until now. She had never seen him before, but something in his whipcord body and hunched stance screamed malice.

"Faroth!" she called to her brother again, and as Alkar tried to block her path she shoved him aside with a desperate sob and plunged forward. "Faroth, stop!" she pleaded. "Stop! Listen to me!" She heard Alkar shouting, and then someone grabbed her arms from behind and held them fast.

"Easy," said the Mongrel into her ear.

"Stop this," she sobbed, twisting around to face her, "please! This isn't your plan—this isn't what you wanted!"

The Mongrel looked down at her with her silver-green eye glinting like moonlight on metal. "What I wanted?" she repeated coldly. "You have no idea what I want. None of you do."

"Dramash," said Faroth, taking his son by both shoulders, "this man's name is Josah. He has something to tell you."

Josah looked down at the boy. "That's the coin the White Wolf gave your mother before they took you away. As soon as you were gone, that soldier—Rho—he cut her throat." He slipped behind Dramash like a shadow and slid his bony finger across the child's neck. "Cut it, just like that—like butchering an animal. I saw it: he killed her like she was nothing."

"It's true," Faroth said, giving Dramash a little shake.

The boy stared back at his father, the color draining visibly from his face.

"Faroth, don't do this," Harotha moaned, fruitlessly tugging against the Mongrel's iron grip. "Oh gods, please don't. You don't know—"

"You can't change the visions," said the Mongrel. Something shifted behind her silver-green eye, some emotion, furtive as a ghost. "I'm sorry."

"I—I waved goodbye to her," Dramash said haltingly. His wide-eyed face dissolved as Harotha's eyes swam with tears for the second time that day. "I saw her—she said it was all right to go. Rho was with her. Rho—"

"That's right," Faroth said, jerking him again, "Rho—he was the one. Josah saw him—he recognized him right away. Rho is not your friend, Dramash. He murdered your mother. Do you understand me, boy? That Dead One murdered your mother! She's dead! She's never coming back!"

"Faroth!" Harotha cried, breaking free from the Mongrel at last. She rushed forward and pounded her fists against her brother's back. "Stop it! *Stop it!*" she screamed.

"Rho is in the temple right now," Faroth continued, ignoring Harotha's blows. Dramash was still staring at his father, slack-jawed with shock. "The Dead One who killed your mother is in there—he *lied* to you, Dramash. He pretended to be your friend when all along he knew what he'd done. Dramash! Do you hear me?"

Faroth stood up and motioned for the crowd around them to scatter.

This time when the Mongrel took her arms, Harotha offered no resistance. She had failed. She could not stop what was about to happen.

Faroth tilted Dramash's head up so he was looking at the temple. "There he is, Dramash, your mother's murderer is up there!"

Dramash turned away from the temple, still holding the coin encrusted with his mother's blood. With the slow, deliberate movements of an old man he sat down on the sand and looked at the coin, and then he looked back at the temple. When he swung back around to face Harotha, she recognized the expression instantly, and she collapsed into the Mongrel's unyielding arms in utter despair.

Chapter Thirty-Nine

A torch streaked down past Eofar's shoulder and he jerked his arm out of the way, unintentionally tugging on the triffon's reins and sending the beast into a dive. *Stupid mistake*, he chided himself; he was flying like a boy who'd never been in the saddle before. Strife's Bane wavered dangerously in his hand, lashed about by his lack of focus and the shifting winds, as if the triffons on the hilt had decided to fly away in disgust. He tightened his grip on the sword, steadied his mind and pulled the reins taut. He was allowing fear to get to him—fear for Harotha, for his child, for the men under his command . . . for himself.

Another triffon loomed up in front of him and he scanned the other rider's saddle anxiously, looking for a scrap of white cloth—thank Onfar for Daem, suggesting that signal; he would never have thought of it himself, and now that the battle had started he couldn't remember anyone's allegiance but his own. He was still looking for the cloth when the other rider picked up speed and streaked toward him. He looped the reins over the pommel of the saddle and secured them with a sharp tug, loosened the strap around his waist and stood to meet the attack. The other rider—it was Kharl—had already drawn his own sword; now he too stood up in the stirrups and both triffons tucked their wings back, allowing their lithe bodies to glide to within a hand's-breadth of each other. Eofar swung, picturing the path of the black blade in his mind, adding the force of his will to the strength of his arms. The straps around his thighs, his only protection against a deadly tumble from the saddle, dug in reassuringly. The swords clashed once and twice, then scraped apart as the triffons' trajectories carried them past each other: no hits. He gulped down a breath of night air and snatched up the reins again.

Both riders turned their triffons around. <Don't do this, Kharl. Frea's gone mad—you have to see that.>

<Shut up,> Kharl replied. <You can't tell me what to do. Lady Frea's going to lead us to glory.> He urged his triffon forward.

Eofar watched him approach, feeling his own triffon tense as they picked up speed. Strife's Bane's blade pulsed like an extension of his own arm. He was the only one in the battle with an imperial sword; he had no excuse for failure. *It's just like the tournaments*, he told himself, *count your opponent's wing-beats. Gauge his speed. Wait—not yet, a little closer.*

Just as Kharl's triffon tucked in its wings, Eofar pulled smoothly on the reins, guiding his beast into a dive underneath the other's nose, bringing them out again on Kharl's left side instead of the right. Kharl twisted in his saddle, caught out by the move, and offered only one ineffective swing in Eofar's direction.

Eofar blocked, but didn't strike back immediately; he was waiting for the instant when his angled climb would lift him above his opponent, giving him a clear shot at his back. Kharl saw it coming and changed his grip to block the attack, but he was too late; Eofar felt the blade digging into yielding flesh before he was pulled away by his speeding beast.

He leaned over the saddle and looked down; Kharl's triffon was spiraling toward a landing spot on the narrow plain between the temple and the edge of the city, but dark figures on the ground had already converged and were waiting for him.

Eofar steered his triffon around to face the temple.

<That's it, hold the line,> he called out to his men, <don't let them get by you.> He scanned the skies, watching the triffons executing the tight little turns that enabled them to stay relatively stationary. The signalmen, spaced out along the line with lit torches, marked out a ragged constellation. They weren't doing badly; they'd managed to push Frea's line back to the temple, but their advantage couldn't last. Frea had so many more men.

<We're too spread out,> Falkar called back, his words pulled into thinness by the distance they had to travel. <We've got to tighten up the line!>

A horrible shriek blasted through the noise of the wind and Eofar looked up in alarm. Directly above him, two triffons had become entangled in a deadly mess of wings and claws and were struggling frantically to free themselves, keening eerily as they mauled each other.

<Lord Eofar, look out!>

He snapped the reins just as one of the triffons, her rider still strapped in tightly, hurtled past him. The falling beast clipped the left wing of Eofar's triffon and sent him into a dizzying, panicked lurch. Mountains, temple, stars, sand, all rushed past at a sickening speed until he forced open his clenched hand and gave the terrified creature his head. The beast took a few more wingstrokes to right himself. Once out of danger, Eofar took in a deep breath and looked down at where the other triffon had fallen. <Who was that?> he asked, glad no one could see how badly he was shaking.

There was a pause before someone close by answered back, <Arnaf.>

Arnaf: his father's personal guard. Which side had he been on? Eofar couldn't remember for sure. He flew back down the line toward Falkar. <Where's Frea? Has anyone seen her?> he demanded, impatiently turning and gliding back toward the beach.

<North and high, behind the center formation,> Rho reported.

<The Mongrel was right: she hasn't left anyone behind guarding the temple,> said Daem. <Should we make for our second position?>

<Too soon,> Rho said, <Eofar needs us here.>

<They're breaking off!> Falkar cried, and Eofar dived away from the line, trying to get a better view.

<No, they're not!> he reported wretchedly, <they're splitting the line—they're going over. Move in! *Move in!*>

<She planned this all along,> said Falkar. <She drew us in.>

<We can't cover; there're too many of them,> Daem roared as Frea's back line, torches now ablaze, turned away. <What do we do, Lord Eofar?>

<We'll have to split our line, too!> he called back, improvising frantically. <First and third groups keep where you are; the rest move up—don't let them get past you!> But it was already too late; Frea's forces were sailing above them, heading out over the city. Some of Eofar's men chased after them briefly, but returned when they failed to catch up.

<Restore the line,> Eofar ordered, <we'll need to hold the rest of them here.>

He guided his triffon upward and again surveyed the battle. The view was grim: Frea's remaining line had tightened up, closing in at either end and trapping his forces in the middle. Behind him, her second group had spread itself out over the city, and there was nothing he could do to stop them now. Daryan, Isa and the Shadari would have to deal with that threat.

He swept behind the line in the direction of the beach. <All right, Daem, take your squad and head for the temple. Let's get at least one part of this plan right.>

<Yes, my Lord.>

Eofar turned his triffon head-on to a gap in the line and urged it forward, thundering, <Make way!> to anyone who could understand him. <By the rules of engagement, I challenge your commander to personal combat.

Make way!> He shot through the line and out the other side unchallenged.

The battle disappeared behind him. Ahead, he saw nothing but the star-pocked sky and the temple's lightless face. He was conscious of the sound of his own breathing, synchronized with the beat of his triffon's wings. And then she was there; he sensed her presence before she spoke, felt her malice before her triffon dove into view.

<Where's the boy, Eofar?> Trakkar swerved dangerously close in front of him and then disappeared somewhere underneath. Eagerness gnawed through her words. <Rho stole him from me and I want him back. Give him to me and I might even let you live.>

<Dramash is dead,> he told the empty air where she'd been. He brought his own triffon around as sharply as he could, but he still didn't see her. <We knew you needed him, so we killed him.>

<You're lying.> Trakkar shot over his head from behind, catching Eofar and his beast in their wake. <That's what I would have done—but not you.>

He clutched the reins. *Remember the plan.* <I'm here to challenge you—>

<Oh, I don't care,> Frea interrupted. She flew around him and again disappeared. <Give me the boy and I'll spare the city.>

<You can't refuse my challenge,> he insisted. He stood up in the saddle and brandished Strife's Bane at the empty sky. <Honor demands it. The rules—>

The air moaned beneath him and Frea shot out in front of him again. <Honor? Rules?> she echoed hollowly. The back of her silver helmet shone in the starlight. Trakkar streaked toward the temple, almost reaching its dark walls before turning round again. <They don't mean anything to me any more. I'm my own emperor now. I'll make my own rules.>

<Have it your way!> Eofar growled, and suddenly the fear that had been spreading its sickly fingers through

every part of him came blazing out again, tempered into hard, cold rage. <Don't accept the challenge—you'll fight me because I'll *make* you!> He spurred his triffon forward, heading straight toward her.

<Do you know why Mother left you behind?> she asked before adroitly diving underneath him again, leaving him advancing on nothing but Trakkar's stinking wake. Both triffons wheeled around.

<I'm not listening to you. I know what you're trying to do> he informed her as he lined up with her position.

<It wasn't because she thought you told on that *thing* she was hiding; it was because you were weak,> his sister continued anyway. <Mother could tell, even then. At least Isa and I knew what we wanted and we did something about it. What did you ever do? What do you think you're going to do now?>

He locked his eyes on the silver helmet and flew toward her. She would not evade him again.

<This wasn't *your* idea, Eofar—you don't even want to be here. Rho and Daem, they propped you up because they needed a leader, someone legitimate for the others to follow—but that doesn't make you a leader: you know it, and your men know it, too.>

He looped the reins around the saddle and gripped Strife's Bane with both hands. This time Frea was prepared to fight, and she swung Blood's Pride around in a tight loop by her side as she came on. The steel blade sliced through the air with deadly promise. He raised himself up a little higher in the saddle and readied his sword. The space between the two triffons closed until both beasts snapped their wings back simultaneously and Eofar swung his sword forward.

She dropped her arm back behind her shoulder and sheathed Blood's Pride, leaving Eofar blinking in confusion at her unprotected torso, and just like that, the two triffons passed each other.

He was left alone in the dark sky, burning with the ridiculousness of his failure.

<You see?> Frea crowed. <That's what I mean: you had your chance and you couldn't take it. It took you two passes to down Kharl even with that fancy toy you're carrying, and even then, you left him alive.>

<Why don't you fight me?> Eofar cried out. He craned his neck and looked behind him. <You're the killer here, aren't you?> he screamed at her. <You killed Mother—so why don't you kill me, if that's what you want?>

The black knife slapped back into her palm and her fingers closed around the hilt: Eofar stared at it in confusion. *When had she drawn her knife?* He unhooked the reins from the saddle and tugged hard to turn his triffon back around—and with a horrifying lurch rocked backward, out of control, as the severed ends of his harness flapped in the wind.

He seized the saddle with his left hand and let the wind carry the useless straps off into the darkness. She had cut the harness with the black knife as the two triffons passed—just like before. Just like she'd done with Mother . . .

<You see?> Frea told him. There was something strange in her voice, something he had never felt from her before. It was pity. <I already have.>

He was still holding his useless sword in his right hand. He tried to sheath it, but in his panic he could not guide the blade into the scabbard. Nothing was keeping him in the saddle except the stirrups and his one-handed grip on the pommel, and now he could feel the wind, pulling at him. He saw Frea's arm draw back, and her knife came streaking toward him across the sky. He hated that knife and he hated Strife's Bane and everything they represented: every pointless hour, day, week, month and year of his wasted life compressed down into the brutal hardness of black steel.

With a strength born of fury and a precision that was only possible with an imperial blade or by the will of the gods, Eofar struck down with Strife's Bane—and cleaved the knife in two. The two pieces went flying off into the night in different directions.

Frea's wrath exploded outward from her, a scarlet shockwave of anger that slammed into him like a wall. Now, finally, she drew her sword and came for him, and his heart swelled in triumph. He had finally succeeded in making her fight him.

It was not until he began to stand up in the stirrups that he remembered the broken harness—but it was too late for him to evade her, so he jammed his boots as far into the stirrups as he could and clutched the pommel with his left hand. Her first blow was a thrust, aimed straight at his chest, but it was only a feint; by the time he had brought his sword up in defense she had aimed a slice across his right side. He managed to get his blade up in time only by releasing it and twisting his arm to grab it after the fact, but it was still an imperfect move and Blood's Pride slid along the length of Strife's Bane with a teeth-shattering scrape. Sparks flew out into the dark sky, then the blades came apart.

And then his left foot slipped out of the stirrup.

His triffon, sensing something amiss in the sudden weight change, bleated nervously and thumped its tail in the air. The air in Eofar's lungs turned to daggers as he saw the beast twist his great head around to see what was happening. The saddle lurched and he grabbed on to the pommel, kicking around desperately, trying to find the stirrup. He needed both hands; he would have been forced to drop a normal sword, endangering the people below, but he was able to guide Strife's Bane into the scabbard built into the saddle. Then he seized the pommel with both hands as the frightened triffon rolled into a turn, but he felt himself sliding helplessly over the side. His right foot was still in the stirrup but it did little to support his weight. Below his dangling body he could see the desert floor rushing up toward him. He wouldn't be able to hold on for long—a few more moments, that was all. A few more heartbeats.

The sky around him was empty. Frea was gone. He was alone.

The triffon's wings hit their downward stroke, and Eofar, suddenly inspired, writhed in the air and managed to wedge his left foot against the thick cartilage where the triffon's wing protruded from its body. With his weight supported at last, he slapped the stray hair away from his eyes and tried to hoist himself back up into the saddle. If he could only get his leg back over the saddle and his foot in the stirrup he should be able to land—but before he could haul himself up, the triffon's wings arched up again and with sickening inevitability he felt his foot clamped tight. He'd waited too long. The triffon's wing came up, his bones cracked and splintered, and he screamed in agony. A dark mist swam in front of his eyes: he was going to lose consciousness—but if that happened, he'd be dead. The wing came down again, and flinging his whole body into the air like a hooked fish, he finally managed to flop up and over onto the saddle. With numb hands he guided his left foot into the stirrup, trying not to notice the strange shape of his boot, hinting at the wreckage inside. Despite the pain-addled haze, he snatched up the flapping ends of the broken harness and managed to tie them around his legs.

He had to go down. It took him a few moments to summon enough breath for a weak whistle, but at last he managed to give the triffon the signal, and the traumatized creature obeyed with an eager relief and sent them streaking to the ground. They hit the sand with a jolt; Eofar plucked weakly at the knots in the harness until he'd got them untied, then he slid from the saddle. He screamed in agony as his left foot touched the ground and he fell face-first into the sand, where he lay beating his fists until the skin had been flayed raw and he'd exhausted his last ounce of strength.

He'd failed them all.

His body crumpled up and he shut his eyes as unconsciousness dragged at him, pulling him like a lead weight.

He wondered why no one came; he thought that the Shadari would have come to finish the job that Frea had started. But then he became aware of a noise in his head, a rhythmic thumping that at first he mistook for his own pulse. As the noise grew louder, he realized someone was walking toward him across the sand.

He opened his eyes and tried to lift his head, but found he could not. In the foreground, only a few steps away now, was a Shadari carrying a coil of leather straps looped over one shoulder. *There was something important about the straps.*

The young man stopped in front of Eofar and looked down at him with a smile: a tight, humorless twist of his lips. In a slow, deliberate gesture, he slid the coil from his shoulder and let it fall to the ground.

"We're done with you," said the Shadari. "Your kind is finished here. It's over." He began to laugh. He hooked his sandalled foot under the straps and kicked them at Eofar. The hard leather smacked into his face, splattered sand into his eyes and mouth.

The Shadari walked away, still laughing.

Elthion: the Shadari spy Isa had chased from the cave. The one Daryan had tied up, making sure the knots weren't too tight so he could reach the water they'd left for him. They'd tied him up because he knew about them—about Daryan and Isa, about Eofar and Harotha. *He knew about the baby.*

Eofar pushed himself up onto his knees and drew his right foot underneath him, placing it determinedly in the sand and standing up. The instant his left foot touched the ground he knew he was going to faint. He began to fall—he had never known it was possible to fall so slowly, or that the world around him could sharpen into such minute details. He could see the separate sparkle of each grain of sand; smell the unmingled scents of smoke and sweat, sea and rock; hear the sounds of wind and wing-beats. And as the ground finally reached up to take him he felt a pressure in his head that slowed time down to an airless pause, wrapped everything up in a bubble that swelled and swelled until he could feel it ready to burst. He had never felt anything like it before in his life, and yet somehow he knew exactly what it meant.

It meant that the world was about to end.

Chapter Forty

"No, the other way—*the other way!* To the left," Daryan cried out. Isa's white braids flapped out behind her, only a hand's-breath from his face. She twisted her shoulders, trying to give her one-handed pull on the reins more force, but she was pulling the dereshadi in the wrong direction, and the rider they were chasing was getting further and further ahead. "Isa, you're going the wrong way!" he shouted again, and she glanced back at him with an icy glare—just as he finally saw the other rider just in front of them: the one Isa was actually chasing. There was a flicker of flames beneath the pierced metal guard as the Dead One brandished his torch.

Aeda's powerful wings flexed beneath Daryan's feet: she was as intent on the pursuit as her riders. He tightened his grip on the saddle, ignoring the muscles cramping in his hands. Isa had assured him over and over again that he didn't need to hold on, that the harness was enough to keep him in the saddle, but surely not when every downward stroke of Aeda's wings tossed him up into the air, and every upstroke sent him crashing back down again onto the hard leather.

He leaned cautiously over to one side, trying to see the ground below—they were flying so low that he could see individual people running through the streets as flames licked at their homes. He chewed his lip angrily. Left or right, it hardly mattered which way they went—what difference could they possibly hope to make? Even if they stopped this Dead One, what of the dozens of others who'd made it past Eofar's defenses?

"He's landing!" Isa's shrill cry flew back to him on the wind, and as she wheeled the triffon around yet again, he felt as if a heavy stone were rolling from one side of his stomach to the other. He tried shutting his eyes for a moment, but that was worse. But then the ground rose sharply beneath them and before he could catch his breath, Aeda had made an abrupt but not ungraceful landing in the middle of a narrow street. He started unbuckling the complicated series of straps, and when he had freed himself he swung his right leg over the saddle. The ground looked much further away than he'd expected, but he gamely pushed himself off with enough force to clear the hump of Aeda's folded wing.

He landed in a sprawl in the dirt, and immediately caught a flash of light moving between two of the houses to his left.

He whirled back around, expecting to see Isa charging past him in pursuit, but she was still in the saddle and he realized with a sharp pang she was struggling to undo the buckles by herself. He started toward her, but she cried out in a harsh voice, "Go—don't lose him!"

Without stopping to think, he plunged into the alley and soon found himself pushing his way through lines of drying clothes and dodging heaps of rubbish twitching with vermin. It wasn't until he neared the end of the alley that the fact that he carried no weapon began to feel important: the only thing he could think to do against an armed Dead One was shout, and he probably wouldn't be able to do that for very long. His mouth dry, his pulse racing, he burst out of the alley, to be greeted neither by a Dead One's sword nor the leap of flames, but by half a dozen strangely dressed women—Nomas—who turned toward him with exclamations of alarm. All of them were carrying things: bundles that looked like clothes or blankets, small sacks and jars that exuded a pungent medicinal odor.

"A man with a torch—a Dead One—did you see him?" he asked them, as he looked around for the object of his pursuit.

"No," said their leader. She wore a large silver medallion around her neck and the blue of her eyes was striking even in the darkness. He and Isa had been checking Aeda's harness when the Nomas had arrived at their makeshift camp in the ruined palace in a riot of bright colors and chattering, incomprehensible voices, as if they'd come for a holiday rather than a battle. With only a few words from the Mongrel, they had quickly and efficiently formed themselves into armed companies, fire brigades and a host of other useful groups—and Daryan was absolutely certain that this imperious woman and her stealthy companions had not been among them.

"Who are you? You didn't come with the others, did you?" he asked.

"No," she confirmed, but she did not seem at ease. "We—"

But before she could continue a tremendous crash sounded from somewhere behind them and they turned in alarm to see a ball of flame shoot up into the air over the housetops and unfurl in a blinding arc of sparks.

"Oh, no!" he breathed. Cursing himself for getting distracted, he leaped down the street in the direction of the flames. He rounded the first corner and a woman darted out at him from a shadowed doorway, hissing "Daimon—thank the gods!" As if the sound of his title were a signal, the district's residents tumbled out of the shadows and bore down on him. They were carrying blankets for smothering the flames, pots and jars for flinging sand, brooms and rakes for beating. They pressed in close, their frightened faces seeking reassurance.

"The Dead One, where is he?" Daryan demanded, seizing the woman's arm.

"Over there." She pointed up the street to a doorway glowing brightly in the dark night; a moment later a house on the other side of the street collapsed inward, sending a cloud of acrid smoke into the sky and exposing the burning interior. A black cloud of fury gathered over Daryan: this was *his* city. These were *his* people.

A muffled scream came from further up the street. Another woman lurched out of the smoke, this one half-carrying, half-dragging three small children. "Dead Ones!" she shouted. "The Dead Ones are here!"

"Get those fires out—don't let them spread or we'll lose the whole neighborhood!" he ordered as he ran toward the fires. Over the crackling of the flames he caught the unmistakable clang of swords, and he chased the sound around the burning buildings, through a tiny echoing alley and into a small square with a boarded-over well. A torch sputtered on the ground, and flames flickered in the doorways of the houses on either side of the square.

Isa was fighting a big, lumbering man with arms like tree trunks—but she had already backed him against the wall of one of the burning buildings. She battered at him relentlessly, the rapid blows coming at him from every conceivable angle while the man lunged and twisted in an almost comical attempt to defend himself. Daryan found himself flushing with stupid pride at her prowess. Just as he was about to call out to the other Shadari to come deal with the fires, Isa plunged her sword into the man's chest.

The Dead One crashed back into the wall behind him, smacking his head against the stone with an unpleasant crunch; his arms jerked and blood welled out from the wound. He dropped his sword as his hands stiffened into claws and he writhed in pain.

She yanked at the blade, but Truth's Might had sunk in so deeply that it took her three tugs to free it, and when she did, the blood poured out and pattered audibly into the dirt at the man's feet. Then he crumpled to the ground, his unfocused eyes and slack muscles leaving no doubt whatsoever that he was dead.

Isa stood for a moment with her sword in her hand, breathing hard, looking down at the soldier's body; then she bent down and methodically wiped the blood from her blade on the dead man's cloak. Only then did she turn around to face Daryan.

And he saw a Dead One standing there in Isa's place, with a blank face and a deadly sword: a cold, silent, remorseless killer. That's what any other Shadari would have seen.

And in that instant the fantasy that he had been stealthily tending in the hidden corners of his mind for the last two days came crashing down: there would be no grand, glorious day when Shadari and Norlanders would celebrate their common victory. There would be no toasts of new-found trust, no speeches about new beginnings, no merry banquet where he and Isa would sit, side by side, in front of the entire world. There would be no time when the Shadari would be able—or willing—to forget what the Dead Ones had done to them.

"Your face—what is it?" she asked, sheathing her sword as she walked over to him.

"Are you all right?" he asked, deflecting her question.

She nodded. "There are more. We must hurry."

He had no idea where they were, but Isa turned with assurance and he followed at her side. They turned on to the street where they'd left Aeda, and the triffon lifted up her huge head as they approached.

"Did you know him?" he asked her.

"Yes," she answered, and her eyes darted to his face, and then away again. "I had to kill him," she added.

"I know."

She stopped, one foot already hooked in the stirrup, and asked, "Could you? Kill someone?"

"Me? I don't know how," he answered with a nervous laugh, but when her gaze didn't waver, he continued, "I don't know. To protect someone I loved? You?" he added. "Yes, I think I could—I *know* I could."

Her silver-green eyes held his a moment longer. "I hope you never have to."

Then she was back in the saddle and he was helping her with the buckles without being asked. Once she was secure, he moved to the back of the saddle and scrambled into his seat. She took up the reins while he strapped himself in, and the moment he was ready Aeda sprang into the air.

The higher they climbed, the more horrifying the sight below them became: whole sections of the city engulfed in flames, panic-stricken figures running in all directions. The aerial battle continued in front of the temple.

"It's just like the Mongrel said," Daryan seethed. "They'll either find Dramash, or they'll make things so bad we'll have to use him. Damn Frea!"

"And the emperor's ship is here," Isa called back to him. "Look over there."

Looking out to sea he could just make out the faint glow of white sails beyond the harbor.

Isa looked back at him, her eyes shining. "Where do we go?" she shouted over the noise of the wind, but before he could say a word the shockwave hit them, pushing them sideways through the air like an angry shove from the hand of a god. Daryan's hands were torn from the saddle and he was knocked to one side as if he weighed nothing at all. He felt the boom in his ears, in his bones, in his head: every membrane in his body thumped like a drumhead. Beneath them, the ground slanted at an impossible angle.

Isa had been knocked to the side just as he was. She dragged her head toward him. Their eyes met. Together, they braced themselves for disaster.

Chapter Forty-One

Daem stepped out in front of the triffon on the blackened stone floor of the stables, his sword already drawn. <No, you're not.>

Rho stood there, trying not to breathe in the soot that their landing had swirled up into the air. He could never explain his reasons to Daem's satisfaction—he couldn't even explain them to himself. <It just feels wrong. I'm sorry,> he tried, lamely. <I should never have agreed to this. I should have stayed out there.>

Anger sizzled around Daem in a white halo. <I thought we were past this.>

<Daem, just let me go back,> he pleaded.

<No. You're not going to do this to me now, or to them.> He glanced at the rest of their pitiful little company, trying to divide themselves into groups to search for the people Frea had imprisoned. <They're all here because of you. You brought them into this fight, and there's no way you're leaving them now.>

<I'm sorry,> he said, <but they're going to do something terrible with that boy. His father— I know you think it's a mistake for me to interfere, and I'm sorry. But I have to.>

Daem took a deep breath. After a moment's hesitation he slid his sword into its scabbard and laid his hand on Rho's shoulder. <I'm sorry, too,> he said.

<For what?>

Before he even had time to flinch Daem had landed a sharp, brutal blow to his purulent wound and pain snatched his breath away, blinding him even as he collapsed. He could feel the flesh splitting apart as the wound reopened, and then a warm, sticky wetness oozing out over his skin.

Daem knelt down by his side. <I didn't want to do that, believe me, but you're as thick as a triffon's ass sometimes. Face it, you're no good to anyone right now. How else could I prove it to you?> He helped him to sit up.

Rho leaned helplessly against him, gasping for breath, but even through the agony he could feel the depth of his friend's remorse.

<If you don't let a physic tend to that wound, you'll die—if I wasn't sure of it before, I'm damn well certain of it now.> Daem's tone deepened to something cool and comforting as he added, <Listen Rho, you're the only friend I've got. We're not much, either of us: that's why we're here in the Shadar, isn't it? Let's face it, life is a battle and you and I surrendered before we took to the field. We're not heroes; when we get to the afterlife we won't be sitting with Onfar in his celestial hall. The best we can hope for is some way out of this mess.>

Rho listened with his eyes closed, feeling the truth of it. Then he tried to stand. Daem took his arm and helped him up, releasing him once he'd got his balance and was relatively steady on his feet. The stables were dark, but there was light enough to see the streaks of black soot mottling their cloaks.

<Now we'll go and find those physics,> said Daem, but Rho walked past him to the triffon, each step tearing at his side. He felt Daem watching as he struggled to mount, and when he finally managed to get his leg over the saddle he couldn't stop himself from crying out in pain. Daem stood silently, not helping him—not stopping him. Rho buckled himself in and took the reins in his hands, then sat there for a long, miserable moment,

staring out over the triffon's head and trying to think of something to say that would make this better.

He whistled, and the triffon sprang into the air. As they spiraled up out of the temple and into the clear night sky he kept himself from looking down. He knew he'd see Daem, standing there looking up at him, and he couldn't bear it.

He wheeled the triffon around in the direction of the city.

A great hollow boom sounded below him, muffled, but strong enough to resonate through his whole body. Then came splitting sounds, layered, one on top of each other, crackling like the sky torn apart by a frenzied lightning storm.

And then the screaming started, raking like claws inside his skull, like every nightmare, every helpless, frozen moment of dread he'd ever experienced.

The screams submerged into a rumbling, thudding roar and a cloud of matter rolled outward from the temple, choking out the stars. At first it looked as insubstantial as smoke, but as it came toward him he saw the tumbling, heaving chunks of stone.

In a single moment, panic stripped away civilization's veneer and reduced him to a whimpering, unreasoning animal. The triffon bellowed in pure terror and flung itself toward the sea, thrashing its wings furiously and streaking over the black water with no concern for the rider on its back. Ahead, the night sky was clear and bright with stars, but fast overtaking them was the hot breath of chaos. Debris whizzed by on all sides, pelting Rho's back, cracking against his bones. He pressed himself into the triffon's neck; all he could do was hang on.

After a while, the beast's wing-beats lengthened. They were far out at sea by now, maybe too far for the exhausted triffon to return to the shore. Rho looked back over his shoulder.

The temple was gone.

There was nothing left but a jagged square of foundations, like a piece of pottery slammed against the edge of a table. The debris from the explosion had buried both the plain and the beach around the temple, and a cloud of dust hung over the site like a veil draped over a bloody corpse. He stared, stupefied. They were all dead—*all* of them. Daem . . . Daem, his friend, was dead. He could still feel the throb of his wound where Daem had struck him, but now he was dead. And Eofar, Frea, all the others that had been in the air—the sky was empty. They were gone. All gone.

<See?> he whispered to Daem in anguish, <I told you so.>

Chapter Forty-Two

Jachad woke up in hell, rocks prodding his flesh and cracking against his skull. He clamped his eyes shut and a scream swelled torturously in his chest, but he couldn't squeeze enough air out of his lungs for anything more than a helpless whimper. He was afraid to conjure up even the smallest flame for fear of sucking up the last remaining gasp of air. He tried to move his arms and legs, but the effort only jostled the rocks against his bruised body and choked him with dirt. Panic squashed his lungs; froze his heart.

Alone, buried under stone and sand, he prayed to his father, far off on the other side of the world, and to the moon goddess Amai and to the Shadari star-gods to take his message there. He prayed to anyone who would listen, and he was still praying when they dug him out.

"Damn! It's just that stinking Nomas," someone said.

Rough hands pushed away the debris until they'd freed enough of his body to be able to hoist him up out of the rubble. A dank, evil-smelling cloth was passed over his face, and then—ah, *praise Shof*—a flask of water was poked between his lips, and he drank.

"That's enough." The flask was yanked away from him, the supporting hands disappeared and he fell back against the rocks. "I'm not wasting any more time on this one. Come on."

His dissatisfied rescuers departed before Jachad could produce even one syllable of thanks. He lay there blinking, watching the red flares in front of his eyes gradually fade away. He could feel no broken bones, and yet he felt shattered: a collection of parts that had never been meant to fit together.

After a while he got up, stiffly and painfully, and looked behind him. He remembered standing not far from the foot of the temple, looking up at the battle in the sky above him, trying to count the number of Eofar's men still left aloft. Frea had succeeded in getting enough of her men through the line to set the city ablaze. Then he had seen one triffon streak to the ground with its rider slumped over in the saddle, somewhere out to the west. The pair had been far away but he had been certain it was Eofar—he had just begun to run in that direction when the world had come crashing down on top of him.

Now the temple slumped in the near distance like a dying thing, wreathed in the dust of its own smashed bones, its torn vitals exposed to an empty sky. Its destruction had effectively ended the battle, both on the ground and in the air. He could not see any living triffons anywhere; he didn't know if they had all been killed, or if they had gone to ground. Now he could see ghostly figures drifting through the piles of debris, stumbling along with their heads bent down to the ground. Wounded of indeterminate race and gender sprawled among the rubble, and many Shadari survivors were sobbing and wailing and clawing at the piles of stone and dirt and detritus. He bore witness to their grief with a strange, emotionless pity. He still had a heart, and a mind, but there no longer seemed to be a connection between the two.

He thought that might be just as well, considering what he intended to do.

After a moment he made out men and women coming

and going from one particular spot, and when he got there he found Omir distributing mining equipment to the stream of blank-faced volunteers. No one spoke more than absolutely necessary, and the atmosphere was as stifling as the smoke hanging over their heads.

He walked straight up to Omir. "The Mongrel—where is she? Has anyone seen her?"

"You and that—" Omir began as a snarl, but stopped when he saw the look on Jachad's face. "In the palace," he said, twisting the loose ends of a shovel's leather-wrapped handle, "with Faroth."

"Just Faroth? What about Daryan?"

Omir's eyes remained as motionless as if they had been chiseled into his face, but his mouth moved tellingly before he answered, "No one's seen him yet."

Jachad turned toward the city.

"King Jachad," Omir called out to him. Jachad waited until the big man found the words he needed; in his still, dark eyes was a savage grief, a living thing that writhed and twisted, struggling to free itself. "Is it over?"

"No," said Jachad, "but it's about to be."

He began picking his way over the uneven ground back toward the city. The terrain had changed completely; what had once been a flat plain of sand and scrub was now all heaps of broken rocks and smashed things that he avoided examining too closely. A weak, sanguine light shone in the sky overhead: not the dawn yet, but the light of the still-burning fires reflecting from the heavy clouds of dust and smoke.

He passed into the city streets where fires still smoldered everywhere. Whole neighborhoods had been reduced to smoking ruins, and most of the landmarks had been obliterated or obscured. People moved about with an aimless confusion he found exhausting just to watch. As he neared the old Shadari royal palace the crowds grew larger. He made his way toward the heart of the ruin, to that same spot where the council of war had been held earlier in the day. Despite their numbers the people were eerily quiet, and the expressions on the faces around him were not the simple, mute fatigue he might have expected, but a feverish, wide-eyed uneasiness that needed only a spark to flare into full-blown hysteria.

He pushed his way forward to the southern entrance of the roofless hall. The broken wall was highest on this side, and he could not see over it.

A Shadari, clearly delighted with his role as sentry, puffed his chest out and crossed his arms when he saw Jachad approaching. "No one goes in. Faroth's orders."

Jachad could hear voices: "You're not getting a damned thing from us," Faroth was saying.

"Pay me."

He winced at the sound of Meiran's voice. He hadn't realized how badly he'd wanted her to be long-gone, away to some distant land where he would never find her even if he spent the rest of his life looking.

Faroth snorted a derisive laugh. "Pay you? For *what*? You didn't win this battle. My son did."

"Pay me," Meiran said again. "The battle is over. You won. I get paid. That was our bargain."

Jachad looked into the sentry's eyes and said, "Move aside."

"Go away, sand-spitter," said the sentry. "No one wants you here."

Beyond the doorway, Faroth answered Meiran with triumph in his voice. "You can't do anything to me, and you know it. If you're smart, you'll leave while you still can. You're not going to get what you want."

"You don't know what I want."

"Of course I do," Faroth snapped. "You want Dramash."

Jachad raised his left hand so that the Shadari sentry could see the orange flames curling around his fingers. "Move aside," he repeated, and this time the sentry's face went slack and he drew back against the doorframe.

"I don't want Dramash," Meiran said as Jachad entered the hall. "I want Harotha."

For a moment Jachad felt himself back underground again, trapped and suffocating, with a knife of pain slicing through his lungs. What could she possibly want with Harotha? Then he reminded himself that it didn't matter, because she wasn't going to get her. No one else would die because of Meiran; that was the bargain he had made with the Shadari gods, under the ground, in exchange for air and light and life. *No one else.*

He saw Faroth standing at the far end of the hall. Five or six men—Faroth's inner circle—were clustered around him, but despite the growing crowd pushing and jostling beyond the walls there was no one else in this vast room except those few men. And Dramash, of course, sitting on the ground near his father's feet, absently tracking his fingers through the cracks in the paving stones. And Meiran, with a gleaming Norlander sword in her hand.

"Harotha? You mean my sister? What does she have to do with anything?" Faroth repeated and he glanced behind him. Now Jachad could see Harotha, rising from where she'd been hidden in the shadows of the crumbling wall. He could see the tracks of tears streaking her face, but they were old tears, already dry. She was staring at Meiran.

"That's what I want: your sister. That's my price," Meiran answered, "and I'm going to take her. Now."

Faroth moved a little closer, staying outside the reach of her sword and staring into her scarred face. *Surely*, thought Jachad, *he'll never let her take his sister, his own twin sister. He'll stop her, and then I won't have to—*

"You want to take Harotha away?" Faroth began to laugh. "You want her? Then go right ahead—take her!"

Jachad's heart shriveled.

"She made her choice. Daryan is dead, and he was the last daimon the Shadar will ever see." Faroth's followers raised nervous voices in approbation and his mocking laughter rang out across the smoky yard. "Go ahead, take her—you'll be doing me a favor."

Jachad finally stepped forward. "I'm not going to let that happen," he announced grimly.

"Jachi?"

One glance into Meiran's silver-green eye and at her lips, still parted from saying his name, confirmed all of his suspicions: she had known exactly what was going to happen to the temple; she had known from the beginning. When he had left her to fight in its shadow, she had not expected him to come back.

"You shouldn't be here," she warned him, speaking in Nomas. "Stay out of this. Stay out of my way, I'm begging you."

"And if I don't?"

"I don't want to hurt you."

"No?" he asked. "Tell me—when have you ever done anything else?" A fireball roared into shape in his right hand.

"King Jachad!" Harotha called out to him from across the hall. From the corner of his eye, he saw her circling toward him.

"Run, Harotha," he cried out to her. "Get away from here!"

Meiran began to advance and he stood his ground, arching the flames toward her. She swung her sword and batted them away as she came, but then she suddenly stopped. Thrusting her sword out toward him, she cried, "Look out—the fire! Put it out!" She had noticed what he had not: Harotha was rushing toward him. He clapped his hands to his sides and snuffed out the flames.

"Harotha, what are you doing? I told you to get away from here!" His fingers still flickered with sparks.

"Something's wrong—you need to stop what you're doing." She laid an urgent hand on his arm but she was looking across the cracked paving at Meiran, whose sword sagged in her hand as if it had grown suddenly heavier. Behind her, Faroth and his cronies watched with the grim anticipation of gamblers baiting dogs. "This isn't what you think. We're missing something. I don't think she wants to hurt me."

"Don't let her fool you," he told her. "I should have stopped her long before now, before all of those people—"

"She isn't trying to trick anyone—it's just something I know," said Harotha, gripping his arm. "I'm not sure why; I can just feel it."

He stared back at her incredulously. If he hadn't known better, he would have sworn she had lost her mind.

"I was there when the temple exploded," he told her. "I was right underneath it. People *died*—in the air, on the ground. People are still dying—"

"And that was Faroth," Harotha said, "I know. I saw him do it." Her voice caught, but she forced herself to say the words. "Faroth goaded Dramash into destroying the temple—it wasn't the Mongrel. She didn't do it."

"She didn't try to stop it, either," he pointed out, lifting her hand from his arm.

She looked like she was about to answer him, but then she inhaled sharply and listed; he lunged forward and caught her in his arms. "It's the baby," she whispered, squeezing her eyes shut in pain.

Meiran darted toward them. "Let me take her, now!"

"Stay back," Jachad yelled, raising his left hand as far from Harotha as he could and launching a plume of flame into the air. Meiran gripped her sword with both hands and held it aloft, but she couldn't move forward.

"I have midwives, everything, waiting for her," Meiran growled. "Let me take her!"

"No," he roared back. The flames died down again, but not by his choice: he had overused his powers tonight and they were weakening. "Elixir be damned—I don't care what you think you saw, you're not going to take her."

Harotha reached up and grabbed the front of his robe, pulling him down to her. "The elixir," she said, gasping for breath, "she's right: you can't change anything. I thought I could—I was wrong . . ." She trailed off.

"Jachi, listen to her," Meiran urged, inching forward. "Don't stop me—you can't—"

He released Harotha carefully and then straightened up. "You keep saying that," he seethed, "but if you really believed it, you could have told me everything from the beginning. So why didn't you?"

Her eye locked into his and he felt himself being rent wide open, like a fish being gutted. When she spoke it was in Norlander, with an onslaught of emotion that burned him like acid, stripping him bare of all of his resolve. <Because I knew that if anyone could stop me, it would be you, Jachi.>

"No!" he grunted in Nomas, pushing her out of his mind. "I don't want to know. It's too late."

"All right, then," she cried, throwing her arms out wide. She tossed her sword away and he heard it clatter on the pavement. Her normally flat voice rose to a shrill pitch and her luminous eye burned behind the smoke. "Go ahead, stop me!" She ripped off the eyepatch and dashed it to the ground. "What are you waiting for?"

He answered in Norlander, too—like her, he wanted her to feel what he felt: to know in her bones exactly what this cost him, down to the last drop of his unnameable feelings for her.

<Dawn.>

He watched the contemptuous expression on her face crumble and fall away. She was the Mongrel, it was true; but he was the son of the sun god, and he could feel the dawn with every drop of his blood. She had been too distracted to notice the subtle brightening of the sky above the smoke-clouds, but he had timed it to the very moment and he saw the pang strike. She tried to steel herself, but her chest contracted as if she'd been struck and she fell to her knees.

He walked toward her, tongues of flame dancing

fretfully between his fingers. He tamped them down: he would not use Shof's gift for this; he needed to do it with his own hands. He needed to feel it.

She fought her way to one knee and tried to drag herself to her sword, but the sickness had full hold of her now and she collapsed onto the stones.

By the time he reached her, she was barely conscious. He knelt down beside her and circled her bare gray throat with his hands. She batted weakly at his arms, but already her mismatched eyes were rolling vacantly beneath fluttering eyelids. Her skin felt dry and feverish and he forced himself to look into her face, to watch the scar on her mouth twitch as she fought for air. From a long way away he heard Harotha, shouting at him to stop. He wanted to pretend that none of this was real, that someone else's hands were around her throat, but he wouldn't allow himself to do that: he needed to make himself remember this, every detail of it, for as long as he lived. That would be his penance.

Then a scream tore through the air behind him and he turned away from Meiran's lifeless face with the feeling of passing from one nightmare into another. Harotha was being hauled to her knees by a Shadari who had a knife pointed at her pregnant belly. Her eyes were wide and glassy with horror. He sprang up with his hands already blazing, but they were too far away. There was nothing he could do.

"Elthion!" shouted Faroth, lurching forward. "What do you think you're doing? Who do you think you are, coming in here like this?"

"I'm doing what you should be doing, Faroth!" Elthion yelled back. His face was cut and bruised and his wrists were covered with bloody scratches. He had his arm around Harotha's neck, holding her fast. "They've made a fool of you!"

"*Nobody* makes a fool of me," Faroth warned, glancing back at the others. "Watch your words."

Her brother wasn't going to do anything to help her; he was angry at Elthion for overstepping his place, not for attacking the sister he'd already renounced. Jachad stared at the knife, trying to think of some way to get it away without endangering her. But then Harotha's desperate eyes found his and he understood that her fear wasn't for the knife at all. She saw the realization on his face and nodded, almost imperceptibly.

"*He knows,*" she mouthed.

"I knew you wouldn't listen to me," Elthion was saying to Faroth, "but I can prove it—I'll cut this—this *thing*—out of her and show you, all of you!"

Jachad sent a mass of flames roaring up to the gray dawn sky. He could sustain the fire for only a moment, but it was long enough to get Elthion's attention.

"I've been looking for you, Elthion!" he shouted, pointing as he advanced on the lanky Shadari with quick, angry strides. "Did you really think I was going to let those things you said about me and my people stand?"

Elthion's mean, narrowed eyes turned to him with a look of almost joyful hatred and Jachad knew at once that he had hit upon the right tactic: Elthion wanted to be important—important enough to be hated and pursued, to have mortal enemies.

"What do you want here, sand-spitter?" sneered the Shadari, flecks of spit flying from his mouth. He still had one arm circled around Harotha's neck and the knife pointed at her belly.

"I'll give you one chance to take back the things you said," Jachad offered reasonably, stopping about ten paces from him. "No one needs to get hurt."

"Do you think I'm afraid of you?" Elthion snorted, responding exactly as Jachad hoped.

"Afraid enough to hide behind a woman, I'd say," he returned. He heard a murmur from Faroth, but no one made any move to interfere. "What's the matter, Elthion, was your mother too busy to let you hide behind her skirts this time? Or did she finally decide it was time to wean you?"

Elthion let go of Harotha, who slumped to the ground in a faint. The Shadari glared down at her with a look of utter disgust, then kicked her in the back with a cruelty that scorched Jachad's blood.

He whisked his knife out of its sheath. "You're a worm, Elthion," he told him. "You're nothing—*nobody*—and I won't waste one spark of Shof's fire killing you."

The Shadari flew at him and Jachad fell back, pulling him as far away from Harotha as possible before standing his ground. Elthion slashed at him with no skill whatsoever, but his arms were long and Jachad had a hard time dodging his crazed attacks. He stayed on the defensive, steering Elthion further and further away from Harotha, conscious that he needed to keep them all distracted while she got herself to safety. He glanced anxiously at her slumped body, praying that he was right in thinking her swoon feigned.

Elthion struck at him, close enough that the knife ripped a gash in his sleeve, but for a moment it caught in the fabric and gave Jachad time enough to grab his arm and thrust with his own knife. Elthion stumbled backward to break Jachad's hold and tripped over the uneven stones. Jachad flung himself down on top of Elthion, squirming to avoid the blade, and they grappled frantically for a moment before Elthion threw him off—he was stronger than he looked. Jachad scrambled back to his feet.

A sharp moan cut underneath their ragged breathing, and both men turned to see Harotha—already halfway to the doorway and freedom—stagger and fall to her knees. There was nothing feigned in her collapse this time.

Elthion whirled back to Jachad, his face twisted into a caricature of loathing. "*Tricks!*" he choked out. "You're with them—you're one of them! I'll kill that whore and her bastard child and I'll make you watch!"

He lunged toward Harotha, but Jachad's hands were already surging with fire and he bounded after Elthion and grabbed for his legs. He caught the Shadari's robe with one smoldering hand and Elthion screamed in outrage, but the dirty hem singed away under Jachad's fingers and sent him crashing to the ground holding nothing but ash.

Elthion rolled on the ground and sprang up again. He loomed over Jachad, brandishing his knife in triumph and shrieking, "I'm going to cut that monster out of her!"

Jachad raised his hands, praying that he had enough fire left to incinerate them both—

—when a strange buzzing skidded along the ground and vibrated through his body, like a sound too low to be heard. There was a thin splintering noise, like the sound of ice breaking, and tiny cracks began snaking through the pavement beneath and around him.

Jachad jumped up in alarm, but a heartbeat later the whole floor shattered into a thousand tiny pieces. Sand bubbled up from the ground like a living thing, submerging the broken shards of stone until the area around them was roiling.

Jachad understood what was happening and he knew that his only chance was to run, but fear immobilized him. The ground slid out from beneath him and he fell to his knees. He could not get up; instead, he was slipping steadily backward, as if pulled by a retreating tide.

"What—?" Elthion cried, looking around him, his mouth gaping foolishly. The sand rippled around his ankles and, with a lurch, swallowed him up to his knees. He kicked his legs, trying in vain to climb out.

Jachad grabbed the ground sloping up in front of him, but his efforts were useless. Sand lapped against his chest, rising up higher and higher as he sank. He and Elthion were caught up in a funnel; they were being dragged down into its depths.

He could hear Elthion screaming for help. The Shadari had long since dropped his knife and was now clawing madly at the sand, trying to dig himself out of the hole that was steadily deepening beneath him. His self-important smirk had given way to a look of abject terror. "Faroth! Faroth, help me!"

"Not again," Jachad prayed, shutting his eyes as the dirt crested his shoulders. "Please Shof, not again. Anything but this—"

A clammy hand grabbed his wrist and he opened his eyes to see Meiran, her lithe body balanced on the slope in front of him as she clung to his arm, her muscles taut with the strain. She clamped her other hand around his wrist and with one massive tug hauled him out of the hole. They tumbled backward together, falling onto more level ground, safely out of the funnel's reach.

"Faroth! Faroth!" yelped Elthion, now up to his neck at the epicenter of the funnel. On the other side, half-hidden by the swirling smoke, Jachad saw exactly what he had expected: a small figure standing tense and still, watching silently, his fists clenched tight.

Elthion's arms flapped frantically over his head as another surge pulled him down to his chin. "Faroth! It's Dramash—Dramash is doing this! Stop h—" And as Jachad watched, breathless with horror, Elthion's pleas changed to a wordless shriek of terror that died away as sand sifted into his mouth and nose. For a moment longer the sand swirled, and then it lay still.

"He wanted to hurt the baby," Dramash explained in a voice too old and too tired to have come from that young body. He turned around and walked back to his father, who was staring blankly at the spot where Elthion had disappeared.

For a moment Jachad thought the others had all gone, but then he saw them, huddled together in the far corner of the room, their faces white with dismay.

Meiran touched his shoulder and said, "We have to go."

He lurched to his feet. She was already sprinting toward Harotha, who seemed to have recovered, at least physically. Her face was red and swollen and fresh tears were streaming down her cheeks.

"We have to help him—he's just a little boy," she told Jachad chokingly as he and Meiran ushered her toward the doorway.

"I know," he said, "but we can't do anything now. We have to get you out of here."

The same sentry was still at his post. He had his back to the doorway, but he turned as the three of them came out. "Was that Elthion shouting?" he asked, glancing nervously through to the courtyard. "I let him in because he swore Faroth was waiting for him. What's happening in there?"

Jachad paused, subtly giving Harotha and Meiran enough room to exit behind him while he spoke with the guard. "Faroth's going to make a speech," he told the sentry in a voice loud enough for everyone in the vicinity to hear. "He wants you to let everyone inside."

"If he wants—" began the sentry, but just as Jachad had intended, the crowd immediately began pushing their way past him into the hall.

Meiran took Harotha's arm and steered her through the press of bodies. She had to squint with her Norlander eye in the absence of her eye-patch. Some people recognized her and cried out or jumped back, but most were so intent on pushing forward that they took no notice of them. By the time Jachad, Meiran and Harotha reached the edge of the palace ruins there was no one else in sight.

"I need to rest, please," Harotha begged, and slumped onto the low stone wall by her side. Jachad watched her in alarm: her face had gone pale, except for patches of hectic color on her cheeks. "Don't worry,

I'm all right," she reassured him, smiling thinly as Meiran helped her to sit. "The pains have stopped again. I'm just tired."

When she shut her eyes, he moved off a little further along the wall to give her a moment's solitude. Meiran joined him. The color had faded from the sky, leaving the unbroken clouds the flat, dull color of smoke; he saw Meiran glance up and rub her arms as if she felt a chill.

"I'm trying to make some sense of this," he said. "You saved my life, even after I tried to kill you—even after you let me go off to fight under the temple, where you *expected me to be killed*." He cleared his throat and focused on the wall, watching the breeze gently rustling the dry weeds poking out between the stones. "Can you explain that? Why didn't you just let me go down with Elthion?"

The heavy silence lengthened, until Meiran finally said, "You know why."

He did know, now. He had felt it in that one unguarded moment they had shared, but he wasn't ready to acknowledge it yet. He unwound the scarf from around his neck, and sand hissed down around him. He shook out the rest from its folds. "She tried to tell me you weren't going to hurt her. I suppose if I hadn't interfered, you could have got her away before Elthion even arrived—and then—what, spirited her away before her brother or the others came after her?"

"That's right."

He looked straight into her mismatched eyes. "So that mess back there was *my* fault, then?"

She held his gaze, but said nothing.

"You're wrong," he told her. He twisted the silk in his hands, pulling it taut. "It's not my fault—it's yours. You expect me to trust you when you give me nothing. Nothing!" He threw the scarf to the ground. "If you had told me what you were trying to do, I would have listened to you. All I've asked you to do is trust me—"

"Why should I?" she burst out.

"Why?" He laughed. "*Why?* What about the years we spent growing up together? What about all the mornings after you ran away when I woke up next to your empty bed feeling like a part of me had been cut out? What about all the stories I had to endure about the infamous Mongrel, knowing all the time that you were out there somewhere, not caring enough to send one word, not even to let us know you were still alive?"

Her face twisted up with contempt. "Don't pretend you think of me any differently than anyone else does," she said. Her raw voice scraped like fingernails across a stone.

"How can you say that? I—"

"Don't!" she cried out, holding up her hands.

"Meiran, I—"

"Don't," she said again, and her shoulders flinched as if he'd struck her. "Don't lie about it. Don't make it worse."

"Worse!" He kicked the wall and bits of stone toppled down around him. "*Worse?* We've nearly killed each other tonight: how could it possibly be any worse?" On a mad impulse he pulled out his knife, seized her hand and slapped the hilt into her palm. "There: if you want revenge, then take it. We're the ones who made you sick: the Nomas, not the Shadari or the Norlanders. We offered you up to both of our gods and they've been pulling you apart ever since. So here," he thumped his chest with his clenched fist, "go ahead, kill Shof's son—make him hate you. Then maybe you'll be free and all of this can finally be over."

She stared at the knife, lying like a dead thing across her palm, and the instant her eyes looked up into his, he finally understood.

"You knew," he whispered. He felt the blood drain from his face. "You knew all along."

Her eyes lost focus; their angry flashing gave way to

that weary, wounded look that had haunted him all these years. "Of course I knew."

"Meiran . . ."

The knife still lay in her hand, dividing them, pushing them apart. She spoke haltingly, and her normally flat voice took on a peculiar, far-away cadence, like surf breaking on a moonless night. "At first I thought, if I just waited . . . I knew why you didn't want me to know." She looked down at the knife. "I knew what you were afraid of."

"I had a duty to my people—" he started, but she stopped him.

"I know. I know what I am, and what I've done." She closed her hand around the leather hilt, turned the knife this way and that, catching the dull light on the blade, making it gleam. Finally she looked up at him again. "I thought you might think better of me, that's all."

Some scorching mix of remorse and hope flooded through him, and he reached out and gripped her shoulders with both hands, holding on to her, feeling as if he were drowning and he needed her to stay afloat. Her arms went slack; the knife dropped into the dirt. "Tell me now," he urged her. "Tell me what you want with Harotha—I swear I'll trust you. I will believe anything you say. Anything!"

Her eyes searched his face, but this time she did not pull away. She hesitated, finding the words with difficulty, until she finally held up her scarred forearm and said, "I've already held him. They give him to me—they *beg* me to take him." Her face took on a strange expression, softer than he had ever seen, but aglow with a possessive, almost frantic exhilaration. "He's mine, Jachi: he's really mine, and I won't let anything happen to him. I won't let anyone take him away from me."

He caught his breath. "You mean the baby."

She nodded. "I felt something. I don't know what to call it. It felt like—like a *reason* to be alive."

He was still holding on to her shoulders; now he gripped them even harder. He had promised to believe her, unconditionally, but still he asked, "Why would Harotha and Eofar give you their baby? Their own child?"

"They don't want him." She leaned in so close that he could see the hectic pulsing of the veins beneath her skin. "They don't, but I do—Jachi, I've seen it all—he needs me. You swore that if I told you, you'd believe me. You *must* believe me—"

They heard a soft cry and turned to see Harotha trying to stand, holding on to the wall for support. Jachad rushed over and grasped her arm. The coldness of her skin shocked him, as did the frightening bluish tint of her lips, and the way her eyes were darting about as if they couldn't focus.

"You said you had a midwife for her?" he called out to Meiran.

"The house—it's not far. Your mother and the others, they're waiting." She circled around to support Harotha on the other side.

Meiran led them through the deserted streets, the two of them half-carrying Harotha. She pointed out a house with a homely light flickering behind its curtained doorway and a few fragrant wisps of smoke spiraling up from the chimney, but before they could reach it, Harotha inhaled sharply and her eyelids fluttered.

"Something's wrong," she muttered.

"What is it? What's wrong?" Jachad asked her, stopping.

"Keep going!" Meiran commanded.

"Something's wrong. I can feel it." She was slurring her words together, then she gasped again.

"Hurry," Meiran pleaded, propeling them on even faster. They were practically dragging Harotha now, and her labored breaths had degenerated into rhythmic moans.

Suddenly the Shadari dug her heels into the ground

and seized the front of Jachad's robe with both hands. "Promise me!" she demanded. Her eyes were stretched wide open, but they were vague, unfocused, like a sleepwalker's.

"Promise you what?" he cried.

"Promise you'll save the baby—if you have to choose. You choose the baby. Promise me!"

"Harotha," he pleaded, "don't talk like that. Everything's going to be—"

She reached out to Meiran. "You'll promise me, won't you? You— Oh!" She stopped speaking and the focus came back into her eyes. She stared into Meiran's face as if she was seeing it for the first time. Her head fell to one side and the faintest of smiles crossed her lips. In an odd, soothing voice, she said, "It's all right. It's all right." She reached out, as if she wanted to touch Meiran's face, but she was too weak to lift her arm. "I know why you're here. I know—" Then she fainted into Jachad's arms.

"Shof help us!" he cried. Between them they lifted her up and staggered toward the house. Now they could hear small, urgent sounds from within: pots rattling gently, a fire snapping, voices speaking in serious undertones.

Meiran rustled the curtain over the narrow doorway and two Nomas women darted out and whisked Harotha inside without a word. Jachad was beginning to follow when he realized that Meiran wasn't behind him. He turned around and found her backing out into the empty street with a ghastly look on her face.

"What is it?" he asked, running over to her. "What's wrong?"

"Everything—it's all wrong," she murmured. "It's just like the visions, but it's wrong."

He seized her arm. "What do you mean?"

Her voice ached with dismay. "I remember it all, every detail. Nisha brings me the baby. She says, 'Eofar can't bear the sight of him. You can't blame him, can you? Harotha wants you to take him away from here. Take him away, and never come back to the Shadar.' "

In the long silence that followed, Jachad heard the blood roaring in his ears. "And you thought it meant they didn't want him," he said.

"But they don't—they *don't* want him," she insisted, clutching his torn sleeve. "They don't want him. He's a mongrel. He's like *me*."

"Meiran, you made a mistake. I know how you feel, but it doesn't matter now. We have to—" But before he could finish, she ran off down the street. He stared after her with a feeling like he'd been kicked in the stomach. Then he walked back up to the house, each step heavier with apprehension than the last. He was just about to push past the curtain when a Nomas woman stepped out to block his path, wiping her hands on a piece of cloth.

"Now, now, where do you think you're going?"

He stared back at her stupidly for a moment. She was an old friend, someone he'd known since childhood, but somehow he couldn't remember her name. "Inside."

"Oh, no, you're not. No place for a man in there. It's going to be a difficult one. I can always tell." She flipped the cloth onto one shoulder and her clear, dark green eyes searched his face; when she spoke again, a hint of compassion warmed her crisp voice. "Best stay out of the way. You understand."

"Oh— Of course," he answered. He still didn't move from the doorway.

"Jachi," the woman said, more gently still, and the sound of his pet name roused him a little. "We'll do the best we can for her. Lucky thing our Meiran had us prepared. Here." She took him by the elbow and led him over to a little bench set against the wall of the house. "You sit here and the first chance I get, I'll bring you out a nice hot cup of tea. How's that?"

He looked up at her sun-kissed face. The morning breeze blew by and shook the scent of the sea from her hair. With depthless gratitude, he replied, “A cup of tea would be lovely, Mairi. Thank you.”

Chapter Forty-Three

Rho sat on a rock, looking out to sea. He wasn't sure how long he'd been there, listening to the soporific pulse of the waves. He remembered that the sky had still been dark when he'd landed his exhausted triffon on the beach and tumbled out of the saddle. Now the eastern horizon had lightened by degrees from black to a deep blue, and the white tops of the waves appeared and disappeared, pale as wraiths. He liked looking at the water. He liked pretending that he was floating on those calm ripples, without any concern for what might be lurking in the deep water underneath.

The thump and snap of wings sounded behind him, but he didn't turn around. He'd been hearing the wings on and off the whole night. There was never anyone there.

<Go away,> he told his ghosts, not unkindly, but firmly. <It's no use haunting me. I can't help you.>

Now that dawn was approaching, he could see the shape of the huge ship more clearly, the tips of her tall masts pointing up to the cobalt sky. Very slowly they had succeeded in turning her back out to sea, but they hadn't got very far yet—the tide must have been against them. They hadn't lowered the boats, or tried to send anyone ashore. He supposed they had been close enough to see that the temple had been destroyed and decided to turn back. Not that it made any difference to him; it was just something to look at, part of the scenery.

<Rho! Rho!>

He heard the sound of someone running across the packed sand behind him, and then a hand seized him and pulled him from the rock. The owner of the hand threw herself into his arms, saying, <You're alive! You're alive!>

Rho dutifully brought his arms up around Isa, but he could only return the mechanics of her embrace, not the spirit. <Yes. I'm alive,> he reassured her, but he had a vague, guilty feeling that he was lying. He had been alive, once. It had felt different than this.

She drew back from him. <You're not hurt, are you?> she asked, her eyes scanning his body, presumably for wounds.

He noticed that her face was very dirty—soot, maybe. There had been fires. Behind her he could see Daryan walking toward them over the sand, looking ten years older than he had that afternoon. He found himself wondering what his own face must look like by now. He marveled that Isa still recognized him.

<We thought—> She glanced over at Daryan and switched to Shadari, "we thought you were dead. When the temple— Daem and the others, where are they?"

He looked back at her, surprised by her question. "They're all dead."

"But you got out. Maybe they—"

"They're all dead," he told her. He was very calm, like the ripples on the water. "They were all in the temple. They're dead. I heard them screaming."

Isa stepped back from him.

He had upset her—he hadn't wanted to upset her, but the calmness—it didn't allow him to be anything but brutally frank.

Daryan touched the tips of his fingers to her back. "We can't stay here. If Frea's still alive she's going to make her move right now. She has no other choice. We have to get to Faroth. If he's got Dramash out in the open we have to do something. If Harotha is there, maybe the two of us, together—I know it's not much of a plan, but what else can we do?"

"But now we have Rho. He can help us."

Rho returned to his seat on the rock. "I can't help you."

<The Shadari think Frea was killed in the explosion, but she wasn't,> Isa told him. <She's still alive, and so are most of her men. Daryan and I saw them, waiting up in the mountains, spying for some sign of Dramash.>

"Eofar can't do anything more—he's still alive, thank the gods, but Frea nearly killed him. We found him and took him to the Nomas," said Daryan, talking over Isa without realizing it. "Only a dozen of the Dead Ones—the Norlanders—on your side are left, and fewer dereshadi. They've taken shelter in that cave Harotha found."

"We know Frea still wants Dramash—but now you're here, and Dramash trusts you. Maybe you can—"

"I can't help you," he repeated as he looked back out over the water.

Isa stood in front of him. "What's wrong with you?"

"It took me a little time to work it out." Out beyond the harbor, the white sails of the ship rocked, back and forth. "It was the coin—you remember the coin, Isa? Faroth must have waited for me to go to the temple, then he told Dramash that his mother was dead and that I'm the one who murdered her."

There was a pause. Then Daryan, standing a little apart, asked in a low voice, "Why would he tell him that?"

The sound of the surf rolled in his ears. "Because I did murder her."

He felt Isa recoil, but just as quickly she pushed her horror away, as he had known she would. "But what happened? You must have—"

"Because Frea asked me to. That's why I did it." He cut off any justification she might have produced, and then went even further, correcting himself, "No, I've been telling myself that, but it's not true. Frea only wanted me to keep her quiet; it was my idea to cut her throat." More of an impulse than an idea; but no matter. "Dramash was already in the air, waving to her. I held her up while she died so he wouldn't notice. She bled on me. You remember, Isa? You spoke to me just after that, in the temple. Her blood was still on me then." It was easy to talk about it now that he no longer had anything to hide. He could have gone on, but when she drew back from him he knew he had said enough. He greeted her disgust and disappointment with relief. "So, now you see," he told them again, "I can't help you."

Daryan had not moved throughout Rho's recitation, but his face had gone very red. "So that's it?" he asked. "Now you're just going to sit here and do nothing? You're not even going to help us save Dramash from the White Wolf?"

Rho watched Isa walk down the sloping shore, toward the water, shells crunching under her heels. Her boots splashed in the shallows. He said to Daryan, "If I hadn't turned on Frea, Daem and the others wouldn't have either—they wouldn't have been in the temple. And without me, Dramash would have had no reason to destroy it. You see? The more I do, the more people die. Daem tried to explain it to me, but I wouldn't listen. And now he's dead. Now they're all dead." He rested his hands on his knees and watched Isa turn and walk along the waterline. "So yes. I'm just going to sit here."

Daryan stepped closer. His face was still red and his hands were clenched into fists at his sides. "You saved my life. I haven't forgotten that." His mouth moved as he tried to compose his thoughts. "There's no excuse for what you did. You can't undo it—"

"I know."

"—but that doesn't mean you're allowed to give up. Do something. *Fix it.*"

The surf was getting rougher. Was the tide going out,

or coming in? Isa walked back up from the water with the spray chasing her heels. Wet sand caked the hem of her cloak as it dragged behind her.

"I'm sorry. You just don't understand," he told Daryan.

Isa walked back toward them—he thought she was coming to join them, but instead she kept walking right by them, making for Aeda, who was dozing in the sand.

"Isa!" Daryan called out, "aren't you going to say anything?"

She kept her eyes straight ahead. "No."

"But he's your friend!" Daryan protested, jogging after her.

She paused with her foot in the stirrup. "That's not my friend. That's not Rho," she said clearly. She turned to look at him over her shoulder. Then she spoke in Norlander, but not with the hatred that he'd wanted and expected, but with love and concern that came stabbing at him with the sharpness of a dagger. <But he *will* be again. And when he is, I don't think he'll be able to live with himself.>

A moment later, they were gone.

And a moment after that, Rho was in the saddle of his own triffon, buckling himself in with hands that trembled with urgency.

There was enough light for him to keep Aeda in sight, but by the time he landed next to her, on a street lined with the blackened lumps that had once been people's homes, the two of them had already gone. He poked around until he found a charred blanket stinking of smoke, took off his sword and threw the blanket over his head and shoulders, concealing both his features and the weapon in his hands. He hurried down the gray street and soon found himself caught up in a steady stream of people heading in the same direction. As they passed through the broken walls of the old Shadari royal palace, he hunched his shoulders and rearranged his makeshift cowl. He avoided the press of bodies as best he could, not trusting the blanket to disguise his Norlander chill. The crowd was hushed enough for him to hear voices: Daryan was already there, speaking to Faroth.

"Dramash has done enough, hasn't he? You've got to get him to some place safe. We have to decide what we're going to do about the White Wolf."

"The White Wolf is dead—and you don't give the orders here," Faroth said. Rho's breath had turned the air under the blanket moist and stifling. Sweat dripped down from his forehead and into his eyes. "Did you think we'd forgotten all those years you spent in the temple, Daryan, getting fat with Shairav? You stood up to the Dead Ones now because you had no other choice. That doesn't give you any right—"

"I never said I was fit to be daimon," Daryan conceded diplomatically, "but are you? What do you plan to do—rule over the Shadar using Dramash to threaten anyone who disagrees with you?"

"He's *my* son and I'll use him as I see fit."

Warm bodies jostled against Rho as more and more people tried to get close enough to hear what was happening. He edged his way forward.

"As you see fit? As you saw fit to destroy the temple?" Daryan's voice rose wrathfully. "What about the Shadari who were still trapped in there, and the others who were buried alive when it fell?" he thundered. "And the Dead Ones you killed—most of them were our allies!"

Suddenly someone tugged at the blanket over Rho's head and he yanked Fortune's Blight a few inches from its scabbard—but he checked the impulse, just in time. He had not been recognized; he was just being pushed to one side to make way for an even dirtier and bloodier group of Shadari men forcing their way through the crowd. From beneath his cowl he saw a heavy rock-hammer swinging in the hand of the man who'd pushed him.

Anticipating disaster, he stepped out behind the man and followed in his wake, keeping his head bowed and his eyes to the ground until he saw an empty patch of ground in front of him that signaled he had come to the front of the crowd. He ventured a glance and recognized the tall Shadari, Omir, stepping into the wide circle that already contained Daryan, Faroth and Dramash. He couldn't see either Isa or Harotha.

"Omir!" Daryan cried joyfully.

"Stay back, Daimon. We came as soon as we heard you were still alive. Faroth has no right to lead us—he's a murderer. He's killed hundreds of Shadari tonight by destroying the temple. He'll kill you, too, before the sun is up."

"Omir, for the gods' sake, put your weapon down!" Daryan cautioned. "This isn't the time!"

Faroth thrust out his arm toward Daryan; his other hand brandished the curved sword that Rho knew so well. "Daryan has betrayed us!" he shouted, and the crowd murmured loudly in response, but not necessarily in agreement. The bodies around Rho shifted as the spectators turned to each other, but he continued watching Omir and his men. They had Faroth encircled, and were slowly drawing the loop tight.

"Stop, stop," Daryan called out to Omir, waving his arms over his head. "Don't come any closer—"

"They're all traitors," Faroth shouted to the crowd, then he bent down to Dramash and whispered something in his ear. The boy looked sharply up at his father, and then at Daryan. Omir saw the look, and with an inarticulate cry charged forward toward the father and son.

"Dramash—*do it!*" Faroth shouted, grabbing the boy and shaking his arm, but nothing happened. He yanked the child around in front of him. "You're not going to get my son!" Faroth roared at Omir. He drew his sword and held it in front of the boy's neck. "I'll kill him myself before I'll let any of you take him!"

"Stop!" Daryan repeated as he ran forward to block Omir's path. "Just wait! This isn't the way—"

Rho looked at the blade in Faroth's hand and felt the

steel ripping into his gut all over again. Wincing at the sudden pain, he looked up into Dramash's face. To his amazement, he found Dramash looking not at Omir or Daryan but straight back at him. It was Frea's bedchamber all over again, only now Rho was the one looking on and Dramash was the one with Faroth's sword pressed up against his flesh. And as surely as if Dramash had been a Norlander, Rho knew that the boy was having exactly the same thought, and was remembering what Faroth had done the last time.

And he knew exactly what Dramash was going to do.

"Rho, no—wait!" Daryan called out as he threw off the blanket and plunged forward.

Dramash was only a few steps away, but to Rho it felt like he was running under water. The ten strides he needed to reach the boy and his father stretched ahead of him like leagues. On the second step he saw Dramash pull away from Faroth. On the third he saw Faroth reach out for the boy and on the fifth, like a bird swallowing a worm, the sand opened up under Faroth's feet and sucked him down. On the sixth step he heard the crowd screaming, and on the eighth he saw them turn and flee from the child, now standing alone in front of the little mound of sand that had closed over his father's head. And on the ninth step, Rho fell to his knees, dropped his sword and began paddling in the dirt under Dramash's steady gaze, but there was nothing left of Faroth. He was gone.

Dramash's smooth, little-boy features were inscrutable. "It's wrong to hurt people," he said.

Rho sat back on his heels and looked up at the child. "Yes," he said, feeling the word burning in his throat. "It *is* wrong."

Dramash didn't respond. Rho dug his fingers into the dirt. The flat ground mocked him with its semblance of solidity. He was waiting for the first sign of a shift, the first lurch of the pull. He had been judged and sentenced, and now his punishment was finally at hand.

"You're bleeding," Dramash told him, pointing a stubby finger at his stomach. He looked down. His wound had reopened and fresh blood had already soaked through his shirt and stained his cloak. With the sight of the wound came the pain, and with the pain came the dizziness. He crashed to one side, falling onto his elbow.

The wings again: he saw them through the purple splotches in front of his eyes. There were triffons in the air—too many triffons: all of Rho's ghosts, coming to watch the ground drag him below. One of the triffons pounced just behind Dramash, and the ground under his legs bounced. And there was Frea, on Trakkar's back, in her white cape and gleaming silver helmet, immaculate as a goddess amid the blood and the smoke.

Other triffons took up positions around the square, not fully alighting, but keeping their claws just off the ground, the concussive flapping of their wings stirring up the sand and soot, their roar drowning out even the terrified screams of the Shadari as they tried to push and shove their way out of the palace hall.

Ingeld, Rho's former barracks-mate, snatched Dramash from before his very eyes, tossed a sack over his head and threw him up onto Frea's saddle.

<I thought you were dead,> Frea said to Rho as her gloved hands deftly fastened the straps around Dramash. The boy sat still, apparently too stunned or too frightened to struggle or fight back. <I could kill you now, but I like it better this way. You have to live knowing that you tried to stop me and failed.>

On her signal, the triffons rose into the air and turned toward the sea. He saw Daryan running after them, shrieking something in Shadari and shaking his fist at the sky. Rho crawled painfully to his feet. The crowd had gone, except for the victims of the terrified stampede lying hurt or insensate on the ground.

A lone triffon flapped out of the gray sky and dropped to the ground in front of Rho, and he looked into Aeda's black, shining eyes.

<I went back to get her, but then I couldn't get through,> Isa told him. <There were too many of them.>

<I know.> He walked around beside Aeda, steeled himself against the pain and pulled himself up.

As he strapped himself in, she asked, <Is that blood on your cloak? Are you hurt?> She tried to get a closer look at him over her shoulder, but his cape concealed the worst of the mess.

<I'm all right,> he promised her.

She turned back around. <We're going to kill Frea now, aren't we?> she asked. Her words had a cold crispness around the edges, like frost.

<She won't give Dramash up any other way.>

She bunched the reins up in her solo hand. He expected her to take Aeda into the air, but instead she said, <I killed someone tonight. In the battle.>

He looked at the loose strands of her soft white hair, moving in the breeze. Her cowl was down and he could see the smooth sweep of her neck.

<I'm glad it's us. I'm glad we'll be the ones to do it,> she told him. <You and I are the only ones who ever really cared about her, so it seems right, doesn't it?> She paused, and he could almost see the air around her shimmering and the crystalline Norland snow falling down around her shoulders. <I think she'd want it that way. I know I would.>

He realized that he had never loved anything as much as he loved Isa at that moment. He leaned forward and lifted her cowl up over her head for her, making sure the folds covered her vulnerable skin. Then she whistled to Aeda and launched them into the air.

Chapter Forty-Four

Isa strained her eyes, searching the sky for Frea and her men, urgency charging through her. The horizon had turned a pearly gray, with the threat of a brilliant dawn waiting not far off to dazzle her, and the further out to sea they went, the closer they came to passing the point from which Aeda would not have the strength to fly back to shore.

<Frea still has at least twenty triffons,> she reminded Rho. <We can't take them all on. What are we going to do?>

<I don't know,> he said, his words short and brittle, and she thought again of the blood on his cloak. She wanted to turn around for another look, but she was afraid to take her eyes off the sky in front of her. <We'll have to make her *want* to fight us.>

Then she caught sight of Frea's neat formation of triffons bearing down on the massive imperial ship. Her sister's silver helmet gleamed from the point of the formation and Isa fought down a surge of panic. <She's in front,> she reported.

<Fly straight for them.>

She guided Aeda up above the formation, and saw when Frea's silver helmet swung around and the black eye-slits trained on them. One triffon broke and wheeled around toward them.

<We'll have to deal with him first,> Isa said, her heart pumping fast. <That's Ongen.>

<All right. Aeda knows what to do. Just stay with her. I'll take care of Ongen.> Rho drew his sword and stood up in the stirrups, his hips rolling to compensate for the movement of Aeda's body, the leather straps around his thighs stretching and tightening, keeping him safe. She noticed with alarm that the bloodstain on his cape looked larger than it had before.

<Rho—>

<Here he comes,> he said, cutting her off. <Get down!>

She ducked as the two triffons passed each other, and he raised his arm to fend off Ongen's attack, his white cape catching the wind and snapping out behind him. Ongen's meaty arm came down in a weighty hack that Isa felt shake the saddle beneath her, but Rho made no attempt to strike back, only blocked Ongen's blow, and did the same with the two that followed it. The moment they were clear, Aeda dropped her head and swooped down so close beneath the other triffon that Isa had to twist out of the way of its sweeping tail, then they immediately rose up again and nimbly turned in the opposite direction.

<Eofar taught her that,> Rho explained as she looked down, stunned, at the reins lying slackly in her hand. They came on Ongen from behind; the soldier twisted around in the saddle and found himself horribly out of position. Aeda tucked in her wings and glided past; Rho feinted once and then plunged his sword straight into Ongen's chest. He was dead before Aeda's tail flicked by his slumping body. Aeda broke away from the other triffon of her own accord and headed away. Isa swiveled around to look behind her.

<Don't look back,> advised Rho, as he collapsed back down into the saddle, breathing hard, but his warning came too late. She saw Ongen's triffon sniff the air and his nostrils flare out as he smelled the blood. He whined

in alarm and started bucking in mid-air, trying to throw the body from its back.

<They don't like dead weight on them,> Rho explained uncomfortably, watching Ongen's corpse flopping around like a rag-doll. Bones snapped like sticks as the body collided again and again with the hard leather saddle.

Isa tightened her grip on the reins and turned Aeda around.

<What are you doing?> asked Rho.

<I'm not leaving either of them like that. Gently, girl,> she said to Aeda, whistling reassuringly as they cautiously approached the terrified triffon.

<Isa, we don't have time—>

But Aeda snorted reassuringly to her fellow creature, and with a nervous whinny he stopped bucking long enough for them to draw alongside. Rho leaned out over Aeda's wing and carefully cut the tethers that held the saddle on the triffon's back. Ongen's body, still strapped in, slowly slid off and plunged down toward the black water. They waited until they heard the splash.

<All right,> Rho said tightly, <I've had enough. Where's Frea?>

She took them higher up and as they neared the ship, they saw that Frea had started her attack. Sailors were scurrying down from the rigging, looking for refuge belowdecks while the Norland soldiers garrisoned on board swept up to the fighting tops. Some of Frea's men had already landed on the vast deck, while others were making feints from the air. The wind was strong and the sea was fast; dropping anchor was not an option. The whole battle was moving rapidly away from the Shadar.

<There! By the mast,> Rho called out tensely, as Frea's helmet flashed. Trakkar was orbiting the ship's mainmast. Dramash was still with her—he no longer had the sack over his head and his arms were free, but he was not struggling.

<Look out for her knife,> Rho advised. <She can control it in the air if she's not too far away from it.>

<I know—but look at the sheath, it's empty. She must have lost it somehow.>

<Eofar?>

<Maybe. He was unconscious when we found him. He wasn't able to tell us what happened.> With her nerves singing, she stood up in the stirrups. <Frea!> she called out.

<No, let me—> Rho began, but she silenced him.

<Frea!> she called again, even though she knew her sister had heard her the first time. She guided Aeda closer. <If you want to go to Norland, go ahead, but you're not taking that boy with you. We're not going to let you.>

Frea circled the mast and turned her triffon around to face them.

<A cripple now?> Frea asked Rho as if Isa wasn't even there. <Varnat told me what she let them do to her. Is that really the best you can do? Do you pretend that she's me when you touch her?>

<Shut up!> Rho seethed as he stood up, and Isa saw the flash of Fortune's Blight as he drew.

<Don't let her make you angry,> Isa reminded him. <It's all a lie—she's afraid, can't you feel it?>

<She feels the same to me,> he replied wretchedly, dropping back into the saddle.

<Yes, I know,> she said. <That's just it . . . >

<Do you think I'm stupid?> Frea asked them. <I know you won't try anything as long as I have the boy with me. You don't want anything to happen to him, do you?>

<I don't know. Maybe we think he'd be better off dead than with you,> Isa replied.

<You're the one who'd be better off dead. Look at you! Garbage—that's what you are. Someone should have thrown you away,> Frea shot back. And there it was again: the fear, like a long thread winding through her every word—Isa couldn't understand how she had

never noticed it before. She felt that if she took the fear in her fingers and tugged on it, Frea would simply unravel into nothingness. Even the silver helmet with its snarling wolf's head was no longer the least bit intimidating. It was like looking at a child hiding in plain sight with her hands over her eyes.

Another triffon broke off from circling the ship and headed toward them. <I'll handle this, Ingeld,> Frea called back. <Take command. Nothing is going to stop that ship from taking us to Norland.>

<Yes, Lady Frea!> he snapped, and turned his triffon back toward the ship.

<Frea, listen to me,> Isa said impulsively, the words rushing out before she had time to think about them. <I understand what happened, with Mother—you were scared. You didn't want to lose her.>

<No,> Rho called out, and she felt a tug on the back of her cloak. <It's too late for this . . . > He trailed off as Aeda turned and they both squinted fiercely against the light, trying to keep Frea in view.

<You condescending little bitch!> Frea screeched. <Is that why you followed me out here? Because you think you *understand* me now?> She swung Trakkar around on an intercept course. <It was all your fault! She wouldn't have taken us out there at all if you hadn't told.>

<I know,> she said as she steered Aeda into combat position. <That's why I wanted you to know that I'm sorry.>

<You should feel sorry for yourself, not me,> Frea told her. <I'm going to Norland—where are you going? Back to your slave friends? The ones who burned your arm? Do you think they care about anything you've done for them? They'll rip you apart. And as for your own people, there's not a Norlander alive who could bear to look at you without being sick.>

Frea meant to hurt her, to drive her to despair, and everything she said was true enough—except for one part, and it was was the only part that mattered. <You're

wrong,> she said coolly. <I can look at myself, which is more than you can say.> She tossed the reins back to Rho and commanded, <Get down!>

He caught the reins and threw himself against the saddle as Frea came on, heaving Blood's Pride aloft. Isa refused to let herself think about the black water churning below; she trusted the harness to hold her, and focused all of her concentration on Frea's sword. She threw every ounce of force she had into her attack: strike; watch; react. The time it took for her sister's arm to arch back and come at her again felt long enough to contain a whole lifetime. Somewhere underneath it all, she heard Rho shouting in Shadari, "Dramash! Slide back—all the way back—and stay down!"

They were just about to slip out of reach when she twisted as far as she could to her left, away from Frea, and brought her hand up past her face and high up over her left ear. Then she swept the blow down and behind her, using the force of it to turn her body almost completely around. But her aim was off; instead of striking Frea's back, she hit the silver helmet with a clang like the rap of a hammer. The force stung her hand so badly that she nearly dropped Truth's Might into the ocean, but the helmet buckled and Frea rocked heavily over the side of her saddle. Isa prepared to deliver the decisive thrust, but the triffons had passed each other and Frea was out of reach.

Rho turned Aeda around again into the sun; beneath her cowl Isa felt the heat of the dawn on her face. The colors were so brilliant that they drew tears from her eyes. The wind had carried the imperial ship further out toward the horizon, and Frea's men were too far away to intervene. Whatever happened now would be played out among the three of them.

<Rho, what are you doing?> she cried suddenly as she noticed him undoing the buckles that held him in the harness.

<I have an idea,> he said. He took Fortune's Blight

and slid it into the saddle-scabbard. By now the straps of his harness were flapping in the air and the stirrups were the only thing keeping him on the triffon's back. <Here, take these,> he said, holding the reins out to her, and when she started to sheath her sword, added, <No, keep it ready—you'll need to keep fighting.>

<Rho,> she said. She could see Frea across the sky, readying Blood's Pride, and she could feel her sister's fury like a soundless roar. <I can't—I can't fly and fight at the same time, not with one arm.>

He leaned forward. The passivity that had always been so much a part of him was gone forever; his assurance was irrefutable and as solid as a brick. <I haven't forgotten anything,> he told her, looping the reins around her thigh and cinching them loosely. He gripped her leg and then turned back around.

Instinctively Aeda matched her wing-strokes to Trakkar's. *Up. Down. Up. Down.* As they came closer Isa could see the damage she had done. The right side of Frea's helmet bore a deep indentation and blood was dripping from underneath it onto the collar of her cloak.

This time Frea struck first, and her attack was murderous, leaving Isa no opportunity for anything but defense, no chance to strike back. She was horribly conscious that if just one blow found its mark she was done for. Finally Frea's sword ground down against Truth's Might, and then snapped away as Trakkar carried her past.

Now she had time to look back at Rho. He had slipped his feet out of the stirrups and brought them up underneath him. His fine, lean body balanced on the saddle for one long, airless heartbeat. <I'm so proud of you,> he told her.

Then he jumped.

She caught her breath and watched Rho's cape, transformed from snowy white to tawny gold by the morning light, swelling out behind him. He wasn't going to make it—his leap was too short . . .

But then his foot came down on the tough cartilage of Trakkar's wing and he used the momentum of its upswing to propel him the rest of the way. He threw himself into the wide space that Dramash had left when he'd moved back, and he'd got one foot jammed into the near stirrup before Frea even had time to react, and the other leg over and secure while she was still trying to get her sword around to strike at him.

Isa looped her fingers through the reins and whistled frantically to Aeda, who sprang forward and executed the same tight little turn she'd showed off earlier, bringing them around behind Trakkar. With the sun behind her everything in her field of vision was soaked with color, and it was difficult for her to make sense of what she was seeing.

Trakkar was flying erratically, alarmed by the sudden extra passenger and by Frea's slack handling of the reins. Rho was trying to wrest Blood's Pride out of Frea's hands, struggling to break her grip on the sword while trying to keep clear of the blade itself. And in a phenomenal piece of bad luck, his cape had snagged on the stirrup, pulling his shoulders backward and leaving his left side exposed to the sun.

<Your knife! Use your knife,> she called as Aeda pumped her wings and put on a burst of speed, sliding her next to Trakkar. She readied Truth's Might to strike in Rho's defense, but as she slipped past Trakkar's tail, her went heart leaping into her throat: Dramash was not strapped in. He was holding on to the leather saddle with both hands, but with each roll of the triffon's body he was sliding back and forth; if the creature bucked or turned too sharply, the boy would surely be flung off into the sea.

Instinctively she reached out to help him, but she still had her sword in her hand and he ducked away from her in fear. "Hold on!" she shouted, then, <Rho! Dramash isn't strapped in!>

But Rho and Frea were locked together, and if he let go of Frea's arm now, he would be dead in an instant.

Isa changed her grip on Truth's Might, and then frantically changed it again as she considered the possibilities. With the two so close together, there was no sure way for her to strike at Frea without hitting Rho.

Then she saw the dull hilt of Rho's knife poking out from under his cape: it was just what she needed, but she had no free hand with which to grab it and in another split-second it would be out of reach. There was no time to sheath her sword.

She opened her fist and let it go.

Truth's Might dropped between the heaving sides of the two triffons and fell away, tumbling down, shrinking until it slid into the dark water below and disappeared forever.

Wasting no more time, she snatched Rho's knife from its scabbard and plunged it deep into Frea's thigh, just a moment before Aeda's momentum ripped it out of her hand. Frea's body went rigid with shock, she lost her grip on Blood's Pride and Rho tore it away from her.

<Now, Rho! You have to kill her!> Isa cried, as Rho swung the sword over his head.

<I can't!> he howled in frustration. <Trakkar will bolt and we'll lose Dramash. Here!> He heaved the sword through the air, and a line of sparks lit a path toward her as the sunlight caught the turning blade. She reached up and the hilt slapped sweetly into her palm. Then Aeda unfurled her wings and they shot out in front of Trakkar.

Frea's silent howl of pain and outrage hit Isa in the back like a savage shove. She straightened up and tried to bring Aeda about again, but maneuvering was more difficult now that both animals were facing in the same direction. As they turned, she saw Frea yank the knife out of her leg and she called urgently, <Rho, look out!>

But he had already slid further back to strap Dramash and himself safely into the harness, and his seat was precarious: he had only one foot in the stirrup, one hand gripping the saddle and his back was turned. Isa whistled desperately to Aeda, but the triffon was already doing her best to bring them back into position.

Frea was trying to reach Rho, but she had buckled herself in too tightly to turn around. As Isa watched, her sister yanked furiously at the sliding buckles, trying to loosen the straps around her legs, and finally sliced through them with Rho's knife.

<Frea,> she called out, hoping to distract her long enough for Rho to get Dramash and himself strapped in securely, <your imperial knife is gone and I've got your sword. You're hurt. Why don't you surrender?>

Frea's rage was no longer rational; there was only a savage hunger to taste the blood of those who had wounded her. Isa felt her sister's madness sucking at her like a whirlpool, and finally she understood that no mercy, no clemency, would be possible. The part of Frea that had been her sister was already gone.

<Rho,> Isa screamed as Frea finally freed herself of the broken straps and lunged toward him, <behind you—she's got your knife!>

Throwing both arms protectively around the boy, Rho kicked back at Frea. His heel caught her leg near the knife-wound and her body jerked in pain, but still she brought the knife back up and slashed at him. He kicked at her again, this time hitting her forearm, and though she kept hold of the knife, Trakkar's reins went snapping out into the hazy air. The triffon felt the change in the tension on the reins immediately and tossed his head with a worried snort.

Rho fastened the last buckle around Dramash's waist and yanked the strap tight, then he thrashed around with his foot, trying to find the stirrup again, but he had slipped too far back in the saddle to reach it.

As the unfamiliar weight of Blood's Pride slid about in her sweat-slicked glove, Isa tried to bring Aeda into battle position, but Trakkar's flight path was too unpredictable. Finally Aeda found a straight line to him, and she put on a burst of speed and pulled in her wings—but at the last moment, Trakkar jerked around again and suddenly, instead of coming alongside, they were facing him broadside.

<Look out!> Isa warned them all indiscriminately, and stood up in the saddle to give her yank on the reins more force, but Aeda had seen the danger for herself and stretched out her great wings with a snap.

Frea's dented helmet spun toward them and she thrust out her open hand toward Blood's Pride as she howled, <That's *mine*!> It was the wail of a broken-hearted child. <Mine! *Mine!*> She tossed aside Rho's knife as carelessly as if it were a broken toy and reached out with both hands.

Aeda ducked her head to fly under Trakkar's belly. In one moment, the saddles of the two triffons would be at equal height.

Isa drew in a deep breath and flipped Blood's Pride around so that her hand was gripping the unsharpened base of the blade. She held the sword out, hilt-first, toward her sister. Time slowed down; each moment had the inevitability of something she had already lived through, many, many times.

The space between the two triffons closed.

Frea leaned out to grab the sword as it came toward her, and Isa held it there steadily for her, knowing that her sister could see or think of nothing else. When Frea's fingertips brushed the hilt, Isa brought her arm back like a fisherman yanking a line, and Frea lunged for the bait. For a moment she hung there, prone, in the open sky. Then she dropped.

Trakkar's claws rose up in front of Isa's face and she threw herself down onto the saddle. A cool wind chilled the sweat beneath her cloak as Trakkar's shadow passed overhead. And then she and Aeda were diving down, down, following the flash of Frea's helmet toward the hungry waves.

By the time Frea hit the water, Isa was close enough to feel the spray spatter her face. Aeda dragged her feet through the swells and then opened her wings and soared upward again. Isa searched among the dipping white-caps for a gleam of silver or the spread of a white cloak.

<Do you see her?> Rho called down from above. His words were raw with expectation and dread.

<No.> She looked up and saw Trakkar's black shape against the bright sky. <Are you all right?>

<Dramash is safe. I've got the reins now. We've got to—>

<Wait! I see her!> She had caught a glimpse of the helmet, bobbing far to the east of where Frea had first hit the water; she had been caught in a strong current. Aeda glided toward her. <Frea?> she called out to her sister. <Frea, can you hear me?>

Trakkar's shadow flicked over the water. <Isa, what are you doing?> Rho asked.

<Frea?> she called out again, ignoring him.

A strange, faint voice answered, <It won't come off. I can't get it off.>

Isa leaned forward and grabbed the reins as close to Aeda's neck as she could. She played out the slack over Aeda's side. <I'm coming toward you,> she told her sister. <Grab hold of Aeda's reins. We'll pull you out of the water.>

<It won't come off,> she said again, and Isa could feel nothing from her sister except childish simplicity. There was no sign that she had understood anything Isa had just said.

She guided Aeda down as low as she dared and leaned out over her wing. <Frea? Can you see the reins? They're right in front of you. Can you see them?>

<Isa?> Frea asked, as if she had just now realized that her sister was speaking to her. <I can't get it off.>

She leaned further out. Now she could see Frea thrashing in the water. She was alternately scrambling with her arms and legs to stay afloat, and pushing and tugging at her helmet. The contrast between the frantic movements and the still, peevish little voice was terrifying.

<Your helmet won't come off,> Isa told her firmly. <It's dented. Forget about it. Listen to me: take your cloak off. It's dragging you down.>

<But the water's getting in,> Frea whimpered.

<Grab the reins, Frea!> she pleaded. <They're right in front of you!>

A wave lapped over Frea's head and she disappeared.

<Frea!> Isa screamed helplessly.

A moment later she bobbed up again, further out to sea.

<Rho!> Isa cried out. <Rho, help me—I'm losing her!>

Frea's cape fanned out over the water, spreading outward. The helmet sank first. Then, inch by inch, the cape disappeared beneath the waves.

A curtain of dread came down around Isa, muting everything but her own voice. <Frea?> she whispered.

<Don't, Isa.> Rho's voice held her up like a strong arm around her waist. <She's gone. It's over.>

A wave slapped up against Aeda's side and the triffon tossed her head in alarm. Isa gathered up the slippery reins and let her climb back to a comfortable altitude. The ship was far out to sea by now; there would be no chance of any of Frea's men making it back to the Shadar on the triffons. For the moment at least they posed no threat to the city. Rho and Isa silently turned Trakkar and Aeda back toward the shore.

The sun was warm on her back. She had no memory of having fallen asleep, but when she opened her eyes, her head was resting on Aeda's bristly neck and the beach was right in front of her. Trakkar was lying in the sand just below the tide line, with the water splashing over his feet and belly. From his exhausted attitude, she guessed that he had refused to fly any further. Rho and Dramash were making their way up the beach on foot. Rho was walking with a pained, lurching motion, and just as Aeda touched down next to Trakkar, she saw him double over and fall heavily onto the sand.

<Rho!> she cried out, tugging at the straps of the harness. By the time she'd undone them and clambered down from Aeda's back, he had hauled himself back up again. Dramash stood a little way in front of him, watching silently. <Rho!> she called again, running up the beach, the sand pulling heavily at her boots.

<Isa,> he called out to her, and then, just as she reached him, gasped out, <Help me—>

She caught him with her right arm as he fell, but she couldn't hold him. She dropped to her knees in the sand, cradling his quaking body against her chest. Using her own body to shield him from the sun, she pulled open the clasps of his cloak and pulled up his shirt.

<No. Don't,> he pleaded weakly, trying to push her hand away, but it was too late. The wound was like nothing she could have imagined. The blood was not the worst of it; it was the swollen, discolored flesh oozing pus that turned her stomach. He was in tremendous pain, convulsing helplessly against her. <Take Dramash to the Shadari—to Harotha, and Daryan,> he begged. <Please!>

<I'm taking you to a physic,> she said rapidly, covering him up again. <The Nomas—they're taking care of Eofar.>

<Isa!> His tortured silver eyes looked up into hers entreatingly. <You'll never get me into the saddle. Take him and go!>

He was right: she couldn't possibly lift Rho into the saddle by herself, not one-handed. But she couldn't just leave him lying on the beach, burning in the sun. Squinting against the glare, she saw a cluster of rocks not far to her right. <I'm going to move you into the shade,> she warned him, and began dragging him over the sand. Every pull and bump increased his agony, but there was nothing else she could do. By the time she had him safely in the shadow of the rocks, his eyes were closed and she couldn't tell if he was still conscious.

<Listen to me,> she said, making him as comfortable as she could, adjusting his cape and cowl so that they

covered him completely, <you wait here, all right?> She felt no response from him, but when she touched his cheek his eyelids fluttered. <Rho! You wait for me; do you understand? I know it might seem easier to go,>—she had to pause as a pulse of pain raced down her missing left arm—<but don't, all right? Please.> She was looking at his face, his beautiful face, and hardly knowing what she was doing, she leaned toward him and pressed her lips tenderly against his. <Please,> she pleaded. She didn't realize that she was crying until she saw her tears glistening on his pale skin.

His lips moved against hers and his eyes opened again. <My sword?> he asked faintly.

She ran back to Aeda, slid Fortune's Blight from the saddle and ran back, but by the time she reached him, he was unconscious again. She laid the sword vertically across his body with the hilt on his chest. Then she took his limp hands and closed his fingers around the hilt.

<*You wait*,> she whispered to him again.

She picked her way over the flaming sands to Dramash. She had no idea what to say to him, how she would convince him to come with her, but he came forward to meet her and followed her without a word, as if he already understood. She helped him clamber up into Aeda's saddle, and he buckled the straps of the harness himself, all the time as silent as a Norlander.

A few moments later they were setting down in the middle of the ruined palace, where a small crowd had re-formed around Daryan and Omir. Most of them scuttled back against the walls as Isa landed, but Daryan ran forward to meet them.

"Thank the gods," he called out in a strained voice as he ran up to Aeda. "You got him back— You just took off after Frea, and I didn't know— What happened? Are you all right?"

Dramash undid the harness and slipped down off Aeda's back into Daryan's arms. The hush in the ruined hall was so intense that the clinking of the buckles rang out like claxons. Then the boy walked to Aeda's huge head and began stroking the fur between her ears. Aeda lowered her head and narrowed her eyes with pleasure.

Isa stayed in the saddle, looking down from beneath the shadows of her cowl at the reins twisted around her fingers.

"My sister is dead."

"Isa," Daryan breathed. He stepped closer to Aeda's neck so that she could see his face as he looked up at her. His dark eyes looked softly into hers. "I'm sorry. I'm sure you had no other choice."

"I must go. I must find a healer for Rho. I had to leave him on the beach. He's hurt very badly."

"No, don't go," he cried, very softly, but turned at the sound of someone running toward them.

"Daimon!" the breathless man called out as he neared them. The messenger caught sight of Dramash and decided to stop a good ten paces away. "Daimon, your wife is in need of you," he said more formally. "They sent me to fetch you—they say you should come at once."

"All right," Daryan said. The messenger moved away from them, but stood waiting for Daryan to follow. "I have to go, too," he told her, staring straight ahead at Aeda's bristly hide.

"Rho wants you to take Dramash. You and Harotha."

"Harotha will know what to do with him," he agreed. He glanced around at the crowd, at the messenger waiting for him, and then at Dramash, still standing by Aeda's head. "They're all afraid of him now." He swallowed, and then looked up at her again. "Are you all right?"

She twisted the reins in her hand. "No."

"Isa," he said, miserably. He made the slightest of movements toward her, and then checked himself. "I have to go." He held his hand out to Dramash and together they walked after the messenger.

She was already losing him.

Chapter Forty-Five

The messenger guided Daryan and Dramash through a district that had largely escaped the fires to an unassuming house with smoke streaming from the chimney and a Nomas woman waiting in the doorway.

"Hello again, Daimon," she greeted him. It took a moment for him to recognize her as one of the women he had encountered in the street just before the temple exploded. He regarded her with unease. Her jaunty greeting felt forced and her face was grave. She moved aside and he started toward the doorway, but then stopped, seeing the Nomas king sitting by himself in the shadows. Jachad was leaning up against the wall of the house and his eyes were trained on the ground. He appeared to be staring at nothing.

"King Jachad?"

The Nomas looked up at him. A glance into his blue eyes, and suddenly the last thing Daryan wanted to do was to go into that house.

Then he heard a faint sound that he had heard only a handful of times before in his life: the mewing wails of a newborn child.

"Harotha had the baby?" he cried out, rushing forward and seizing the Nomas woman by the arm. "He's all right?"

"He's more than all right," she whispered significantly.

Her mouth broke into a wide smile as she pulled back the curtain and ushered Daryan and Dramash inside. "He's the most beautiful baby I've ever seen."

The interior of the house was dim. Three more Nomas women were inside: one silently stirring a pot of tea over the hearth, a second on her knees replacing instruments and pots of medicines into a case and the third sitting with her back against the wall outside the curtained sleeping chamber, absently plucking at some linens jumbled up in her lap. A breeze rustled the curtain next to her as they entered, revealing a murmur of voices and a flicker of lamplight in the small chamber beyond. Then Daryan noticed the familiar shape of Strife's Bane, with its twin dereshadi climbing the hilt, leaning up against the wall in its tooled scabbard.

"Eofar! He's here?" Daryan cried out.

"Of course he's here. He's with his wife and babe, where else?" the woman who had greeted him tossed back.

"Brigeth," cautioned the woman by the fire.

"Oh, what's the point of pretending?" she said dismissively. "I don't know how they managed to fool anyone at all—anyone with two eyes can see what they are to each other. Praise Amai, she brought him right to where he was supposed to be."

"So everything's all right," he exhaled in relief. "Everyone's all right."

The Nomas woman stirring the pot stopped with her spoon halfway to her lips. The woman with the linens in her lap turned her head away.

Brigeth stepped close enough for him to smell the wild, briny sea in her hair. She laid a callused but gentle hand on his shoulder. "Harotha won't live, lad. I'm sorry. There's nothing to be done about it."

He looked into her clear eyes and saw no chance for appeal. Her features melted into a blur and he found himself kneeling on the carpet, still clutching Dramash's small hand.

"It was too much for her," he blurted out in an agony of self-recrimination. "I should have kept her out of it. I should have—"

"Belay that!" Brigeth interrupted with spirit. "She could have spent nine months in bed and it might have ended just the same. No one can know what would have happened. There, now."

He dropped Dramash's hand. "Does she know?"

"Hm." Brigeth sniffed respectfully. "She knew before we did. Not much gets by that one, I'm thinking."

A faint voice from the other room called out a name, and the woman sitting on the floor dumped the linens out of her lap and slipped inside. A few moments later she came out again.

"What is it, Raina?" asked Brigeth.

"She wants to see him."

Daryan stood up. He tried to take a deep breath, but his chest was so tight that the air stuck in a lump and would go no further. "All right," he told Raina, "I'm ready."

"Not you," she said, pointing at Dramash. "Him."

Daryan looked down at the boy doubtfully. Exhaustion showed in the puffy flesh under his glassy eyes and he didn't appear to be paying any attention to the adults' conversation, but then he looked up at Raina and without a word shuffled into the next room. Daryan followed behind him, but his courage faltered as he got to the curtain.

Inside, a familiar voice was speaking in the earnest, cajoling tones he knew so well: "— but she will love him, you see? That's what she's wanted all along. She's never had anything else to love. It's not just his safety I'm thinking about. And you know you have to go, otherwise the emperor—" and then in an entirely different tone, "Dramash! There you are! Daryan, are you out there? You come in, too."

He pushed the curtain aside and saw Harotha, lying back against the cushions. She looked up into his eyes and instantly he stopped trying to think of what he was going to say to her. He didn't need to say anything; she knew it all.

Eofar was lying next to her, a limp remnant of his former self. His face was haggard and one of his legs was heavily bandaged. He had his arm around the cushion behind Harotha's shoulders, not quite touching her, and was brushing her damp hair with the tips of his fingers at compulsively regular intervals. His eyes were fixed on her face and he never looked up, not even when Daryan entered the room.

But the baby. Oh gods, the baby.

Brigeth had not exaggerated. He had expected him to look either Norlander or Shadari, or some discordant mix of the two, like the Mongrel, but no: here, all was unity. His skin had the warm glow of the desert sand at sunset, and his head was covered with delicate curls the color of beaten gold. His round eyes, which at the moment were wide open, were a silvery blue around enormous black pupils, and ringed with thick white lashes.

"Oh, Harotha," he breathed, dumbstruck.

She cuddled the swaddled baby closer to her breast, beaming with pride. The baby made a snuffling little sound and she leaned her flushed cheek against his tiny head with a soft coo.

Eofar's eyes never left his wife's face.

"Come here, Dramash," she called over, patting the cushion next to her. The boy tottered over and plopped down by her side. "I want to talk to you." He was staring at the baby, and now he gave the child a little wave. "Dramash, are you listening to me?"

Daryan thought that he detected some truculence in Dramash's swollen brown eyes, but the child nodded in response to her question.

"It's about your friend—what's his name, Rho?"

"Harotha, no!" Daryan burst out, but she flashed him a warning look and he clamped his mouth shut.

"Rho did a very, very bad thing," she continued, in

the same carefully modulated tone of voice. "A very bad thing. You know what I'm talking about, don't you?"

The boy hunched up his shoulders protectively and a deep frown creased his brow. "I guess."

"You're angry, and I understand that. I'm angry, too." She glanced up at Daryan, and then back to Dramash. "But I'm going to ask you to do something—something very difficult—and I want you to promise me that you'll do as I ask. Dramash?"

After a long moment, he finally answered, "I promise."

"Good boy." She looked up at Daryan again, holding his eyes for a moment, making sure of him. "Daryan is going to take you to see Rho. He's going to leave the two of you alone together. And you can say anything you need to say to him. But after that, Rho is going to be your protector. He's going to look out for you, from now on, just as he did tonight."

Dramash and Daryan were both listening to the steady rise and fall of Harotha's words as if she held them under a spell.

"But that's not the hard part. That's not the part I asked you to promise me about." She nestled the baby closer to her breast, freeing up one arm so that she could lay her hand over Dramash's. "I want you to promise me that you'll try to forgive him."

"Harotha," Daryan exclaimed, aghast, "you can't!"

Again she silenced him with a look. "I want you to forgive him," she repeated slowly. "It's going to be very hard. It might take a very, very long time. But I want you to promise me that you'll try." She reached out and touched his little dimpled chin with the tips of her fingers, turning his face up so that she could look into his eyes. "Do you think you can promise me that?"

The boy's frown deepened as he looked back at his aunt. After a few moments' thought his face relaxed and he nodded, then without pausing another beat he asked, "Can I hold the baby?"

She sank back against the cushions with a little laugh. "Of course," she said. "He's your cousin, you know." Daryan sprang forward and helped transfer the little bundle into his eager arms. "Hold his head," she reminded both of them. Daryan heard the slight slur in her speech and glanced up in alarm. Her eyes were closed, and now that he was closer, he could see the high color in her cheeks and forehead and the feverish trembling in her limbs.

"Dramash?" he said softly, and the boy looked up from rocking the baby in his arms with a bit more enthusiasm than was necessary. "Are you hungry?"

He looked down at the baby, and then back at Daryan. "I guess," he admitted.

"All right," Daryan said, "give the baby back to your aunt and then go and ask the Nomas for something to eat; they'll find something for you."

Dramash handed the baby back to Harotha with exaggerated carefulness, but not before planting a sweet kiss on his golden curls. Daryan held the curtain aside and waited for him to shuffle out into the main room, then he glanced at Eofar. He hadn't changed position, but now his head rested on the cushion next to Harotha's and it was impossible to tell who was comforting whom.

Daryan knelt on the spot that Dramash had just vacated and lowered his voice. "Harotha," he said, "you can't ask that boy to forgive Rho."

"I have to," she answered. Her dry, feverish eyes burned into his. "Saria was more than just my friend—she was the closest thing I had to a sister. It's the only thing I can do for her or her little boy now."

"I don't think you know what you're saying. You're asking him to forgive the man who murdered his mother—"

"And what about the person who murdered his father?" she interrupted. Suddenly tears were streaming down her face, but she spoke as if oblivious to them.

"Did you think I hadn't heard that my brother was dead, and how? How long do you think it will be before Dramash feels the weight of what he's done? How many souls does that little boy already have on his head?" She took a deep breath and went on more evenly, "If he can find a way to forgive Rho, he'll be able to forgive himself one day—think, Daryan: do you want another White Wolf on your hands?"

"The White Wolf?" he asked, confused. "What does she have to do with it?"

"It was the guilt, Daryan. Can you imagine what Dramash could become if we let it fester in him like it did in her? In that case it would be better for everyone if we went out there right now and stabbed him through the heart!"

"Harotha," Eofar murmured, and she turned to him and met his eyes, then sagged back down against the cushions.

Daryan rocked back onto his heels. He couldn't tell her that Rho had been badly hurt, that he might even be dead. He got to his feet. "There's something I need to do," he told them hurriedly. He bent down and kissed her tenderly on the forehead; her skin was dry and impossibly hot. "I'll be right back," he reassured her, and then brushed his fingers against the baby's smooth cheek. "He really is amazing," he whispered, feeling the bitter tears snaking down his cheeks.

"He is," she agreed, smiling.

He ducked through the curtain. "Brigeth?" he called out, fighting to keep the panic out of his voice.

She looked up from breaking off some pieces of dried fish for Dramash.

"There's a Dead One—a Norlander—badly hurt, on the beach somewhere—I don't know exactly where. He needs help. I should have said something before, but . . ." He trailed off, feeling horribly guilty—the thought of Rho burning to death on the beach had felt like justice. Now he felt like he'd betrayed both Isa *and* Harotha.

"Oh, don't worry about that," Brigeth reassured him, "that pretty friend of yours was just here; Mairi went with her. She's our best healer; if anyone can save him, she can."

"Thanks." He looked into her open, honest face. "And thank you for everything you've done. We're in your debt."

Brigeth frowned, saying sternly, "You're in no such thing. We helped you because it was the right thing to do." She pointed an accusatory finger at his chest. "Your people say we only care about money, but you're the ones who turn everything into a transaction. I hope things can be different now, Daimon. I hope we can learn to understand each other better."

"I do, too," he answered, managing to smile. He moved to go back into the sleeping chamber, but Raina held up a hand to stop him. She peeked quietly around the curtain, and after a brief look inside she tugged it closed again.

Hardly knowing what he was doing, Daryan grabbed Brigeth's hand and squeezed it tightly. A strange silence fell over the little house, broken only by the occasional snap of the fire. Dramash was asleep on the floor, or pretending to be. They waited together, listening, and the silence lengthened until Daryan became conscious of a dull ringing in his ears. And then he heard something, a heavy, rhythmic thumping: the sound of a fist striking a clay wall, over, and over, and over again.

Brigeth gently removed Daryan's fingers and slipped out of the front door. Raina went back into the sleeping chamber. He heard the baby crying, and then she reappeared cradling him in one arm and supporting Eofar's hunched, limping body with the other. Blood shone wetly on his knuckles.

"No, no—you don't understand!" Daryan cried, though no one had spoken to him. "I can't do this myself—this isn't how it's supposed to be. She *knew* what we were supposed to do. She *always* knew." He glared at

Raina as if she were arguing with him. "People aren't just alive one minute and talking to you, and then dead the next. It's ridiculous." He lunged at Eofar. "I don't know how to do this—I need to talk to her!"

Daryan felt the grief crushing his heart in his chest and he clutched Eofar's arm, needing the pain and the cold, holding on tighter the more deeply it bit into him. His former master grabbed his shoulder and sagged against him. "I didn't even say goodbye to her," Daryan gasped.

"All right, all right," a voice behind him murmured, and gentle hands disentangled him from Eofar and sat him down on the carpet. He was too blinded by his tears to see the warm cup someone pressed into his hand and then guided to his lips. The aroma wafted up into his face with homely familiarity and he grabbed the cup with both hands and gulped down the steaming liquid.

"This way, Nisha," Brigeth said, and he smeared the tears from his eyes and looked up. Jachad, his face drained of all color or expression, had come in and was standing next to the door. Then the regal woman Daryan had spoken to in the street, the one with the silver medallion around her neck, swept into the room. She took the crying baby from Raina, nestled him against her breast and began clucking and murmuring to him in Nomas. The infant settled down immediately.

"All right: we're telling them outside that we lost both of them, so we'd better keep this little one quiet," she said, her musical voice assuming a tone of quiet command. The sea-blue eyes she turned toward Eofar were shining with sympathetic tears. "Everyone's been told to go home, just as we discussed. We told them their daimon wishes to mourn in private for now. My girls are shooing them away. She'll come in as soon as it's safe."

"She?" Daryan asked.

The two women exchanged a private look. Then Brigeth turned back to Daryan and said, "The Mongrel, as you call her."

"The Mongrel? Why is she coming here?"

Eofar slumped back against the wall, ignoring Raina's soft urgings for him to sit down. "She's coming for the baby."

"What?" He vaulted to his feet. "You can't be serious! She's—she's—"

"She's my sister," Eofar reminded him.

"It was Harotha's decision," Raina interjected.

"Eofar!" He hurried over to his friend. "He's your son—yours and Harotha's! You're not just going to abandon him, are you?"

Eofar's silver eyes were dull. "It's for his own good."

"That's what they told *me*," Daryan retorted hotly, "when they took me away from my mother. They were *wrong*."

"What do you want?" Eofar cried out, his voice breaking. He threw out his hand toward the infant. "Look at him! Anyone who sees him will know what he is. He can't stay in the Shadar. He needs someone to protect him."

"What about you? You're his father—"

"I'm going to Norland," Eofar told him, glancing over at Nisha. "Someone must go to the emperor. If he hears the Shadari have revolted, there will be another invasion. Someone must go and speak with him. It has to be me."

"Is this really what you want?"

"What I *want*?" Eofar rasped, and turned away.

Daryan looked at the helpless little baby lying in Nisha's arms. Harotha had figured out everything before him, just like always. Angry, impotent sobs took hold of him again. Eofar hobbled slowly back toward the sleeping chamber. Raina laid a hand on his arm to stop him, but he looked at her and she took her hand away.

"Wait," Nisha called after him, and he paused with his hand on the curtain. "We need to know his name."

Eofar opened his mouth to speak, and then stopped. The Norlander closed his eyes and stood there, deathly still, for a long moment, then he turned back to Nisha. "What's the Nomas word for 'victory?' "

The Nomas women chanted simultaneously, "Osha-rad."

"Call him that," he said before disappearing inside.

A slice of daylight split the room as the curtain over the front door shifted, and the Mongrel slid inside. She stopped in the middle of the room and stared at the baby in Nisha's arms.

"Meiran," Nisha said, in a voice husky with emotion. She cleared her throat and then went on more glibly, "Well, here he is, my poor, beautiful babe." She looked down at the baby and wrinkled her pretty nose for him, then laid him against her shoulder and softly patted his back. "Eofar can't bear the sight of him. You can't blame him, can you? Harotha wants you to take him away from here. Take him away, and never come back to the Shadar."

The Mongrel's scars shone silver in the firelight as she slowly held out her arms. It might have been a trick of the light, but Daryan thought he saw her trembling. Nisha nestled the baby boy's head in the crook of her arm, and then paused, her hands resting on her shoulders, beaming at her with such overwhelming tenderness that his own sore heart swelled with longing. He would have given anything to see his own mother again, just for a moment.

The Mongrel whispered, "I knew you were going to say that."

Daryan looked around the room. Suddenly he realized that he was in the presence of a conspiracy, witnessing the culmination of a story in which he had played a part, but that he still barely understood.

Ignoring the eyes that turned to follow him, he trudged across the room, lifted the sleeping Dramash off the floor, and said wearily, "Can we go now?"

Epilogue

Eofar stood on the deck in the stern of the Nomas ship *Argent* with the strong, cool wind blowing into his face. He was watching the Shadari's fires twinkling in front of the mountains, which were just visible as purple humps in the evening starlight. All around him the ship creaked and groaned uneasily, but he had already grown accustomed to the ceaseless torrent of sound. It blended into the background of his thoughts, as did the bright voices of the Nomas sailors attending to the needs of their vessel.

The cabin door behind him squeaked open and he heard the uncertain steps of his cabin-mate coming to join him.

<Have they started yet?> Rho asked as he leaned against the railing.

<Not yet.>

They stood together for a few more moments, lost in their own thoughts, before Eofar looked at Rho and recoiled. <What—? What have you done to yourself?>

Rho's wounds were finally beginning to heal, but he still couldn't straighten to his full height. The resulting slouch echoed his former disinterested posing, but there was no mistaking the fact that he had turned his back on his birthright: his head was a mess of choppy white spikes. It looked as if he had used his knife to hack off his hair by the handful.

He was unfazed by Eofar's reaction. <It seemed like the thing to do.>

Eofar remembered something. <Isn't that what they do in Norland? To criminals?>

Rho said nothing in reply, but his thoughtfulness deepened and Eofar shifted the subject of the conversation. <Is he asleep yet?>

<What do you think?> Rho asked in despair, but there was more than a hint of amusement, too. <Look over there.>

He turned and scanned the immaculate deck, illuminated by lamps swinging from the rigging. Underneath the billowing sails, a dozen steady-legged, strong-armed Nomas women were going about their business with their usual air of unflappable efficiency. In their midst, Nisha stood with one arm resting easily on the ship's great wheel, the other supporting Dramash as he tried to turn it under her laughing tutelage.

<Any sign of the emperor's ship?> asked Rho.

<Not yet—they've nearly two weeks' start on us, and we don't even where they're heading.>

<They don't have too many choices. If Ingeld and the others did manage to take the ship, they'll have to find a place to hide out where people don't ask too many questions. What else can they do?>

<They can go to Norland,> Eofar reminded him. <They can tell the emperor some lie about what happened here, and make themselves look like the loyal ones. Then we'd be walking right into our own tribunal.>

Rho tried to be dismissive, but without much success. <Ingeld's not smart enough for that. Besides, Nisha thinks we still have a good chance of catching up with them in the straits—although I think she may be boasting.>

They turned back to the receding view of the Shadar.

<I'm grateful to her, you know,> Rho said after another lengthy pause, and Eofar understood that he was not speaking of the Nomas queen. During one of the

interminable, sleepless days that had followed the battle Eofar had found himself confiding everything that he had kept hidden for so long. <Can I ask you something?>

<All right,> he agreed, afraid he already knew the question.

<Why did you and Harotha stay in the Shadar? Why didn't you leave before any of this happened?>

Eofar looked down at his hands on the railing. <I wish I knew. I can't stop asking myself that.> He stamped one foot, sending fresh spasms through his bandaged ankle, as if the pain would bring enlightenment. <Does it matter now? It won't change anything.> He looked back out across the water. <Maybe we were both tied to too many other things. Maybe neither of us could let go of the past.> The stars looked brighter at sea than they had from the Shadar, and the sea air was fresher and cooler. For the first time in a long while, he felt the stirrings of hunger.

<What's the plan when we get to Norland?> Rho asked.

<I haven't the slightest idea.>

<Well, you should have a lot of time to think about it. It's going to be a long voyage.>

<What about you?> Eofar asked. <You know a lot more about Norland and Ravindal than I do. You've been there, at least.>

<I'm just along for the ride,> Rho reminded him firmly. <I go where Dramash goes, that's all. I'm not interested in politics.>

<But you still have family there, don't you?>

<Oh, they've probably all killed each other by now,> Rho joked, but his levity was no more convincing than his optimism. <Let's hope it doesn't take long to persuade the emperor that the Shadar outpost is no longer worth his trouble, not now that the ore is nearly gone. Or else . . . >

<A demonstration from Dramash should help persuade him to leave the Shadari alone.>

<If we must.>

Eofar leaned forward. Something was flickering on the beach. <You know what? Norland, the emperor . . . they're not what's worrying me.>

<No? What is, then?>

He saw a new light spring up, larger than the rest, and closer; it flared up higher, hotter. His keen Norlander eyes made out the wisps of black smoke snaking up from the pyre before they thinned out into the purple sky. <I don't seem to care about anything any more.>

<I know that feeling.> Rho leaned out over the railing and stared down into the dark water. <Pity it doesn't last.>

Isa looked down at the crowds of people heading toward the beach. The light was gone and she had finally been able to peel off her cloak and single white glove. The evening breeze cooled her skin beautifully and she closed her eyes, listening to the insects buzzing and chirping in the mountain's scrubby underbrush. Somewhere behind her, Aeda was also enjoying the cool solitude of the mountain ridge; she could hear her tail thumping contentedly in the dirt.

Maybe he wouldn't come.

She sat back down on the ground to wait and looked around again, checking the landmarks, making absolutely certain that she was in the right spot, then, satisfied, she stretched out on the ground with her balled-up cloak as a pillow and watched night descend over the city.

She awoke to Daryan's warm hand brushing her hip and his dark eyes smiling into hers.

"Sorry," he whispered as she sat up beside him. "I hated to wake you. You were sleeping so peacefully."

She rubbed her eyes and stared at him in confusion. He wore a splendid purple robe, gaudily embroidered with shiny constellations of stars. A thin gold band circled his newly trimmed curls and his wrists were encased in a pair of wide gold cuffs. A heavy gold medallion swung from a chain around his neck. He should have looked ridiculous, but he did not. He looked noble.

"I couldn't change," he explained. "It would have made them suspicious. Don't worry, I brought a plain robe." He waved at a large sack lying nearby and began stripping off the jewelry. "Is everything ready? Do you have everything you need?"

She picked her glove up off the ground and smoothed it out in her lap. "How was the funeral?" she asked.

He sat down heavily on the grass beside her. "They didn't *know* her—they have no idea how brave she really was, or what sacrifices she made for them. They anointed her and prayed for her and laid her body on a bonfire because they thought she was the wife of a daimon. If they had known the truth, they would have torn her apart, and me, too." He turned to her. "I looked for you. I thought you might change your mind."

She looked out over the city. The Shadari had offered her a place of honor at Harotha's funeral: the latest in a string of awkward gestures intended to repay her for saving Dramash and killing Frea.

"The *Argent* sailed before sunset. I needed to say goodbye to my brother and Rho," she reminded him. She would never admit how close they had come to persuading her to join them. "And Dramash. I'm still surprised his family let him go."

"*Let* him?" Daryan asked bitterly. "They're so terrified of him they couldn't wait to get rid of him. They were singing songs about his heroics all the while they were pushing him into the landing-boat. It's all such a mess." He sat there in silence, staring down at the city.

The drumming began, and Isa listened expectantly for the rhythm to take hold. From every corner of the city, one drummer after another took up the complicated rhythm and kept it going, made a subtle change, passed it back again, like a vibrant but amiable conversation. She found it all strangely uplifting, and now it helped her summon the last ounce of courage she needed.

"I have to tell you something." She swallowed painfully. "I'm not going."

Daryan looked over at her sharply. "What?"

"We should stay in the Shadar." She faltered. She knew him too well to mistake the crushed look in his eyes. "We should stay."

"What's the matter?" he cried. "Don't you want to be with me? You know it's the only way we can be together, don't you?"

She intertwined her fingers briefly with his, feeling the heat wrap around them before she pulled her hand away. "Now, it's the only way, but things will change."

He stared down at her knees. "I don't understand," he whispered. "We've been planning this ever since Harotha died." He looked up at her, his eyes bright with welling tears. "Did I do something wrong?"

She pushed down the impulse to stop, to give in. "I knew when you walked away from me, after Frea died—I knew it had to be this way, but I just didn't want to believe it. I let myself pretend for a little while, but I can't pretend any longer."

He began to speak, but she went on without allowing him to interrupt her. "You are their king—you think you can't be, not without Harotha, but you're *wrong*. You're their king and we can't change that."

"Yes, we can," he responded forcefully, kneeling down in front of her. "We *have* to change it. Nothing's going to get any better for us here—do you want to end up like Eofar and Harotha? We have to get away—"

"We'll *make* it better," Isa said with equal force.

"Let them do it themselves then, if that's what they want!" he shouted. "I never wanted to be their leader, Isa. I did the best I could, but this is the end of it. I'm finished."

"You're not," she insisted, "and you're wrong. You'd

find it out soon enough if we left: you would know you'd abandoned them and it would poison everything. We would never be free of it. We'd never be happy—and it would be too late to come back. No. We have to stay."

"*Have to?* Who are you to tell me what I *have* to do? Am I still your slave? What about me—what about what *I* want?" He seized her and pulled her close, squeezing her in his shivering arms until she cried out. He released her at last, saying, "Can I not have something I want, for once in my life?"

"We'll work for it," she whispered, desperate for him to understand, to believe her, "until they don't need you any more. Then we'll be together."

He knelt there for a long time, and gradually she saw his shoulders relax and she knew that she had reached him. Now that he understood, there would be no more talk of running away. She scooted close enough to him to feel his warmth and waited while the moon rose, the sky grew brighter and one by one the drums left off beating. The chirping of the insects slowed and grew drowsy.

"I have something for you," she told him, and reached for the packet she'd concealed under her folded robe.

He took the flat bundle with a look of surprise and unwrapped the cloth. "What is—? Isa! Where did you get this?"

"From the Nomas," she said happily as he lifted the top sheet from the stack of paper and held it up for them both to admire. "You can start your book again. You can write down everything Harotha told you about the past, and when that's done, you can write down everything that's happened here now."

He ran his fingers over the sheet. "It's so *smooth*."

"It's from Daringal. The Nomas told me it was better than our paper—the best paper you can get. It's made from the pulp of some soft tree."

"But how did you pay for it?"

"Lahlil. She gave me some money before she left."

"And you bought me a present. I don't know what to

say. It's beautiful." He carefully placed the sheet back in the stack with the others, then looked up at her and said huskily, "Come here."

They lay back in the scrubby grass then, and made love on his purple robe, not with the desperate, grasping awkwardness of the first time, or the frantic haste of their few secret trysts since then. This time they were exploring each other, testing their limits, seeking out the bliss that they knew waited on the other side of the pain; they were two people for whom the world would wait.

"You'll be a good king," Isa reassured him, tangling her fingers in the curls on the back of his neck, just as he did when he thought no one was watching. "And we will be together, when the time comes."

He laughed a little, and flashed her a thin smile. "Thanks—but that's not what's worrying me." His expression darkened. "What's worrying me is who we'll have become by then. People change. We don't know what's going to happen to us. How are we supposed to keep it all from pulling us apart?"

She stretched out on the grass beside him and gazed up at the stars, searching for the answer.

Lahlil was concentrating on being still. As the Mongrel, she knew how to be still. In combat, it was often essential, and in scouting, always—but that kind of stillness was preparatory to action; it was finite, and she controlled when it began and when it ended. This was different. This wasn't about action. It wasn't even about waiting. It was just about being still.

Slowly she drew in a deep breath, and just as slowly let it out again. The baby in her arms puckered up his rosy mouth and made a few tiny smacking sounds. Then he fell back into a deep sleep.

She went back to being still.

A gray haze drifted over the mountains and dissipated over the desert long before it reached her. The rich color of the sand around her shifted as the pre-dawn light grew stronger.

A swish of sandalled footsteps approached from behind, and her heart, feeling as new to the world and as defenseless as the baby in her arms, swelled in anticipation.

"Is he asleep?" Jachad whispered. She felt his warm, wine-scented breath on her neck as he knelt down behind her and peeked over her shoulder. She turned her head and caught a glimpse of his face: his eyes were red-rimmed and swollen. "Shof help me, he's too beautiful to be real. Osharad. I like it—a little odd, perhaps, but it suits him." He knelt there for a few moments more, staring down at the tiny baby, his hands unconsciously resting on her shoulders. "Do you want me to take him for a while, give you a break?" he asked hopefully. More gently he reminded her, "You're going to have to give him to me in a little while, anyway."

He lifted his hands from her shoulders and for a sinking moment she thought he was going to go away again, but instead he sat down behind her in the sand and wriggled his back up against hers.

"Here," he suggested, "lean on me."

She did as he advised, and the slow, burning pain that had been spreading through her lower back began to fade.

"They hauled out every tedious ritual they had for Harotha's funeral. I left early," he said. His voice was light and quick, but she had seen his eyes, and she could feel the grief moving just below the surface. *He's hiding it from himself*, she thought, *not from me*. "But it was quite the spectacle. The wine was terrible. Nobody asked after you." He gathered his thoughts and then went on, "The *Argent* set sail in the afternoon. Nisha said to say goodbye to you. Again." She felt him shaking his head, and he laughed. "I still can't believe she volunteered to take them to Norland in her own ship. What a show-off."

She felt the rhythm of his breathing slow as he watched the sand blow around them in the dawn breeze.

"What if I had never come back?"

He sighed, long and deep. "I knew that's what you were thinking."

She waited for him to give her an answer.

"If you had never come back, things would have been different. That's all you can know. Better for some, maybe worse for others. Who can say?" His voice roughened; the grief was threatening to break through. "You came back because you needed to, and I came with you because I needed to. We both have to live with that now."

They sat together in silence while the eastern sky slowly brightened to a silvery gray. As he stirred at her back, she told him, "Not yet," and he grunted and settled back down again.

"Nisha said she spoke to you about your illness," he said quietly, after another pause. "She said you've never actually asked Shof and Amai to be free. You might try that, you know—what have you got to lose? They might finally leave you alone."

Lahlil felt the first sign, a shiver running up and down her legs. "Exactly."

His fingertips crept over her shoulder and squeezed it gently. "You're not alone. You know that, don't you?"

"I know," she said. "That's not what's worrying me."

"No?" asked Jachad. He leaned further back and twisted around so that he could see her face. "What, then?"

Lahlil looked over her shoulder and into his sea-blue eyes. "I think I'm happy."

Coming in 2015

FORTUNE'S BLIGHT

Shattered Kingdoms Book 2

Evie Manieri

Read on for a preview!

A TOR BOOK

Daryan was asleep.

Isa leaned over him and touched his shoulder with the tips of her fingers. The smooth fabric of the robe pulled up over him like a blanket was thick enough to shield him from the chill of her touch, and he didn't wake. A gust of wind blew over the ridge and set the prickly grasses brushing against her skin as she shifted her body, trying to get away from a sharp rock gouging into her thigh through her worn trousers. The straggly bushes dotting the slope clacked their dry branches: an urgent conversation in a percussive language that was only just beyond her understanding. Isa slid her fingers gently down Daryan's chest, noticing how the moonlight drained the color from the fabric.

The rumbling wasn't very loud, but she still heard it: she heard it because she was listening for it, every day, all the time, even in her sleep. A moment after, the ground beneath her gave a slight tremor, as if a heavy stone had rolled by.

Isa sprang up, wincing as a bolt of pain shot down through her missing left arm, and ran through the tall weeds to where Aeda waited, still saddled. She breathed in the pungent scent of the triffon's bristly hide—sea air and musk—as she checked the harness for faults.

"What was that?" asked Daryan, sitting up with a squirm of his back and a groan before fumbling in the stiff grass behind him and fishing out the gold circlet that had left its impression in his back. "Damn. I fell asleep, didn't I? You're already dressed. Where are you going?"

"It's the temple. It's collapsed again."

"Oh no. No, no, no—I've got to get down there—"

She stopped to fish out one of the dense little green balls from the pouch around her waist, not allowing herself to remember that she had already taken one when she and Daryan had sneaked away up here for a few precious hours together, or that she had only a few left and ought to be saving them. There was no telling when the Nomas would be back with more. She tasted the medicine's bitter tang the moment it touched her tongue, and made herself chew slowly, wanting to get the most benefit from the herbs and roots and whatever else made up the concoction.

"Just wait," Daryan hissed, whispering even though there was no one but the goats on the next hilltop over to hear him. "I'm almost dressed."

She jammed her foot in the stirrup and swung herself into the saddle, grateful that she'd found a way to fasten the harness so that she could wriggle in and out without having to manipulate the buckles one-handed. She wrapped the reins around her hand and whistled Aeda into the sky while Daryan was still struggling back into his robe. "I'll take a look, and come right back."

A moment later, she was in the air with Aeda's wings beating their slow rhythm beneath her. She still found the ascent to be the worst part, when the angled climb slid her backward on the saddle and the harness was the difference between life and death. She held on to the pommel and pushed her feet down against the stirrups. She had been too terrified to get on a triffon's back for years after watching her mother fall to her death, so it was ironic that the only job she was now fit for was to fly Daryan around to whatever part of the Shadar was currently in crisis. In three months she had done enough flying to make up for the previous seventeen years; she would have a hard time guessing whether she or Aeda was the more exhausted.

Still, anything was better than skulking in the cave with the other Norlanders, watching them do nothing but dive to the bottom of their wine casks.

The city below looked peaceful in the dark, but dawn would reveal the stark truth: the neighborhoods reduced to scorched rubble, the bleached skeletons of fishing boats wedged among the rocks, the crowds of hungry people washing like a muddy tide toward the scaffold-covered palace for their daily rations. She doubted that whatever the ancient ashas had been protecting their people from by dooming them to ignorance could possibly have been worse than this.

She flew north, toward the temple. The darkness hid the cloud of red grit that had been kicked up by the collapse, but she could still smell it in the air. She couldn't tell where exactly the ruins had settled. The debris from the temple had fanned out in a wide ring, but the bulk of the structure had fallen back in on top of itself. The lowest levels of the temple were still mostly solid despite their cracked foundations. The rest was a great unsteady pile, the remains of endless rooms and broken walls and corridors and staircases. Among the rubble was everything from straw mats and broken broom handles to massive carved chests and sacks of coins from her father's imperial treasury, the promise of all that buried wealth luring people to their ruin.

Somewhere in that rubble lay her burned left arm, still wrapped up in Eofar's old shirt. Maybe it was nestled among other remnants of her mother's tomb, like the carved lid of the sarcophagus that Rahsa had turned into her torture table, or even her mother's broken body. Maybe it was surrounded—watched over by the undiscovered dead.

Another triffon rose up from behind the hills and crossed their path, beating back the cold night air with its leathery wings. It had no saddle: it was one of the others, the ones who had gone feral after their berths in the temple had been destroyed, when the Shadari were too concerned with keeping their people alive to look after the frightened creatures. Isa could see the moon reflected in its shiny black eyes. Then a second one broke away from the summit of the next hill over, tumbling down like the shower of ash before unfurling its wings and sweeping back up to join its companion, and the two flew off together. The Shadari kept arguing about whether they should be tamed again or killed outright, but no one had come up with a practical plan for doing either. If they didn't make up their minds soon, there wouldn't be a single goat left in the whole of the Shadar.

Isa looked back over her shoulder. Tiny points of light—torches and lanterns—had appeared around the ruins like a new constellation.

Daryan was pacing the ridge when she landed. He hurried toward her, sending small stones skipping away down the slope toward the city. "How bad is it?"

"I couldn't tell," she said. "It was too dark."

He moved his hand toward the hair curling over the back of his neck, but stopped short. He had decided the old gesture was a childish tick, hardly befitting his position. "I'd better get down there before they trample each other to death over who gets a copper chamber pot."

He climbed up behind her and looped the harness over his shoulders. She watched his hands as he tightened the straps, remembering the way his touch made her feel as if her skin was melting from her bones. The urgency of satisfying their passion made everything else—even the constant pain—irrelevant. She pitied ordinary couples whose embraces cost them nothing; whose love-making came so cheaply that they could undertake it on a whim and forget it just as easily. They couldn't know what it was like to have a lover's arms circle around the small of their backs like a pair of blacksmith's tongs straight from the fire, or have kisses rain like a shower of embers.

He unbuckled a strap, untwisted it, and buckled it again. "Why did you let me fall asleep?"

"You were tired."

"I don't have time to sleep. You knew I was supposed

to be down at the beach, talking to the resurrectionists. How am I going to explain to Omir why I didn't show up?"

She let go of the reins for a moment so she could grab them higher up. "Omir isn't king. You are. You shouldn't have to explain."

"I couldn't manage any of this without him, Isa. You know that."

She whistled and took them back up. She had no difficulty spotting the four pyres blazing in a line along the shore. *Resurrectionists.* A strange feeling fizzed through her empty stomach: they fascinated her as much as they repulsed her. Some of the bodies they'd exhumed were decades old, with no one left to remember their names. Omir distrusted them because they claimed to have no leader, and would say only that a common purpose had brought them together. He suspected them of some motive beyond giving the Shadari dead a proper funeral.

Daryan, she knew, envied them. The resurrectionists had been able to bring people together with apparently no effort whatsoever, while every attempt Daryan made to mobilize his people to action failed for one reason or another. When he'd asked them to donate food to a common store to help feed the destitute, they'd said they didn't have enough for themselves. When he'd asked them to work the mines so they could make weapons to defend the Shadar, they'd accused him of trying to bring back slavery. And on it went.

The number of lights around the temple had tripled in that short time, and now many of the Shadari had grouped into a column winding through the nearby streets. There was another audible rumble, a sign that the pile had not yet settled back into equilibrium. Sometimes it went on like that for hours.

"This is bad," Daryan shouted over the wind. "Probably that little prick Binit, winding them up again. Why do they even listen to him? Everyone knows he was one of Faroth's cronies. He knows I have to go down there. He wants a confrontation."

Isa brought them down low enough for the crowd to sharpen into individual figures. Relatively few of them carried torches or lanterns, which meant that the procession was much larger than Isa had thought at first. They shouted when they saw the triffon.

"Land on that side street over there," Daryan said, pointing, and she did as he asked. He unbuckled himself and slid down and was adjusting his robe when she leapt down beside him. They started off down the street when Daryan stopped suddenly and turned back to her.

"Where's your sword?"

It wasn't *her* sword. Her sword was at the bottom of the ocean. Blood's Pride was *Frea's* sword, and always would be. "I left it on the saddle."

"Isa," he hissed, drawing out her name in the way he did when he was really angry with her. "You *promised* me. You know it's not safe for you to walk around without it."

"I don't want them to be afraid of me."

"You knew what it was going to be like if we stayed. . . ." He started to stay something more, then his mouth closed and he stood for a moment, not moving. "I shouldn't tell you what to do. I know how much you hate that. I just don't think you understand what losing you would do to me. That day in the temple . . . I can face just about anything, but not that. Not again . . ." He tailed off and looked anxiously down the street.

Suddenly she felt ashamed, which was what he wanted. Staying in the Shadar had been her idea. She had convinced Daryan that his people needed him, and so far they had been doing everything possible to prove her wrong—unless what they really needed was someone to blame. She went back and transferred Blood's Pride from the saddle to the scabbard across her back.

They came out of the side street just in time to cut off the procession. Daryan had been right: Binit was in the lead, his flabby arm sagging under the weight of a stinking torch. She let Daryan go forward while she stayed back in the shadows between two of the houses. No one noticed her. She was a ghost: one of those misguided spirits who had turned their backs on the doors of the Norlander After-realm to cling to a life that had already begun to forget them.

"No one is going near those ruins," said Daryan, squaring off against Binit in the middle of the street. He didn't appear to care that Binit had at least three hundred people behind him, while he was alone.

"Our dead are buried in those ruins," said Binit. The remains of Faroth's revolutionaries had oozed out of the crowd and congealed around him. So far, their contribution to the rebuilding effort had consisted of trying to convince people that Daryan wasn't a "real" Shadari because he had spent most of his life as a servant in the temple. Isa hated every one of their smug faces.

"We can all look for our dead in the morning," said Daryan, "when we can see, and the ruins have settled. It's madness to go anywhere near there in the dark."

Omir appeared with about a dozen armed men, each carrying one of the first black-bladed swords produced since the uprising. "Why don't you just admit the truth, Binit: that you're looking to get hold of any loot for yourselves. Anything found in the temple goes into the treasury. That's what we all agreed."

"Of course, here come the enforcers," Binit shouted for the benefit of the crowd, "with the same weapons that made slaves of us for the last thirty years."

"You know full well that I would shut down the mines right now if people with the asha powers would just come forward," Daryan told him. "We need some way to defend ourselves against the emperor—and anyone else who decides to make a grab for us. What else have we got? Some half-built walls in the mountain passes that wouldn't hold back a herd of goats? Twenty-six Dead Ones who are only waiting for Eofar to straighten things out with the emperor so they can go back to killing people like good little soldiers? We *need* the ashas, and instead, you and your friends are out there telling everyone that even trying to use the power is blasphemy—even after Harotha risked her life to show you how it was all a lie."

"Oh yes, Harotha's 'visions'," said Binit, provoking an insincere laugh from his supporters, although not many others in the crowd joined in. Harotha's story, of a beautiful and self-sacrificing queen dead before her time, had only grown in importance in the months since her death.

Daryan started to reach up behind his head again, but then he jerked his arm down. "If there was one bottle of the elixir—no, one *drop* of the stuff left anywhere, anywhere in the world—I would give you all the proof you needed."

"I'm sure you would. You would think Harotha might have thought of that, before she drank it all. Or, maybe . . . she did?"

Omir's shoulders rolled back and he looked as if he was about to draw his sword, but Daryan held up a warning hand. Instead he walked out further into the street and gestured for Binit to come closer. Binit handed the torch to one of his companions and came out to meet him.

"You want to get into those ruins, don't you?" Daryan asked him. He spoke too quietly for any of the other Shadari to hear him, but Isa's hearing was far sharper.

"What if we do?" answered Binit, matching his tone.

"If you'll wait until dawn, I'll let you."

"What, with Omir and his toy army right behind us?"

"No, I'll let you and your people go in on your own and do whatever you want—you can steal the governor's monogrammed napkins for all I care."

Binit crossed his arms and looked from one side of the street to the other. "What do you want in return?"

"Stop spreading these rumors about a plague. There is *no* plague."

"So you deny it, then?"

Isa didn't need to see Daryan's face to know his teeth were clenched. "No one is sick."

"I know. Suspicious, isn't it?"

"I've got to hand it to you, Binit," Daryan said with a dark little laugh. "Not many people could convince a mob that there's a plague because there *aren't* any bodies. Every time some family moves house, you and your friends are out there the next day parading up and down in front of the palace, claiming we've carried them off in the night. Gods help us, don't you think people are scared enough already? What are you trying to do with all of this? What's the *point* of it?"

"The Shadar needs to go back to the way it was before the Dead Ones came," Binit answered. "You want to change everything. You want to change what we've believed for hundreds of years. I say what was good enough for my father and my grandfather is good enough for me. Who do you think you are?"

"I don't think; I *know* I'm the daimon. And I think you're afraid."

"What did you say?" said Binit, curling his fleshy fingers around the hilt of the dagger sheathed on his hip.

"What was good enough for your father and grandfather didn't help them when the Dead Ones came. It didn't help my father either, or anyone else's father. That's the kind of thing people say when they don't think they're smart enough to learn something new. It's a lot easier to make ignorance a virtue, isn't it? That way you never have to worry about looking stupid."

Binit sneered and his lips moved, but he couldn't come up with a retort.

"Now, why don't you tell these people to get some sleep and come back at dawn," said Daryan. "Omir will be glad to help you with that."

He turned around and walked away without waiting for an answer. The hard lines Isa saw on his face as he came back towards her were becoming all too familiar. This wasn't her Daryan; this was the daimon.

"It's not too late to talk to the resurrectionists," he told her, leading her into a dark alley between two abandoned houses.

"All right. I'll take you," she said.

He looked back over his shoulder, toward the beach. "It's not far. I can go on my own."

Cool air snaked up underneath the untucked tail of her brother's old shirt, but she still felt the itch of sweat on the back of her neck. "Why? Don't you want me to fly you?"

"I was going to tell you before I fell asleep"—he lifted his head stiffly, as if he was forcing himself to look at her—"I don't think it's a good idea to have you flying me around for a while."

Daryan wasn't a Norlander, so he couldn't feel the burning flush that swept over her body. She reached down and squeezed the little pouch, feeling the shapes of the pills inside. Only four left.

"They're angry, and they're looking for someone to blame," he explained. "It's just for a while—just until things settle down again."

"They will never learn to accept me if I stay shut up in the ashadom." She and the other Norlanders had moved into the cave with the constellations and writing painted all over the walls, the one Harotha had discovered, after several attempts to house them elsewhere had ended in regrettable encounters with the locals. Daryan had finally decided to move them up to the cave he'd dubbed the ashadom, because the superstitious Shadari still refused to go anywhere near the place.

"Sometimes I forget how stubborn you are," he said, shaking his head. "Will you just—?"

She hooked her fingers into the front of his robe and yanked him toward her. She knew it was a mad, reckless thing to do with so many people around, but she couldn't stop herself from kissing him. He made a soft sound deep in his throat even as his shoulders stiffened from the shock of her cold skin. He seized her waist. She wanted to melt into him until nothing was left of her but a pool of water; melt out of existence . . .

"Isa," he said quickly, pulling away from her. She stepped back with her heart thumping, afraid they had been caught, but Daryan was backing out into the street with his head tilted at the night sky. "Wings. It's the Dead Ones. If they show up here, now . . ."

. . . there was a good chance there'd be a riot, just as there had been on three other similar occasions.

"I'll stop them," she said, already running back to Aeda. She saw the other riders heading toward the temple as soon as she was aloft. There were six triffons—the only ones left beside Aeda who would still tolerate being saddled—and they rode doubled- or tripled-up. Falkar, Frea's erstwhile lieutenant and their effectual leader, led the formation.

Isa spurred Aeda on. <You have to go back,> she told them, beating back a flash of panic as she flew in front of them and saw the triffons' massive heads streaking toward her. <Daryan doesn't want anyone in the ruins until dawn.>

<Of course,> Gyr called out, pulling his triffon up and over her head. <Dawn, when he knows we'll be stuck hiding in that stinking cave.>

<Falkar, that's our stuff in there,> said Arvald, appealing to the lieutenant. The other Norlanders almost never spoke to her directly, a fact that she had carefully kept hidden from Daryan so far. <Those're our friends, buried under there. We have the right to take back what's ours!>

<You know what will happen if you go down there now,> Isa told them. The moon was setting over the water, lighting a rippling trail towards the city. She turned Aeda back around toward them, but kept her distance. <There are hundreds of Shadari down there, and they're already angry. Falkar, just go back.>

He flew toward her out of the line. He was the only one of them still clean-shaven, and the only one who was bothering to wash his clothes on a regular basis. He was proud, and he had followed Eofar because that's what the rules told him to do. Now Eofar was risking his life in Norland trying to negotiate the Shadars' freedom, and Falkar had been left behind without even truly knowing which side he was on.

<Our people have been buried in there for three months.

Every time those rocks move, there's a chance we could find some of them,> he said. <They gave their lives in battle. They deserve proper graves.>

<The only reason *we're* still alive is because of Daryan's protection—because he promised my brother that nothing would happen to us. Do you think that's easy? How far do you think you can push the Shadari before they stop listening to him?>

Falkar flew over the crowd in a lazy circle, taking its measure, then doubled back and gave the order to return to the ashadom. Isa felt the others griping, but they had just enough discipline left to obey him.

Falkar brought his mount alongside her. Instinctively, both triffons fell into formation, timing the beats of their wings in unison. <What do you think they see, when they look at you?> he asked. It was the first time any of them had spoken to her directly in weeks, and it felt as if someone had crept up behind her and put their hands around her neck. <What do you think they see?>

He flew away.

She took in a great breath of the cold air as soon as he was gone and tried to focus. Daryan needed her. She wouldn't think about anything else. She wouldn't think about the pain shooting down from her shoulder into her missing arm, or what she would do when the pills were gone. Above all, she wouldn't think about the fact that she would eventually have to go back to the cave, to these people who despised her, because she had no other place else to go.

She flew above the ashadom, where the rock was sheer and smooth. The moon was behind her, still setting over the water, and she caught sight of her shadow on the cliff face, elongated by the moonlight into a silent, stringy-limbed giant atop a gigantic winged beast. The leaning cross of Blood's Pride poked up over her shoulder, stark and menacing. Where the face should have been was nothing more than a blank oval, incapable of seeing anyone's suffering or offering any pity, and yet she knew it was looking right back at her.

Acknowledgments

My dear friends and family, too many to name now, for their excitement, encouragement and general awesomeness. There are two more books in this series, so there'll be loads more to come. For now . . .

My agent Becca Stumpf, recipient of my 99th query letter (I think there's a lesson in there somewhere), whom I can never adequately thank for rescuing me from the slush pile or for her tireless work and reliably cheerful support ever since . . .

Jo Fletcher of Jo Fletcher Books and Stacy Hill of Tor Books, for taking a chance on me; for their marvelously insightful and sensitive editing, and for the magic trick of providing amazingly different but never contradictory notes; and for putting up with my rookie nonsense with remarkable patience . . .

Fellow author and unspeakably lovely person Laura J. Snyder, who blithely assured me that my book would be published the very first time we met, but who otherwise seems perfectly sane . . .

My amazing mother Joanne Manieri, for always believing that I could do something wonderful provided I took adequate precautions against natural disasters, terrorists, deer ticks, black ice, under-cooked poultry and killer bees . . .

My daughter Prudence, who at nine years old is the kindest and most compassionate person I have ever met.

Her good qualities will serve humankind well when she rules over us all as Goddess of the Uber-Nerds . . .

My husband Lou Flees—penultimately, of course, since that's his favorite word—for being unfailingly gracious when awakened at 4am to inspect suspicious moles or identify distant beeping sounds. Without his support I could not possibly have written this book, or have had the chance to describe him in print as "Clooney handsome" (his phrase) . . .

And finally, the steadfast and true Lisa Rogers, who loses ten points for almost completely derailing this project by introducing me to Howard Overman's *Misfits*, but gains a million points for making me a snowglobe with Simon's picture in it. I can always rely on her to tell me to get down off the ledge, out from under the covers or away from the keyboard, as the situation requires—now being one of those times.